THE OPAL
CAUSEWAY

THE OPAL CAUSEWAY

D. H. Yeats

The Book Guild Ltd

First published in Great Britain in 2022 by
The Book Guild Ltd
Unit E2 Airfield Business Park,
Harrison Road, Market Harborough,
Leicestershire. LE16 7UL
Tel: 0116 2792299
www.bookguild.co.uk
Email: info@bookguild.co.uk
Twitter: @bookguild

This work is entirely fictitious and bears no resemblance to any persons living or dead.

Typeset in 12pt Baskerville

Printed and bound in the UK by TJ Books LTD, Padstow, Cornwall

ISBN 978 1915352 057

British Library Cataloguing in Publication Data.
A catalogue record for this book is available from the British Library.

For Jenny

PART ONE

———

In the Pink and Re-Energising
Notting Hill Dawn

He paused by the top of the spiral staircase leading up from the platform. He could now hear the sound of another's footsteps echoing off those grubby, white-tiled circular walls as replicating his own; they made their way up those two hundred or more steps from down below in that stuffy, airless capsule embedded in the London clay.

Jesus, was I that noisy? Dead give-away or what?

Yet, fear of discovery was negated by welcoming, cool air on the face. Because, having run all the way up, he'd broken out in a sweat, something he hoped to avoid. All that devious effort, just to save a bob or two, and he was still going to be late. Mel and Baz would be wondering where he was. Well, Mel would. He imagined her gently furrowed brow quietly demonstrating her inward concern, but Baz... well, to be truthful, did he much care about anything?

He made his way to the exit, his eyes on lookout for lurking ticket inspectors, but the coast was clear. Stepping out onto the pavement, he was blinded by the setting sun and his eyes took some moments to refocus before noticing the already lengthened shadows. It was later that he imagined.

Momentarily confused, not familiar with this part of the city, he waited by the entrance, gathering his bearings. He'd only been here twice before – it was night-time on both occasions – but, then, across the road the façade of Marine

Ices came into focus and things started to become familiar. He wouldn't forget *that* café in a hurry. Baz and Mel took him there. They still raved about the aromatic pizza and delicious ice cream to be had there.

So, where's the Roundhouse?

He imagined it being more or less in front of him. He must have come out through the wrong exit, then. Turning right, making his way along the pavement, he traced the curving wall of a dust-encrusted building and the familiar sight of that quintessential relic of a bygone age came into view.

He'd gone to a gig there in his teens a few years back, hitching up from the coast with his childhood friend Nicola. A trip it was billed and a trip it was for all their naivety. They'd not owned up to it then, but a lot going on that night went way above their heads, just like the revellers and pranksters floating by them in their day-glow finery. It was also the first occasion either of them stayed out all night and, after the gig finished, they wandered through the buzzy city streets till, in Oxford Street, they found a greasy spoon open, full of right dodgy-looking people. Nicola so got off on that.

This evening the Roundhouse was decked out in oriental décor. Red and gold pennants, lanterns, paper fish and dragon-type creatures were rustling in the light warm south-westerly breeze and glinting as they caught the long rays of the departing sun.

Now which way? he wondered as his eyes surveyed the pleasing contours of that former railway shed. *Up the road to the bridge with the Roundhouse to your left*, that's what had Mel said, so he started to leg it.

But, just as the bridge came into view, realising he'd forgotten something he planned to do earlier, deep thoughts and a human body having distracted him, he stopped. And now, the sudden realisation that he'd again fucked up made him sigh loudly.

'Shit! You prat! You forgot to ring the old man again!' he said, out loud.

To be true, he tried to call earlier during the day, but there was no answer. However, he reckoned the old man was perhaps up at the orchard. But he should call right now; it would be too late if left till after. His grandfather would be in bed. Asleep. And he'd told him he'd ring that day. He'd promised.

His eyes started searching for a phone box.

How could he have allowed himself to forget Mémé when, in the morning, after he got up, he'd determined to remember her the whole day long? It was his duty, he'd told himself, to show a silent, poignant respect. And he hadn't even been able to get it together to telephone the old man, on this important anniversary, let alone remember. He cursed himself.

Deep down he knew why he'd forgotten and started to feel remorseful. But then, the thought came to him that Mémé wouldn't have minded, would've laughed it off with that familiar sweep of her hands because she would have approved of him having the good time which he'd been having these last few months so long as he paid proper respect to his grandfather.

Then a realisation hit him. The immense grief that he'd shared with his grandfather, a grief which bound them together, he'd borne for months, suddenly and silently, had dissipated. Because of new, exciting distractions. And at this, he started to feel base, traitorous, for his grandfather was alone in an empty house, surrounded by decades of memories, still mourning, in a lachrymose condition, lost, unmotivated.

But then, was it right that he should feel bad about feeling happy, feel bad that all this positive movement in his life had cushioned, in fact stifled the feeling of loss so it had become a comfortable melancholy?

The reason for this important telephone call was because it was the first anniversary of Mémé's death. Though, in fact, his step-grandmother, it was she who had brought him up, had mothered him ever since he could remember. Her illness and subsequent passing had been so sudden that the shock was seismic for both him and his grandfather. And, now, as his eyes searched around for a telephone box, some words she once said to him rang out in his head: *Peter, il faut que tu comprends quelque chose. Tu es jeune et tu peux rebondir plus facilement que ton grand-père et moi; surtout ton grand-père.*

He recalled the emphasis she placed on the words *especially your grandfather* and how, as she said it, her eyes got big and her eyebrows darted up her forehead as she lifted up her head.

He looked around for a telephone box but couldn't see one. But as he was thinking that he best go back to the station, a sudden splash of red caught his eyes. There was one on the other side of the road in the shadow of a large plane tree. As he ran across, paying scant attention to traffic, he felt for change in the pockets of his tight sailor's bellbottoms, dyed pink and bought the day before in Kensington Market. He prised out a couple of sixpences and, as he reached the heavy iron door, he prayed that it would work.

It stank inside – naturally – but blocking his nose with thumb and forefinger, he wedged the receiver between his head and shoulder, dialling the number with his other hand.

As it rang, he visualised his grandfather getting up from his chair, methodically making his way to the hall. He could now see him picking up the receiver with that certain precision, that kind of reverence the old man held for such an invention. He imagined his familiar quizzical look which always came to his face as he lifted up the apparatus to his ear just before he spoke.

It rang seven times before he answered but any preliminary assessment of his grandfather's state was prevented as his response was interrupted by the pips. Pete fumbled with his change and pushed in one of the sixpenny bits.

'Granddad, it's me. I said I'd ring. How are you?'

'Oh, Peter, fine, yes, fine.'

However, to Pete, he didn't sound fine. There was an almost reedy quality to his voice. His fears were confirmed. But before he could continue the conversation, a raucous voice piped up in the background, drowning out whatever it was his grandfather was trying to say.

'Who's that then, Mr Jones? Would that be Peter? You must tell him about Nicola. He'll want to know,' it blurted.

'Yes, son, Mrs Strachan popped by,' his grandfather whispered.

'Oh, that's nice,' Pete slowly replied.

Nice? No way! The idea that someone else was there slayed him and, in an attempt to disguise his disappointment, his voice just trailed off. Connie Strachan's presence was obviously contributing to the old man's hesitant reply, for his grandfather was a private man and Pete knew that he wouldn't much talk with her around.

In fact, her flummery, as Mémé and his grandfather termed it, had come, increasingly but silently, to irritate the latter over the years, and while his wife was alive, he was often seen to beat a hasty retreat at Connie's approach. Out like a whippet through the backdoor, he was, and up to the end of the garden or further still up to the orchard by the way of the public footpath by the side of the house.

Of course, Connie no doubt thought she was being kind, doing the right thing because she would have known what day it was. But, somehow, she would still, despite good intentions, bend his grandfather's ear about something or other. She did so burden others with her nonsense; there was evidently some gossip about Nicola. And, with that thought, Pete started to feel neither would he have no further chance of finding out how his grandfather really was nor of raising the old man's spirits. He again cursed himself for not ringing earlier. How could he talk about Mémé knowing that Connie would be straining to hear every word?

But what was that about Nicola? he wondered. He was curious as Nicknick was one of his best friends, like a big sister to him, ever since he could remember, and although they did not see each other so often now, they were still close.

'You're getting on all right then, son, are you?' his grandfather asked.

'Yeah, Granddad, so-so,' he replied nonchalantly, although in all reality he was bursting to tell his grandfather about the brilliant time he was having. 'Well, I'm just on my way to a concert with Mel and Baz. You remember them, don't you?' he continued, as if it was of no consequence.

'Melanie, of course, son, is she there with you? You mustn't be keeping her waiting.'

'No, I'm meeting them there. She would've wanted to speak with you if she was. But you know what? She said she'd like to come down and visit you sometime soon.'

'Now I'd like that.'

Mention of Mel was like a shot of medicine for the old man; the tone of his voice was quite altered. He'd taken quite a shine to her when they met a few years back. Very much to Mémé's amusement, for Zénaïde, with a deadpan expression on her face, had said when they were all sitting around the table that she would have to take care now she had a rival. But of course, she never had any competition. She and Albert had been completely devoted to one another, steadfast, like a rock. And Pete was always included in that equation, as Mémé always used to tell him while giving his bath when he was little that he was their rock, *leur pierre*, the abandoned child that they took in and brought up.

Eh ouais, mon petit, toi tu es le ti pierre d'Albert et Zénaïde qui nous lie ensemble. Il suffit de penser que, te comprendes?

But Albert's interest in Mel, and Zénaïde's also, was because they initially were under the mistaken belief that she was Pete's girlfriend and hoped something would come of it. However, that was before they knew Baz was on the scene. Still, the old man never gave up hope and started to enquire about Mel. Was she still working in the library? Yes, she was welcome down there at any time. And, then, surmising that she was no doubt at that very minute waiting for Pete, he started to chastise him for keeping her waiting.

'So this concert you're going to with her, son?' Albert continued.

'Nothing you would like; in fact, nothing that you would consider being music.'

Pete felt encouraged by a chuckle coming from the other end of the line. At last it seemed the call had started to do some good.

'It starts late then, son?'

'At seven thirty.'

'Well, you are late, aren't you, son? It's nearer eight o'clock by now.'

'Oh no, I didn't realise. I'm sorry. In that case I'll have to go. And we've hardly talked.'

His revelation he was oblivious to his lateness caused more chuckles and Pete felt gratified as he recalled that his dream-induced lateness, as Albert termed it, was always an amusement to his grandfather, as it had also been to Zénaïde. Yet, Pete lingered there in the telephone box, desperately searching to find the right words to terminate their conversation. Some comforting words about Zénaïde to appropriately finish it off and to make his grandfather realise he knew it was the anniversary of her death.

But he couldn't think of anything; his mind was blank.

'I'll tell you what, Granddad,' he said, after a pause. 'I'm not working in the morning. I'll ring you then. That's okay, isn't it? And then we'll be able to talk more, if you know what I mean.'

'I'd like that, son. The morning, you say?'

Pete could tell by his inflection that his grandfather favoured that solution, but then the old man added, 'But are you sure, son? You'll need a few coppers for that.'

'That's okay, I got loads in a jar back at the squat. But it won't be too early.'

'Well, then. I'll say goodbye. Remember, son, let the dog see the rabbit.'

'Tomorrow then, Granddad,' Pete said, and then, as Albert was about to put down the receiver, he added quickly but quietly, 'Oh, by the way, Granddad. I do remember, the day, what today is?'

'Yes, son, of course. I know you do, and I appreciate you calling,' Albert said, calmly.

Pete put down the receiver. As he pushed open the door, he sighed. Everything seemed unsatisfactory; he felt like a bad person. Emotion welled up inside him; tears formed in his eyes. He still couldn't get his head around the fact that he would never again accompany his grandfather down to the port to meet Zénaïde off the passenger ferry from a voyage across the Opal Causeway, that magical path of such salty, and sometimes milky, iridescence which had led his grandparents to discover each other. He also always expected his grandfather to die before her; in fact, in his early teens, his grandfather actually once drew him aside and said as much. His words still ran crystal-clear in Pete's memory.

'I won't last long, son, but I'll see you through school,' the old man had said.

As he walked away from that telephone box, Pete determined there and then he would go down. A visit to the old man was overdue; besides, there was something he wanted tell him. During a fleeting visit a few weeks back, the opportunity to talk had never been right, again partly due to Connie Strachan, although his hesitation hadn't helped. But now he would speak to Mel about going. He had some days off soon. Maybe she could take some too.

Shit, Mel, he must be really late by now, so, making his way up the road, he crossed the railway bridge and found himself on Regents Park Road. The only sounds to be heard were the distant yells of kids out playing late, strangely echoic but innocent and thus soothing.

No way threatening or violent.

Albert Jones replaced the telephone, making sure that the receiver was correctly positioned in the cradle. A feeling of desperation welled up inside of him, but a lifetime's discipline made him suppress it. Like his grandson Peter, he also wished that Connie hadn't been there when the boy called.

He'd been neighbours with her since she was a child, long before he and Zénaïde married. She'd been Connie Roberts then and lived with her widowed mother. The late Mrs Roberts had been a lady whose slight, delightful Edwardian form was sadly spoilt by a Victorian sternness, and Connie's clumsiness, just one of many defects attributed to her by her mother, irritated the old girl to no end. Appalled that she'd given birth to such an ungainly, sluggish daughter who seemed quite incapable of mimicking her own airs and graces, and who lacked her perception of good manners or appreciated her refined tastes, Mrs Roberts meted out punishment to Connie that often seemed to Albert and his first wife Queenie to be in the realms of cruelty.

In consequence, as she grew to adulthood, Connie was to play up her despairing mother surreptitiously, slyly and with a constant regularity. When, in her thirties, she made an inappropriate marriage, at the time when most people in their town were more concerned one way or another in helping get the troops back from the beaches of Dunkirk, Mrs Roberts made sure that the marriage didn't last a day. Indeed, Albert himself witnessed the old lady, having been told she now had a son-in-law by her inebriated daughter just back from celebrating in a public house, wielding a hatchet with which she saw off, in no uncertain way, her new relative. But Stanley Strachan eventually came back after she died and Connie's life began a spiralling descent as she struggled to bring up a child and work, something she was ill prepared to do, while never knowing whether her husband would be at home, and, should he be, wondering what kind of alcoholic stupor she would find him in, or whether he would had taken off on his travels, which was something he did frequently, more often than not in the summer, and with no warning whatsoever.

Of course, Albert recognised deep down that Connie, despite being strangely limited, was a good sort. But, tonight, on the anniversary of his beloved Zinny's death, Albert could have done without her dropping in because he wanted to be alone with his memories. As he walked back into the living room and returned to his chair, Connie was already in full flow about Nicola and grandson Darren. It was so garbled and he couldn't follow it at all, so he just nodded and smiled despite feeling all churned up inside.

It happened so quickly, Zénaïde's passing. It hadn't been fair. His Zinny had been a person full of life. He always imagined that she'd live to be a ripe old age; he would be the one to go first. After all, he was ten years older than her. Of course, they didn't realise it then, but it all started on their holiday in the south of France in the spring six months before, when they were staying with Zénaïde's sister-in-law Ghislaine in Cagnes-sur-mer.

He smiled to himself as he remembered how the boy had clamoured for three of them to go there, ever since he returned three years previously, at the end of the summer holidays, enthusing about the Fondation Maeght and Matisse's chapel in Vence.

The boy was about to start his A-Level year then and it was that visit that determined he would go to art school. Albert couldn't recall why they hadn't gone earlier, not that it would have made the blindest bit of difference. Perhaps something to do with their work, but in fact, by the time they went, Peter was already in the second year of a photography course in Manchester.

It was inside the Chapelle du Rosaire, while gazing up with admiration at the yellow and blue stained-glass windows, when Zénaïde suddenly fell. Naturally, she made light of it, but it did worry Albert at the time, for it was so uncharacteristic of her. Her balance and poise were quite like that of someone twenty years her junior. Of course, with hindsight, Albert now realised that she had been profoundly disturbed by it. When he snatched furtive glances at her in the remaining days of their visit before taking the *Train bleu* home, she seemed to have quite a look of confusion on her face, as if she were lost. Yes, there'd been a kind of flicker of uncertainty about her.

That journey was to be the last time they travelled back together across their sublime Opal Causeway and the last time they passed through the docks where a chance meeting almost thirty-five years before changed both of their lives forever.

And, it always seemed painfully poignant to Albert that the last place Zénaïde had asked to go, in that first week of the July before her death, was to the wild strawberry woods.

How thin she'd become by then.

The boy came too, and Nicola and Darren, and while they went off to scavenge for those tiny nut-flavoured fruits, Albert sat down with her on the picnic rug on which they'd sat down so many times before, and in almost the same place where all those years before their union was consummated.

The boy even took the old wind-up gramophone with them.

What an effort Zénaïde made that day!

She was made up and as always so well dressed.

'Albert, it's a good thing that I bought those pretty little turbans in Nice, don't you think?' he remembered her saying.

For, by that time, she'd lost so much hair and the turbans had become indispensable.

In the following days, it seemed as if she was getting better. After the picking, there was that year's batch of wild strawberry jam and jelly to make, which she undertook with her usual determination. There had only been one year since they'd married that circumstances had prevented her: her unforeseen absence during the war. Of course, both the boy and Nicola were a great help; they knew all the runnings because they'd helped with Albert and Zénaïde's fruit and flower enterprise from an early age.

But Albert had not touched a pound of that last batch of jam and jelly she'd made. He could not bear to. So the full jars remained there on the shelf in the larder in well-ordered rows as if they were an offering to the household gods.

Hell's bells, how he missed her!

'Mr Jones? Mr Jones? I'll be going now. I can see you're tired,' Connie said, as she rose from her chair. 'I've got to see to Nicola and all that, in any case. No, don't get up now. I'd thought you'd dropped off for a moment. I'll call by tomorrow.'

As she made her way through the door, Albert felt she seemed strangely spectrelike. There was an unreal quality about her, as if she was floating. As silence again descended, a sense of relief shot through him, and in that silence, he was, at last, able to cast his mind back to the day of that ferocious gale when he and Zénaïde had met, and of how that meeting led to a rare, undreamed-of happiness.

Neither of them never quite understood how it had happened but blossom it did. And just as they thought that it couldn't have got better, having the boy come to live with them a decade or so later, made their life seem even more complete.

Ah yes, the boy!

That boy, now in uncharted territory, paused to gather his bearings. Being Sunday, the streets were deserted.

'Turn left after the bridge, sort of slightly downhill,' Mel had said.

He turned left, noticed an incline and, quickening his pace, began to make his way down it. The street had that end of a dry summer dusty sheen to it; overhanging limes were still secreting their sticky emission onto the pavement, causing the soles of his plimsolls to feel tacky. Underneath these trees, unkempt privet hedges hid the cracked tiles and flaking white paint on porticoes that led into once-substantial residences, while further along end-of-season hollyhocks with furry beige stalks, laden with heavy seed pods and one last tiny wilting flower, saluted him as he passed. A scattering of browning leaves were being lethargically blown across the street, a precursor of what was soon to come.

Yes, summer seemed to be fast disappearing, and as if to emphasise that thought, his nostrils were assaulted by a whiff of autumn in the early evening air. It disturbed him that the evenings were drawing in. Despite there being many summers yet to come, he could only lament the passing of this summer because it had been the best ever: best as everything seemed to be coming together for him and best even if he didn't know precisely for where he was bound. For, at last,

17

he had begun to feel at one with himself; the awkwardness of his teenage years quite gone and he knew he was going somewhere – right ready for it, he was.

As he retraced the sequence of the summer in his mind, he found it hard to believe how so much had happened in such a short time. His diploma show over, he'd left Lowry's dwindling chimneys behind and, after standing in the teeming rain with thumb outstretched on the road leading to the M6, turned up six hours later at the door of the squat in a sunny Powis Square to be greeted by an overjoyed Mel, a grumpy Baz and a group of assorted freaks, some suspicious, others welcoming.

Now everything seemed to lead to somewhere, something or someone, and he felt he'd arrived at a great ocean, an ocean in which he could dive, swim or sail across, and which allowed him fluidity, a certain kind of weightlessness. Yes, he'd experienced so much in the last few months; he definitely felt to be a different person from the one back at the start of it. It was unbelievable. Falling into that job at the adventure playground was a right eye-opener for him too. What a bunch of kids! Rough, raw and bold! He'd imagined that headlice and worms were things of the past, but despite that, it was brilliant there, and what photos he'd taken! Grainy and honest, he felt he had captured both motion and the moods of the kids, but was he actually doing anything for them, he wondered? Or just using them? Yet, he was dead chuffed with those prints, even more so when the head of the Christian mission whose project it was, asked for copies for their records, for publicity, presumably, and was prepared to pay for them.

His time, now unburdened since graduating, became as long a ball of string. And it was a ball he had under those dusty, leafy glades around Portobello, going to gigs, impromptu parties or just hanging about with new, interesting mates, rapping, getting stoned and staying up late to welcome in the pink and re-energising Notting Hill dawn while listening to all kinds of neat, progressive sounds and patiently waiting as the rising sun engulfed the Italianate pepper-pot tower of St Peter's.

There'd been encounters too, seemingly meaningful at the time, particularly in the deep of the night when seductive words spoken took on more significance. But, in the end, it was all so hit-and-run as, come the realities of the day, hardness and a sense of distance returned, and an awkwardness pervaded until each went their separate way, faint-hearted promises thrown away across doorways or down creaky, rickety staircases. The only thing he regretted was not meeting that special someone, but he always remembered what Mémé told Nicola, that she would know when it happened. He believed that he too would know.

With all these thoughts buzzing about his head, Pete, for an instant, forgot both where he was and where he should be. However, he was rudely brought back to reality by a clapped-out old Humber belching out poisonous smoke passing him; raucous laughter from inside was mingling with its aggravated revving.

He searched his pockets for the flyer about the gig which Mel had given him but couldn't find it. What number was it? Perhaps he'd walked straight by. Did Mel say something about metal steps up the outside of a building, kind of set back from the road, sort of wedged in between the road and the railway just before the bridge over the canal? He thought she had.

He now noticed the Humber pulling up beside a pub further down the road. Maybe its occupants knew where the place was. He quickened his pace, and as he did, he saw three skinheads get out of the car, joking and cursing and looking as if they were on the same leash, like an image of some mythical beast. They were making their way through the door as he drew alongside the pub. He was about to ask if they knew the gaff when the last of the three, a scrawny, pale individual who weirdly eyed him up as he approached, shouted out, 'Yer long-haired git! Fucking poof!'

Of course, after all that effort, the arsehole, hot on his mates' heels, darted into the pub, and Pete breathed a sigh of relief. He lacked what Nicola once termed the art of confrontation.

'Fuckin' hell, Petey, you should've biffed that geezer. Why you always walk away? You's always too nice to people. I know it worked for Mémé, but she always could stand her ground,' she'd once said to him, but then admitted her confrontational behaviour often got her into more trouble than out of it.

But in all truth, he never felt much antagonism towards guys like that skinhead or even felt fear. He knew from Nicola's husband, Ernie, that guys like that could be right timid when alone without their mates to egg them on, with no one to show off to. Their strength was always in numbers, and three was not enough, at least not before they were bevvied up. And this he'd found out recently walking down Shaftesbury Avenue late one night, when he'd come across, in the car park of a hotel, a group of about eleven guys that looked like they were in the same football team, all snappily dressed and drunk, presumably celebrating a win. One of them clocked him and shouted out, 'Poof!'

Momentarily emboldened, Pete turned towards them and said, 'So who are you calling a poof then?', and then carried on down the street. Three of them splintered off from their core and ran after him, one punching him in the gut, the second on the chin while the third kicked his shins. He immediately fell the ground while they ran back to base. But he just got up quickly, dusted himself down and determined to walk the five or so miles back to the squat. He did feel sore the next day, though.

But in all truth, he felt those kinds of people plain sad, and knew that he, Pete, well, he had so many more options in his life. That was something Zénaïde had instilled in him from an early age; her words *toujours essaie de réaliser ton rêve d'enfance* often passed through his mind. *And don't let anyone prevent you*, she'd added. He wasn't going to.

His eyes once again scanned down the road and now a hump became clearly visible. Was that the bridge over the canal? Further scrutiny revealed a gap between two buildings to the left just before the hump; his stride now became purposeful.

On reaching the gap, he saw a metal staircase running up the side of the building. At its bottom, he stopped, looked up, eyes searching for the way in, but because by now the whole side of the building was in shadow and there were no lights, the entrance was obscured.

He began to climb the steps but a sudden lack of confidence overcame him. He stopped halfway, becoming doubtful as to whether it was the right place at all. No sounds whatsoever were coming from the inside; there were no signs, not even one poster advertising a gig. It was like just another seemingly derelict building in a city of derelict buildings, as taking any random bus ride demonstrated.

Just go back to the squat. Oh, but what about Mel?

He knew she'd be disappointed if he didn't show. But where was that flyer she gave him? All he could remember were phrases like *mind-blowing sounds* and *a journey through space and time*, and a smudged photocopy of some guy called the Wizard Geezer.

Chronic procrastination set in. Pete, halfway up those steps, still unable to make out any sounds coming from inside, became totally bewildered. The eerie silence around him unnerved him. He turned to look back up the street. Not one person to be seen, no traffic, few parked cars, and those apart from the Humber looked like they were abandoned. It seemed like a scene from a sci-fi movie.

Perhaps he misread the time; the gig started earlier. If so, it would probably be over. Or maybe it was cancelled; perhaps nobody turned up.

I should at least try the door, he thought. Bracing himself, he continued up the steps. Mindful of not making too much noise, but also trying to look like he belonged as he'd no wish for a passing copper to suspect him of attempting a break-in, he reached what had the appearance of a stable door. But now the clothes he chose earlier, the bellbottoms, his top, a purple skinny ribbed tee-shirt, now felt inappropriate; his body tingled unpleasantly under them. He felt awkward, ungainly. Stopping a second to inhale and flick back his curly tawny shoulder-length hair, he pushed the door hesitantly. It swung open easily. But any chance of anonymous entry was eliminated when it began to make a most horrendous creaking noise.

Once his eyes adjusted to the dimly lit interior, Pete saw a group of people sitting in silence on the floor. The door's creaking evidently disturbed them as a number of faces turned in his direction. He blushed as his eyes searched for Mel and Baz. He spotted them just as Mel saw him, her brow wrinkling up with a list of questions before her face broke out into a smile. Tiptoeing over, he squeezed up beside them on the floor. Being more involved, as most of the audience seemed to be, in tracing some projected blue bubbles running across their bodies, Baz gave him a cursory nod, but Mel leant over to him.

'You took your time, Pete. Still, you've not missed much,' she whispered. 'One of the tape recorders broke, then some fuses blew. It's been like this for a quarter of an hour.'

'Okay, mate. It's fixed,' some guy yelled down from a ladder leant up the facing wall.

'So what happened, Pete? Did you get lost? I was beginning to really get worried,' Mel continued.

'Well, it took me time to find the gaff, and then, I had to stop by a phone box to ring Granddad, I forgot earlier, you see, it's the anniversary… I felt really bad…'

'Oh yes, so how was he?'

'Well, I'm a bit concerned about him. Mrs Strachan was there spouting something or other about Nicknick, so it made it really difficult.'

'Oh, she's not left Ernie again?' Mel asked him, her brow endeavouring to anticipate Pete's answer.

'Who knows? But I was thinking of going down. I was wondering whether you got—'

His words were drowned out by some harsh electronic sounds. No further communication was possible. And because of the increasing drone, Mel's brow briefly quizzed him before her attention was diverted by the performance cranking up around her.

Slowly acclimatising himself, Pete cast his eyes up to the rafters. *It's like an old farmyard building*, he thought. He could see gaps in the slates letting in the last diffused rays of the sun which, filtering through masses of ancient cobwebs and dust particles, contrived to be creating their own micro-performance; nature's own light show played out above the man-made one below. What a studio it would make! A building to die for!

His eyes turned to the audience: about thirty-five or so people, all mostly around his age, but inter-weaved in between them were a few venerable relics of the beatnik generation. All were covered in projections. Pete's eyes, quickly drawn to the varied sources of these, clocked several slide projectors around the room. Not only were they facing the audience but some were lined up facing a screen on the far wall, below which a dais was situated. On this was a trestle table with a couple of tape recorders resting on it, surrounded by rubbery cables. Various small wind and percussion instruments were lying nearby encircling a large gong.

A man with waist-length hair and a plaited beard, the Wizard Geezer, presumably, suddenly started to rush around the equipment with great panache. Initially, he conjured up an image of Gandalf, but as he manically moved, Pete found him increasingly disturbing. Despite a splendid full-length robe of many hues and patterns, a rather fine creation, he had an unattractive quality about him, His physicality, his choreographed movements seemed just too poncey.

His first exposure to electronic music, Pete was not prepared for what now followed. Harsh sounds assaulted him, invaded his senses and, despite trying to concentrate, he found it impossible. Usually open to most things, he allowed himself to defer judgement, always trying to appreciate the effort that went into creative processes, but these sounds seemed like a CIA-devised torture. He felt uncomfortable and, perhaps because it was a Sunday, a memory of a dark, depressing sermon at Nicola's Methodist Sunday school came to mind, and of how, like this, it seemingly went on for hours, with Nicola and he trapped in the front row with the preacher's spittle raining down on them.

But others, indeed most of the audience, really seemed into it, their dilated pupils gleaming in appreciation. *Dilated pupils, of course*, Pete thought, *yes!* Most were no doubt lulled into the whole trip, bathed in projections and sound like they were immersed in a Badedas bubble bath and anticipating the things that would happen after.

After what seemed to be an agonising age, defective decibels defecating, the Wizard Geezer appeared to be bringing the proceedings to a close. A succession of tape machines were turned off and then, after a single beat, battered out by a girl with Pre-Raphaelite corkscrew curls, the Wizard Geezer, stretching to his full height, delivered a mighty crash on the gong. Its sound reverberated for some time after. There followed blissful silence.

Any anticipation of it being the finale, however, proved precipitate, as now the Wizard Geezer approached another tape recorder. Another switch was flicked, and a resonate, distorted voice was heard methodically, repeating two words: *Organic ecstasy*! Slowly at first, but gradually this incantation sped up, the volume upped, with the Pre-Raphaelite Chick joining in. Swooping frenetically around the audience, she was imploring them to join her, her dress and scarves swirling as she leant over, mouthing those words at them: *Organic ecstasy! Organic ecstasy! Organic ecstasy!*

Slow to respond, when, at last, the audience succumbed to her entreaties and, as the sheer volume seemed to cause the whole building to shake, the Wizard Geezer, by some mercurial application, added more distorted versions of those two words. It became too much for Pete. Almost unconsciously, he found himself standing up. After stepping over a number of ecstatic bodies, he made his way to the exit. The creaking of the door, as he passed through it, was the sweetest melody to his ears.

Outside, he remained on the top step; the fresh night air felt cleansing. But then, a whiff rose from the nearby canal, reminding him of a wider world and, looking up to the purple sky, he noticed stars delicately pulsating and he wished for an instance that he was back by the Opal Causeway, lying on the shingle gazing up at the heavens, waiting for dawn and hoping for a glimpse of *Gris Nez* or *Blanc Nez* with the sun rising over them.

His first instinct, now, was to flee, but what about Mel and Baz? He should wait for them. Yet he would prefer not being there when the audience came out. Like, what would he say if asked whether he liked the gig?

His thoughts were interrupted by a cough; looking down the steps he could just make out in the shadows beneath him a smiling face. Pete nodded.

'So yer couldn't take it, huh?'

The accent sounded American and sent butterflies to his stomach.

'I suppose I wasn't in the mood,' he replied. 'My mates in there, Mel and Baz, were raving about the Wizard Geezer. I thought it was going to be something special.'

'Jeez, that fruitcake, that's how I come to be here. A guy I stay with told me about him; I kinda thought I'd get a story for a paper back home.'

'You're a writer. Oh, wow!'

'Well, to make some bread to see me through school, you know. I been studying in Germany. On my way back home for my final year, now. I want to be a journalist eventually, but I don't think I'll write anything about that gig,' the stranger said, laughing.

His laughter was infective.

'I just couldn't take that organic ecstasy business. I had to get out.'

'Yeah, it was too much, man. I was on my way out when that crap started.'

'I didn't understand the point of it.'

'There was a point, man?' said the stranger.

'I dunno, it was all so confusing. And then when they all started to writhe on the floor.'

'Get away! Please! Am I glad I got out of there.'

'Yeah, they did, but what I was going to say was,' Pete started a little nervously, 'because of that, I got really confused, thought it was something to do with Wilhelm Reich and the stuff he wrote on orgasms, but then I realised dur orgasmic is not organic. So what was it all about? It was like the action went against the notion. Organic is organic. You can't induce it, organic ecstasy, surely, coz it's not natural, not organic, if you know what I mean.'

'Yeah, but let's not get too hung up about it, man!' the stranger said, laughing again.

Then, walking up the steps towards Pete, he held out his hand. His self-confidence was awesome.

'I'm Brad Brewster. Say, who are you?'

'Er, Pete… Pete Jones,' Pete said, shaking Brad's hand.

As Brad got closer, Pete got a better look at him. He was drop-dead. Pete was fascinated; lust and blood seemed to be rushing everywhere throughout his body.

'Say dude, who's gotta cute smile? Wanna toke?' Brad said, offering Pete a joint.

Not yet nine o'clock, but Albert slowly walked upstairs. Once so active and consequently an early riser, he was used to waiting until after the nine o'clock news before turning in. But these days, he increasingly was of the opinion that the news on television seemed trivialised, the images distracting, often not very relevant. During the Depression and the Second World War, folk would reverently listen to the radio, dwelling on every exaggeratedly enunciated word as if they came from the mouth of a benevolent uncle, but they were able to read between the lines. Then, however, there was always the belief that things would eventually get better if people strove together. To be true, things had got better for many, but for all the change, people seemed to have changed. It was like they didn't care so much. Respect was wanting.

Besides that evening, the outside world held no interest for him. He was not taken with what he saw; enthusiasm was in short supply, especially with Zénaïde gone and the boy off making his own life. Too much was happening in the world that shouldn't be: too many people in distress, strikes and the increasing acrimony between the classes worried him. Famines shouldn't be happening. And those pointless, continual wars. The world was fast changing but he had no wish to change with it, for it seemed not to be the world which he fought for during those two wars. Hadn't he fought in the first one to end all wars?

If depression had been a word in his vocabulary, he would have realised what had happened to him over the year since his wife died.

He passed from the corridor to his bedroom, got out his pyjamas from under his pillow and laid them on his bed. He then sat on the edge of that double bed contemplating its emptiness before leaning down to untie his shoelaces. As he was bent over, he momentarily flinched feeling a sharp pain in his lower rib cage. It passed quickly, but he found that he ached more since Zénaïde's death. Shoes and socks off, placed in perfect symmetry under an upright wooden chair near the window, he continued undressing. His despondency was not yet enough to break a habit of lifetime: the immaculate arrangement of his clothes, ironing out any creases with his hands, laying them out on the chair ready for the next day, trousers being slipped onto an old wooden hanger and hung behind the door. Instilled in him by his mother from an early age was the concept of properly looking after things.

After getting into his pyjamas and putting on his dressing gown, he walked back into the corridor and then the few feet to the bathroom. In this pink-painted environment, which was Zénaïde's favourite colour, with its scallop-shaped light fittings, he stood for some time above the toilet bowl wanting to pee, but, being unable to, became suddenly annoyed with himself and profusely swore before giving up. He washed his hands and face, which he did with the smallest amount of water. The gardener that he was knew of the preciousness of that commodity.

Back in his bedroom he walked over to Zénaïde's dressing table, picked up his pair of handle-less hairbrushes and, looking at his reflection in the mirror, brushed his hair from each side of his parting till he was satisfied that not one hair was out of place, even though he knew that, by the time he awoke, his thick white mop would give him the appearance of someone who'd had a bad shock.

Once in bed, sleep did not come easily, however. His mind jumped from thought to thought and he began to make a mental list of all the things that he'd neglected to do since Zénaïde's death, chastising himself. How he missed her expert planning, her encouraging ways, her subtle way of coaxing him. He still worked in the back garden, kept rose bushes trim, aphid-free, the flowerbeds tidy and mowed the lawn. But the business, which he told her he would continue, he simply couldn't carry on without her, as she had been the business. And he felt so ashamed, as the orchard, that they had tended together, was now become like a jungle: brambles encroaching from every corner, clumps of stinging nettles and buddleia appearing like they'd come out from behind a puff of magician's smoke, much to the delight of countless cabbage whites and common blues.

That orchard had been their life, their livelihood, the key component of the market garden business they'd begun together. Freeing both him from his work as a porter in the docks, and her from the onboard shop, it allowed them to do something of which they'd really only previously dreamt.

And it was all down to a ferocious gale, an unforeseen storm that had totally changed their lives thirty-five years before. For on that day, Zénaïde's ferry was kept in port and she was left stranded on dry land while he, at a loss as what to do, went to the buffet in the Marine Station and there she was, and it was there they'd exchanged their lives for a smile, instantly falling in love.

Finding that they both had similar dreams of running a smallholding, it was only driving out to the countryside one day and coming across the pinewood in which wild strawberries in abundance grew that determined that they go ahead with their plans. And, once married and settled in the house in the shadow of the Downs with a splendid, indeed, a magical view of the sea, their own Opal Causeway, and lucky enough to find an orchard for sale within walking distance of their house, they began to cultivate flowers and fruits.

Zénaïde's experience of previously being a florist on transatlantic liners put her in good stead and the local shop jumped at the chance of employing her as well as purchasing their blooms. But it was how she turned the soft fruit into preserves that became the core of their business and, within a few years, demand for her bottled fruit, jams and jellies outstripped what they could grow and they would visit outlying farms to buy fruit in the appropriate season.

However, it was that discovery, in the pinewood, of those wild strawberries turned so expertly into jam, and so well sought after, with which she made her name, became synonymous with her.

As Albert tossed about in his state of half sleep, he recalled that moment in a gossamer dream, when they drove out to the countryside on that auspicious day at the beginning of July and discovered the pinewood in which the wild strawberries grew. Now he was again under that cathedral of pines and Zénaïde was coming towards him with eerie shafts of sunlight flickering, dancing about her, complementing her graceful movements.

It really was her. She was still alive. Her death was just a fallacy, but on reaching out for her and attempting to fold her up in a tight embrace, she slipped away from his grasp and evaporated. And all there was left was pool of water.

Then Albert suddenly woke up, quite disoriented, desperate to go to the lavatory. As he walked to the bathroom, he wondered what the boy was getting up to now. Had Zinny been right about him all along? She usually was.

As the studio door opened, its creaking almost frantic, it occurred to Pete standing halfway up those steps that never was there enough time to be alone with someone when you really wanted to be, to solidify the contact.

He felt such a tremendous chemistry with this mysterious stranger and their furtive glances at one another soon become bold stares and then, quickly the broadest of smiles came onto both their faces. Already mutually exchanged details of their lives made him feel that he just somehow met up with a long-lost friend; freaky or what?

He always remembered those two Americans that Mémé met on the ferry once and bought home. They were really cool. One night they'd scored some choc, as the guy who sold it them in the little Greek café on the high street called it, bought some beers and, he being in procession of the key to Connie's beach hut, had gone in there, got blasted and had fabulous sex. That was when he decided that if something like that was so beautiful, it never could be neither wrong nor wicked.

Yes, he and Brad had clicked right away. But, being a secretive, self-conscious sort, now with the audience starting to file past them, that clicking was becoming curtailed.

Of course, he did believe in destiny, in significant occasions. Zénaïde installed that sense in him from an early age by always maintaining that it was predestined that she should cross the Opal Causeway and meet Albert, that together they'd make a new life and that Pete should come to live with them. It had been written eons before, she'd once said, when all three of them were stargazing up in the orchard one fine autumn night.

And what Pete had already found out about Brad sent him reeling. The guy seemed so confident for a start, just so upfront; he had absolutely no hesitation in his voice when he spoke. For not only was Brad from California and gay, but he seemed so positive, proud about being so.

'Yeah, man,' Brad said, fixing Pete with an awesome stare. 'I live in Berkeley. Where that notorious university is, the biggest circus in the universe, you know, where west meets east and east meets west. But you know what I miss? Other than the sunshine, that is.'

'What's that?' Pete asked.

'Going to Gay Liberation Front meetings and rapping about it all. There weren't any groups in Europe when I was there. Is there someplace here?'

Pete didn't know. He was hardly aware of Gay Liberation, though he'd come across references to it when reading about the States and California. However his interest in the West Coast had been growing. He was increasingly drawn to all the great art and music coming out from there. A potter friend from college had travelled out there the year before, and wrote him long, enthusiastic letters about the life. San Francisco was far out, the climate great despite fog on the bay, and life there seemed to be so outdoors: open, free and appropriately technicoloured. And since being in London, Pete had been harbouring a secret dream of travelling there, and meeting this so utterly upfront, admirable bloke, not only from California, but the Bay area to boot, there and then clinched it for him. And perhaps, just perhaps, Brad was that special person that Pete had been seeking all summer long.

'So that's where you got to, Pete. I thought we'd lost you again for a mo.' Mel's concerned voice echoed above them as she walked down the steps towards him.

She was followed by Baz; others of the audience began to squeeze past them.

'Here's Pete, Baz. I found him.'

'I can see, Doll,' he replied. Slight irritation could be detected in his tone.

Mel's emergence and that of the others made Pete again blush. Brad, noticing this, grinned provocatively.

'Fancy going to that pub up Regents Park Road?' Mel, hesitantly yet quickly, volunteered to no one in particular, becoming embarrassed by such lustful grins. 'Half hour till closing, I said I would. And, there's a party in a house nearby, some squat opposite, Baz says, didn't you, Baz? Everybody's going, you coming, Pete?' Then, looking at Brad, said with a contrived innocence: 'Perhaps you'd like to? Sorry, I don't know your name.'

'This is Brad,' Pete said, nervously.

A beaming Brad leapt up the steps to greet her, saying with total charm, and before Pete could introduce her, 'Hey, you must be Mel. Really pleased to meet you, and yes, I would like to come to the pub with you all.' And then, looking further up the steps towards Baz, he held out his hand to the latter, saying, 'And I guess you're Baz. How you doing, man? Wow, you know, I sure think I've seen you somewhere before.'

Again, Brad's incredible confidence amazed Pete.

However, Baz became quite standoffish and would barely look at Brad.

'I very much doubt it, mate,' he replied tersely, and turning to Mel, he said in a really pissed-off tone, 'Got me rolly, Doll?'

Mel sighed. She was always looking for things he'd lost. But she delved into her vast shoulder bag to search for his tobacco all the same. There was so much in it that she had to set it down on the steps to rumble through the contents. Out came an extraordinary assortment of articles. There were several books, including one by Tom Wolfe, *The Electric Kool-Aid Acid Test*. While this was happening the audience continued to stream by.

'No, love, it's not here,' she said. 'Sorry, sure you didn't leave it back in the music lab? Why don't you run up there and have a look? And we'll wait here.'

Pete's eyes followed Baz as he passed through the creaking door. *What was with him?* he wondered. Always contrived to cause an atmosphere, didn't the fucker realise he was lucky to have Mel? So patient with him, she was, always smoothing things over and putting up with those lengthy periods of moodiness as well as tacitly accepting how he suddenly had to go away for work. She'd never given him a hard time. And now he'd acted really off with Brad.

He sneaked a look at Brad to gauge his reaction. Nothing indicated that he was perturbed by Baz's antics. Their eyes met; they grinned at each other.

'So Brad, you do fancy coming to pub with us then?' Mel asked, her voluminous bag again heaving.

'Not changed my mind yet,' he said, with consummate charm. 'Hey *vamos*.'

Mel hitched up her long floral-patterned skirt and linked her arm through Brad's.

As they moved off down the steps together, Pete felt it was as if they too were connecting like long-lost friends. Feeling a pang of jealousy, he hurried to catch them up at the bottom.

'Where's Baz got to?' said Mel, now on the pavement.

'I'm here, Doll,' Baz said, bounding down the steps, his mood quite changed.

'You found it then?'

'What, Doll?'

'Your baccy. What else?'

'Yeah, yeah,' he said, waving his packet of Dutch tobacco at her.

'You still want to go to the pub, Baz?' Mel asked, as Pete sidled closer to Brad, almost fearful he might evaporate.

'Of course, Doll. So what we waiting for?' he replied, teasingly as he drew abreast with her, linking her arm through his.

'Oh, Baz, honestly!' said Mel, giggling.

'You're going, right?' Brad asked Pete.

Pete smiled in reply but his thoughts were on Baz. He was sure that baccy was in his pocket all the time. He'd been up to something, but what?

'To the pub then?' cried Mel. 'Follow me, your great, intrepid non-navigator.'

'So you really are reading that book?' Brad said.

'I am,' replied Mel, taking the book from her bag and flashing it across his face.

'Yeah, I saw it. Trippy, man. Those guys sure had some fun,' said Brad, as he winked at Pete.

Again Albert awoke, this time due to a commotion in the street below. A car screeched to a halt, its engine revving loudly before the ignition was switched off, after which a door banged. It jerked him out of what was a rarity – a peaceful slumber. How long he'd been asleep, he wondered; it was still dark, though.

He sat up, turned on the bedside light and then gazed at the alarm clock. He sighed. Hell's bells, it wasn't even midnight. How he wished it was already morning. Now disgruntled, he turned off the light and laid back his head onto the pillow. But no sooner had he closed his eyes than shouting started up; angry slurred swearing followed by violent banging on a door. It was coming, he was pretty sure, from the house next door, from Connie's. He turned back on the light, got out of bed and, putting on his dressing gown, went to the window to investigate.

'I thought as much,' he said out loud, as he recognised Ernie below. His mind went back to earlier that evening and, unscrambling Connie's rambles, he remembered she'd said something about Nicola leaving her husband and coming back to live with her. Still, he mused, it wouldn't be the first time.

In fact he clearly remembered that first time Nicola left Ernie. Darren was hardly a toddler then. Albert and Zénaïde had been standing by their front door, having been collared by Connie about something or other, when he noticed a figure struggling with a suitcase and pushchair turning the corner at the bottom of the hill.

With hair blown by the wind, the figure turned into Nicola clopping up the street in extremely high heels with a look of determination on her face. She, constantly experimenting with eye make-up at that time, seemed to have taken it to extremes that day. Her eyes, ringed in thick black mascara, had painted on lashes above and below, giving them a millipede-like quality, the tears she was evidently trying to suppress beginning to make them appear smudged. She was also wearing a miniskirt.

It was the first time that both he and Zénaïde had seen anybody wearing one. Of course, Connie, who was always berating her daughter for taking everything to extremes, erupted at the sight of her. Albert and Zénaïde joked about it afterwards as Connie was habitually showing off her slip and rolled-down stockings, oblivious to the amusement or contempt of all. But it had to be said that her daughter's dress was more like the scantiest of negligees, rather than a skirt, and hardly covered her buttocks. Her panties were quite visible particularly when she bent over Darren in his pushchair. And Connie, red as a beetroot, had her daughter in the house as quick as a knife.

However, as Albert surveyed the situation from his bedroom window, he was aware this time of a new development. There was evidently a change to the pattern of things as Ernie, no doubt emboldened by drink, had come in the middle of the night to reclaim his wife. Usually he stayed away and she went back after a day or two.

'Nicola, Nicola, I know you're in there,' Albert heard Ernie yelling as he continued to pummel the door. Then he heard the sound of a window opening.

'Belt up, Ernie. You're right out of order. Just go away and leave us alone! Else you'll wake Darren and my mum,' he heard Nicola hiss.

She should never have married him, Albert thought as his eyes looked over to Nicola framed in the window. Still, he hadn't thought that at the time, nor had Zénaïde. At the time, they both thought that the young couple had a chance of making a go of it. But, in all truth, Nicola'd been too young, but there was no other option. She had been determined to keep the baby and Connie, despite the irregularities of her own marriage, wasn't the type of woman to let her daughter keep a child out of wedlock. And Nicola, once she knew the score, would not even consider giving up the child for adoption. Besides, it had been all promising at first, despite their youth. Everybody came together to help them. Their wedding at the local registry office, although hardly a grand affair, was, due to the antics of the groom's family, particularly those of Ernie's miscreant brothers, a bit of a disaster, though.

But Zénaïde, of course, had a hand with the arrangements, steered things in the right direction, helping Connie with the catering, as well as altering for Nicola a beautiful Edwardian dress which had once belonged to her grandmother. Albert provided the flowers, which Zénaïde made up into the most exquisite bouquets and buttonholes. As Nicola's dad had died about four years before, she asked the boy to give her away. He'd just returned from France on the day she asked him, from that trip to the Fondation Maeght and the Matisse chapel. He'd been over the moon about doing it.

Albert recalled with a smile how close Nicola and Peter were as children. The former was often to be found around at the Jones' house. Indeed, before she went to school, Zénaïde looked after her whenever Connie went to work. And that gap still remained in the hedge, between the two households' gardens through which the two of them used to go back and forth. Albert never had the heart to close it, especially now, as it was used by Darren. But it had to be admitted that Nicola had been a wild child.

'Come down here, Nicola, I want to talk to you,' Albert heard Ernie's half-forceful, half-whining voice continue.

Another window opened and then Albert heard Connie's voice.

'Ernie. Pipe down or I'll call the police,' she hissed.

By the sound of it, he guessed, she had not put back in her teeth.

'Fuck off, you old frump!'

'That's it! I'm not being cheeked like that; I'm going to call—'

She was interrupted by Nicola.

'Ernie, don't you go calling my mum a frump!'

They'd been happy to begin with, Albert thought. But that was before Ernie went the way of his brothers and the windswept borstal up on the cliffs claimed him, and subsequently being up before the beak and prison became a regular feature of his life. Of course, the situation probably wasn't helped by Nicola having to live with Ernie's family. For a start, Nicola never had any chance with his mother. *That woman*, as she became known, was someone that even Albert and Zénaïde were more than happy to avoid.

'Nicola, just get your gear and the nipper and come home with me now.'

'Shush, Ernie, you'll wake the baby,' hissed Connie.

'He's not a fucking baby, you stupid cow, he's six,' Ernie retorted.

Albert found it curious how Connie always persisted in calling Darren a baby, particularly as it upset the little lad.

'He's my son and I want him. He should be with me,' Ernie, in a now extremely agitated state, carried on.

'Take a hike, Ern. I can't talk to you in that state,' Nicola shouted, as she started to pull down the window and then, before it was properly closed, she hissed, 'Go on, fuck off, won't you? Do one, Ernie!'

Albert ceased being shocked by the language Nicola used, but he still recalled how she'd been a polite little girl despite her mother's constant scolding and cuffing. It all started after she'd failed the 11+ and ended up at a rough secondary modern. Such a shame, as she showed much promise. Albert still retained a clear image of her on the floor by their bookcase pulling out all sorts of books. She would be engrossed in them for hours. Both Albert and Zénaïde, of course, recognised her deviancy always increased when her erring alcoholic father was at home as she strove to take him on in any way she could. And, because he and her mother were both ridiculed by their peers, by the slurs of most of their neighbours, she developed a hard exterior towards the outside world, which, by the time she came into her teens, was perfected. She became impregnable; even boys feared her. She'd not been a child to know physical fear herself, in any case, and was certainly not cautious like Peter. But, strangely enough, though, Albert now reflected, whenever she entered the Jones' house, it seemed like she felt she could drop her guard.

Of course, Albert recognised, Zénaïde had been the main reason for that. They'd formed a close relationship from even before the boy came to live with them. She worshipped Zénaïde, who showed her the more feminine side of life, showed her things that her own mother couldn't be bothered with. Yes, it was true. She became a quite different person with Zénaïde and, quietly, sought her advice even if she didn't always take it. And Zénaïde had sheltered her, often secreting her in their bedroom, especially when Nicola was fleeing her dad, who, regularly taking umbrage at any slight misdemeanour she committed, would turn up in hot pursuit of her at their front door, puce and shaking with rage.

Albert walked away from the window. Now he felt wide awake but he desperately wanted to sleep. He decided to go downstairs to make himself some Horlicks, inwardly laughing, as he'd done countless times before as he remembered Zénaïde's Gallic contempt for such drinks. She herself always made a tisane, more often than not a *verveine*; maintaining too much milk on the stomach was not a good thing at all, last thing at night. But he liked the soothing texture of his preferred drink, which seemed to do the trick.

Back upstairs, and he found the pantomime continuing. Ernie was relentless and there was no reasoning with him. As his slurred imploring rose to a crescendo, more and more lights in houses down the street came on. Albert could tell that Connie was exasperated by now and had ceased to answer. Nicola's window remained fiercely closed, but Connie, although she left her window open, suddenly disappeared from view and Ernie was left talking now incoherently to himself, and, in his drunken stupor, muddling his words into imitation pearls of confusion.

After a short while Connie came back to her window.

'Here, Ernie, come here! Maybe there's a solution,' she called out to her son-in-law.

As he walked along her tiny front garden, Albert saw Connie lift up a large preserving pan and set it on the window sill. Ernie looked up and, as he did, she tipped a few gallons of icy cold water all over him, took back the pan into her room and, quickly, slammed shut the window. The shock of the cold sent Ernie reeling to the ground and there he stayed, moaning and cursing, till his alcohol intake anaesthetised him to sleep.

Albert finished off his Horlicks and, relieved, got back into bed. The noise over, he soon was asleep. The last thing he remembered thinking was that Peter would call the next day. Was it in the morning, he said? He thought it was but couldn't actually remember.

'Phew! That was a close one, folks!' said Baz as the four of them started to emerge from along the path that led from the back entrance to the squat where the party had taken place.

By the time they were on the pavement, the paddy wagon was wailing its way around the corner at the end of the road.

'Poor bastards,' Baz continued. 'Can't think they can get them for anything. All the same they'll probably be duffed up. But there was nothing there. Jesus, call that a party!'

'To be fair, Baz, we didn't contribute anything ourselves,' said Mel.

'Yeah, Doll, but you know!'

The party had turned out to be in some derelict flats, above an empty shop, just across the road from the pub, where Pete, Brad, Mel and Baz had stayed till closing time. They found the door on the latch when they arrived and, trooping in, also found after bumping into some unidentifiable piece of furniture that there was no lighting. Beckoned by the sounds of a stringy guitar, they made their way up the stairs. In that opportune darkness Brad brushed up against Pete; they both felt their bodies tingling in anticipation of what was to come.

On the first floor, they came across a room with a huddle of freaks sitting cross-legged in a circle on the floor, staring at a minuscule piece of hash, evidently lamenting its shrinking. Nobody responded to their greeting, and if this was a party, it was difficult to tell as there was neither booze nor food; indeed, not even a salty peanut, for that matter. And as for the music, somebody facing a corner was playing the blues: a Robert Johnson tune, on a guitar very badly, wailing not weeping, and certainly with no tears dripping down his leg. They stood like mugs in the doorway for a short while, and then, realising that acknowledgement would never be forthcoming, decided to carry on up the stairs to the second floor.

The contrast of this floor to the one below was unbelievable. It was like they were entering another world, that of souk or harem. Rich, luxuriant oriental carpets covered the floor and walls; loudly patterned cushions were strewn about inter-spaced with candles, lanterns and exotic plants, triffid-like, ensnaring and softening the dimensions as they cast a series of even more complicated patterns and textures on the already richly decorated walls. They all gasped simultaneously when, out of the shadows, a figure, tanned and healthy-looking, emerged. He was wearing just a pair of shorts.

He spoke, saying with a great credence that he was a horticulturist, though it sounded he was more like a gardener as apparently he made his living tending the gardens of the liberal rich up the hill in Hampstead. But his passion, about which like a preacher he regaled them, while sucking on a hubbly-bubbly pipe, was the study of Islamic gardens, and he spent most of the winter in Morocco, he told them.

And it was while he was talking about Morocco that they heard the heavy bangs and shouts, tell-tale noises of oppression. Gathering what appeared to be his stash, the horticulturist quickly led them up to a flat roof, from where a rusty wrought-iron spiral staircase took them down to safety at the back of the building, and where they remained in silence until they felt the coast to be clear. Yes, it had been a close one.

'Thing is now, Doll, I wish you'd never persuaded me to take the bus. Hiding from the old bill's made us miss the last one. And forget the night buses. From Camden to the Gate? We probably have a stopover of two days at Trafalgar Square.'

'Oh, Baz, honestly! We could walk. It would be fun,' said Mel.

'Doll! No! It wouldn't. I'm telling you.'

'You all want a ride in my VW bus? I drove here. You're all welcome to,' said Brad, his eyes on Pete.

'Nice one, Brad,' said Baz, beaming.

'It's parked somewhere nearby that music lab. But I'm fucked if I know where.'

As Mel and Baz led the way along the pavement, Pete and Brad stopped simultaneously; their grins became synchronised and their eyes shone as they turned to look, the one at the other, and then, under a spluttering lamppost, they kissed.

I hope he feels the same as me, Pete thought, as they continued walking back towards the music lab. The bus was quickly located in a street nearby on the other side of the canal.

'I hope you're okay to drive, Brad,' Mel enquired. 'That barley wine we had in the pub is strong, you know.'

'Jesus, Melanie!' scoffed Baz. 'That was hours ago. Of course he's all right to fucking drive.'

'If you say so,' said Brad, laughing, as he unlocked the door and held it open in a cavalier fashion.

They piled in: Brad, Baz, who knew the way, with Mel between them in the front. Brad started up the van and followed Baz's directions. Pete was up behind, leaning over the backs of their seat as they chatted on their journey back to Powis Square.

'Where exactly are you from in California, Brad?' Mel asked after a while.

'Berkeley.'

'So where's that exactly?'

'Just across the bay across from San Francisco, Northern California. I'm studying there. In that notorious hot bed of radicals, wowee!'

'Oh yes, I know. I read something about that uni in *Rolling Stone*. Or *Time* magazine. Some Republican senator was slating it something chronic. Calling everybody a bunch of red commies. Yes, there's a lot of demos there, aren't there? Anti-war ones. And so what do you study, Brad?' said Mel.

'Jesus, Mel, what's with the third degree?' interjected Baz.

'No, it's all right, man. German and literature. I just finished my third year, which I spent in Germany. Wow, did I *ausgeflipt* there!' said Brad, suddenly bursting into infective laughter.

'*Ausgeflipt?*' queried Mel, her brow furrowing up.

'Oh, it just means flipped out. They have some real neat sayings over there! We all used to joke about them. I sure had a great time anyway. Travelled around a lot in Europe with a few of the guys: Munich, Paris, Spain. Now, Ibiza, that's some place. You all been there?'

'Never,' three voices said, in unison.

'Now that is a helluva fabulous place to hang out. It's so unspoilt. The sea, it's so blue, just awesome. And those beaches!

The freaks! Joni Mitchell was hanging out there when I visited, you know. Yeah, we all had great adventures going down there, travelling on the ferries and everything. In this ol' jalopy. Sure did, and I got to be the one that got to keep it. That's how I came to London. Drove and got the ferry. My buddies all went home. But I stayed. I wanted to do some more exploring. Since I've been over here in Europe, I've been writing articles for a local Berkeley underground paper on gigs and cultural stuff, to make extra bread. That's how I come to be here tonight. But tell me about you, Mel? What do you do?'

'Oh, I just work in a library.'

'Neat. Libraries are good. Important. So how'd you all meet?'

'In Manchester,' said Pete. 'Baz and Mel were at the university there and I was at art college. We had rooms in the same house my first year.'

'Say what d'you do, Baz?' asked Brad, slowly.

'Oh, this and that, mate.'

'Meaning?'

'What I say! This and that!'

There was once more a tone of irritation in Baz's voice, an up-tightness. Pete, who sometimes found it difficult to restrain himself when he felt that Baz was being unnecessarily unfair with Mel, clocked this frostiness from Baz towards the American stranger and he was confused as to why. He'd acted like his best friend when he heard he'd got wheels.

'Oh, Baz, honestly!' Mel cut in, trying to defuse the atmosphere. 'No, Brad, he's got a market stall in Portobello selling collages he makes from junk, old clocks and things like that. And kinetic stuff. They're brilliant. And he also imports antiques from Belgium.'

'Ah, an artist and connoisseur then!' said Brad.

'If you say so,' retorted Baz.

'Hey, that's where I saw you. Amsterdam, man. Were you there last spring? I'm pretty sure of it now, man.'

'I don't think so, mate.'

'But you were in Bruges in April,' Mel reminded him.

'Yeah, but Bruges ain't fuckin' Amsterdam, you stupid cow. It's not even in fuckin' Holland,' said Baz, with such vehemence that Brad was persuaded that it was time to change the topic of conversation. They had reached Swiss Cottage by then and the lights just turned red as the bus drew up to the crossing.

'Damn, the traffic lights in this city! Always red! So, Pete?' said Brad, as he turned round to look at Pete.

As he did, he drew his top teeth over his bottom lip, which so got to Pete.

'So, Pete, what is it that you do?'

'Me?'

'Like, are there any other Petes here?'

'Well, I—'

'They're green now, mate,' said Baz.

Brad turned to look straight ahead and escalated across Finchley Road.

'So, Pete, you were saying?'

'Well, I just finished a photography course in Manchester. And I've been looking for photography work since. Actually, I've been offered a job doing a mail order catalogue, but I've not decided whether I want to do it. It's so straight, not at all creative, and besides, it's back in Manchester. And I'm not sure if I want to go back. It was a great three years there, but I kinda want to travel a bit.'

'You must tell him about the adventure playground, Pete,' said Mel.

'The what?'

'Oh, yeah, the adventure playground,' said Pete. 'Well, it's not a proper paid job actually. But yeah, I'm volunteering at an adventure playground. It's something new, started for the kids with nothing to do in the holidays, when their parents work. Supposed to keep them off the street and out of mischief. Well, sort of.'

'Serious grassroots then!'

'Yeah, probably more for the playleaders than the kids, you know, *their* credibility,' Pete said.

'Oh, Pete,' said Mel, tutting.

'So how did it all get started?' asked Brad.

'Mel knows more about that than me.'

'Well, Celina, a Jamaican woman I know from the library, came in one day for information about things happening for kids,' said Mel. 'We got talking and she told me that she wanted to start a playgroup for the toddlers. I got her the numbers of useful contacts, councillors, people working in the council, churches, etc., and, well, to cut a long story short, she got a small grant and a donated hut which she was allowed to erect, under a small closed-off section under the motorway, by Portobello. That was last year. But it put a lot of ideas in people's heads and, as a result, they started opening up adventure playgrounds for older kids on disused sites all over the place. But Celina really has to be given the credit for it all.'

'So you work round Portobello Pete?'

'No, in Hammersmith, down Fulham Palace Road. The kids are older there, from about ten, eleven to sixteen. I am due there tomorrow afternoon. You can come with me if you want. I'll show you around.'

Brad drew the bus up at the lights on Kilburn High Road and braked. Tossing back his thick blond hair, he turned again to look at Pete, flashing his shining brown eyes at him. Pete was slayed by the gesture.

'I'd like that. And hey, maybe I might write something about it,' he said, with deliberation.

'You have to turn left here, mate, and then sharp right,' Baz said, abruptly.

Once across the road, Brad was about to put down his foot on the gas when Mel shouted out for him to stop.

'I want to show you something. I forgot we went past here.'

Brad screeched to a halt by a Number 28 bus stop and Mel insisted that they all get out and lined them up on the pavement. Getting a torch from her bag, she shone it on a memorial of sorts.

'Look, boys! This memorial is dedicated to all the animals that lost their lives in the First World War. There were just so many of them: horses, camels, donkeys, dogs, even pigeons. Look at that list. It's so sad. They couldn't even be conscientious objectors.'

Tears started to form in her eyes, and Baz, in a rare moment of tenderness, put his arm around her shoulders.

'Yeah, Doll. It stinks, but...' he said, and starting to grin, he turned to Brad and Pete. 'She sometimes goes way over the top about animals. I mean, that time when we was staying in a cottage in Wales, and I come downstairs and find Mel with a sheep in the kitchen, by the range, as she thought it was cold!'

'Oh, Baz, it'd just been sheared, the poor thing.'

'But Doll, it was the middle of June.'

They all chuckled.

It's true, Pete thought, *she can be somewhat over the top when it came to animals.* But he didn't think it appropriate then to bring up the story of the time when he and Mel were in a crowded bar at Euston station, waiting for the Manchester train, and Mel espied a lone silverfish, marooned on the carpet, to whose rescue she leapt. She had carried off the little creature to the ladies' toilet as she maintained it needed to be near a source of water. Pete was never quite sure whether she hadn't managed to extinguish its little life on the way there.

'So, Brad?' Mel asked, as they set off again. 'What was your most favourite place you visited in Europe?'

'It's difficult to say. I found that I liked different places for different reasons. But France, Paris sure is interesting. The museums! Fantastic, but the French can be difficult.'

'Pete's half French.'

'I'm not really, Mel. No, my step-grandmother was French. She brought me up. The truth is I don't know what I am. My dad is English. Not that I see him. When he left the navy, he retired to Australia with his second wife.'

'What about your mother?' asked Brad.

'I don't know. I can barely remember her, just sort of have a vague memory of someone wrapped in a swirly patterned purple-coloured cloak. She disappeared one snowy day. Nobody knows what happened to her.'

'What, did she just up and left you alone? How old were you?'

'Still a baby really, nearly two, I think. But I wasn't alone. I was with Granddad and Mémé, Zénaïde, that is, my step-grandmother.'

'Zénaïde. Wow, that's an unusual name. I like it.'

'She didn't. She cursed her strict Catholic mother for it. She was named after some nineteenth-century novelist called Zénaïde-Marie-Anne Fleuriot, whose works were intended for good Catholic women and girls like her. Mémé was forced to read them as a child and hated them. Apparently, it was Zénaïde-Marie-Anne Fleuriot's aim in life to furnish people with unobjectionable reading. That's what Mémé told me, in any case – literature for nuns, she said.'

'I've never heard of her. So you speak French then?' Brad asked.

'Yes, as a child, always with her. And besides, we were always going over there. Or relatives were coming to us. Back and forth across the Opal Causeway, as she called it.'

'The Opal Causeway? That's neat. So what's that then?'

'The Straits of Dover, or Pas de Calais, depending which language you use. It is the name of the sea by which we lived.'

'Why did she call it the Opal Causeway, Pete?' Mel asked. 'I never did know.'

'Because of the constantly changing colours in the sea – have a look next time you go across.'

'Oh, so you *do* speak French, then?' Brad repeated.

Speaking French, or rather, not speaking it, had been something Pete had been thinking about during the previous day on the anniversary of Zénaïde's death. He lamented the fact he didn't speak it much now she was gone. The last time he'd been to France was when Zénaïde had that fall, and he'd not been in touch at all since with his cousins Françoise and Jean-Luc, Zénaïde's niece Germaine's kids, with whom he and Nicola had spent seemingly endless summer holidays.

For, strangely after going to Manchester, he'd fallen out of sync with them. Despite *mai soixante-huit*, he found, without even realising at first, he was turning his back on France. He no longer found people there cool anymore. They were too into smart clothes, naff aftershave and chauvinism, although he was naturally always the first to defend them if some ignorant English person attempted to ridicule them. In fact, he had stood up for them, as Nicola had for them and him, despite her lack of French, ever since he went to school, ever since he could remember. Yes, like Josephine Baker, he did have *deux amours*.

But the world had become a bigger place for him after he travelled with some students from his college to Amsterdam and Germany and found himself being drawn to the culture there, particularly the fine but relaxed sense of order that pervaded everything in Holland. But lately it was really the strident sounds and images, the music and words that were coming out of America, and from California and the West Coast in particular, that were really interesting him. So it was with a very keen interest that he surveyed Brad's head from his position from the back of the bus. Brad's total upfront manner seemed to him to encapsulate all that he admired from over there.

'Wow!' exclaimed Brad. 'Another canal. Sure are a lot here.'

'Same one, mate,' Baz replied, as they drove over it. 'Now when we get to the bottom of the road, you turn right and then it's no distance at all to the squat.'

'Squat? I keep hearing this word squatting. So what's a squat?' asked Brad.

'That's where we live. In a squat. With a group of people

we've occupied an empty derelict property,' Mel pronounced. 'Reclaimed it for the people.'

'Kinda like a cooperative then?'

'On the good days,' said Pete.

Mel made a tutting sound and then laughed.

'Oh, Pete! But it's about trying to redress something. It's all about being fair. As there's a severe housing crisis in this country, you see, and some people live under the most appalling conditions or have no place to live while there are so many empty properties and not enough council housing. A lot of these houses have been empty since before the last government came to power and cracked down on unscrupulous landlords; in fact, some have been empty since the Second World War. Left in a terrible state by their owners. There were some horrendous landlords, outrageous ones, in the last years of the fifties and the early sixties, that used violence and extortion, especially against the Caribbean community; that Rackman—'

Baz cut in now. 'All right, Mel, enough of the social history lesson. Turn left here, mate, and drive straight down.'

'That's where we live,' said Pete, pointing to a tall white painted and obviously once impressive building as the bus drew up by the side of the pavement. 'And it's a mansion inside. There's even a conservatory at the back. Although when we have a heavy rainstorm, it does leak a bit.'

'A bit, Pete? More like a lot!' jibbed Baz, as they all got out of the van and walked in single file up the steps.

Once in their room, Baz and Mel crashed out immediately, but Pete and Brad in Pete's room were awake and very alert until dawn.

Albert had paced the length of his house's ground floor several times since he'd breakfasted. He'd risen with a dull headache and, as a result, felt uncharacteristically fidgety, like he should be doing something or other. But what? He couldn't recall. He hadn't even been able to settle down to his newspaper; the form of horses running that day at the nearby racetrack holding no allure for him. At least, it seemed that Ernie was gone; his car was no longer in the street. But the previous night's interrupted sleep hadn't given him the rest that he craved. He felt disorientated.

After looking out of the window again to check Ernie's car was really gone, his sense of relief was short-lived, as he now imagined Connie relating in great detail her no doubt complicated, confusing interpretation of last night's shenanigans, at some point later on that day. His pacing came to a halt by the mantelpiece, where he was attracted by a small framed black and white photograph. It was of Zénaïde with Peter and Nicola in the wild strawberry woods. It couldn't have been taken that long ago, but how those kids had grown! Wild strawberries made him think of the orchard.

Perhaps I'll go up there after the boy calls, he thought. *That way, if Mrs Strachan comes around to clobber me, I won't be home.*

He looked at his watch. After ten thirty. He'd remembered

on waking that the boy said he'd call early, that he had to go to work later. He should have called by now, then. But perhaps he'd difficulty finding a telephone box working. Albert stared at the black Bakelite telephone on the hallway table willing it to ring. There was so much he wanted to ask Peter, to discuss with him.

What was this agitation he was feeling? Was he ill? He felt flushed. It wasn't like him. He sat down in his armchair in the front room and tried to read his paper once more. The clock on the mantelpiece ticked away, lulling him, hypnotising him into half sleep, that kind of daytime slumber when the soul is confused as to whether it sleeps or not.

But there he was, half his age again, down at the docks, walking along the Prince of Wales pier, with the waves cascading up around him. It felt invigorating, cleansing. There was a ferryboat being tossed about by the swell like a bird in a dog's mouth as it attempted to enter the harbour. The Opal Causeway was angry, angry like when on that fateful day he met Zénaïde.

He was roused from this unaccustomedly long slumber by the sound of someone starting up a lawnmower, and, looking up at the clock, he realised it was midday. Had he been asleep all that time? Still Peter hadn't called. Surely, the phone's ringing would have woken him. By now, the boy would be working, but best not to worry; there was always an explanation. He had to give the boy some slack, but he wished he'd returned home this summer instead of going to London. He wanted to pin him down about that job, the one with the catalogue company in Manchester. He hoped the boy would take it. He wanted to see him settled. Such an opportunity should not be thrown to the wind.

And why was the boy squatting? He didn't care for that. And the adventure playground malarkey was all well and good, but it was only seasonal, and as for the photographers' cooperative that had apparently been set up in one of the nearby squats that Peter had enthusiastically told him about a couple of months back, well, he'd not said much at the time but he did wonder where the wages would come from. It all sounded like an upbeat version of Mr Rye's setup down the road, but it was a hobby for him; he'd a proper job. Mr Rye had been the first to encourage Peter to take up photography, but it had been Zénaïde who convinced Albert there was money to be made from it.

'Look at the number of new glossy magazines, colour supplements and catalogues,' she'd said, and so there was, the Manchester job just one, and it was important the boy paid his stamp. He would if he took that job. Yet he did sense that Peter had an aversion to the job. He'd said it was too straight. Straight, what did he mean? All this talk about freedom and expression, these young people had these days, and doing your own thing; well, they didn't know how lucky they were. His own dad would have beaten him just for disagreeing with him, for refusing to do what he was told. But that was in a different era, and besides, his father had died by the time he was thirteen, and then he'd been responsible for his family. And he'd eventually done what he wanted. To be true, with Zénaïde's guidance.

Yet, if the boy went to Manchester, it was a long way; he wouldn't much see him. Yes, Manchester was far, not a journey Albert relished making, certainly not by car. Those motorways! He'd only been on the M2 twice, only from one junction to the next. To be truthful, latterly he'd barely driven west of the Medway, let alone the Stour. Maybe the boy would be better off with something around here. But would he find anything?

No call and the clock's ticking, he thought. *Perhaps I'll phone Melanie.* The boy mentioned the night before that she wanted to visit. She'd know where he was; they lived in the same house. He had her work number; Peter gave it to him for emergencies. Now where was it? As he searched about for it, his mind went back to the boy. He was proud of him.

He and Zénaïde never expected to bring up a child. But fate took a strange twist when Albert's daughter-in-law and the boy, around two at the time, were left with them by Georgy, while he went off on a tour of duty and, not long afterwards, Sara disappeared without a trace, leaving the child. Albert never knew where Georgy met Sara: Malta, Gibraltar or further east, perhaps. Zénaïde always remarked that the boy had a slight oriental look about him.

But once Georgy left them, she became distant to both baby and them, and much as they tried, they were at a loss as what to do about her. It was during a snow storm that she disappeared, wrapped up in the purple paisley-patterned eiderdown from her bed. There was a sighting of someone like her on the cliffs later that day, but the only evidence, found sopping and decaying near the cliffs some months later, was the eiderdown. To begin with the boy missed his mother, but because they were already besotted with him, had quickly fallen in love with him, he responded to them. He started to imitate what his grandfather did and was keen to help him in his chores in that hindering way young children do. When Albert did eventually hear from Georgy, Georgy asked him to hang on to the boy till he got back on leave and could sort it out. But somehow, it never did get sorted out for some years, and the boy became the biggest part of their lives, became their child by default.

They were both devastated when the boy, then about eight, was reclaimed by his father. Georgy was by then posted to a nearby naval dockyard, had a new Australian wife, twin girls and an older step-daughter from his wife's first marriage. The boy, curious about his father, jumped at the idea at first, but it didn't work out and he ran away. And so he came back to them, continuing to live with them right through till the end of his school days.

How proud they were of him when he passed his 11+ and went on to the grammar school, although to begin with, he wanted to join Nicola at the secondary modern. And with his eight O and three A-levels later, he became the first in his family to go on to further education. But where was that number?

Albert started to rummage through a pile of papers on the hall table. What a mess it all was! Zénaïde used to keep things in such good order. He again felt bad about letting things go, but he just did not have her method, that way that she was able to *ranger ses affaires*. He was about to give up but, noticing some papers had fallen to the floor behind the small table, he peered down and Peter's handwriting beckoned up to him.

Albert dialled the number with some feeling of guilt. It was not in his nature to make trunk calls during the day. It rang four times before a terse voice answered: 'Kensington Public Library, the head librarian speaking.'

'Good afternoon. I would like to speak to Melanie…' Albert hesitated, as he couldn't remember Mel's surname. 'Who works there if I may?'

'Is this a personal call?' came the brusque reply.

'Yes, it is.'

'We don't normally allow our staff to take personal calls. And in any case, Melanie is at lunch. She's not due back for another forty-five minutes.'

'I wonder if you might be able to give her a message. I would be much obliged. Can you tell her Peter's granddad rang? Mr Jones, that is.'

'Peter's granddad, well, well, I see. I'll make an exception this time, but please don't ring again if it's not to do with library business. We're not a messaging service, you know,' the haughty voice on the other end said, before the line went dead.

What an unpleasant woman; there's no need to be like that, Albert thought as he put down the receiver.

He went into the kitchen to get some bread and cheese for his lunch. As he just sat down at the table there was a tap on the backdoor. Surely not Connie Strachan! It was too early for her. But then a meek-sounding voice cried out, 'Mr Jones? I hope I'm not disturbing you. Can I talk to you? It's Nicola.'

Thanking his lucky stars that it wasn't Connie, he went over to the door and, opening it, found both Nicola and a grinning Darren on the other side.

'We came through the gap! And I've come to apologise. Sorry about last night, Mr Jones. He's up in court again today,' she sighed. 'He's too much. I am confused about it all.'

Albert brushed it off by going to the gas cooker and putting on the kettle.

'I'll expect you'll be wanting a cup of tea then,' he said.

'You sit down, Mr Jones. I'll make the tea. Continue with your sandwich.'

'There are some biscuits and a bottle of squash over there. I expect the young scallywag would like that,' said Albert, winking as he lifted his sandwich to his mouth while gesturing towards the Easywork dresser. Darren beamed.

He was an unusual child, Albert had always thought: way older than his age, not at all like his dad and not much like Nicola either. Albert was impressed by how he had such a retentive memory. From an early age, Darren had declared he was going to be an astronaut when he grew up. He also loved pets and longed to have a puppy. But Nicola put her foot down about that, their flat being no place for a dog. But he still badgered his grandmother about getting one and keeping it at her house, but she always told him he was too young. But he did own two gerbils, one called Telstar and the other Sputnik, and a goldfish called Gemini, which were now safely installed next door.

The kettle came to the boil and Nicola made the tea.

'Any news of Petey, Mr Jones? Is he taking that job?' she asked Albert, as she set the teapot, mugs, milk jug and sugar bowl down on the table and started to pour the tea.

'He said he'd ring today but hasn't yet. So I don't know, but I think he should. It's been offered to him on a plate. He did say he is coming down soon to stay a few days.'

'Fab!' said Nicola. 'We should go on a day out, like we always did when Mémé was...'

She stopped in mid-sentence, concerned about his feelings. She too had remembered the anniversary of the previous day and she too missed Zénaïde. How she wished she was still around now her problems with Ernie had escalated.

Albert smiled at her.

Nicola had been such a part of their lives and it always touched him that she, like the boy, called Zénaïde Mémé. A lot of the children in the street had when they were younger, although with their East Kent vowels, it sounded more like my-my.

'Yes, I'd like that,' he said. 'I think his friend Melanie is coming too. The one who works in the library, with the Flash Harry boyfriend, you know, the Julius Caesar from Carnaby Street.'

'By herself?' asked Nicola.

'I believe so,' replied Albert.

'Oh, I see,' Nicola said, with a trace of disappointment in her voice, because she'd fancied Baz something rotten the last time.

While Darren went out to play in the garden, Albert and Nicola chatted away, reminiscing about the days out taken when she and Peter had been children and about the times they had spent up at the orchard and how days seemed less carefree now. The visit cheered Albert up no end and he began to feel a certain contentment.

'Talking of the orchard, Nicola.'

'Yes, Mr Jones.'

'Well, I'm planning to go up to it in a little while. Do you think that Darren would care to accompany me there?'

'I think he might,' Nicola replied.

She went over to the open door and called out to ask her son, who came running inside in a heightened state of excitement at the prospect.

'In actual fact, Mr Jones, you would be doing me a favour as I got to go home and get some things and find out what happened in court. And Darren would only get under Mum's feet. He so enjoys being with you. He always comes back full of ideas.'

So Nicola went off to do her errands, leaving an overjoyed Darren jigging about all over the show while he waited for Albert to get himself ready.

It was the shrill call of a peacock that woke Pete from his slumbers on the grassy area behind the King George VI Memorial Youth Hostel. He sat up and watched a group of Japanese tourists, weighed down by cameras, the make of which he could only dream owning, encircling a guide who seemed to be talking with an exaggerated enthusiasm about the partly ruined Holland House.

As the guide led them away and they filed past him and the sleeping Brad, Pete heard the guide say, evidently in a reply to a question from one tourist, 'Oh my goodness, yes! The mansion was at one period in the late eighteenth century the hubbub of British political life.'

'What is a hubbub?' another of the tourists asked.

Pete didn't get to hear the reply as the party quickly moved off towards Holland Walk, but by the exasperated look on the face of the guide, it would have seemed that he was quite digging himself a hole in which to fall.

It was a beautiful late summer's afternoon, and the grass surrounding him was parched and dusty. He and Brad had been playing Frisbee for about an hour before flopping down on the grass to snooze.

Pete looked at his watch. Three. Mel wouldn't come for another hour yet. They'd arranged to meet her there when she got off from work. He glanced over to the edge of the wooded area and noticed three brown rabbits each running in short bursts as if playing some kind of game, until a Jack Russell streaked off in their direction and they quickly scattered into the wooded area. He looked down at Brad. He looked so peaceful. Was it really only two days since they'd met? It seemed longer.

If what had happened the day before had not been a fire he would have called it fortuitous because now he had the rest of the week off. And he could spend it all with Brad.

However, his conscience was nagging him as because of all the excitement, he'd neglected calling his grandfather. But he would do it later.

The previous morning, after strolling down Portobello, pointing out to Brad places of interest, local quirky features, the two of them had set off for the adventure playground, getting the tube at Ladbroke Grove for the couple or so stops to Hammersmith. The jovial ticket inspector there, who Pete knew from a meeting he went to with Mel at Celina's playgroup, waved them through as if he was ushering them into a church wedding.

Brad was astounded.

There was a slight warm west wind blowing and it was pleasant walking down the streets over dry brown leaves disintegrating into dusty powder under their feet. They felt so relaxed, at ease with each other, and every so often one of them would catch the other sneaking covert glances and big grins would be exchanged. After about ten minutes, they turned the corner by the Greyhound pub. However, further up, as they reached the playground's eight-foot corrugated iron fence and turned another corner, their idyllic state began to become polluted by some strange sort of vibe, nothing they could touch on, though.

'What? Wow! This is an adventure playground?' Brad exclaimed, after they drew up to the hefty corrugated iron gates which were half open.

Pete didn't know what he was expecting – maybe they'd better facilities for kids in Berkeley; he imagined they might well do – but still, he could forgive Brad for being taken aback. For despite the project being set up through the worthy efforts of a Christian mission down the road, it quite resembled a bomb site, and certainly would have been a totally appropriate location for a scene in an Ealing comedy.

Situated on a corner of two streets where a right angle of terrace houses once stood, the local council, having compulsory purchased the block, had let the mission have the use of it, although it was earmarked for future development. There was no smooth, freshly laid asphalt to be found; it had neither climbing frames nor swings, not even was there one blade of grass visible. It was just a desert of rubble surrounded by the high corrugated iron fence on two sides, an occupied house on a third and by part of a derelict building at the back.

This derelict building had a ladder inside which leant onto a frameless first-floor window and was where the most daring kids, kept in line by Paco, a kid both wiser and harder beyond his years and with little respect for Brian, the project leader, spent their days, swinging out on a rope which was somehow attached onto the top of the window. They would eventually let go and fall on to a heap of old, smelly, stained mattresses down below.

There was a queue of mainly boys waiting to take turns when Brad and Pete arrived.

Once inside they were greeted by Brian.

'Cor, I'm glad you're here, Pete!' he said, while casting an inquisitive eye over Brad. 'They's fucking manic today. Maybe it's the wind or someit.'

While Pete was introducing Brad to Brian and the other workers, he noticed Maria, Paco's sister, pass by them carrying a bucket which contained what looked like some pieces of coal. Because some of the kids brought all sorts of weird things with them, it didn't seem strange at the time. Maria and the other girls were usually to be found either inside or around a makeshift hut on the right side of the gate. This was their den and they brought different precious items daily to embellish it. Still, Pete cursed himself for not seeing it happen. But then, no one did.

For very soon, a whiff of smoke coming from the hut was quickly followed by a sudden exodus from inside of it of about ten terrified girls squealing out, 'Fire! Fire!'

Within seconds, the smoke was bellowing thick and dark, and while Brian started throwing a bucket of sand and rubble onto the fire and another play worker directed the kids out on to the street, Pete, with Brad behind him, was desperately searching for a telephone box.

Luckily, they located one working not too far up the street and Pete was able to get through to the fire brigade first time. However, by the time they got back to the playground, they found the fire had devoured the little hut and that its flames had fiercely started to lick their way up the side of the occupied house adjacent to it. And it seemed to be taking hold.

With sirens clanging, three fire engines arrived and, suddenly, firemen were everywhere. Luckily, they quickly got the fire under control while Brian took a roll of the kids to check they were all there. One or two of the littler girls were crying and were being consoled by their elders. It was just then that the man from the mission arrived on the scene. Asking Brian if all the kids were accounted for, he was told one was missing.

Just as a recount was being taken, and it was realised the unaccounted-for kid was Paco, a noise, like a distant rumble of thunder, sounded behind them. Alarmed, everybody revolved towards the direction it was coming from and were just able to clock a brief image of Paco, yelling like Tarzan, as he swung on the rope through the frameless window before the whole wall of the building to which the rope was attached started to lean precariously and then quickly caved over with a thud to the ground.

Pete's heart stopped; everybody froze, fearing the worse.

But as the dust subsided, a smudged, cheeky face looked up and smiled. Miraculously, Paco had landed on the mattresses, and the wall had landed completely all around him; indeed, he was perfectly framed by where they window should have been. He had no injury whatsoever, not one mark, no scratch on his body.

Getting up, he shook the dust off his clothes, and then, before anyone was able to say anything, strutted out of the playground with a right cocky look on his face while all and sundry looked on in disbelief.

'Paco, hey, come back,' Brian called out.

'Fuck off,' came the reply as two fingers were lifted.

It was then that the man from the mission decided that the playground should be closed for the rest of the week.

The peacock shrieked again and woke up Brad this time.

He looked up at Pete, who was seated cross-legged at his side.

'You know, I was dreaming a wall nearly fell on me. I wonder why?' he said, while gently stroking Pete's thigh. 'You know what else? I really like this place. And the market. It's a pity I'll have to split before too long. We'll have to do some more exploring.'

Pete knew that Brad had to get back for his new semester, but he forced that knowledge from his mind. What was important was now. He felt they were like kindred spirits, particularly as when out walking and observing, they seemed to have the same reaction to things.

It had been such a ball showing Brad the area around the squat, as they talked about all those things two people opportunely thrown together talk about: excitedly exchanging experiences, about people and places, about fears and desires, and of the beauty and the unfairness of the world in which they lived. Pete was fascinated to hear more about gay liberation and how it was for gay people in California. They appeared to be so strident, without fear. Bold.

But Pete reflected that although he'd spoken at great length about his grandfather and Zénaïde – and of how he grew up in their care and about the life they led together, about his mucker Nicola, about the Opal Causeway and France and how he often felt French even though he wasn't French – he realised that, although Brad talked a lot about his life in Berkeley and the people there, he volunteered very little information about his own family.

Maybe, in his own heightened state of enthusiasm, Pete surmised that perhaps he'd monopolised the conversation.

But he couldn't help it, for suddenly it seemed that there was so much to talk about. And all was interesting, all significant.

'So will Mel be long now?' Brad asked.

'No. About half an hour, I guess.'

'Neat. It's just I want to get over later to the American Express office in Piccadilly. I got some errands to do,' said Brad, yawning and lying back down again as a more distant peacock shrieked.

'Jesus, those peacocks!' he said, putting his hands under his head and closing his eyes.

Pete looked down at Brad again. It was earlier that morning when he'd woken up, buzzing with calmness, and was gazing around his frugal room that he hatched a plot. As when glancing down at Brad, transfixed by the alluring contours of his slumbering body, snugly ensconced under an old green eiderdown which he and Nicola once used as a prop for the hills around Bethlehem in a nativity play they put on one Christmas, he decided that he would take the job in Manchester and save as much up as possible so he could go to California the next year. Brad said he was welcome anytime and, suddenly, it seemed the right thing to do.

Opal-clear, it was. No longer contented with black and white, he wanted now to experience a life of glorious technicolour and leave centuries of acquired hang-ups behind. Both cluttered hippy-style-anything-goes and the fine, uncomplicated and very modern lines of David Hockney paintings of youths by swimming pools beckoned him. There in California it seemed to him he could be what he wanted to be. *Who was it that said or wrote 'Go west, young man'?* he wondered.

Mel glanced up at the clock. Four at last. Yippee!

After she tidied up the work surface, she bent down to retrieve her bag and jacket from under the counter and started to make her way to the exit.

'Not quite yet, Melanie, I need a word with you,' a voice called out to her.

She was stopped in her tracks by the stentorian tones of the Dragon Librarian. She had come to find that a word from her boss was not a word but more of a rant or a lecture, and always thoroughly unpleasant.

'Yes, Miss McPherson?'

'Now, Melanie, you are aware that we do not permit our staff to take private telephone calls during working hours, aren't you?'

'Yes, Miss McPherson.'

'Well, in that case, perhaps you can tell your friends and associates to please not telephone you here! Is that understood?'

'But no one has telephoned, Miss—'

The Dragon Librarian sliced in. 'Yes, but someone did yesterday, a Mr Jones, Melanie? Does that name mean anything to you? The grandfather of that long-haired friend of yours who is always coming in here to see you or loitering outside at the entrance phoned.'

The Dragon Librarian's face quite screwed up as she mentioned Pete.

'Oh, Pete's grandfather, Miss McPherson. What did he say?' asked Mel, wondering once more why her boss was so hostile to her friends.

'Nothing, Melanie.'

'Nothing, Miss McPherson?'

'He just called and asked for you, Melanie. There was no message.'

'Well, thank you for telling me, Miss McPherson.'

'Don't let it happen again, Melanie. That's a good girl. It's all very tedious,' replied the Dragon Librarian, as she swept back to her seat of surveillance.

Mel sighed as she started to make her way to the exit. She felt deflated, desperate to get away to join the boys in the park. Try as she might, she always ended up being upset by these unpleasant encounters. The woman was so picky, so prickly, and Mel never seemed able to please her. As she started to walk down the outside steps she was completely embraced by the sun and stopped to allow its warm rays penetrate her skin.

'In trouble again, Mel?' said a voice, coming from behind her.

Mel jumped.

'Oh, sorry, Mel, I didn't mean to scare you.'

As Mel turned around, she caught the sight of a striking woman with a mass of red curly hair which, although quite lacked the symmetry of an afro, was equally impressive, framing as it did a creamy freckled face. It was Hazel, whom she had met through Celina, who ran the toddlers' group under the motorway.

'Oh, I didn't see you there,' exclaimed Mel, as she cast her eyes over this new acquaintance of whom she was somewhat in awe.

That day Hazel was wearing a pair of men's voluminous blue overalls over a man's equally voluminous collarless blue shirt with its sleeves rolled up to the elbow. A leather belt was strung round her middle, some wooden Hindu prayer beads hung round her neck and she was wearing bovver boots.

'I'm just going to the reference library,' said Hazel. 'I hoped you'd still be there.'

'Well, I would've been normally, but today I'm off early. I'm going to meet some friends in the park.'

'Oh, well, the next time then, Mel? I was going to ask if you wanted to go and eat at that new macrobiotic restaurant in All Saints Road sometime.'

'Ooh, yes. That would be great. Yes, why not?'

'Well, I best get cracking,' said Hazel. 'There's a lot I want to get done before it closes. I'll be here a lot during the next few weeks so I'm bound to see you.'

'Yes, well, goodbye then. See you,' said Mel shyly as she watched Hazel enter the library and nod very brusquely in what she imagined to be the Dragon Librarian's direction.

That woman seems so confident, Mel thought, as she turned around and made her way to Holland Park.

The park was only a stone's throw away and she was in Holland Walk in no time, underneath the tall beeches and elms. She never ceased to love this place from that first time when, out walking alone one day, she came across it. Its fine shrubs and flowers, the contrast between the formal and the natural, its scents and the sweet, adorable little bunny rabbits, which she would have taken home if she could have caught them, never bored her.

It had quite become a haven for her since she came to live in the city, a refuge from the squabbles of the squat and the tongue of the Dragon Librarian. It was also a place she came to when she needed to get away from Baz, during those times when he got a right strop on. And every workday, as long as the weather was good, she came there in her lunch break. Indeed, on some days she would get up really early and walk the long way round to work so she could spend some precious quiet moments there watching the sun as it rose higher in the sky, its heat gradually drying the dew on the grass. Sometimes, in early morning, if there was a low-level mist and no one else was about, she immersed herself in it, Ophelia-like, dancing and slicing at it with strange, convoluted arm movements. And, being a devotee of the Glastonbury Legends, she at times sat there on a bench fantasying that she was Guinevere, waiting for Sir Lancelot to come riding out of the mist and woods beyond.

But it was back to Baz she returned, always knowing that he would never scoop her up on to his horse and gallop off with her to some Celtic hideaway, where there were waterfalls, mountains and holy springs, and lambs, plenty of them, for her to care for.

As she reached the gate by the youth hostel, a wolf whistle dispersed her thoughts, and she suddenly found herself confronted by a bunch of German students, in similar leather cowboy hats, hanging out there, smoking cigarettes. Or perhaps something stronger, her nose discerned as she drew abreast to them. As she passed, one of them, no doubt in an attempt to impress her, danced up to her, evidently fancying himself as Hendrix, playing an imaginary guitar, goofing up his teeth in that familiar way. Feeling like she was being undressed by their eyes, she smiled meekly, lowered her head and blushed simultaneously as the leering group slowly parted to let her go by.

How would Hazel have dealt with a situation like this? she wondered.

On reaching the grassy area, she squinted and her brow furrowed as she looked for Pete and Brad. Shielding her eyes, she soon espied two figures lying close together at the edge of the wooded area. It looked like Pete and Brad to her, and as she drew nearer she could see that their bodies were more than close as Brad's thigh was lying heavy over Pete's side.

She smiled. They looked so innocent, so free.

When she reached them, she stood silently, uncertain whether to disturb them. But then, she coughed weakly and, suddenly, sensing a shadow cast over them and evidently hearing the cough, Pete and Brad were brought back to life and simultaneously looked up to find her standing above them, smiling with sunlight highlighting the back of her head in a halo.

'Wow, it's a visitation, I'm sanctified,' said Brad. 'I hope you've not come to tell me I am gonna have a baby.'

'So how are you two?' Mel replied, laughing, and then, without waiting for an answer, she continued, 'Oh, by the way, Pete, I'm really sorry. The most terrible thing happened. I think that Miss McPherson breathed fire down the phone at your granddad. She only told me as I was leaving that he rang. Yesterday lunchtime apparently.'

'Oh, shit!' said Pete, as a feeling of guilt surged up inside. 'I keep forgetting to phone him. As it's a year since... I said

I'd go down to see him. And now I've got the rest of the week off…'

'Well,' said Mel, 'I've got this Friday off. I'd love to go and visit him. I like your granddad. I wish he was my granddad. It'll be good to see the sea too.'

'What's Baz up to? Maybe we can drive down on Thursday night and stay a few days.'

Mel pursed her lips. 'I'm not sure. I expected him to call by at work. He's sorta disappeared again. Perhaps Brad would like to come?'

She addressed this to Pete but was looking at Brad. Pete turned and looked at him too. He had been thinking of asking Brad if he'd like to come but wasn't sure whether he would want to or not and was simply scared of rejection. But now Mel was making it easier for him.

'Hey, how do you fancy going down to the coast? We could go on Thursday evening. That way we would have three full days there.'

'I was wondering when you were going to ask, Booby. Of course, that would be neat and, say, we could all go in my bus. Wow, yeah, it'd be great. I get to see more of England. Like, London's great, but…'

His face broke into a smile for an instant and then a more serious, almost dark expression superseded it.

'Listen, folks, I'm gonna have to split. I've got to get to the American Express in Piccadilly before it closes. Let's all meet up later in a pub later? Are there any gay bars in the neighbourhood?'

Pete scratched his head and thought for a while, and then, as they started to make their way back to Holland Walk, he said, after some consideration, 'Well, there's that one on Bayswater Road, opposite the private road with all the embassies, but it's a bit straight and I rarely go in there as people stare at me like I'm from another planet.'

'Well, that's quaint. Only in the UK would you get a straight gay bar! Meet you there round nine, say? Yeah?'

Both Pete and Mel nodded.

'Okay, great! So how do I get to Piccadilly?'

'Take the bus from Kensington High Street.'

'You all going my way?'

'No, we have to go in the opposite direction.'

'See you later then. Say, which way is it?' said Brad, as they reached the heavy metal gate by the youth hostel.

Pete indicated to the right. They hovered there for a moment and then, Brad leant over to first kiss and hug Pete and then Mel.

'Yeah, you'll find a stop on this side of the street at the bottom.'

'Hum! Get you,' said Brad, slapping Pete's butt before setting off down the path.

Mel and Pete watched him stride off, impressed by his total sense of purpose. Then they started off in the opposite direction. They were silent going up the path which, bordered by the thickly wooded area of the park on one side and a high wall of grimy yellow London brick on the other, suddenly seemed dark and sombre, damp and spooky.

'You know,' said Mel, 'this part of the park has always reminds me of an Arthur Rackham illustration or a scene from one of those German fairy stories where the trees take on the form of evil witches or spirits. Especially when you hear the peacocks' cries through the undergrowth of ivy and brambles.'

As the path started descending again and the imitation

countryside became more like town, Pete suddenly blurted out as he broke out into a big grin, 'You know, I really like him, Mel.'

'I can tell,' Mel replied.

She smiled at him and then they carried on in silence, each of them thinking about their own situation: Mel wondering whether Baz would be home while Pete eagerly looking forward to seeing Brad in the pub.

They crossed over Holland Park Avenue and started along the tree-lined Ladbroke Grove.

'Wow, it's like a roller coaster,' Pete said.

'Meeting Brad?'

Pete stopped and laughed out loud. 'Well, I suppose that is too. But no, I really meant that I always find Ladbroke Grove seems like a great big roller coaster. But it's a pain you can't get a bus all the way up it. Don't make sense.'

Mel nodded her head in agreement and they carried on again in silence.

When they eventually arrived at the squat, they found Baz unloading a large quantity of boxes from his car.

'Give us a hand, Doll, will you?'

'What's all this, Baz?'

'This and that. You know.'

'Is it stuff to sell on your stall?'

'Something like that. Hey, what's with the third degree?'

Something in Baz's manner stopped Mel from pursuing her questioning and she docilely started to pick up one of the boxes. It was far too heavy for her and Pete rushed to her aid. He scowled. The way Baz treated Mel sometimes, yes, okay, she could be nosey, a bit too effusive sometimes, but she only meant well, eager as she was to help all and sundry.

'I'll do this. You go in. You've been working all day,' he told her.

'Are you hungry? I was thinking of cooking some rice and vegetables. I went to the wholefood shop.'

'That would be nice,' said Pete.

'Baz?'

'What do you think, Doll? I'm bleeding starving.'

'She only asked you if you wanted to eat, man,' said Pete, rising to Mel's defence.

'Yeah, yeah,' said Baz. 'Got things on my mind, Doll, things on my mind, I'm sorry.'

But he didn't sound it.

Still, Pete let it be and they continued to unload the boxes in silence, which they eventually stacked up in Mel and Baz's bedroom.

Finished, there was only a small corridor leading to the bed, and when Mel came up to tell them dinner was ready, she was taken aback.

'Oh, Baz, how long are these going to be here?'

The charming side of his nature came to the fore.

'Not long, Doll, a couple of days or so. You do want to go travelling, Doll, don't you, Doll? Like you've always dreamed of, Doll? Hey?'

He went over and took her hand to his lips, kissed it, and Mel naturally melted at such a gesture.

'Baz?' said Mel, as she lingered close to him, hoping for a hug.

'Yes, Doll?'

'We're going to that gay pub in Bayswater Road later on. Want to come?'

'Why the fuck would I want to go there, Melanie?'

'I only asked, Baz. Honestly. Still, fancy going down to Pete's granddad's Thursday night? We were planning to go in Brad's bus.'

Baz frowned slightly. 'Busy, Doll, sorry, things to do. You go, yeah?' he replied, as a slight smile came to his face and he sauntered over to her and kissed her full on the lips.

After they'd eaten, Mel and Pete decided to make it into an occasion and dress up for the pub. Back in her room, Mel chose a long floral-patterned dress; she'd bought in the Laura Ashley shop in Shrewsbury with some birthday money from her gran when visiting her there. She complemented it with a feather boa and floppy hat, bought for less than a pound down the market one Saturday.

Baz was still busy with his boxes when she had finished getting ready.

'How do I look, Baz?'

'Great, Doll,' he replied, without even looking up.

He seemed so preoccupied by what he was doing that she didn't dare to protest, even gently, just telling him that she would see him later before making her way to Pete's room.

'Wow, you look great!' exclaimed Pete.

'Snap!'

Pete's mix and match consisted of wearing a pair of extremely wide bellbottom jeans, a thick brown leather belt, brown leather boots and a Biba top with mutton-chop sleeves that suggested a medieval look. He was in the process of tying a bandana round his head when Mel entered. They both took one last look in the mirror before making their way out to the street. It was nearly dark and the sky had that purple tint above the glare of the orange street lamps.

'Hey, Pete, what about your granddad?' Mel suddenly said.

Pete, whose mind had been solely on Brad, felt mortified at his forgetfulness and, quickly locating the nearest phone box, dialled the old man's number.

'Two five eight six five.'

'Granddad, it's Pete.'

'Hello, son.'

The old man's voice sounded a bit distant. *No doubt a bad line*, Pete thought.

'Mel said you called her at the library. I'm sorry. I was going to call you, but there were problems at the adventure playground. We had a fire.'

'A fire, you say, son? Well, what about that?'

But the old man didn't really seem seriously to take it in.

'Granddad, I'm with Mel. We both got this Friday off and wanted to come down on Thursday night to see you. We could stay over the weekend? Is that all right?'

'I'd like that, son. Melanie as well? You won't be hitching, son, will you? I don't like the idea of you doing that with her.'

'Not this time. We got a new American friend who's got a VW bus.'

'A what?'

'You know, like a dormobile, a Volkswagen. His name is Brad. He's really keen to see different parts of the country, Granddad. He's been studying over here, well, in Germany actually, and travelling around touring Europe in the bus. He's a really nice bloke, Granddad. I think you'll like him.'

'A Yank, is he? So where will you all billet down?'

'Don't worry, Granddad. The bus has a bed in it. Listen...' Pete looked at Mel while he was talking, 'now, we probably won't arrive until quite late, as we can't leave till after Mel gets back from work and gets her stuff and things, and then it's best to wait till rush hour is over.'

'Righty-ho, son, I'll expect you when I see you. I look forward to it.' The old man sounded excited.

'And Granddad, if we—'

But Albert put the phone down before he could finish his sentence.

'Oh, he's put the receiver down,' said Pete to Mel, who was holding the door ajar for him in an effort to diminish the stench. 'Still, I can't remember what I was going to say anyway.'

They started to wend their way through the back streets of the gate up to the Bayswater Road, lapping up the end-of-season scent of roses and lavender coming from the communal gardens of the larger houses by which they passed. But it was the dahlias, chrysanthemums and Michaelmas daisies which drew their attention. It was their season and their blooms formed thick and luscious. It had become quite dark and the air suddenly felt quite chilly. Something about the dimly lit route they chose to follow rekindled Pete's feelings of summer drawing to an end. Once in the pub, they ordered drinks and sat down in the saloon bar. It was well after nine and soon the pub suddenly started to fill up. Brad reached there about fifteen minutes later and Pete, on seeing him at the entrance, leapt up to greet him by the bar.

'Wow, so look at you!' exclaimed Brad.

'What do you want to—'

The word drink was suppressed by Brad leaning over and kissing him. It was a lingering kiss full of passion, one to which Pete eagerly responded. To their mutual bewilderment, the landlord, a burly, middle-aged man of over six feet in height, suddenly came at them as if from nowhere. Grabbing both of them by their collars like they were a brace of ensnared quarry, he half-pushed, half-marched them to the door and thrust them with considerable force out into the street. So taken aback they were, so shocked, resistance wasn't possible and they both hit the pavement with a thud.

'We'll have none of that in here,' the landlord barked. 'This is a respectable establishment. We don't like hippies and weirdos in here, and you certainly can't behave like that.'

And with that, he then went back into the pub, roughly bumping into Mel, who was in the process of rushing out to see what was happening. He pushed her rudely out of the way and she promptly burst into tears.

'Respectable. That bunch of fag dinosaurs,' Brad said, as he got up from the pavement and dusted himself down while looking for bruises or grazes.

'So you know now why the world needs the gay liberation movement,' he said, looking at Pete in the eye.

Things never seem to go as planned, and although Mel rushed back from work on the next Thursday eager to get down to the coast that night, she found Brad, Pete and Baz in the street outside the squat, struggling to get the spare tyre on the front left wheel hub of Brad's bus.

'We got a flat,' Brad said, looking up at her and shrugging his shoulders.

'And this spare's a dud 'n' all,' said Baz. 'You can't drive with that, mate. No way!'

Baz, who took many risks in his own life, was always emphatic about safety when it came to cars. He even agreed with Barbara Castle when she introduced seatbelts, putting up with much derision from his mates; Backseat Baz, they called him for quite a few months after.

'Does that mean we can't go then? It's too late to get the coach, and the train's too expensive. I've not much bread. If we hitch it'll be difficult with two boys. We'd have to split up and it gets dark earlier now,' said Mel, fretfully.

She had been looking forward to the weekend.

'Isn't there anything you can do, Baz?'

'This one is definitely threadbare. One skid on the motorway and... well, I don't like to say what will happen. I'm not having you going in this van, Melanie. The others can if they want. It's a bit late to find a garage open now, but let's see...'

Stroking his chin, Baz thought for a moment.

'Oh, I know, I'll call Tiny. He'll help us out. Owes me a few favours.'

'Who's Tiny? Have I met him?' asked Mel.

'Yeah, you know. Got that garage up Crouch End. This pile of junk should make it up there okay. I'll go and ring him.'

Mel knit her brow, trying to think who Tiny was. Baz seemed to know some many people. It was hard to keep track. She watched him as he started to walk up to the phone box.

'Are you sure he'll be open now, Baz?' she called out to him.

'He will be for me. Just have to make sure he's got the type of tyre needed.'

Baz came back presently and told them Tiny was working till late in the garage as he had a bunch of MOTs to get through.

'Dodgy, no doubt,' he added. 'And yeah, he says he'll sort you out a spare. In fact, two…'

'Wow, man,' said Brad. 'That's terrific. Only thing, how much is it all gonna cost?'

'It's sorted, mate. As I said, Tiny owes me a favour or two.'

'Aren't you coming with us?' Mel asked him.

'Can't do, Doll, got things to do. You know how it is,' Baz replied.

'So how do you get there?' asked Brad.

Baz explained the best route from Notting Hill to Crouch End, and in no time, they were gingerly cruising up towards the leafy lanes of North London.

'Some big old mansions here,' commented Brad, a few minutes later, as they were driving up along Millionaires' Row.

Mel and Pete agreed. Hampstead seemed a far cry from the dereliction of Notting Hill.

Once they'd arrived in Crouch End, they astonished themselves by easily finding Tiny's garage and were soon cruising into the forecourt.

As Brad drew the bus up to a halt, a man wearing a dark blue boiler suit, the same colour as Hazel's overalls but covered in axle grease, came out of a workshop rubbing his hands with Swarfega. He greeted them with a nod and a suspicious smile.

'We're looking for a bloke called Tiny. Baz rang to say we were coming,' Pete said, leaning out of the van window.

'That's me. The verwy man,' replied Tiny, who evidently had some kind of speech impediment as he pronounced his Rs like a W.

'You don't look like you're tiny to me,' said Brad.

'You taking the mick or something?'

'No, man, I mean you don't look small.'

Tiny guffawed in a bored way and then frowned. 'Yeah, yeah, verwy funny. I hearwit all the time, mate,' he said.

Tiny was at least six foot six inches tall and had hands the size of dinner plates. His size made him look very intimidating, someone definitely not to be messed with.

'Oh yes. I remember him now,' whispered Mel, from the back for the bus. 'He's as gentle as a lamb when he opens up.'

'So you need a couple of tyres for this old crock, do you? Got the verwy ones.'

The changing of the tyre was accomplished in no time at all, and with a new spare installed upfront. As he went about his work, the boys could tell that Tiny seemed much taken with Mel. He treated her with gentleness and a respect which left Baz far behind, and she responded with effervescent kindness. Looking at his watch, Pete realised that they wouldn't make it down to the coast before Albert's bedtime. They were all starving by now, so they decided it would be best to go back to the squat to eat, have a rest and then set off after midnight. That way they would arrive in the early morning.

Tiny let Pete use his phone to call Albert to alert him of the change of plan.

'And you know what,' said Pete, as he put down the receiver. 'We can arrive at dawn and go up to the cliffs to watch the sunrise over the Opal Causeway. It'll be stunning. If it's not cloudy, that is.'

Consequently, they took up Tiny's offer of a cup of tea and a joint in his workshop.

'Nice smoke your Baz got me, doncha think?' Tiny said to Mel.

Mel's forehead wrinkled up in surprise. 'What, you got this from Baz?' she asked.

'Yeah. Oh no, I don't think I were supposed to tell ya.'

When they eventually all piled into the bus and Brad started up the engine and they were saying their goodbyes, Mel leant out the window.

'Yes, bye bye, and thanks ever so much, Tiny. Oh, by the way, you did remember to tighten up the bolts, didn't you?' she mischievously said.

'Oh no, shit!' replied Tiny, scratching his head. 'Glad you reminded me, Mel.'

And he wasn't joking.

Bolts at last firmly secured, as Brad negotiated the bus out of the forecourt and the other two waved farewell to a beaming Tiny, they could hardly keep their faces straight. And when they got a respectable distance from his garage, Brad just had to draw up aside the kerb and stop the bus as they'd all become utterly convulsed in laughter: hysterical till it hurt.

'Gosh! We were lucky,' said Mel. 'Still, it wasn't really his fault.'

She was always the champion of the underdog.

'Not his fault, Mel?' replied Brad. 'The trouble was that he was paying more attention to you than the bus. I think he's smitten.'

'Oh no, surely not,' said Mel, beetrooting. 'He's a mate of Baz.'

'So? What's that got to do with anything?'

'Yeah, I think he was, Mel,' said Pete. 'You could tell he really fancied you. Still, it was a close one. We could have been goners going down the motorway.'

While Mel and the boys were on their way back from Tiny's garage, Baz was rummaging around in their room in the squat. After rearranging some of the boxes and pushing the old wrought-iron bed a few feet across the room, he rolled up the rug under it, and, taking a screw driver from a tool box, prised up a floorboard. Extracting an old shoe box from the void under the floorboards, he opened it and pulled out a brown envelope containing a wedge of notes. Counting them, he put about half in his pocket and returned the rest to the envelope. He put it back in the box and put the box back under the floorboards, slipped the floorboard back and rearranged the rug and bed. He then went over to the chair over which his jacket was slung. Rummaging in the pockets, he eventually pulled out a screwed-up postcard. Straightening it out, as he started to read what was written on it, a big grin came to his face.

'Yes,' he shouted as he jumped in the air as if he'd won the pools or ERNIE.

He kissed the postcard with a display of affection he rarely used on Mel and then, with little care, shoved it in the back pocket of his trousers.

Looking round the room, he spied his Pan Am flight shoulder bag, which he packed with fresh underwear, socks and a jumper, toothbrush and his address book. Tearing a page from a pad, he penned a note to Mel. This he placed on the white-painted dressing table, standing it up in front of her box containing beads and other jewellery. He gave himself a quick once-over in the mirror, flicking back his hair, smoothing down his face.

'You're not a bad-looking fellow, Baz, if I have to say it myself,' he said.

But as he was preening himself, he inadvertently dislodged from out of his pocket the screwed-up postcard. It floated noiselessly to the floor, landing in Mel's floppy hat.

Picking up his brown leather jacket and the Pan Am bag, he swung them, with an exaggerated bravado, over his shoulder and made his way down to the street. Getting in his car after giving it a rev up a few times, he drove off at some considerable speed in the direction of Victoria and Vauxhall Bridge.

'Oh, well, it can't be helped. A flat tyre, these things happen,' Albert said out loud, as he made his way back to the sitting room.

Yet he was disappointed, as the prospect of the imminent arrival of young people had quite perked him up on rising that morning. But now, tired after a long day, he began to feel crumpled, depleted of energy. They were still coming, though; Peter would soon be home and there was the added bonus of seeing Melanie again.

And there was the American too. He was curious about him, this new friend of Peter's. He wondered whether he would be like those two young Americans that Zénaïde once met on the ferry and invited back. They, too, had also been travelling around Europe and ended up staying a few days in the house under the Downs. They all – he, Zénaïde, Peter, Nicola, the toddler Darren – had really taken to them, especially Peter, he seemed to recall. For a number of years, he and Zénaïde exchanged Christmas cards with them, but the cards stopped the Christmas after they both were drafted to Vietnam. He often wondered what happened to them. He hoped no harm.

He often reflected on how curious it was that in many ways Peter was so like Zénaïde, despite the two of them not being genetically related. They both made friends easily, for a start, with all manner of folk too. He often thought of all those people Zénaïde befriended on her travels to and from France; their address book was full up with names he now hardly recognised. But he still heard from people all over the globe; postcards would suddenly drop through the letter box, Christmas and New Year cards too. *Yes, Zénaïde's approach to life had definitely rubbed off on the boy,* he thought as he walked into the kitchen.

Good thing he'd waited to put the pies in the oven, those steak pies Peter liked so much, which he went out especially early that morning to buy from Dorothy's, the bakery, just down the street from the florist shop where Zénaïde once worked. He now put them back into the fridge.

He was keen to see Peter again. He'd gradually left the nest and this was the first summer he'd not come home. Previously he spent much of the holidays undertaking various seasonal jobs: a deck-chair attendant on the promenade or, if he applied early enough, a steward on the car ferries. He earned good money on the latter, saved a tidy sum.

But now he'd finished college, Albert recognised things would be different. Yes, Manchester was far away, Zénaïde hated it when he first went there, but he hoped that the boy would take that job. He wondered whether the boy knew how lucky he was.

It had not always been plain sailing when the boy was growing up; they had their moments when they collided, but Zénaïde had been there to smooth it all over. And Albert took pride in believing he was a realist. He certainly recognised how the world had changed since he was a lad. Then, there was no such thing as a teenager; he'd gone to work at the age of fourteen to support his widowed mother and young siblings, and straight after into the army, as there was a war to fight. It had been the same with his son, Georgy. He'd joined the navy not long before the outbreak of the Second World War. Both of them had missed out on those carefree days of youth; they both had to grow up fast. He recognised the boy had superseded Georgy in his affections, for they had always been close, whereas with Georgy, his relationship was always distant, difficult. Georgy rarely contacted him, whereas the boy always rang him regularly; indeed, at least once a week since Zénaïde died, despite often reversing the charges.

Yet he worried about the boy when he was a teenager on several counts, but Zénaïde always pulled him up about it.

'Does it really matter if he is, Albert? There are worse things to be in this world. Like being a member of the Gestapo or a fascist. Remember what happened to Charles-Hippolyte,' she'd said. Charles-Hippolyte, her first husband, had been shot trying to escape deportation.

And in all truth, the boy never really got into trouble, and although he was brought home by the police one night when out late – they said he was loitering with intent down by the harbour – he certainly wasn't the terror of the neighbourhood. The company that Nicola started to keep vouched for that. And it was also Zénaïde who pointed out to him that, when it came to boys growing up, they became like a combination of lighthouses and foghorns, very visible and extremely loud. He felt sad to think that Zénaïde would never see the boy properly grown; he always imagined that they would grow very old together.

Thinking of Zénaïde, he began to daydream.

A rap on his backdoor, then its creaking open, and then a loud voice suddenly woke him.

'Mr Jones? Have they got here yet? I don't see a van,' Connie's inharmonious tone was calling.

How long had he been sleeping? *Hell's bells*, he thought, *I'm in no mood for her.* Yet being the gentleman he was, he asked her into the living room. She was followed by Darren.

'So not here yet. What time do you expect them?' she said, looking around the room as if Albert might be hiding them somewhere.

'Peter telephoned. The American's bus, as he called it, got a flat. They won't be here till morning.'

'Well, isn't that a shame? They won't have so long now.'

While his grandmother was talking, Darren had made a beeline for the bookcase and was looking with longing at an atlas.

'Baby, get away from there! Don't you be going and interfering with Mr Jones's books,' snapped his grandmother.

'No, that's fine,' said Albert. 'You want to look at that big atlas, don't you, young Darren? Take it down. He's very interested in the page with the map of the night sky.'

'Oh, this thing about books with him, he always wants to look at books. I don't know where he gets it from,' said Connie.

'His mother? I seem to remember that Nicola always was interested in books at the same age when at primary school… Nicola often came here to look…'

Yes, Nicola had always made a beeline for the bookcase as a child, Albert thought, *at least before she failed the eleven plus and lost any interest in school.*

'Now, don't you talk to me about Nicola! I despair of that girl. She's left him for good,' Connie said, and then launched into a rant which Albert found very difficult to follow. Eventually she got to the real reason she'd come round. She wondered what he planned. Nicola suggested they might go for a picnic in the wild strawberry woods, if fine, and of course she was sure that the American would appreciate seeing some sights, the castle, the cathedral, the cliffs.

'They like things like that, Americans do,' she said. 'What do you think, Mr Jones?'

She looked up at Albert. It seemed that he'd fallen asleep. He was snoring quietly.

'Oh dear, Mr Jones has fallen asleep. Put back that book! Come along, Baby,' said Connie, as she made her way to the backdoor.

Darren replaced the atlas and walked over slowly to scrutinise the sleeping Albert. Albert's eyes suddenly opened and he winked at Darren while lifting his right index finger to his lips before closing his eyes again.

'Hurry up, Baby, stop jigging about! Get a move on.' Connie hissed from Albert's backdoor.

Once back at the squat, Mel rushed to their bedroom, eager to tell Baz about Tiny and the near-miss they had. But he wasn't there. There was something strange about the room; things seemed somewhat disturbed. She couldn't quite put her finger on it, but were the bed and rug not in a slightly different position? Fewer boxes? It was only when she walked round the room for a third time she noticed a note laying up against her trinket box on the dressing table. She went over, picked it up and read it.

Doll, have to go away for a couple of days.
Should be back on Sunday or Monday
or Tuesday at the latest. B

Although used to Baz's disappearing acts, a feeling of being deserted came over her. She sat down, note in hand, on her bed; tears came to her eyes. Of course, she recognised it was his spontaneous behaviour, his just getting up and going out at any time of day or night, which she'd initially found attractive in him. But she'd always imagined that he would somehow change, change because they were together, and change because he would want to have a baby with her and settle down. And she'd always thought she'd be the one to change him, but after nearly four years since they'd met during her first year at university, he'd remained exactly the same.

Lately, however, she found there seemed something different in his behaviour.

He was moodier; the extreme shortness of his temper becoming frightening. Previously, he usually smoothed things over quickly when they were heading for a collision, and weave long, charming tales as to why he was doing something or going somewhere. And then afterwards he would tease or tickle her so she would fall into laughter, and then miraculously things didn't feel so bad after all.

Yet behind her laughter, despite the tickling, his declarations of love, deep inside, she came to wonder whether he did stuff just to keep her sweet. But she was forever forgiving, for subconsciously since childhood she was made to feel that she was the one who bore the blame, a condition she was beginning to realise was, in the main, influenced by her exposure as a child to the constant berating of her mother by her father. Her mother had always backed down, often apologising for what should have required no apology, for what she had no culpability.

But this current situation with Baz confused Mel as he did seem more closed. He could be abrasive during the times leading up to periods of absence, but there was something different about now, something definitely fishy about his behaviour. *Oh well*, she thought, as she went out to ask the boys whether they wanted to eat, *I will be away until Sunday so we wouldn't have seen each other in any case.*

The boys were still in Pete's room and she didn't think she should disturb them, so she decided to surprise them with her tuna, mushroom and macaroni casserole. When ready she took it into Pete's room, but although the boys scoffed it down, she found she had no appetite.

'I won't have any. I feel like eating fruit just now,' she said, starting to peel an orange. 'In fact, after reading about the mercury content in tinned tuna and about the way they catch them, I am thinking that I shall become a proper vegetarian and give up fish altogether. What time are we going to leave?'

Brad and Pete looked at each other.

'Well, what about four? Then we can have a decent kip. I'll put the alarm on,' said Pete.

'Great, then I'll go and have a lie down,' said Mel.

'Good idea, Mel. We will too,' said Brad. 'We'll come and wake you, yeah?'

Mel smiled as she left Pete's room, thinking that they had already done just that, had a lengthy lie down, but remembered how much time she and Baz spent in bed when they'd first met, and her brow ruefully furrowed up.

Once she had closed the door, Brad looked at Pete quizzically. 'She's okay, right?' he asked, after he was certain that he'd heard the door of her room close.

'She gets fretful when she doesn't know what Baz is up to. I kinda think he might have done one of his runners. He was acting like he was psyching himself up for it.'

'Does he go off a lot then?' Brad asked, and then he smiled knowingly.

'What?' said Pete.

'You know, I really find his face real familiar. I really do think I know him from somewhere.'

'Maybe in another space, another time,' said Pete, as he went to lie down on the bed.

'Joker,' said Brad.

He picked up a pillow and playfully began to hit Pete with it.

'But seriously, Pete, I do find he's kinda sharp with Mel. You'd get more than this if you behaved like that to me.'

Brad now pinned him down with his knees and hit him harder with the pillow.

'Surrender?'

'You mean I haven't?' Pete said.

Their lips brushed.

'Yeah, it's true. Baz can be really nasty to her,' said Pete. 'He puts her down such a lot. I really don't understand why he's like that. She really helps him out. But you know, the other day when you'd gone to the American Express, she asked him an innocent question and he just lost it. It makes me angry when he gets narked with her for no reason at all. And because she gets all upset and tries to make amends, he just gets worse. And she starts to look like one of those wounded animals she is always trying to save. I kinda wonder about him, like, what he's up to all the time? He's always off somewhere and he's definitely never short of a bob or two.'

'A what?'

'Oh, a bob is a shilling.'

'Jeez, the money here is complicated enough without confusing us foreigners with slang terminology too. Still, I take your point about him and bread, though. Maybe he's dealing. You know how surprised she was when Tiny said that thing about his hash.'

'Yeah, I'd been wondering about that. He did a little up at uni, not much, though. I guess he could be; it would explain all those sudden trips.'

'He's a good-looking guy, though,' Brad said.

That took Pete by surprise and he experienced a pang of jealousy.

'Yeah, I guess in a regency, rakish sort of way,' he said. 'Mel told me that she fancied him as she thought that with those lamb-chop sideburns and wavy black hair, he looked like he was a character in a Jane Austen novel, especially the way that he used to comb it before he grew it longer.'

'You know what, Pete? He's a closet case.'

'A what?'

'A suppressed homosexual,' Brad slowly replied, enunciating every syllable of the phrase like an Ivy League academic.

'Oh, I hadn't thought of that. No, surely not. There's a rumour he's knocked off half the woman in the squats, though Mel's not the wiser.'

'So maybe he's fucked half the blokes too,' Brad said in an exaggerated London accent.

'Surely not?' said Pete.

'Hey, enough of Baz and Mel,' said Brad, as he manoeuvred himself, snakelike, on top of Pete. 'It's you I'm interested in. You know, I just love the way you're always smiling.'

Meanwhile, Mel was sorting out the clobber she wanted to take with her. Soon packed, she was pondering on what jacket she should bring. She definitely needed something waterproof. Her eyes suddenly focused on her Laura Ashley dress hanging on the back of the door. What a shame she couldn't take that with her, but it was torn from when that pub landlord pushed her and needed mending. Oh, but her floppy hat? Where was that? She started to rummage around for it. Noticing it on the floor beneath her dressing table, she bent down to pick it up. As she lifted it towards her head, tossing back her hair at the same time as she put it on, she saw in the mirror in front of her the reflection of a screwed-up postcard float down to the floor. Picking it up and unfolding it, she saw the image was of the Cloth Hall in Bruges, which she'd once visited with Baz. She'd loved the sound of the carillon in its Belfry tower. She started to smooth out the creases in it, but as she turned over the postcard, she suddenly stopped, stunned by some smudged words that jumped out at her:

> *Barry, my friend, great news. So when are you coming over again, man? We need to talk. I got the beautiful Marieke here now; she's desperate to meet you. She's a right real cracker, in great shape. That's how you English say it? Right? You'll love her and I'll know she's just what you want. She'll meet your every need. Definitely! Telephone soon.*
> *Tot ziens, Jan*

As Mel reread the text, she began to feel sick, dizzy. Marieke? Who on earth? Marieke? It was definitely the name of a Dutch or Flemish girl. Was Baz cheating on her? He'd been going to Belgium a lot recently. That had to be it: he was seeing a girl there and that was why he was evasive when she'd asked to go with him the last two times. What had he said on those occasions?

'Not the best of times, Doll, I'm doing boring stuff, later on in the winter, yeah?'

Tears started to fall down her face, fast and furious. She

tried to suppress her sobs as she didn't want to either wake the boys or let them hear her distress. Feeling alone, she lay down on the bed, but she didn't get much sleep.

But the boys were not sleeping. They were lying on the bed, facing each other, rapping.

'You know, if anybody had said to me last week that I would meet someone like, no, not someone like, but actually you,' said Pete, 'I would have not believed them. Do you believe in fate?'

'Well, I suppose.'

'You know, I really, really like you – well, more than like you.'

'Yeah, me too, Booby, so I guess it's all right then if I stay here till I go back home? I really want to spend time with you.'

A despondent feeling flushed through Pete. He'd only just found this guy and he was already talking about going back home. But it passed and, rationalising he knew the score, he remained silent. Brad had his studies to finish. Besides, he didn't want to know anything finite like the date of Brad's impending departure. He was only getting to know him and was curious to learn more about the guy.

'So does your family live in California? You haven't really talked about them. Like, do you have any brothers and sisters? And what do they do?'

A pained expression came on Brad's face and although he didn't understand why, Pete felt that that he'd overstepped the mark.

'I don't see them much these days, you know. They live back east.'

There was an awkward silence.

'I really don't care to talk about them much either. It's all in the past,' he added, as he turned from his side onto his front and stared towards the open window.

Pete found the inflection in Brad's voice at the end of the sentence so affirmative that he remained silent. He started to trace his fingers along Brad's backbone. Brad turned around to look at him and weakly smiled.

'Hey, Booby, I like the shape of your eyes. They're so cute. They're like kind of oriental-looking?'

'Mémé told me they were like my mother's.'

'Where was your mother from?'

'We never really knew. Well, I guess my dad did, but no one said much about it. I imagine she had Anglo-Indian ancestry. Or Malay, possibly? I don't know. Still, the kids at my primary school obviously thought they looked oriental as I used to get teased something chronic about my "chinky" eyes. But Nicknick, the girl next door I told you about, put a stop to it early on. She always looked out for me. And then, it never was an issue. She was like my big sister. She was in our house all the time.'

'So you don't see your dad?'

'No, never, he's lived in Australia with his second wife since he left the navy. I did go to live with them when he was stationed in England. But I ran away.' Pete chuckled.

'That's heavy. Why are you laughing?'

'Because I can now.'

'So how come you ran away?'

'I didn't like it there. I was only there two months. The twins, my little half-sisters Isobel and Jane, were okay, but Cynthia, my step-mother's daughter by her first marriage, was a bully and really good at getting me into trouble with my dad.

So I'd get the blame for things she'd done. But, in any case, Amber Mae, my step-mum, that is, didn't want me around. It was so obvious. So I ran away. It was around the time that the Russians launched that dog into space and, while waiting for the train, I remember looking up at the moon as it was a very clear night. It was so beautiful and it led me back to Granddad and Mémé. They were eating when I arrived, and Mémé, without saying anything, just got up and laid a place for me. I remember that she'd baked this incredible pork pie and its shiny crust reflected the flames of the coal fire in it. It was Bonfire Night, Guy Fawkes, you know, I told you about it before, and after eating, we went to see the fireworks on the recreation ground like we'd done ever since I could remember. I was back home. I'd missed them so much. I guess there was some discussion about it, although I have no recollection of it as I just stayed there. I never went back to Georgy's. I think Amber Mae had my stuff packed up all ready in any case…' Pete stopped.

'So how old were you?' Brad asked him.

'About seven. Yeah, I think Amber Mae was so keen to get rid of me, she'd probably already raised the issue with Georgy, my dad, that is. Anyway, Nicknick is more like a sister to me than my dad's kids. My French cousins are closer to me too. They are like my family, my brothers and sisters, despite none of us being blood-related. It's weird.'

'So you don't remember your real mother at all?'

'Not really. I just have a memory of someone wrapped in a purple cover. Mémé said it was a paisley-patterned eiderdown that Sara, that was her name, used to keep warm during the winter, when we first arrived. But anyway, I always considered Granddad and Mémé to be my parents and I never wanted any others. I hope you like the old man. You see what you get with him. But he's not as active as he used to be when Mémé was alive. They were such a team and both worked so hard. I told you about the market garden and jams and all that.'

'Yes, it was like back to land before back to the land.'

'More like they never left, and they certainly never left the sea,' said Pete, smiling.

'So you said you went to France a lot, right?'

'Yes, in the summer holidays and every other Christmas, special family occasions, yes, a lot. You know what the first thing was that I remember about France?'

'Say what?'

'Well, a box of sweets you could get there in the *confiserie* was shaped like a French matelot's hat, with a red pompom on the top, and the sweets inside were shaped like pebbles you find on the beach. They were so scrumptious. And I also remember that first time crossing over with Mémé, when she went to visit her mother, and how we talked about the colours in the sea as we were sat by the funnel. The sea was like the most exquisite opal, she said. I remember those words so well. That's why she called it the Opal Causeway. But it's strange, as since Mémé died I've felt kinda detached from France. But I so love travelling.'

'Me too, Booby.'

'You know you were saying about me being able to stay with you? Well, I was thinking that,' said Pete, with a certain hesitation, 'if I took that job in Manchester, saved the money, I could save to come out next summer.'

'Now, I'd like that more than anything in the world,' said Brad, and he rolled over off his front and onto his side.

They started kissing; speech was no longer necessary as, for the fourth time that day, a more frenetic and very physical, sybaritic form of communication kicked off again.

The teeming rain in London, which had clattered down on the roof of Brad's bus as it slowly lumbered up Shooter's Hill, disappeared completely once they were across the Medway, and by the time they arrived on the cliffs just before dawn, there was no evidence of it at all.

The sky to the east was of a clear blue-grey colour with a streak of red hanging over the horizon, an indication the sun was about to ascend. The bus parked, glad to stretch their legs, they tumbled out, making their way to the cliffs' edge. Sitting cross-legged, the three of them watched this perpetual spectacle of day unfolding, recognising that, although they'd seen it happen many times before, it never lost its allure; it always seemed a new experience.

The red of the sky soon started to become more intense as wafts of orange, pink and blue suddenly appeared from nowhere and the horizon completely disappeared as sea and sky momentarily merged.

'Hey, far out, man!' said Brad, flourishing a familiar combustible in his hand. 'Say, who wants some of this doobie?'

He lit it, took a draw and then passed it to Mel.

'You know, I've never seen the sun rise over the sea until now. Only set,' he said as he slowly exhaled. 'The sunsets over San Francisco Bay are phenomenal, man, with the Golden

Gate glinting and Mount Tam silhouetted all powerful and solid in the distance. But this, wow, there's no land, no shapes, only colour. It's just ether, pure space, like a gaseous vacuum of colour.'

They gazed at this amazing one-off natural occurrence, mesmerised by it, feeling it firmly fixed them in the present.

'It makes one feel so insignificant,' said Mel.

'Sure does,' Brad said. 'Yeah,' said Pete, at the same time.

They sat in peace, anchored to the environment of which they keenly understood they were but a minuscule part. And then, almost as fast as it had disappeared, the horizon once more became visible and, like a jack in a box, the sun popped up over it. They gasped in unison, so taken aback they were, and now, it was as if their gasp blew some strange magical powder out in front of them as the colour of the sea below gradually faded to that opal sheen that was such a familiar characteristic to this part of the straits, those schizophrenic straits, that Opal Causeway which was both such a bulwark and such a conduit. And a new day had begun in the real world.

As they made their way to the house under the Downs, Mel's mind was in turmoil, and on the journey down, from the safety of the back of the bus, she'd taken a number of glimpses at the crumpled postcard as she tried to suss it out. It occurred to her that Jan, the name with which the card was signed, was a girl's name. She didn't recall Baz mentioning a mate called Jan, but besides that, this Jan seemed to imply that Marieke, whoever she was, was desperate to meet Baz. And about meeting his needs? In this context, was it meant sexually? It sounded kinky. Maybe that's why he'd become so secretive lately; he'd got into something kinky and one or both of these girls was a Miss Whiplash type.

She decided she would confront him about it when he got back. She was beginning to admit to herself she was increasingly unhappy about the state of their relationship. They needed to talk. But how would she undertake it without it becoming messy, disjointed? She had a sudden brainwave; she'd join one of those new women's assertiveness groups. She'd ask Hazel for advice, unaware that during the weekend, she'd be presented quite a demonstration of assertiveness from Nicola, a girl she'd only met once before, and by whom she had felt intimated.

A heatwave occurred during their three days on the coast and it felt that summer would last forever. The storm of the previous night had brought well-needed rain and now, every plant, tree and lawn was freshly green again while any indications of imminent autumn seemed outright fraudulent. Being by the sea, the young people took on a holiday mood, which completely captured Albert, Mel's attentiveness to him, without a doubt, playing a big part in this, and the spring in his step returned. Even Connie eased off a little, softened slightly and became almost relaxed.

They made a strange sight going out on their daily trips, a bizarre convoy led by Albert, driving his pre-war but pristinely kept Austin Seven, followed by the bright orange VW with its German registration plates, teeming with hordes of weirdos, hippies and foreigners, as one neighbour remarked to another. Mel sometimes rode with Albert, much to his delight and to Connie's jealousy, but sometimes, she joined the young in the bus.

Darren was really made up to be with grownups who actually took him seriously. It was ace to be riding in the front of the bus, lording it over the passing world, especially when he spotted a few schoolmates. On the way to the beach that first day, he interrogated Brad incessantly about the USA. Had Brad been to the Cape Kennedy or Mission Control? He wanted to know all about the Grand Canyon and cowboys and Indians, and if it were true that Indians had no fear of heights and built the first skyscrapers in Chicago. And why was it that the Americans fought a civil war? He needed facts, facts and more facts, and he started to graduate to the most obscure questions, the answers to which often evaded Brad and left him really amazed at the knowledge and curiosity of someone so young.

Nicola had met Mel the time she visited with Baz while Zénaïde was still alive but never struck up a dialogue with her. In all truth, she was a bit suspicious of her, for Mel had gone to university while she'd left school at fifteen. Mel also seemed so treacly nice, the type of girl she would have relentlessly taken the piss out of when younger, definitely a Miss Goody Two Shoes. But this time, possibly because Baz was not there, she began to warm to her and the two paired off when walking along the promenade or around the harbour.

On that first day, they were following Pete, Brad and Darren down the steps on to the beach when they noticed that Pete had suddenly stopped to show Brad where a strange couple of caged recesses under the promenade were located. These, Nicola and Pete when kids used to pretend were inhabited by invisible lions and tigers and caused them an inimitable amount of pleasure and play-acting when Zénaïde and Connie brought them there on a fine summer's day.

'We had to drag them away screaming. I should say,' said Connie, who'd been keeping up the rear with Albert and arrived just in time to hear the story told. Mel, not quite understanding what was said, turned to Nicola, who repeated Pete's recollections.

'Oh, really!' she exclaimed. 'That's so weird, such a coincidence, you know, Nicola, as where we went on family holidays in Pembrokeshire, there was something similar, and my brother used to scare me by saying they were dragons deep down inside, but you could only see them at night.'

Nicola looked at Mel; they simultaneously smiled; they clicked.

'Mel?' asked Nicola, as they were walking across the sand. 'Where's your fellow these days?'

A pained look came across over Mel's face and she began to sense Mel was not happy.

'Oh no, have I made a boob? You split up, right?'

'No, we haven't,' Mel said, defensively. 'He's gone away for a few days, for work, you know, for a business-type thing ...'

She hesitated. Nicola scrutinised her face.

'No, we're alright really,' she murmured, looking away.

Well,' retorted Nicola, 'don't seem like it by what your face's saying.'

Tears formed in Mel's eyes. Nicola noticed and bit her lip, cursing herself. She was just about to say something to try and make amends when Mel cut her and turned around to talk to the others.

'Hey,' she said, bright and breezy again. 'This would be a nice place to sit. Don't you all think so?'

Later that afternoon, however, the atmosphere was defused when Mel and Nicola went in search of ice cream.

'Sorry about before, Nicola, I'm really upset, actually,' Mel said, as they were walking across the sand with 99s for everybody, ice cream running down their fingers and onto their hands and wrists.

'No. I'm sorry, Mel, that's me, the worst of me mum and dad in me. I didn't mean to upset you.'

'Well, Nicola, the thing is, I think Baz is having an affair. I haven't told anybody yet. It's all so confusing.'

And she told Nicola about the postcard. Nicola, who put up with Ernie sniffing around other girls' skirts since not long after Darren was born, became right indignant for her.

'Well, I know what I'd do with the bastard. Have it out with him when he gets back, don't let him get away with it, Mel. I put up with it for so long, but it was difficult for me as I was living with a baby at his mum's and she'd let her little darling get away with murder. But that's why I am at my own mum's now. Well, until I can afford to get a place for me and Darren.'

'You should come and squat with us.'

'Maybe I will and all,' said Nicola. 'Now, that would make my mum go ballistic.'

But it was the next night that Nicola gave Mel something really to think about and set her mind in serious motion. Nicola came to Albert's to ask them if they wanted to go down Gear, a blues club that she and Pete used to go to when he still lived at home.

'That was the place I was telling you about, Brad. The one where bands like The Yardbirds, Fleetwood Mac, Cream, John Mayall's and Laurel Aitken's bands used to play,' said Pete.

'Well, Brad, don't you expect them tonight. They've gone on to better pastures,' said Nicola. 'Still, you want to come?'

'Sure,' said Brad.

By the time they'd got ready and ambled over there, making a detour by the Greek café on the high street and the beach, Gear was in full swing. Some local band was playing.

'I've not heard of them, Petey,' Nicola said. 'I'm slipping up or what? I hope they're good.'

In fact, they were good, and more important, very danceable too, and dance was what they did, the four of them in the middle of the floor.

Mel, at last, felt relaxed, her anxieties somewhat anaesthetised as she swayed. But then, glancing across the dancefloor towards the entrance, she noticed a tall rocker type slouching against the wall. He was snarling and, at first, she thought he was snarling at her. It frightened her, but she soon realised the boy's eyes were set in Nicola's direction. A concerned frown naturally came to Mel's face; her eyes screwed up, one more than the other, as her brow furrowed. Nicola, clocking this strange look, turned about to see what was eliciting it.

'Oh, fuck, it's Ernie,' she said, quietly.

Once Ernie clocked she'd seen him, he made his way across the floor, lurching left and right, not caring who he bumped into, so pissed he was.

'So who's the bint with the squint?' he shouted over the pulsating sound to Nicola, gesturing to Mel. He looked well pleased by his joke.

Nicola frowned and let out a sigh of frustration, but before she could react, Ernie noticed Brad's eyes looking at him in a quizzical manner.

'Yeah, and who's this geezer then, Nicky? Who the fuck you dancing with?' he shouted, and began to menacingly look at Brad. 'Listen, pal, you fucking taking liberties with my wife or what?'

'Fuck you, Ernie. Sling your hook. This is Pete's friend.'

'Oh, Pete's friend, is he? Well, ain't that fun for you! Nicky, I come to fetch you home.'

By this time, Pete, having gone to the bar, was on his way back with drinks and could see Ernie starting to forcefully grab Nicola by the arm. However, Nicola managed to slither out of his grip and, visibly growing taller, her birdlike frame assumed a Charles Atlas proportion as she made a fist and, like lightning, and certainly before Ernie could suss out what was happening, landed a right hook on his jaw that even Mohammed Ali himself would have been proud of. The impact sent Ernie rolling across the floor.

'You got some right daft moves, Ernie Fagg,' she hissed at him, as the doorman came rushing across to check out the fracas.

'Listen, Ernie,' she continued, as she now calmly stood over him like she could go for the kill, 'I told you before and I swear I ain't saying it again, do us a favour, get the fuck outta my life.'

She then turned her back on him and recommenced dancing, quite ignoring his protestations to the doorman that she was the one out of order, she was the bitch what needed throwing out and not him.

'Listen, mate, she's my wife. I come to get her.'

'Yeah, pal, but don't seem she wanna go with you,' said the doorman as he manoeuvred the stumbling Ernie towards the exit. And then, with the assistance of another of the staff, they almost lifted Ernie off his feet and threw him out of the club.

Back inside Mel was reeling. She'd never seen a woman deal with a situation in the way that Nicola had, and although she abhorred violence, she was impressed. That such a small woman could have such been so forceful with such a large man and then just continue dancing like nothing had happened she found truly inspiring.

Their last day, Sunday, was the hottest and they decided to take a picnic to the wild strawberry woods after visiting the castle in the morning. It was only there that Pete plucked up the courage to tell his grandfather about his plans. And, more importantly, about Brad and him.

He noticed Albert seated on a bench, scrutinising the harbour below and the Opal Causeway beyond, and detached himself from the others and sat down beside him.

'Are you enjoying your day, Granddad?' he asked.

'Yes, son, looking down at the docks has been jogging my memory. They've changed so much since my day. Look at those car terminals. When I met Zinny, they used cranes to get a car onboard. Look at those ferry boats. They hardly look like ships anymore and what with this common market business the port's only set to become bigger.'

They became silent as they surveyed the activity below them. Pete wondered what was going through the old man's head. He knew how rooted his history was to that bustling place. Other than his work as porter in the smoke-filled marine station, the story of that fateful storm was imprinted in Pete's mind from an early age, and how his grandparents' comings and goings between the two coasts, their crossing of the Opal Causeway, made them maintain that, in their own domain, the sea was as much important as the land because for them there was nothing as hateful as a barrier.

'Do you think they'll build a tunnel, Granddad?' Pete said, quite suddenly.

'Be a miracle if they do, son. They've wanted to do it for over a hundred years. Remember those bore holes I showed you down below the cliffs that time? Maybe they will. As I said, everything's changing fast these days.'

'Granddad, do you remember the times when we'd go to the docks when I was a little boy? When we were meeting people then, we used to be able to wait at the bottom of the gangplank for them.'

'Yes, that was because we were often meeting exchange students from off the boat to see them to where they were staying. Zinny used to interpret for the families. And of course, some of them stayed with us in the early days.'

'Yes, I remember. But I also remember that time a policeman, one that we'd never seen before, came over and asked what we were doing there and Mémé said she was waiting for someone or other from off the boat. But he was having none of it and sent us back to wait in the station the other side of the customs. I always thought that things changed that day. The world became different. We were never allowed to wait on the quay again. He was so rude to her, I remember. He said horrid things about foreigners.'

Albert laughed. 'Well, I don't expect it was the first time and it definitely wasn't the last! Now listen, son, I'm glad I've got you alone. I want to ask you something. Well, a coupla things. It's about Zinny's ashes, and mine, for that matter—'

'Oh, Granddad, no—'

'These things have to be spoken about, son. Now our wish is for our ashes to be split into two halves and one half scattered from up here and the other from the French cliffs, after my death, that is…'

Albert grinned.

'…then mine should be mixed with hers. Zinny's are in my bedroom. I'd appreciate you doing that for us, son.'

Pete felt choked up inside. Although he realised it was inevitable, he didn't like to consider the prospect of his grandfather's death. He remained silent, as he could find no immediate reply. And then in his mind he suddenly saw himself travelling across to France on the ferry carrying an urn. Would he have to put it in a bag? What would they say at customs?

His grandfather coughed. 'Well, son?'

'Of course I will,' Pete said.

'Maybe cousin Germaine will do it with you. Now, son, the second thing, that job? Maybe it doesn't appeal to you, but you've been offered it, and on a plate too. When I was your age, I would have jumped at the opportunity. And you know, I'm worried about all this squatting too; you don't want to get into trouble. You have your fun this summer, but you have to get on with your life now. You have had so many opportunities, opportunities that we certainly never had, and, son, don't take this the wrong way, but a decent haircut wouldn't go amiss.'

Albert suddenly seemed to lose track and his face betrayed a trace of confusion.

'I was going to tell you, Granddad. I've decided take that job.'

'Attaboy.'

And with that news, the old man's face broke out into a wide smile and he looked genuinely relieved.

Pete, although he was working his way up to it, never did get around to telling Albert why he was taking the job, about his plan to visit Brad in California, and most importantly about Brad and him, as Connie came puffing up and sat down on the bench beside them.

Well, plenty of time to tell him before I go, Pete thought.

The wild strawberry woods were less than half an hour's drive. They parked in a small lay-by, and once a suitable spot was chosen, Albert and Connie were amazed by what was conjured out of the VW. For other than their picnic, the young people had brought sleeping bags and cushions, two decks chairs, rugs, a transistor radio and a tent, as well as Zénaïde's wind-up gramophone and some seventy-eights that Pete had hidden under a picnic rug.

Up went the tent, down went the sleeping bags, cushions and rugs while Melanie produced, from her voluminous bag, some pieces of Indian cloth and a string of temple bells which she and Nicola attached to various trees and shrubs. Two tree stumps made excellent tables and a space was created they could call their own. It was made complete once two deck chairs were erected and Albert and Connie requested to be seated. Albert was delighted by it all, but Connie was a bit nonplussed. She found it a bit odd!

It was a fine old spread that was laid out, and they were soon on the attack. The sight of the old thermos flasks full of scalding hot coffee and the bottles of Bing's red and white lemonade sent off Pete and Nicola into reminiscing about picnics past. Mel sweetly declined the liver paste sandwiches that Connie made for her.

'They're not meat, they're liver,' said Connie.

'Oh no, thank you, Mrs Strachan, but I couldn't eat another thing. A shame, as they look so delicious,' Mel said.

After their picnic, while Albert and Connie dozed off listening to songs of bygone years, Darren pleaded for a game of hide and seek. His rules were extensive and had to be listened to with great seriousness. In fact, the game turned out to be long and drawn out as other sub-games developed, particularly as Darren and Mel found a small pit, a small camp of sorts evidently dug out by other visitors, which, after gathering up broken branches and leaves and covering it with them, they hid underneath.

Nicola found them first and they waited in silence, but Brad and Pete didn't come. They had been unable to resist each other's advances and, in the undergrowth beneath a very old yew tree that Pete remembered once climbing, made exceedingly fast, almost desperate love.

'Well, Booby, that was best yet,' said Brad, after they unravelled. 'Say, so where are all these wild strawberries?'

'It's a bit late in the season,' said Pete as he fastened his jeans while his eyes scanned the forest floor. 'Ah, here's a couple.'

Bending down and picking them, he handed them to Brad to taste.

'These were the bedrock of Mémé's business.'

'Okay, the jams? Say, they're yummy,' said Brad.

It was Darren's giggling that drew them back to the game and eventually led them to where he, Nicola and Mel were hiding.

Re-joining Albert and Connie, Pete rewound the gramophone, putting on Albert's favourites: Paul Robeson singing 'Jerusalem', Mistinguett 'Mon Homme' and Gracie Fields 'Come Back to Sorrento'. The sound of the wind-up strangely complemented the sounds coming from the woods: the cracking of twigs, rustling in the trees and cooing of wood pigeons. But when it ground to a halt, those natural sounds became louder, seeming almost deafening, and with the balmy, soporific atmosphere under the trees and the intoxicating fragrance of the pines lulled them. They spread out on the sleeping bags staring up at the arboreal cathedral roof while Darren, now in the tent, stared at the shafts of sunlight that fell through the pines, making witch-like shadows on the canvas. They dozed for almost an hour.

When he awoke, Pete realised it was time to return to London and three idyllic, harmonious days were over. On their way to Albert's they were silent and, after unloading the bus and Albert's car and putting everything back in order, Mel doing all the washing up, it was time to leave.

Darren cried to see them go. He'd such a great time. Nicola promised him, as she hugged Mel, that they'd come up to visit. Darren ran after the bus as it made its way down past the White Horse pub, while Albert, Connie and Nicola didn't stop waving until the vehicle had turned around the corner where the dairy had once been.

Pete sat up front with Brad, rapping about their plans for the next few days, but Mel remained in the back, thinking. She was glad of such an interlude, but she was going back to Baz and reality. And she had something important to do. She felt jittery but she must confront him.

However, when the bus eventually rumbled into Powys Square, there was no sign of Baz's car, and when she got back into the squat, there was no sign of him. And what's more, no one there had seen him for days.

Pete was on his way across Holland Park to the library. Earlier that morning, he'd arranged to meet Mel and Brad there around the time Mel finished. He was a bit early, but it was starting to rain, he'd no jacket and the equinoctial winds were making him shiver. It would give him time to check out some new books about photography Mel told him just came in.

Mind-blowing, they were, she'd said.

Since returning from the coast the previous Sunday, the weather had turned. The feel of autumn was everywhere. And he was feeling at a bit of a loss as what to do now that the kids were back at school and the adventure playground closed. On his last day there, he learnt the playground wouldn't open up again, not at least in the same place, as it was planned to start building houses on the site by the next summer. Although Pete began to feel really close to those kids by the end of the summer, he wasn't at all sure whether overall he did anything that constructive for them. Like they were still in the same place, their situations weren't any different and he hadn't been able to give any of them photos he'd taken. Still, it probably looked good on some people's CVs.

Brad had gone to the American Express office to see if there was any response to the ad he'd stuck up on the bulletin board there. During the last few days, he and Pete had been doing the rounds of various joints where travellers hung out, leaving ads for the van. Brad was desperate to sell it now; he really needed the bread, so they'd made two large for-sale signs: one for the van's back window, and the other leant up inside against the windscreen when the vehicle was parked.

Pete was apprehensive about Brad's imminent departure but appreciated that, after a year away, Brad felt homesick. He certainly was missing all his home comforts, and the backwardness of England and Europe, particularly the bathing facilities, or to be more precise, the lack of bathing facilities in the squat, which once seemed quaint to him, just plain irritated him now.

Curiously, two nights before, BBC2 TV had shown a concert by Joni Mitchell in which when she sung a bunch of new songs she'd written during her travels in Greece and Ibiza. Brad got really cut up about the one song 'California' with its lyrics about wanting to go home. That and the song about missing clean white linen really brought it home to him, and when the concert was finished, and after they'd all sat around and far-outed the poignancy of the lyrics, the skill of the song-writing, he told Pete that it was time to go.

But Pete knew now that he was California-bound the next year and convinced himself that the split wouldn't be so hard, particularly as when he got to Manchester and started with the catalogue company, he had an immediate goal to work hard and save money. He contacted the boss the day after he came back from the coast and had a starting date.

Both boys were concerned about Mel since she told them about the crumpled postcard. She burst into floods of tears as she recounted her fears and was inconsolable. Nothing they said seemed to be right. Three days since, and Baz still missing, Mel seemed consumed by a mix of anxiety and anger. Her brow looked permanently wrinkled. She was off her food.

Pete entered the library and, having found the books of which Mel told him, quietly sat down at a table. At first, Mel was nowhere to be seen, but she was soon to appear from the recesses of some hidden repository with the Dragon Librarian hot on her heels. Pete nodded to her, but she barely acknowledged him, her head demurely remaining down as she went about her duties.

He knew why. Apparently ever since Albert's phone call, the Dragon Librarian had been on her case something chronic and watched her every move.

The Dragon Librarian now spotted him and her face twisted up in disdain, but soon her eyes were attracted elsewhere. Her attention was diverted by the conversation going on between two West Indian boys from the local comprehensive, one of whom had an uncontrollably shrill voice on account of it being in the process of breaking. Probably both aged about thirteen, they seemed to be excitedly looking, and with what Pete considered extremely inquisitive eyes, at some large art books.

'Wow, bwana, look at this,' Pete heard one say to the other.

'Hey, bwana, incredible, looks like a painting by Beauford Delaney?' said the other.

The Dragon Librarian bore down upon them like it was D-day, quickly shooing them out of the library.

'We don't talk in public libraries. I've warned you before. Can't you read the signs? You must have learnt by now what the word silence means,' she said.

They tried to protest that she hadn't warned them before, which was most likely true as Mel told Pete that the Dragon Librarian considered all black people to look alike. But she was having none of it and was emphatic that they leave. The boys, no doubt having better things to do than waste their time arguing with her, ran off after calling her an ugly dried-up old prune.

Pete stifled a laugh.

Raising his head a minute later, some words jumped out at him from a badly folded newspaper on the periodical stand just the other side of the table at which he was sitting.

'Wow!' he exclaimed.

The Dragon Librarian glared at him and he was quick to bury his head in his folded arms to protect himself from her hostile looks but, once out of her radar, slowly getting up, he got the newspaper and, sitting back down again, began to read it.

Apparently a meeting, organised by a gay student who visited New York earlier in the summer, had been held at the LSE. Inspired by the Gay Liberation Front meeting he'd attended there, he determined to set something up in London. *So Gay Liberation has arrived in the UK*, thought Pete, *unbelievable or what?* He carried on avidly reading. A slight cough behind him brought back him to the real world. He looked up.

'How long have been you been watching me, Brad?' he whispered.

'Why yer whispering, Pete?'

Pete nodded his head in the direction of the Dragon Librarian's desk.

'Look here, read this. A group of guys has founded a GLF group here. At the LSE. It's all in this paper.'

Brad laughed and thrust a photocopied flyer at Pete.

'Snap! Guess what someone gave me?'

Pete took the flyer and started to read the stencilled hand-written words out loud:

THE GAY LIBERATION FRONT DEMANDS THAT ALL
DISCRIMINATION AGAINST GAY PEOPLE, MALE
AND FEMALE, BY THE LAW, BY EMPLOYERS, AND
BY SOCIETY AT LARGE, SHOULD END, THAT ALL
PEOPLE WHO FEEL ATTRACTED TO A MEMBER OF
THEIR OWN SEX BE TAUGHT THAT SUCH FEELINGS
ARE PERFECTLY NORMAL, THAT SEX EDUCATION
IN SCHOOLS STOP BEING EXCLUSIVELY
HETEROSEXUAL, THAT PSYCHIATRISTS STOP
TREATING HOMOSEXUALITY AS THOUGH IT WERE
A PROBLEM OR SICKNESS, THEREBY GIVING GAY
PEOPLE SENSELESS GUILT COMPLEXES, THAT
EMPLOYERS SHOULD NO LONGER BE ALLOWED TO
DISCRIMINATE AGAINST ANYONE ON ACCOUNT
OF THEIR SEXUAL PREFERENCE, THAT THE AGE
OF CONSENT FOR GAY PEOPLE BE REDUCED TO
THE SAME AS FOR STRAIGHTS, THAT GAY PEOPLE
BE FREE TO HOLD HANDS AND KISS IN PUBLIC, AS
ARE HETEROSEXUALS. GAY IS GOOD. ALL POWER
TO OPPRESSED PEOPLE! COME OUT – JOIN GAY
LIBERATION FRONT!

'Amazing!' said Pete, after a pause. 'Apparently they're going to hold meetings every Wednesday from now on. Look.'

'I've already read it, Booby,' said Brad absentmindedly, as he was still reading the newspaper article.

Once finished, he looked at Pete in the eyes. They both grinned and then, spontaneously hugging each other, they did a little dance of celebration right there.

'Right on!'

They swung round in the direction from where the words came and a strikingly tall woman with lots of flaming curly auburn hair came into view. She smiled at them. What they didn't see was the Dragon Librarian, back from searching for some title kept in the reserve stock in the basement, bearing down on Mel, and because of their excitement, heightened by the amazing upfront stance of the red-haired woman, they didn't hear her being ordered by her boss to remove her friends from the library at once.

Mel, who was quite unaware as to what just took place, got very confused.

'Er! Yes, Miss McPherson,' she meekly said. 'Then is it all right if I leave now too? It is time.'

'Yes, Melanie, by all means, just as long as you make sure you take them with you,' said the Dragon Librarian disdainfully as she eyeballed the other three.

'Well, goodbye, Miss McPherson,' Mel said, still blissfully unaware as she went behind the check-out to collect her bag. But the Dragon Librarian did not reply.

She made her way over to the boys and now noticed the tall woman with the flaming auburn hair.

'Hazel! I didn't know you knew…' she whispered, with surprise in her voice. 'Listen, she wants you all to get out. We got to split before she goes ballistic. I don't know why, but she's told, well, ordered me to remove you.'

They all made for the door, with the Dragon Librarian, while continuing to type as if she was trying to detonate an imaginary bomb under them, never taking her eyes off them until they were through the door.

'Twisted old dyke,' said Hazel, once outside.

'Hazel, surely not—'

'You wanna bet. Oh, well, at least it's stopped raining,' said Hazel, laughing.

Mel now introduced her to Brad and Pete. She was glad to see her new friend as, not knowing where she lived, she'd been hoping she would turn up in the library as there were so many things about which she wished to consult her.

'You must come to the next meeting,' Hazel said to Brad and Pete, as they walked up towards Hazel's squat in Vicarage Gardens. 'We need all the support we can get.'

And as they paired off, Brad and Pete together in front, and Mel and Hazel dawdling in intense conversation a little behind them, Mel, for a short while, forgot all the heartache Baz was causing her.

As it turned out, although in the following days Mel spent most of her spare time with Hazel rapping, listening and hanging on her every word, Brad and Pete never did get to the GLF meeting; circumstances decreed otherwise and, strangely, it was Baz who determined in a roundabout way those circumstances.

When some days later Baz eventually returned, Brad was still fretting as he would soon have to be in Frankfurt to get his plane, having not sold his bus. It was a Saturday afternoon and he and Pete were sitting with Mel in her room drinking coffee, while listening to music. Earlier, they'd been down Portobello Market, where they met up with Hazel and bought some patties at the Jamaican Patty Company and other provisions from Ceres. Hazel had to get back to Vicarage Gardens for a house meeting and afterwards planned to go to Brighton to visit friends. She'd ask Mel to go with her but Mel declined. She felt she had to wait it out, but as Hazel was going to be away for a week, she did wonder what she would do without her.

As the record came to end, the sound of footsteps coming up the stairs could be heard but they paid no attention to them, presuming that it was another of the squatters. However, the door handle turned, the door opened and in walked Baz, grinning. He then winked.

Mel looked up at him with an exaggerated frown.

'You fucking bastard, Baz,' she shouted, trying to be assertive, but her power to be so was understandably undermined by anger and tears, and her confusion as to whether she should act like Hazel or Nicola. 'You could have told me—'

'Steady on, Doll.'

The boys thought it best they let Mel and Baz have their own space and left the room.

'Baz, where have you been? And what is this? I need to know. I've been going crazy. You can't imagine what it's been like for me.'

She got out the crumpled postcard from her bag and thrust it in his face.

'Well, fuck me sideways,' said Baz, with a big grin on his face. 'I been rumbled.'

He laughed and then started to look right pleased with himself. Mel found this totally humiliating and, bursting into tears, she collapsed into a heap on her mattress.

'I knew it. You are having affair with this Dutch girl, aren't you?' she sobbed. 'I don't deserve to be treated like this. Does this Marieke know about me? I bet she doesn't.'

'Ah, Marieke, yeah,' said Baz. 'I've just come to take you to meet her. You'll really like her, Doll. Really, really like her. I promise.'

'How can I? When she's…'

Mel's voice faded into noisy sobs again, and almost choking with panic, she was unable to carry on with what she wanted to say. Baz, in a rare moment of gentleness, went over and folded her in his arms, and she continued to sob while he rubbed her back and stroked her face.

'Hey, Doll, come and meet her. You won't regret it. Trust me. We'll go now. What do you need?' he said as his eyes scanned the room, looking for her jacket and bag, which were on the bed.

Letting her go, he picked them up and then, standing right in front of her, held them up to her and said, 'Hey, put these on, come along, Doll. You won't be sorry. I promise you.'

Her crying now reduced to an occasional sob, Mel, despite being perplexed, started to feel cleansed as if all the anxiety of the last ten days had been released, had run down her cheeks. She took the jacket, meekly put it on and then, retrieving her bag from his hands, as if in a trance followed him out of the room, down the stairs and out of the house to his car.

Pete and Brad watched from Pete's window.

Mel waved up to them. Pete found it disturbing.

'What's he up to? The shifty bastard!' he said.

Brad laughed.

Baz revved off in the direction of the Bayswater Road. The railings on the park side were, as usual, full of bad paintings and, as usual, being seriously scrutinised by hordes of tourists. They passed Marble Arch and cut up behind busy Oxford Street, full of its Saturday-afternoon punters, and in no time, it seemed to Mel in her dreamlike stupor, they were beyond High Holborn and were cruising into the strangely ghostlike city. They remained silent, Mel hoping they'd quickly reach where they were going, and that this fateful meeting would soon be over. Her face was twisted in confusion and her eyes looked right ahead in uncertainty. Right, she knew Baz was a wind-up merchant, always had a rabbit to pull out of a hat, but what was this charade about? To what was he going to subject her now?

On past Whitechapel, with its street market still bustling, they went and then Baz turned off the main road and they were now by a row of derelict warehouses. Mel was lost. Where was he taking her?

Eventually, he drew up to the kerb and stopped the car; leaving its engine running. Mel watched him as he got out, walked over to a pair of tall wooden Victorian gates, painted in British Railways green, and took out a key from his pocket, unlocked the padlock on them and pushed them open. He then got back into the car, drove it into a deserted yard and parked.

'We'll have to walk from here, Doll,' he said.

'But Baz,' protested Melanie, 'nobody lives here. Surely—'

'You'd be surprised, Doll.'

They walked a few yards, turned a corner and Mel realised that they were in a disused dock.

'Close your eyes, Doll.'

'What?'

'Go on, close your eyes,' Baz said, reaching out for her hand.

Her eyes closed, Baz led her around the next corner.

'You can open them now,' he said.

And she did.

'There's Marieke. *De Mooie Marieke*, isn't she a beauty? And you know what? *Mooie* means beautiful in Flemish, yes, beautiful, just like you. And you know what, Doll, we're going to live on her,' he told her.

When Baz dropped Mel back to the squat, she couldn't wait to tell the boys about *De Mooie Marieke* and ran, at top speed, up the staircase to Pete's room. She was bubbling with excitement as she rushed in and, to start with, she made no sense whatsoever to either of them.

But it was dream come true for her. Ever since reading *The Wind in the Willows* as a little girl, she wanted to live on a barge and was totally bowled over by *De Mooie Marieke*: the sheer size, the spaciousness in the hold and her galley with its beautifully carved cabinets and brass work. The stove, in reality a small range, she was in ecstasy about.

'I'll be able to bake bread in the oven,' she said. 'And there's room for a little garden on the roof. I can grow tomatoes and marrows. And you can store bicycles and things on there. Hang out the washing. It'll be bliss. Roof? On a barge? Is that what you call it?'

The boys had no idea.

'So when are you going to move in it?' asked Brad. 'I hope I see it before I go.'

'You will. Now, I'm going to move in now,' said Mel, jumping up and down, hardly able to contain her excitement. 'Yes, now. You see, that's why Baz was so long. It was a surprise. After he sailed her over from Belgium, she's a Rhine barge originally, he did a lot of work on her. Painting, bringing things up to scratch, sorting out the lecky, etc., you know, those sorts of things. So, now she is ready. For me. He did it for me!'

Her brow now became furrowed. It was fixed in her pleading mode.

'Well, you see, Baz has gone off to see Tiny about something, and when he comes back, we'll pack up the car with our stuff. But I was wondering, well, we were both wondering, Brad, because then we wouldn't have to make two trips, whether, if you didn't mind…'

Melanie sweetly smiled at Brad.

'…if we could use your van. That way, with two vehicles…'

'Sure, Mel, far out, be happy to. This way I get to see this fabled palace on the water.'

While Mel returned to her room and started to pack, the boys went down to Portobello, now deserted except for the street cleaners, bin men and a hippy who only answered to the name of Jesus, looking for cardboard boxes and orange crates to help her on her way.

'You know, he always has an ulterior motive,' Pete said on their way back.

'You think so?' said Brad.

'I know so,' said Pete.

Baz was back at the squat by the time they returned and was halfway to filling up his car.

'Great, lads!' he said, as the boys put down the boxes. 'Much appreciated.'

Within an hour Mel and Baz's room was empty, and both Baz's car and the VW were filled to the brim and ready to leave.

While Mel and Baz were on the pavement saying goodbye to fellow squatters, Baz noticed the for-sale sign on Brad's van.

'Ah, I see you're selling your van, Brad?' he said.

'Yeah, but I've had no luck yet, and I gotta be in Frankfurt in a week.'

'Well, I gotta to go back to Belgium at the end of next week, you know. I'll tell you what, I'll buy the van off you. Tiny says it's in great nick and he's a man I trust about motors. And, well, the *autobahns* in Germany are great, once we hit Ostend, we can be in Frankfurt in no time. How about it, mate?'

Brad was stupefied, Pete was more than stupefied and Mel just beamed, pleased that her little tribe was reunited.

And so by the next week, Mel was living on the *De Mooie Marieke* and, when not at work, spending a wad of cash Baz gave her on materials, to make on her grandmother's old sewing machine curtains and cushions for the barge, and Baz had bought Brad's bus.

Pete and Brad spent their last night together on the barge in the large hold, not once letting go of each other. In the morning, after a breakfast of bread just freshly baked by Mel in the stove and piping hot Dutch coffee, the VW was loaded with Baz's Pan Am flight shoulder bag and his haversack, Brad's sophisticated bright orange backpack with his hiking boots strung onto its side, a picnic prepared for them by Mel and other stuff needed for their journey.

After a lingering farewell with Pete, Brad joined Baz in the bus. Brad turned on the ignition, that familiar sound was heard echoing all around the deserted dock and the VW rumbled its way out of the yard on its way again to the coast once more.

Mel and Pete waved until the bus was out of sight, then they hugged and Mel went back into the barge to continue her sewing while Pete made his way back to the squat to pack up his belongings

He finished this task in time to catch a late afternoon train to Manchester. He was feeling somewhat hollow without Brad but also excited, being able to draw strength from the fact that by the end of next spring, he would be in California and they would be reunited.

PART TWO

These Pearly Stores
Streaked with Foam

Pete just made it onto the plane.

Despite going to bed early, being excited, he only fell asleep as it got light. Consequentially, he slept through his alarm and had the unnecessary expense of taking a taxi to the airport. Rushing through from immigration, his new beige suede running shoes betrayed their phoney sportive pretensions. Lacking any substantial grip on the shiny surfaced floor, they sent him sliding past the entrance to the steps down to the bus that would take him to the plane.

'The New York flight?' an official called out, his tone terse, his eyes scornful. 'You're lucky, lad, I was just about to close the gate. You better hurry.'

But now, seated in keen anticipation, Pete wondered whether his marathon had been necessary because take-off was delayed. Waiting for clearance, the pilot had announced some minutes earlier.

He'd not flown before and, quite suddenly, the thought came to him that being on a plane was like an act of betrayal, like he was rejecting the cross-channel ferries of his childhood, obliterating those borrowed memories of Zénaïde's many transatlantic crossings some forty years previously when, on those floating palaces, she'd sailed out of Cherbourg and Le Havre in exactly the same direction he was now going. But no, he surmised, it was okay; he was joining the modern world.

The never-ending winter, which had dragged on with relentless monotony, seemed now to him like a distant, hazy dream. As the prospect of seeing Brad in less than twelve hours' time became a reality, that constant longing for his physical presence was replaced by an intense nervousness. The memory of Brad's scent, which had been with him off and on, being triggered by recollections of their intimacy, now could no longer be conjured up and, sitting on the plane with time to think, appalling thoughts plagued him.

What if he didn't recognise Brad? For now Brad's image, which had been so fixed in his memory since the previous summer, was no longer clear. He couldn't envisage his face. And in his haste that morning, he'd not even had the time to read Brad's letter which he'd found on the doormat when leaving the house. He now retrieved the light blue airmail from his pocket, scrutinising it as he smoothed out the crinkles on it.

Up until Christmas, regular airmails, full of reminiscences about the previous summer, had arrived. But curiously, Brad had not been so forthcoming in reply to Pete's questions about the proposed visit, although at the time, Pete'd put this down to Brad being West Coast laidback.

And so, when after Christmas there was a postal strike and means of communication severely curtailed, Pete carried on regardless planning his trip. He tried telephoning Brad a few times via Baz's mate who worked in the GPO's international exchange, but whenever calls were placed, there was no answer except once when an English-sounding voice answered and said he had the wrong number. Weighed down with coins, he also tried calling from several phone boxes in the area of Manchester where he was staying, but getting through proved impossible: either his coins got stuck or the line just went dead.

He'd actually deliberated about booking his flight, maybe he just should not go, but when he found a good deal going out of Manchester at the end of April with a change in New York, he felt it was meant to be. He would go, despite the strike being over and no letter forthcoming from Brad. He paid for the ticket and sent a telegram to Brad telling him of when he was arriving.

The reply was short. It just said: 'Sure. End of month best. Will write soon.'

At last he was on track. But it was only at Easter, while in the house under the Downs, he told Albert as his contract was not being renewed (which wasn't quite true), he was going. On hearing this, Albert was silent.

'Well, it's your life, son,' he then said, somewhat tersely.

However, by the end of the Easter weekend, he came around to the idea, indeed seemed quite excited by it, and when Darren called round on a wet Easter Monday afternoon, they got out the big atlas and peered over it, conjuring up images of the Golden Gate and Hollywood, orange groves and redwoods, Monument Valley and the mighty Mississippi, the Statue of Liberty and the Empire State Building as they tried to determine which course the plane might take.

At last, the plane started to cruise towards the runway. Pete looked down at the letter and weighed it back and forth in his hand before taking his penknife from the pocket of his maroon Levi cords and slitting it open. He started to read as the plane, now positioned at last at the end of the runway, came to a halt.

Dear Pete,

    Since I got your telegram I've found it difficult to write to you or know what exactly to say. And so I've allowed a long time to elapse in a period in which your uncertainty, apprehension and perhaps feeling of betrayal, I dare say, have been aggravated by my silence. I feel guilty now as I know I chose not to answer all your questions in the letters I got from you before the postal workers' strike. I have been negligent, selfish, and it's inexcusable. So not a good situation, an extreme one allowed to develop out of an original close and good one! Of course you are welcome to stay with me when you come to California. I'll be delighted to have you here; it'll be so fine showing you around, seeing your reactions to things. Your responses will be refreshing to me.

Pete found the opening tones of the letter disquieting. Feeling guilty, what was that all about? It definitely seemed kinda heavy. It took him off-guard, was bewildering. But he was reclaimed for the real world by the voice of his neighbour, a businessman en route to Charlotte, North Carolina.

'The seatbelt light's on, young man. You must do up your seatbelt,' he said.

Now his attention was diverted by an air hostess announcing the safety procedure. He raised his eyes to see the cabin crew, in automated boredom, embark on a strange, mime-like ritual. This procedure he promptly forgot as his eyes lowered and got back to the more pressing subject of Brad's letter:

There is one thing, though. And that is I have exams in the middle of May and it would be better if you could come out towards the end of the month.

Oh, Brad must have meant the end of May in his telegram, and not April, he thought. He read on:

> *Early May I'll hardly be able to spend any time with you and I'll also be very uptight about the exams so not in a very accommodating mood. But after I'll have all the time in the world to spend with you and maybe we could go off travelling somewhere like Mendocino, Big Sur or Yosemite. There's a great deal to do and see here. Berkeley is real fine around June, and San Francisco and the bay are the whole world in themselves. From the hills behind Berkeley, San Francisco seems like the celestial city alight across the water and west through the Golden Gate beyond the ocean is the garden of the Hesperides – or so it would seem when one feels most optimistic about the world and oneself. There's also Marin County with its Pacific beaches. It's the real Wild West in landscape. Everyone here is from somewhere else and here to get themselves together. It'll be good to see you when you arrive on these pearly shores streaked with foam.*

Pearly shores streaked with foam, wow, that's so wistful, Pete thought.

As the plane went into full throttle and started hurtling down the runway, he smiled as confusion turned to relief at what he'd just read, and because of that, his curiosity could only but avert his eyes from the letter to look out of the porthole. The terminal building now seemed far away and the grass, within the airport perimeter, had a strange hue as if a transparent, oily film of pollution was fused over it. He sat back in his seat feeling good. It was going to be all right. Obviously Brad was freaking out about his exams and wouldn't have time for him until after. That was fine; he'd find stuff to do, places to explore, people to meet, photographs to take.

The noise of the plane now became encompassing and it started to shudder, and for a short instance, it seemed that it would never make it off the ground, but then, all of a sudden, it was in the air, and Pete's stomach felt like it was being whipped around his body, and as he gripped the arms of his seat, his ears popped and sounds became muffled. Everything felt different as gravity was denied.

Then his ears popped once more and sounds became normal again. And in no time at all, the airport seemed like a toy model, and very soon the earth disappeared out of view as the plane passed through dense grey clouds.

Wow, unbelievable, I'm actually on my way, he thought.

The plane glided on up above the clouds and far into the blue ethereal heaven. As he looked out of the porthole, he became transfixed by the fluffiness, the whiteness of the clouds below. They looked inviting enough for him to bounce on.

Surely just like those pearly shores streaked with foam, he thought.

His head buzzing, he stared out for a while before looking back at the letter to continue reading it:

Gay life here is particularly good. You'll have to go along to some Gay Liberation Front meetings as well as to some of the gay bars in the city, which are totally full of freaks. Always crowded at weekends, they get very exciting when they get going; it'll blow your mind. There're no places quite like them, as far as I know, in London. There are also some gay rap groups which I go to where people get together to feel good about being gay, encounter each other, discuss their problems and go through sensitivity and awareness exercises. They are really fine and always leave you with a very good feeling about your sexuality. There you can meet other gay guys as really full human beings and not simply as sexual objects in the cruising, sexist ways that some bars encourage. And yes, one thing if you like hiking at all (I can't remember!) we must go to Point Reyes in Marin County. It's very beautiful countryside there. Perhaps we could take a tab together.

Pete wasn't too sure whether he would want to do that: trip. He had twice before but it always seemed a power struggle developed in the group and he kinda felt, in fact, knew he saw the beauty in the things surrounding him anyway. He'd seen the Opal Causeway many years before. Mémé had shown it to him on his first crossing to France, and what could be trippier than that? *Still, don't rule anything out yet,* he thought as he lowered his eyes to continue reading the letter:

Well, since last summer I hope you're been doing things and getting things on with people. But one thing, please don't get too hung up on me; we only met for a short time and will do again for a few weeks. It's unrealistic, and my life's here and yours there, and all I was was a star passing in the night. There are people every bit better than me for you over here. It's all in the head in the end.

If you could, but perhaps it is too late now, set back the date of your arrival here, I'd appreciate it. Nevertheless, I look forward to seeing you when you come, but I'm rather apprehensive about your coming over at such a critical time for me as we hardly know each other at all and the images of each other now cannot be but fantasies, fed by almost a year's separation. It will most certainly be like starting again new and like meeting someone for the first time. We will have to be open and honest with each other and work it out if it should start to go bad. During my exams I'll have to trust you to your own devices, but I know you are quite industrious on your own. I hope I'm not labouring the point, but I don't want my psychic time weighed down with feelings of responsibility and guilt. Let alone with thinking on how we're getting along with each other. But I'm sure everything will be OK. Of course I'll meet you at the airport.

   See you soon,
   Love, Brad

Pete's stomach felt like it was being whipped around his body but this time not by the plane. How could Brad say that they hardly knew each other at all, when the summer before he'd said that he felt like he'd known Pete all his life?

This sounded like a different Brad, a stranger, and Pete's initial feelings, as he started to reread the letter, returned. Procrastination certainly hadn't been a quality he'd remarked in Brad before. But he felt now Brad almost begrudged having to ask him to stay when the previous summer there was no question of Pete not staying with him. And all the talk about guilt, what was that about? He was trying to get his head around it when the stewardess came along to offer him some coffee.

'Nervous, huh?' she said, reading his face. 'Most are on their first flight.'

'I guess so,' replied Pete, as he let down the folding table from the back of the seat in front of him.

'Milk and sugar?'

'Please.'

'Here you go. If there's anything you need just push the button above you,' the stewardess said, starting to wheel her trolley further along the aisle.

As he started to sip his drink, he spilt a spot of coffee on the airmail. He wiped it with the paper napkin the stewardess provided, but some of the writing was smeared and was now unreadable.

No, the letter really didn't sound like the Brad he'd met last summer and suddenly, months of complete certainty in the future were dissipated as they ran like the coffee-stained blue ink, in which the blue airmail was written, into an incomprehensible blot.

Once he'd finished his coffee, Pete folded up Brad's letter, and, deep in thought, slipped it in the blue Pan Am flight shoulder bag which Baz had lent him when he called in on *De Mooie Marieke* on his way back from Albert's at the end of Easter weekend. He closed his eyes and tried to sleep.

He had a two-hour wait at JFK. No time to visit the city, but he had a fine view of Manhattan and the Statue of Liberty during the plane's descent. Looking down at the piers where Mémé's ships had docked all those years before, he imagined her walking those pavements, riding the subways, catching taxicabs. Those thoughts conjured up an intense sense of her spirit, that somehow she was there with him. Yes, he had arrived in the land of the free, and what a vibe he felt. As he was ushered through immigration, the officer looked him up and down as if he were an alien arrived off a UFO. But he didn't care: he'd arrived.

On the shorter flight to San Francisco, his thoughts about Brad became less fixated as he was fascinated, the further west they got, by the chequer-board pattern of the land far below and the shadows cast over it by the ever-setting sun which the plane seemed to be chasing. He recalled Gertrude Stein had written something about that phenomena after her first flight.

How was it possible, he wondered, *that such a vast land could be divided up so precisely?* Only the winding rivers seemed to be organic realities and only the highest mountains, the Rockies, defied that human-imposed symmetry, but by the time they'd reached them, the sun had gone; it was pitch-black. *What had*, he mused, *the Native Americans made of this severe application of geometry to their scarred land?*

It was dark when the plane touched down in San Francisco and the quality of darkness reminded him of being at Aunt Ghislaine's in Cagnes-sur-mer. Collecting his luggage from the conveyor belt, he was through to arrivals in no time. As his eyes scanned over the concourse looking for Brad, other passengers were quickly reunited with family or friends, and soon the terminal building was quite empty: desks were shut down, lights turned out and he felt very alone.

He located a phone. But it took him a while to suss out how to work it and it was a long trek to find a concession stall to get a nickel, but finally he dialled Brad's number.

'Hey, you arrived already, Pete, be really good to see you. Hold on. I'm waiting on my friend Will. He's got a car. He's got delayed. We'll be there soon.'

Brad sounded distracted.

I've probably interrupted his revision, Pete thought.

He put the phone down looking around for a place to

wait. He felt weary. It would be the middle of the night back home. He'd been up for nearly twenty-four hours and just travelled halfway around the world. He settled down on a bench feeling strangely detached from reality as extreme apprehension returned.

He had to wait around an hour before Brad turned up, and it certainly wasn't the greeting which he'd been anticipating. Brad looked thinner, paler and seemed nervous. But if he held back, Will, his friend, didn't. He was beaming and big with masses of blond curly hair and a beard. He greeted Pete warmly.

'Yeah, it's great that you're here. I can't believe it,' Brad said, palely echoing Will's exuberant greeting afterwards. But with the content of the letter still consuming him, Pete had doubts about his sincerity. He was like a different person from the previous summer.

'You know, I only got your letter this morning,' Pete said to Brad, as Will hauled his luggage into the trunk of the car.

'We'll talk about it later, man,' Brad said, opening the backdoor for Pete, after which he slid himself up front beside Will, who was already revving up the motor.

'You all ready?' Will asked, turning briefly round and flashing a great big grin at Pete, as he accelerated off at a fast rate. They were soon out of the airport complex.

Only small talk between Brad and Will was exchanged on that journey to Berkeley. Pete was too zonked to make conversation, although his head constantly turned while he tried to make out the form of the city as the car swept him through the darkness. Staring at the back of Brad's head, the thought occurred to him that perhaps Will and he were lovers. Brad did seem uncharacteristically meek in Will's presence and dwelt on his every word. But at that moment, it was too much for Pete to speculate.

From the backseat of the big, spacious car, his first impression of this new land was definitely the white lines of the freeway as they reflected the light from both passing vehicles and the neons on the buildings above. With its shadowy dwellings, the city seemed nebulous, lacked strong definition for him in that light, and he was surprised to find, when Will mentioned it, that they were driving over the Bay Bridge.

How weird it is, he thought, *to be travelling across a bridge over San Francisco Bay, a place so celebrated in many songs, and not realise.*

They were soon cruising into the Berkeley city limits and eventually turned up a hill onto a treelined street. Intermittent street lamps shone through the leaves, casting blue shadows on the two-storey wooden houses and their surrounding yards. Hardly anybody was walking in the street, but cars passed up and down with regularity. Will drew up and swung the car over alongside a detached house on the other side of the street.

'My apartment's up on the first floor,' Brad said, pointing to a couple of darkened windows. The windows below, in contrast, were bright, and the sound of both loud music and laughter were drifting out from them.

On getting out, Pete noticed an old settee on the scrub lawn in front of those windows as he followed Brad and Will. Skirting around the side of the house and up an exterior wooden staircase they went, and through a door into a small kitchen with a large cooker and a fridge of even larger proportions. Will dumped Pete's luggage down on the floor of the living room adjacent to the kitchen and turned to Brad.

'Hey, man, gotta split! I'll be by tomorrow. Bye, Pete, good to meet you.'

Pete noticed a doleful look on Brad's face as Will went to hug him.

He extended his hand to Pete. 'Thanks for picking me up. I don't know how I—'

'Hey, no worries, man, you have a great stay now, you hear?' he said, and was out the house and down the steps in a flash.

Brad and Pete awkwardly stood in the middle of the room as Will's car started up and roared off up the street. It was the first time he'd seen Brad in bright light since his arrival and, yes, Brad did look different, sort of tense, pained. But now these observations were diverted by a door opening, from which a guy with waist-length hair came out. He wore thick steel-rimmed glasses which made his eyes seems minuscule. He nodded to them before going into the bathroom.

'That's my roommate,' Brad said. 'He's very quiet. You won't know he is there. He works during the day and by night is strung out on angel dust most of the time.'

Angel dust, what was that?

'You only got my letter today then?' Brad said.

'Yes,' Pete replied, no longer sure what day it was.

'So you do understand about my exams? I just can't get into anything else. Here are some leaflets. There's one about a gay awareness group in the city. They meet every Tuesday, yeah, tomorrow. Maybe you want to go? Or maybe you can travel around a while? You know, till I'm through, I'll be no company for you at present. I'm too hung up on my exams right now.'

Although he'd time to think about it on the plane, these sudden changes in Pete's plans, his aspirations, caused utter confusion; besides, he was dropping.

'You know, I'm dead beat,' he said.

'So you brought your sleeping bag?'

'Yeah,' Pete replied, although he'd never expected to use it at Brad's.

He watched Brad as he went over to the settee positioned along the side of the living room's backwall and pulled it out into a narrow bed.

'This okay for you? I'll fetch you some pillows. Extra covers?'

He didn't wait for Pete's answer but went into what must have been his bedroom, closing the door the moment Angel Dust vacated the bathroom. Pete fished out his washbag and towel from his baggage and took Angel Dust's place. Locking the door after vigorously brushing his teeth, he climbed up into the old bathtub and turned on the shower. The water was hot, its pressure soothing.

'Hey, you in the shower? It's all on the sofa. Have to crash, man. See you in the morning,' Brad shouted.

When Pete came out of the bathroom, the living room was empty, the door to Brad's bedroom closed. Although disturbed by how the day had unfolded, Pete's disappointment was numbed by extreme tiredness. Soon he was in his sleeping bag and, after a strange kind of half slumber, when he felt he was free-falling through fluffy white clouds and was being caressed by the foam of pearly shores, and with the still very real vibrations of the plane's engine infiltrating his nervous system, he eventually fell into a strange, uncharted sleep.

Something woke him. At first, Pete imagined he was still on the plane, but on opening his eyes, confused as to where he was, he saw Brad, already dressed, on his way from bathroom to kitchen. Yawning, he turned his head and reached over to the table beside him for his watch. It was already past ten and, incredibly, he'd slept for over ten hours.

'Oh, I'm sorry,' Brad said, glancing down at him. 'Did I wake you? I'm running late for my tutorial. Slept well?'

Pete stretched, blinked a few times and then sat up. His eyes felt sore and sticky.

'Yes, I guess,' he said. 'But I dreamt loads.'

'I do after long flights.'

A car horn sounded in the street.

'Ah, there's Will. Not sure when I'll be back. The leaflet about that group is on the table there and there's a city map by it, San Fran, that is. Berkeley's easy to get around. The campus is, like, up the hill and to get to the city just go down this street as far as Shattuck and put out your thumb. When someone stops just ask for the Bay Bridge. Gotta go and, oh, there's a key by the stove, and the coffee's still good.'

And he was gone.

After taking a quick shower, he went through to the kitchen, where he found the pot of coffee. He poured himself a cup which, after slipping back into his sleeping bag, he drank. As the momentousness of the previous day's developments rose to the surface, his confusion resurfaced.

Brad, his letter and unanticipated change, as well as the lengthy journey and months leading up to it, all seemed to be contriving to plummet him to the depths. But no, he would not go there, and pushing up through that strata of negativity, and knowing the sun was shining brightly outside, he became excited by the prospect of this new world ripe for exploration, in which he had just arrived, and where he'd so often dreamt of being, Brad or no Brad.

So, with his camera slung around his neck, light meter in shoulder bag, he ventured forth. He would grab hold of the day, as Albert would have said, and his stride became purposeful, like someone who belonged. His eyes circled around him as he clocked his new surroundings and found himself going in the direction of the campus.

With its leafy avenues, Berkeley was built on the side of an increasingly steep hill. And like the chequer-board pattern viewed from up high while on the plane the day before, he initially found the city's unsubtle grid system startling. But now, he saw the chequer board come to life as he passed streets and avenues dissecting each other in obsessive asphalt symmetry: no lanes here originating from sheep paths or other animal tracks.

Drawing nearer the campus, he realised the city was dominated by the university, as the campus evidently cut it into two. Its main buildings appeared to have be positioned and been constructed in such an architectural style as to emphasise their status, in the same way as an imposing mediaeval cathedral or castle. And on the peripheries of the campus, like stationers around a medieval cathedral or a market in the shadows of some town wall, Sproul Plaza, at its main entrance, and Telegraph Avenue, stretching down from beyond the campus gates, appeared to be a hive of activity.

There was such rhythm to the place, an exciting buzz, both futuristic yet somehow invoking the past. Serious, earnest street politicians were interspersed between a miscellany of freaks and hawkers, street performers and pranksters, who gave the whole place the impression of being some recently created, zany, technicoloured Speakers' Corner. Many alternative lifestyle products were being hawked around, and as he carried along the pavement, street merchants stepped out into his path in predictable regularity, offering him wares such as homemade candles, joss sticks, organic carrot juice and underground newspapers while saffron-robed Hare Krishna devotees danced.

Pete noticed others of dropped-out consciousness basking like lizards in the sun, and at a second glance, it became obvious to him that some of them had definitely spent too long in wonderland and reality now permanently evaded them. It was all utterly fascinating, though, and he snapped away. He stopped to listen to a preacher telling the passing good-natured students, 'You socialist sinners, get off the streets and go find yourself some religion.' No one barracked the man; he was left alone to his proselytising.

What Pete was also wowed by graffiti he came across:

'To make it a better world, make yourself a better individual.'
'Every little boy can grow up to be the prez – can every little girl?'
'We are the women men warned us about.'

He'd started to make a collection of slogans back home and these were excellent additions. One, *Fuck Santa Rita*, he found mystifying. He'd never heard of a saint called Rita before, but his attention was distracted by coming across a wall of murals displaying images of the world's oppressed, and of Che, Iranian dissidents, guns, ban the bomb signs and flowers.

After this intoxicating onslaught, Pete's head started spinning in a similar way as it had when he'd first viewed an exhibition of Pierre Bonnard's work, and he decided to move on and find some quiet place suited for contemplation, so after walking back through the campus, he turned right and started climbing up in the directions of the hills.

After a couple of blocks, he stopped to catch his breath, and turning around, he cast his eyes for the first time back down the hill. From this point, at last, he was able to see how the city stretched towards the shore and that San Francisco was clearly visible on the opposite side. And Brad was right: it was the celestial city afire.

After taking some shots, he carried on up.

In a weird way, he was reminded of the south of France, as roses and geraniums were already blooming. And as in the south of France, nature could only win in the end, for he noticed that, as the roads continued up to the hills and the hills got steeper, it became impossible for them to run straight anymore. For then the layout of the built environment took on a more ancient look, more higgledy-piggledy, as roads continued Mediterranean hairpin-bend style before petering out, unable to run another yard.

But did this symmetry, he wondered, pervade all human life here? Did it affect how people were; how they saw things and carried on with their daily lives? If so, it surely had to determine how the American dream was dreamt.

Quite suddenly, he recalled Brad talking of a rose garden and had an urge to find it. Stopping a passer-by, he asked for directions.

'Hum, sure thing, let's see. Now, go straight up this street and when you get to Euclid Avenue, turn left. Carry on to Bayview Place, and it's right there next to Codornices Park. You got all that?'

'I think so,' Pete replied.

'Well, you have a nice day now.'

'You too, and thank you.'

The passer-by hurried on, books underarm, towards the campus as Pete set off towards the Rose Garden. After a few minutes, he reached Euclid and arrived by the garden gates. Once inside, as he sat down on a bench contemplating this first morning in the USA, it became quickly apparent to him that all Brad said about this Rose Garden was true. The whole panorama of San Francisco Bay, the Bay Bridge and the city, and Marin County, dominated by Mount Tam, was truly magnificent. And as for the roses, well, Pete only wished Albert were there to see them. The scents bombarded, called out to bees and the rest of the insect world to come buzz, hover and suckle.

Getting up from the bench, he began exploring further. The main section of the rose garden was of a classical design with wide stone terraces and a semi-circular pergola made of wood, which extended the full width of the garden and allowed vibrant climbing varieties of rose to cast shade on benches on which other people sat and contemplated the view which, now he could see it in its entirety, was categorically crowned by the Golden Gate glinting in the morning sun. He quickly finished off his film.

His camera reloaded, Pete snapped away until, through his lens, his attention was caught by the figure of a girl leaning in a position of devotion over one particularly large fine-looking pinkish orange rose. Her stance was so intriguing that he couldn't resist a couple of shots. But the girl suddenly became aware of him and beckoned him over. As Pete approached, it became apparent to him that she was out of it.

'Hey, man, just look at this beauty,' she called out. 'It's fantabulous, it's like a chakra. Watch it pulsating? Look, man, trippy, wow, it's fucking far out!'

Once, Pete reached her and scrutinised the object of her adoration, he could only but agree that it was indeed a most incredible specimen. The girl now turned around and stared at him and he noticed dilated pupils and felt she could see right through him. She wore a long renaissance-style dress and around her head was tied a patterned silk scarf. Large earrings, circular and gold, hung from her ears, and she had a stick onto which a bundle was tied and from which a bell hung. Its jingle accompanied her every movement.

'I'm Leah,' she said. 'You wanna hang out? I'm planning to hitch over to Point Reyes later.'

They chatted for a while, mainly in superlatives, but Pete, in all truth, was a little freaked by her and, excusing himself, left her to continue her communion with the beautiful rose while he made his way back.

He drew closer to Brad's apartment, which he had no trouble locating because of the settee in the front yard. It was now occupied by a bunch of freaks. They warmly greeted him once he reached the house.

'Hey there, you the dude who's visiting from England? Far out!' the girl in the group said. 'Hey, come on, join us, please sit, we're neighbours.'

It turned out that two of the group were brother and sister: Jim and Susan, originally from the Midwest. It also turned out, a little to Pete's relief, that they didn't know Brad too well, as they'd just recently moved in.

There were two dogs scampering around; one had a blue bandana tied around its neck: Susan's, called Tamu, named out of solidarity with Angela Davies, because Tamu was the alias she used on the run from the Feds. Jim's was called Erica, after Erica Huggins, yet another victim of the system's ugly discrimination.

After their friends left, Pete got down to some serious rapping with them. Susan was an upfront woman with long ash-blond hair parted in the middle. Her skin appeared very clear, there was no trace of make up on her face and, under her tee-shirt and pair of blue and white-striped workers' dungarees, she evidently was not wearing a bra. Her brother was quieter, a more studious type.

They invited him into their apartment to smoke some reefer, real strong reefer, and hear some sounds. Pete listened as they fed him with their stories and a bowl of granola, a type of cereal which was new to him, covered with chilled milk and sweetened with thick local honey.

When Pete explained about Brad, his exams and the mix-up and that he was thinking of taking a trip somewhere, they clapped their hands in unison. Pete was confused, but Susan, noticing his look, was quick to dispel his confusion.

'Wow, man, it's so far out. We're only laughing as it's a coincidence, predestined, you could say! We're planning a trip too. Hey, man, why don't you come along? A bunch of us are planning to take a campervan down to Southern California, and come back through Vegas and Death Valley. Go where we fancy, you know. You should come. There's room for another.'

'Wow, that would be brilliant, but are you sure?' Pete said.

'Of course, are you around tomorrow or the next day?' Susan asked, now getting up. 'We got some errands to run and I go to my job at the telephone company later. We can talk about it then, yeah? But it would sure be great if you could.'

'Well, yes,' Pete said, smiling, as he made his way to the door.

'Sure, tomorrow.'

Pete made his way up the steps, wondering if Brad was back. But the apartment was empty and he wondered when they'd have time to be free, open and frank with another.

This new encounter somewhat defused the confusion surrounding his arrival. Now a new agenda was set, a sudden fork in the freeway appeared, a different path had been hacked open and he could again envisage the direction in which he was going. Brad or no Brad, he felt that he was reclaiming his sense of purpose. So after a nap, he shaved, again showered and set out to hitch to the city. He'd go to that group Brad suggested.

He was amazed how quickly he got a lift.

The meeting wasn't a gay liberation one in the political sense about rights and so forth, but more about inward liberation, about being at ease with one's sexuality, one's physicality and, more importantly, accepting that of others. Part of the evening was taken up with Gestalt therapy exercises exploring feelings and scrutinising one's reactions to other gay men. And by the end of the session, Pete was feeling good about himself and the spectre of Brad had become distant, almost irrelevant. He felt light, unburdened as it dawned on him that perhaps the way things turned out were for a reason, not a reason he understood but, nevertheless, a reason all the same, and a reason that one day might be revealed.

Once the session was over, as he was on his way out, a guy standing by the door with whom he paired up to do an exercise about listening to your partner, nodded to him. He was talking with another participant, but as Pete passed, he reached out and touched him on the shoulder.

'So how you getting back to Berkeley, man?' he asked.

'Hitching, I guess,' Pete replied.

'Well, we can't take you all the way, but we can take you to the slip road that leads onto the bridge. You're bound to get a ride from there easily.'

By the time he was dropped off, Pete felt he'd known Gene and Kurt for years, and as there was an exhibition on Picasso's *347 Gravures* which Gene had seen written up in *Avant Garde* magazine and was ecstatic about, they planned to meet at the Museum of Modern Art the next day and, after visiting the museum, hang out together, see the city.

'We'll meet you in front of the museum at noon, yeah?' Gene called out, as Pete was getting out of the car. 'You know, it should be really neat – these engravings are a series of pictures portraying every aspect of sexual pleasure.'

'Oh!' said Pete.

'Yeah, apparently it was something Picasso wanted to do for a long time. I read one critic commented about the difference between Picasso's view of sex and the sniggering, guilt-ridden American pornography of today. I think he got it so right. Well, tomorrow then, man, yeah?'

The next day, this time in daylight, found Pete again hitching to the city. A late spring day with neither wind nor cloud, the sky was a seductive velvety azure. As he stuck out his thumb, Pete basked in anticipation of summer and, once cruising over the top tier of the Bay Bridge with a fresh breeze coming through the open window onto his face, was able to properly appreciate the approach to the city.

The bay beneath was sparkling in sunlight. Boats with white tails of rippling surf bobbed up and down on the water and beyond, San Francisco looked magnificent. The exit from the bridge was close to Third Street where the museum was located. Consequently, Kevin, who gave him the lift and with whom he'd been pleasantly chatting, although he twice removed a wandering hand from his thigh, dropped him off outside the museum, right beside a bench on which Gene and Kurt, enwrapped in one another, just happened to sitting.

Gene was wearing an array of anti-war badges. The one which impressed Pete the most was inscribed with the slogan: 'Suck cock and beat the draft'. They both jumped up when they saw Pete and hugged him.

'Hey, buddy, how you doing? There're two exhibitions, you know. I hadn't realised. Other than Picasso, there's an exhibition of some work by a photographer I've not heard of.

And as you're a photographer, maybe you'd like to see that, Pete. What was his name, Kurt?' Gene said.

'Chauncey Hare,' Kurt replied.

'Well, I was really looking forward to seeing the Picasso, but any mention of a photographer, yeah, why not? But how about you?' Pete asked.

'Cool, fine by us. We got till evening,' Gene said. 'Say, so what kind of photography you do?'

'Well, it's kind of complicated. I sort of lost my direction lately as I was doing this soulless job for the last year with a catalogue company having to take shots of trashy objects I had no interest in. Still, it paid for me to get here, but it's stagnated me.'

'Stagnated? Say, how?' Kurt asked.

As they made their way towards the museum, Pete started to explain how, in his last year at college, he had been doing really interesting multimedia work for his dip show but then he lost track and felt he'd ended up a dead-end street.

'I feel adrift now. The thing is that I allowed myself to get too distracted and lost the point of what I was doing. I got attracted by too many shiny things, superficial and flaky. It all got too precious.'

He carried on to explain his idleness despite the shots he'd taken at the adventure playground after that intense final year at college and the relentless monotony of the work for the catalogue company, however good or worthy it might be considered, had resulted in him finding himself in a creative void. Although he was enthused by the last few days, he felt he was going around taking photographs with a vague hope he might eventually select something good from a contact sheet, but he had no theme, no concept to follow. And he felt he'd gone wide of his ultimate goal and this had caused him doubt about his ability, about his talent. It made him wonder whether he wanted to continue with photography at all.

'But I do now. These last two days have confirmed that for me. Hey, but what about you two?'

'Well,' said Gene. 'I do the switch on a gay helpline. I'll take you there one time.'

'I'd like that. And you, Kurt?'

'I'm a waiter in a diner in an old converted cable car up near Castro. You should come for lunch one day.'

'I'd like that too.'

'And we live in a gay commune, nine gay men together, and they'd all have you for breakfast,' Gene said, laughing.

'Wow!' said Pete, smiling.

They went into the Picasso first.

Although Pete admitted to them Picasso was not his favourite painter, he was impressed by his black and white engravings. Dark, some sombre, they seemed sculptural, despite the thin, scratchy lines. It took time for them to recognise the activities in which the subjects were involved and then, when Kurt suddenly realised, he exclaimed in a loud voice, 'Jeez, man, they're fucking.'

'I guess he was influenced by sculptures on Hindu temples, or by nineteenth-century Japanese prints,' said Pete. 'These are very reminiscent of those. He's a clever man, Monsieur Picasso. However, I always wondered that if the genius Gertrude Stein claimed he was was because of his ability to assume other people's ideas, ideas from other cultures, styles and forms, and from them somehow contrive to create art which he owned?'

'Heavy, man, I'll have to think about that,' said Gene.

Despite that, the *347 Gravures* did have appeal for Pete; the images stayed with him. But it was Chauncey Hare whom he found more fascinating and who became the catalyst for his own artistic resurgence, although he was not to realise it until some time later.

Apparently, once an engineer for an oil company, Chauncey Hare became increasingly disillusioned in his work and turned to photography. His prints were almost spooky, catching quite unaware as they did many of their subjects as if almost skewering them to the background through the use of flash and shadows. Using an extremely wide-angle lens, the photos showed a certain sense of pathos, a brutality, behind the American dream, despite there being a real connection with the subjects. Seeing them made Pete think about his own photographs taken in the adventure playground and whether he had made any connection with his subjects at all, and if not, wonder whether he was a bad person.

They spent much longer in the museum than they'd anticipated, and because he said he'd see Susan and Jim that evening about the trip, and Gene and Kurt had to go to work, there was no time to hang out in the city. However, they offered to show him around another time, so he arranged to meet up with them soon.

As he made his way back, Pete could hardly believe that it was only the night before that he had met these two guys with whom he'd just had such a good time. He felt like they were on the same planet.

Once back in Berkeley, before climbing the steps to Brad's apartment, he knocked on Susan and Jim's door. Getting no answer and being hungry, he walked back to Shattuck

Avenue to Harry Ramsden's, where he ordered some fish and chips, a kind of strange thing to do, he thought after, as he really wanted to try one of the head cafés up near the campus, but he didn't know which one to go to, and besides, he'd started to feel jetlagged.

So after eating in Harry Ramsden's, on his return to Brad's, after a short, confusing discourse with Angel Dust, he crashed out.

Although not at all in the way which during the past winter he'd anticipated, the following two weeks turned out to be a whirlwind for him. It was as if his meeting with both Susan and Jim, and Gene and Kurt, catapulted him into Californian life big time, as back and forth across the bay he travelled to hook up with his new friends.

All the time wide-eyed, ensnared by California's collective charm, he was like a piece of blotting paper soaking up everything he came across. All the people, he encountered seemed so laidback, totally upfront, not at all hung up.

He didn't see much of Brad. As it was, Brad was often up at Will's studying, sometimes staying over. They passed in the apartment, talked from time to time, but it was almost like they were polite strangers. Pete did wonder whether they both were too wary to talk, in case something unpleasant rose to the surface. But as yet nothing had got bad. Still, he did wonder what happened to *being open and honest with each other and working it out*. He knew Nicknick would've said *sort it, Petey* but felt it best not to rock the boat. Once Brad's exams were over, he surmised, there would be ample time to rap and, besides, because of the fun he was having, it really didn't seem important. His ego had dealt with worse.

He loved the freedom of hitching in California. Somehow it had a different dimension from hitching in

England and France. But then, everything did actually, and despite warnings about weirdos, he found that the people who stopped for him were genuinely nice, right on, even the ones who came onto him, for unlike people from whom he sometimes got lifts back at home, people here did not seem to hold back. Their agenda was placed upfront and didn't seem pervy at all.

'Hey, man. I'd like to ball with you,' was a phrase often said to him, and sometimes he acquiesced and the day would develop another dimension, while sometimes he might not.

Two days after the museum visit, he hit the streets of San Francisco with Gene, Kurt being at work. Gene was really into architecture and pointed out to Pete the smallest of features on many of the buildings they passed, features that Pete could have quite easily missed if he'd been wandering around by himself.

If the layout of Berkeley defied its natural environment, the streets of San Francisco, with its cable cars, seemed more like a long, complex roller-coaster ride. The grid system here was taken to extremity. Only the most cunning natural features such as Telegraph Hill were allowed to impede development and defy rules, although Gene told him there were once plans afoot to level it.

As they approached Coit Tower, Gene displayed considerable reverence. The tower was a magnificently tall, circular art deco building, and was, he with glee exclaimed as he rushed to hug the thick reinforced concrete base, very phallic. The views from the tower were fabulous. A sweep of the eye or the click of his camera took in other famous city landmarks round about and the financial district, Russian and Nob Hills, Golden Gate Bridge and the piers, with

Alcatraz out there, all tiny and winking across the bay. Gene told Pete people were not so enthusiastic about the nearby evolving Transamerica Pyramid. Pereira's Prick, they called it, apparently after the architect who designed it.

San Francisco was, for Pete, an extraordinary place in which to be. For a start, he found it to have such energy, its own peculiar vibe, quite unlike any place he'd visited before. Like Venice sometimes didn't appear to be part of Italy and looked towards the Orient from which it derived its wealth, Pete wondered if San Francisco perhaps somehow contrived to defy definition as an American city as it seemed to look across the mighty Pacific for so many of its influences and ideas.

After such a long hike around the city, it was very welcome to reach Kurt's work and sit down to eat with his new friends in the very pleasing-looking converted street-car restaurant before setting off to hitch back to the East Bay.

Pete made two more trips to the city. The next time was when he arranged to meet both Gene and Kurt by the museum and they took him for a stroll around Chinatown, where they ate fresh, steaming-hot spring rolls.

After that, they went to browse among the shelves of the famous City Lights Bookshop. There, Pete picked up a copy of *Three Lives* by Gertrude Stein, some Beat poetry unavailable at home and a slim volume of Emily Dickinson's poetry for Mel. Then it was on to sift through the latest albums at Tower Records.

'Oh no, postcards! I keep forgetting to buy some. I've not sent any yet except to my granddad when I arrived,' Pete said, as they were leaving the record emporium, suddenly remembering again he told Albert he'd write every week to let him know he was safe.

'Didn't you call them when you got here?' Kurt asked, in a surprised tone.

'No, I didn't,' Pete replied slowly as it dawned on him how different expectations in America were.

The idea of Mémé, or even him, calling Albert to say that they had arrived safely in France seemed inconceivable. Germaine, Françoise or any of his cousins would have got in touch soon enough if he or Zénaïde hadn't disembarked from the ferry, or were not to be found amongst the crowds struggling with their baggage down the platform at the Gare du nord or Cagnes-sur-mer.

'Say, now, you can get some over there in that drugstore,' Gene said.

The three of them crossed over to the other side of the road and entered the store, where Pete soon found a rack of postcards. He chose carefully. Albert's was a general view of the city from the East Bay with a lot of shipping visible, for Connie he found one of a view from the Fairmount Hotel, and for Mel and Baz a dreadfully corny 'groovy' flower-power design. Darren's was pre-ordered: the Golden Gate.

'They're not bad,' Kurt said. 'Oh, I see you got one of Alcatraz too.'

'Yeah, I had to buy it,' Pete replied. 'You see, it's for my main mucker, my best friend, that is, Nicknick. She always is saying she wished her husband Ernie was locked up there. You know, far away and surrounded by water. If you met Ernie, you'd know why!'

And over a pitcher of weak beer in a little nearby gay bar, Pete regaled the two of them with tales of Ernie and his feral brothers.

Later, back in Berkeley, he found Susan and Jim seated on the settee in the front yard in the twilight. He'd not seen them for a few days – they'd kept missing one another – and he was eager to find out more about the trip.

'Hey, Pete, man! At last! You're sure difficult to track down. Having fun, I guess. How you doing anyway? Still interested in coming on this trip?' Susan asked.

'Sure am,' Pete replied, realising how easy, after a few days' residence, it was to be seduced by the vernacular.

'Well, we plan to leave Saturday or Sunday. Is that good for you?'

'Sure is.'

During the next few days, Pete continued his exploration of Berkeley. Jim lent him his bike; he was able to cover more ground that way. It was like he'd been kick-started, and all the experiences he was having, particularly Chauncey Hare's exhibition, made him totally determined to come up with ideas. He reminded himself how Mémé fought with Albert to let him take up photography, and now she was gone, he owed that to her.

As he moved about, he began to envisage having a proper studio, perhaps up in Manchester or maybe somewhere in London, yes, in the East End, near to where *De Mooie Marieke* was moored. Or perhaps, yes, perhaps in California – was that too inconceivable? He was so taken with the place: the life, the vibrancy and its countless sources of inspiration. But then he remembered Albert. He couldn't be that far away from the old man, not at his age, and with that thought, a sense of reality curbed his reveries as the logistics of it all began to figure in the equation.

On one of his jaunts cycling around, he found himself in Oakland and realised that both the cities, Berkeley and Oakland to the south of it, were actually joined together. However, despite that union, he noticed that where the city boundaries lay was all too apparent. Not because of any noticeable signage, but because it was where the mighty grid system came to demonstrate another more shameful aspect of American life: where it highlighted the great inequality in this land of the free. For like the graded colours of the rose garden, the nearer he got to the core of Oakland, the darker the people became and the state of houses, the infrastructure totally changed; everything seemed poorer, run-down.

This was a big shock for Pete, as he was in California, not the Deep South, from where, during his teenage years, TV reports by journalists like Charles Wheeler recorded the progress of the Civil Rights movement and had given him the idea that segregation was a thing of the past. Having got flak as a child for his Gallic connections, as well as his own mysterious origins, he felt sadness, even anger. In this land, that was so proud of and so vocal about its fight against tyranny, about its revolution and its democracy and which constantly criticised and judged the conditions and situations in other less happy countries in the world, double standards were still distressingly evident. Yet the majority of its people seemed to take it for granted, even many of the enlightened.

But he was uplifted by a further visit to San Francisco, uplifted to see a group of gay men had proudly set up home together and felt that there was nothing to hide as they strove for equality. Invited for dinner at Gene and Kurt's, as he turned into the street where the commune was located and started to walk along the pavement, he suddenly became excited about a sense of something to come, an idea that the world was becoming a different place, from where hatred and discrimination would be banished, and people would eventually live side by side in harmony and not in judgement.

As he drew closer, he could see their house, constructed of wood, was going to be in a traditional San Franciscan turn-of-the-century style. Once up the steps and inside, he found its rooms exquisite. Light, airy and painted in white, lengths of cloth of either muslin or organdie were to be found hung from the ceilings, appropriately positioned, contriving to soften, to refract the light. At the back of the house, there was a large kitchen with a large table and several bulletin boards on which various rotas were pinned. From it, a door led out to a yard, which sloped upwards, with a small garden, in which both flowers and vegetables were cultivated and where two outbuildings had been converted into living accommodation, providing two extra bedrooms, one of which was Gene and Kurt's.

As the yard was a storey or so higher than the road level, from it the view seen of the city and across the bay was simply stunning. It was a long way from the squat in Powis Square and seemed a whole lot more together. It was a great place to hang out. All the communards made him feel at home. They quizzed him about life in England and Europe. Pete was really impressed by their confidence, their self-assuredness about their sexuality, their sense of purpose. As they sat down to dinner, Dennis, whose turn it was to cook that day, explained to Pete about their house rules and how chores were shared.

It was not only the chores that were shared, as acceptance of free love was a prerequisite of gaining membership of the commune. Although conventional paring-off was tolerated, the collective interests of the group were paramount, and sex was considered to be like art: an expression, a happening, a positive energy, something good that should be shared.

The solidarity that Pete felt from sitting down to eat with nine other gay men as they rapped and put the world to rights was stupendous. He found a togetherness that was lacking at Brad's and no comparison to the company of Angel Dust, with whom Pete rarely exchanged more than a few sentences, and then only during the former's well-worn route between bedroom and bathroom.

'Hey, I know, let's take Pete in the truck on a special tour of the city, take in the sunset there by the park, yeah, Pete, how's about it?' Gene said, once they finished eating.

Thus Pete, Gene, Kurt and the others found themselves piling into an old pick-up truck driven by Dennis. They set off down the hill. Sadly, the sun beat them to it this time, as it had finished setting as they reached the park. Pete wasn't too remorseful, as it was an ace way of touring the city. Lying back in the truck and staring up at illuminated buildings and skyscrapers with streetlights and neons casting ambient shadows about him, he was quickly lulled into a soporific state by a strong combustible substance. This fairground ride of life eventually finished off at a Nickel Odeon, where they, totally stoned by now, watched old cartoons, laughing uncontrollably until their sides ached and tears ran down their faces.

'Hey, Pete, wake up, we've arrived.'

Jim's smoky, resonant voice jolted Pete's slumber, causing a sudden involuntary movement.

'Well, it seems like you completely crashed out, man. Sure wish I could do that on a long trip,' Jim added.

Pete opened his eyes and blinked. He started to rub them as they were heavy with sleep dust.

'What you mean, like, I missed like the whole journey?' he asked, while struggling to sit up.

'Yeah, man, you sure did,' said Mickey, a friend of Jim and Susan's from the Midwest who, with his girlfriend Melinda, had come along on the trip.

'That's a shame. I was looking forward to seeing the scenery,' said Pete.

'You're too much. It's not like you missed it, Pete, it was dark,' said Susan, laughing.

'Yes, but I like to see where I'm going.'

'Pete, you couldn't have. As I said, it was dark?' retorted Susan.

She had a look of great bemusement on her face and then broke out into raucous laughter so infective that it caused everybody to laugh.

Pete looked out of the window of the battered old chrome camper. They were parked by a beach and he saw for the first time what had to be the blue Pacific before him; its large breakers were cascading over a sweep of golden sand which seemed as if it were caught in the giant pincers of some large, craggy rocks. The whole place had a very Mediterranean feel to it; the temperature definitely felt several degrees warmer. But as he could now tell it was evidently early; the heat was soft, suggestive to him, urging him out of his slumber, calling him to get out into the sun.

'So are we in LA?' Pete asked, as he put his trainers back on.

His fellow travellers broke out into laughter again.

'Way past it, man,' said Susan. 'We're at Laguna Beach. Who's coming for a swim? I can't wait no more.'

And with that, she leapt out of the driver's door of the campervan and, landing on the sand, started to run across the beach towards the inviting waves. Discarding her clothes near the water's edge, they watched, cheering her, as her bikini-clad, lithe form dived into the surf.

The others now followed suit.

One by one in order of their alertness, they made their way in a more restrained manner down to the water's edge. Still sleepy but determined to take the plunge, Pete was the last to immerse his body into the turbulent ocean. He'd never encountered such strong waves before and found the water a little chilly.

It was a Saturday morning.

It was a spontaneous decision they should leave the night before. Pete, thinking they were to leave the next day, didn't find out until, turning the corner into Brad's street, he saw a number of freaks congregated outside the house and a couple of bright orange rucksacks leaning up against its exterior wall.

'Yeah, Pete, Mickey and Melinda just got here,' Susan called out. 'Hey presto, the last piece of the puzzle is in place. You know, man, we're thinking of like leaving now, well, in an hour or so. That way, we'll get there in the morning and we'll have more time. Jim, Mickey and I will share the driving.'

Despite not really knowing where *there* actually was, Pete was, nevertheless, happy to be started on the road and, after a brief discussion, excitedly ran up the steps to Brad's apartment to collect what he was going to take with him on the trip. As he started to pack some stuff into the Pan Am bag Baz had lent him, Angel Dust made a predicable foray towards the bathroom. However, he suddenly stopped in his tracks as if he'd seen a vision.

'Wow, that's so weird,' he said, intently staring at the bag through his thick glasses, while scratching his head.

Pete looked up at him just as Brad came out of his bedroom.

'What's so weird?' Brad asked.

'Well, you know that other English guy who visited had a—'

But Brad cut in, with what Pete thought was an unnecessary tone of irritation.

'For fuck's sake, he was German from the university I was at over there. Surely you must have realised that.'

And then, looking towards Pete, he grinned as a confused Angel Dust carried on to the bathroom.

'Hey, you remember those German friends I told you about? The ones I travelled around Europe with,' he said. 'Yeah, well, you know, they visited back in January. Hey, but I thought you were leaving tomorrow. I didn't realise you were going tonight.'

'Nor did I,' Pete replied, while trying to recollect what Brad had said about his German friends.

In fact, in the end they didn't leave until near enough midnight, and it turned out that before heading off to Vegas and Death Valley, they were to visit friends of Mickey in Laguna Beach. And the reason why Susan wanted to get there in the morning was because on every Saturday morning, Mickey's pals and other community-minded folk got together for recycling and she wanted to see how they organised it as she hoped to set up a local scheme.

So now it was morning, and after their ritual immersion in the ocean, followed by coffee and doughnuts in a nearby café, they made their way over to Mickey's pals and walked right into an army of freaks, all busy sorting out bottles and plastic, cans and paper, old clothes and materials – indeed, anything remotely recyclable.

'Come on, join us,' a hearty earth mother type called out, and Susan, followed by the others, soon got into it with gusto.

Pete had heard about the recycling movement and was greatly impressed by this show of community spirit. *Concern for the environment is long overdue and people back home could certainly learn from it*, he thought.

These thoughts were interrupted by Susan.

'You know, it's real sad,' she said to no one in particular, as she held up a plastic carrier bag. 'In fact, tragic to think that this plastic bag represents five thousand years of machine history, and like then, they are often only used once and take at least five hundred years to decompose.'

Although most laughed at the sheer ridiculousness of this fact, the utter foolishness of such a circumstance, the profundity of her words didn't go unconsidered.

They stayed three days with Mickey's friends, mainly lolling around the beach, before they took leave of their hosts, setting off on the road to join the San Bernardino Highway, which took them high up over the Sierra Mountains.

This spectacular route seemed like it had been devoured out of the mountainside. It led them higher and higher until the mountain pass was reached. The chugging camper seemed out of place there, surrounded as it was by lanes of cars storming by in perfect symmetry, each containing the only visible human presence in this vast landscape. And every car that passed them had clothes rails strung across over the backseats, with men's light summer suits and tuxedos and women's evening finery hanging from them, all pressed or permapressed, and so evidently waiting to hit the casinos, clubs and circuses, for Vegas was purportedly hot, classy and to be enjoyed.

Down the mountain the old camper swept, out onto the purple, hazy, never-ending desert. This was no golden sandy desert like the Sahara but a heavy, foreboding place, stony with intermittent scrub and cacti. As they pressed on, Pete's eyes focused on the road ahead, presuming that, by the time the horizon would be reached, the landscape would have changed and there would be some different features in front of them. But it proved not so, for when they reached where he thought the horizon had once been, both to the left and to the right as well as to the front everything just looked exactly the same. On and on, the intimidating desert stretched out before them. It was if the car was not moving and seemed to Pete that the desert's main purpose left on the planet was to defy mankind.

Come on, put them up, it seemed to say, *but beware, I, the earth, will win in the end.*

Their first sight of Vegas was when the shadows were lengthening and they could just make out the neon-illuminated oasis spread out before them. As the camper protested, negotiating its way into the city, they could see mankind, with the aid of sprinklers and air-conditioning, had succeeded to tame this tiny corner of desert. Pete wondered if, perhaps, it might be a prototype for a city on the moon. Casinos and theatres abounded, and although he knew that the selling of marriages and divorces was a great commodity there, he found the marriage parlours totally weird. They had more of an appearance of poodle parlours, he felt: all pink and fluffy, fluorescent and sterile, cluttering up the pavements as they did as if they were the purveyors of the most essential of necessities. The throwaway society was evidently thriving in Vegas.

They checked into a motel. Two-tiered, with an outside balcony spanning the length and width of the building overlooking a quadrangle, with a small pool right bang in its centre, it was like a set from a 1940s black and white gangster movie. It was still hot as they climbed the stairs to their room. Quickly stripping and changing into their swimming costumes, they went down again to immerse themselves in the tepid water of the pool, before returning to shower and rest.

It was late when they hit the sultry pavements, pavements impregnated with bottle tops and chewing gum, and as they went, they gazed inside the casinos, creasing up with laughter at the rows and rows of near-synchronised arms as they inserted coins in the slots of one-armed bandits. The communion here was definitely with machine. Then, their stomachs started to call; they needed filling.

After an hour or so in a small, unpretentious diner, Jim suggested they go out again to explore. Mickey and Melinda were up for it, but Susan declined.

She wanted another beer and Pete said he'd join her.

'We'll see you back at the motel,' she said.

As Susan and Pete watched them all link arms and walk away in the direction of the Golden Nugget, a brassy bombshell of a waitress came over and asked if there was anything else they wanted.

'Two beers, please.'

'I'll have to see your ID now,' she said, fiercely.

'But we've already had beers,' Susan retorted.

'Yes, but I've only just come on.'

Pete took out his passport and handed it to her.

'What's this? You not got a drivers' licence?'

'I'm British, this is my ID,' Pete said, opening his passport on the right page, so she could check he was over twenty-one.

'Oh, okay, so you're British. Hum! Well, ain't you cute, honey?'

While she was getting the beer, Susan leant over to Pete and whispered, 'She kinda sums up Vegas for me, so plastic.'

The waitress came back with the beer. After she left, they remained silent for a while and then both started to speak as the same time.

'No, after you, Susan.'

'Well, I guess that seeing that we are in Vegas I just want to put my cards on the table. The thing is, I really like you. You know, like, really like you.'

'And I really like you, Susan,' Pete slowly replied, instinctively knowing where this was going.

'Why do I feel there is a but coming on?'

'Well, the thing is, Susan, I'm gay.'

'Cool, just my luck. Why is it that all the best guys are gay these days?'

Pete didn't answer.

He felt all choked up. He was in this weird city, in the middle of a desert, far away from home, and suddenly felt overwhelmed. Ever since arriving in California, he'd suppressed his feelings about Brad. But now, he felt completely gutted by it. He'd travelled a long way to be with him. But he wasn't and it had all gone desperately wrong and his dreams, his mapping out of a future over the last year, were shattered, blown to smithereens, and everything was feeling temporary. Homesick, he yearned to be back with Albert, beside the Opal Causeway. At the thought of his grandfather, and that beloved sea, he started to silently cry.

'Pete?'

'Oh, it's nothing,' he said, taking a handkerchief from his pocket to dry his eyes.

'What's wrong, Pete? I'm a good listener, you know.'

'Well…'

Pete started hesitantly and then he suddenly found himself spewing it all out as he told Susan about how he met Brad, about their *undying love*, how they planned for him to visit and how Brad had changed and he didn't really understand why.

Susan listened, she didn't interrupt him, and after he'd finished, he felt like a large burden had been lifted. He felt cleansed.

'I have to say,' Susan said afterwards, 'I've not talked with Brad much. We only moved into the apartment a few months ago. He seemed to have company for the first week or two. Quite a few parties went on, or that's what it seemed like.'

'I expect that was the Germans he was at university with,' said Pete.

'Germans, maybe? I dunno, maybe they were, I didn't get to hear them speak,' she said, as she looked at her watch. 'Hey, man, it's getting late. I guess it's time to hit the sack if we want to get going early tomorrow.'

So after paying the cheque, they made their way back to the motel.

The next morning, at an early hour, the battered chrome camper, with Susan at the wheel, could be seen chugging out of Las Vegas, this time northwards on the route towards Reno through the Amargosa Valley.

They'd fortified themselves with pancakes at a Howard Johnson's near to the motel before they left, as they had a long journey in front of them. The route, again, was straight, the scenery predictably similar. This was Nevada, sparse and formidable.

When they reached Beatty, they changed direction and turned onto the road which led back into California. The only trace of human habitation they came across was Scotty's Castle, where they stopped, toured the interior and spent some time contemplating the logic of living in such isolation. Pete wondered whether it wouldn't have been one of the loneliest places on earth to live, for there was nothing to sustain humanity nearby, seemingly for hundreds of miles. Scotty's Castle, a large mansion designed in a Moorish style, an oasis of architectural folly in the desert, was built by a likeable trickster, whose grandiose plans the desert had seen off. And now, it just seemed as if it were a memorial to a long-ago-unachieved dream. However, this was not their final destination. No, nothing as mundane or temporary as that, for their goal was to experience one of nature's extraordinarily exquisite creations.

Only Jim had been there before and knew what to expect. But the others, getting his vibe about the place, realised that it had to be special. Because if that first ride through the desert to Vegas gave them such awesome impressions of the natural world, of its absolute longevity and staying power, and its constant thirst for movement and change, and consequently, its ability to continually demonstrate how totally insignificant human life was to it, those first few miles driving through Death Valley were not only so completely humbling, because of the harshness, the wildness of the very environment, but they found, they agreed afterwards on their way back, there was something about the unremitting brightness, *that great light*, that contrived to evoke feelings in them intrinsically spiritual. They were dazed by the valley's tremendous beauty, by its colours, by its shades and textures.

When they arrived at Ubehebe Crater, their special destination, they gasped in unison, for it was immense. Over a half mile in diameter and five hundred feet deep, its most extraordinary feature was the many different coloured bands of rock on the crater walls. It seemed strangely like a primeval amphitheatre.

'It was created over six thousand years ago by a powerful volcanic explosion,' Jim told them.

And then, Susan, who'd studied geology in college, took over from him and recounted how it was actually the largest in a series of craters to be found in the area, all formed when molten lava came in contact with groundwater, causing a series of powerful steam explosions.

'You see those mountains over there?' she continued, gesticulating towards the horizon. 'Well, they're constantly eroding, like they're sending rubble out into the valley and then rainfall sends torrents of water carving paths through the rocks, subtly but methodically, constantly altering both form and tones. You know, this is one of the places I've wanted to visit for so long. Wow, it's so trippy, now I'm here.'

She went on to explain that the whole area had once been covered by seas and that you could find fossils of all sorts of marine animals.

'And the reason why salt is so visible is because, during the Ice Ages, the valley was periodically filled by large lakes and their waves carved terraces on the bordering rocks, and as they evaporated, alternating layers of deposits of mud and salt were left.'

The five of them sat in a row by Ubehebe's rim in awesome silence until it was too hot to remain there. Mickey and Melinda sought the shade of the camper, Jim and Susan scoured the ground for fossils, while Pete, after gazing down, mesmerised by the abyss, strolled off.

He felt the need to be alone. Such an overwhelming place, with so much sky, made him feel insignificant. A heat haze danced all around him, everything sizzled and he felt like he was being forced down through to the rock by the sun, now right overhead. Despite the incredible brightness of the light, he took a few shots, although he wasn't confident that they'd be good.

Then, a gravelly sound caught his attention and he looked down and noticed a small lizard scuttling by his feet. His presence was of no concern to it; he smiled at that realisation before making his way back to the others.

It was too hot to remain outside any longer, so seeking the shade of the camper, this time with Mickey at the wheel, they sped off down the only road, as a welcome breeze was whipped up by their speed. Their humbling experience had fired all of them up about the plight of the planet on which they lived and a lively conversation about the environment ensued.

'You know,' Susan said, 'the earth could get on very well without human beings, but humans could never get along without the earth. I just can't believe what people are allowed to do to this beautiful planet. It makes me sick.'

'Come on, guys, don't bring me down,' said Mickey.

Pete noticed how Mickey managed to cushion himself from the reality of the world's problems.

'But Mickey, what about all the animals?' Melinda pleaded. 'Like the whales and the dolphins, you have to do something for them.'

'Yeah, man, have to make a stand,' Jim said.

'Yeah, exactly like the demo coming up soon about the park,' Susan interjected.

'The park? What's that about then?' Pete asked.

'People's Park – in two weeks' time, a demo is being held to commemorate the second anniversary of when the pigs shot dead an innocent bystander there.'

'What shot dead? How come?'

'Well, People's Park was a vacant lot of land owned by the university,' Susan started to explain. 'Quite a large plot, one whole block long and wide and it hadn't been used for years, except as a temporary parking lot. Then suddenly, there were rumours going about that the regents of the university planned to give the go-ahead to sell it to some dubious real-estate developer. So, one day some freaks got together, decided to reclaim it for the people. They went up in there and started to turn it into gardens. It was far out; all the sorts of flowers and vegetables were cultivated there. But one night, the pigs went in, trampled them down, completely trashed it. All hell broke loose the next day, so many people demonstrated; it was far out.'

She made a clenched fist before carrying on.

'It was all peaceful until a pig, on the roof of a building, shot a bystander dead. This demo coming up will be on the second anniversary. All this arguing about stolen land makes me so sick, coz you all know whose land it really is, who it really belongs to?'

'Who?' Melinda and Pete asked, at the same time.

'The Costanoan Indians, they were the first people to live in the area around Berkeley, and you know what? They had no concept of land ownership. They believed the land was under the care and guardianship of the people who lived on it, used it. But once the missionaries came, they started to take away the land from them, although no agreements were made or papers signed. They ripped it off in the name of God. And then the Mexican government—'

'Oh, was California part of Mexico? I didn't realise,' Pete asked.

'Not only California, the entire south-west. That's why there're so many Spanish names. Anyhow, the Mexican government took the land away from the church. Of course, they had guns, an army, and weapons are stronger than God's word. They, consequently, drew up some papers which claimed they owned the land. Naturally, no Indian ever signed those, but these papers didn't fool the good ol' US of A, who had an even stronger army. They thrashed the Mexicans in a war, seized the land, wrote new papers of their own and made the Mexicans sign those. Then they went and sold the land to white settlers, made a tidy profit.'

'But what about the Indians?' Pete asked.

'Well, there were some who were still around and who still laid claim to the land, but most were killed. And gradually, those pieces of paper that said whose land it was were bought by rich white men. Maybe some were interested in taking care of the land, but most made money from it. Finally, the regents of the university bought the land, and there you have it. And do you know that the state auditors' office is at this very moment investigating charges that two wealthy regents exploited university tax-exempt status to cut their own tax load? You have to make a stand. It's more than about the park. I'm gonna be at that demo, man, for sure.'

'But, Susan, do you think protests work nowadays?' said Melinda. 'They disregard so much protest now, cover it up.'

'What else can you do? It takes years to organise politically, and all the while, youngsters are being given napalm and guns and shipped out to other parts of the planet, to where there are people that might have wanted some of our garbage, might have wanted some bit for themselves but they sure don't want it now. It is quite clear that this war, and gluttony, greed, lack of compassion, have caused America to become the most despised nation on the earth. And you know what?'

It was a rhetorical question and Susan carried straight on. There was an admirable passion in her voice.

'It could be the hope of all. America has it in its power to be that. We have the power and technological know-how to stem the environmental damage; we have the money to eradicate famine and disease. But it's like, people are so inward and the right are so anti-education now. It's like knowledge scares them. Watch them; they will go for the education system.'

'How?' asked Mickey.

'Cut-backs and, of course, that affects research. What is taught today is yesterday's research, that's how. And now, you got these hicks going around saying that uni offers a four-year course in sex, drugs and treason. It's outrageous, especially as their concept of what is morally right is so evidently built on such blatant excess.'

There was now a lull in the conversation as everybody reflected on what Susan had just said.

The camper continued to wend its way down the only road out of the valley, and after a night camping in a secluded spot by the side of the road, they eventually joined the freeway back to the Bay Area and returned home to Berkeley after dropping off Mickey and Melinda at the airport on the way to get their flight home. *Back to their boring life in that boring redneck town*, Susan said after they'd waved them off.

However, the few days they'd been away, Pete felt, had created a sense of solidarity in the group, and he'd really begun to feel close to all of them, especially to Susan.

'Pete, we're fixing to go. Say, you ready?'

Jim's voice resonated up the outside stairway to Brad's apartment. It was a beautiful summer's day, but the atmosphere inside was chilly. A couple of weeks had passed since the trip, and Pete was off to the demo. Walking through to the kitchen door, he felt Brad's eyes bearing down on his back as he called down to Jim.

'Almost, I just got back. I'll be down in a sec. Just talking with Brad.'

The previous night, Susan invited both he and Brad to supper. Her moon breakfast, she christened it, as all the colours of the food were predominately green: spinach lasagne, green peppers, lima beans and courgettes with a cheese sauce made from Sage Derby and a green salad. Pistachio ice cream and hash brownies made from the recipe in her Alice B Toklas cookbook and topped with green icing were for afters.

Since Pete returned, he and Brad seemed cool and, for a number of evenings, rapped well into the small hours. Pete began to feel that he was rediscovering things about Brad. More at ease in each other's company, they reminisced about incidents that had occurred the previous summer, like about Tiny, the tyre and his infatuation with Mel.

But they'd not talked about *them* and Pete didn't feel like rocking the boat by bringing up the subject, particularly as

194

he got the vibe Brad was reticent to delve. Besides, he *was* less hung up about it; the trip had distanced him from it, permitted him to examine his own motives, and he began to wonder whether, in fact, his attraction to Brad was initially influenced by the fact Brad came from a place which he'd always wanted to visit. And because he was now in California, as Brad put so succinctly in his letter, there were simply hundreds of guys who seemed just as interesting as Brad. Of course he knew Nicknick would've told him *to have it out with the fucker*. But as his confusion was now in a process of metamorphosis, he'd no wish to broach the subject, open up the can while they were getting to know each other afresh.

After Susan's dinner, he and Brad, both understandably high, ended up going out to the White Horse pub. Brad's exams were all over bar one and he claimed some light relief. There, they ran into Will.

With hindsight Pete wondered whether Brad knew he'd be there, but in any case, Brad left early while Pete stayed on chatting, drinking and dancing with Will and some other guys. Will and he'd not talked much before, and one thing led to another, and Pete found himself going back to Will's pad, and after being persuaded by Will that he'd no involvement with Brad, that they were just good friends, *Brad's got some guy in someplace in Europe that he's so secretive about,* he'd said, which momentarily puzzled Pete, they slept together.

When he arrived back to Brad's apartment that morning, he found Brad pacing the living room. Seeing the look on his face made Pete freeze inside.

'So where you been?'

'Will's, I crashed there.'

'I bet you did,' Brad said in a queeny sort of way.

But Pete detected more than an element of vehemence in his tone and there was a silence as Pete struggled to find a suitable answer. He was about to apologise, for what he wasn't quite sure, when Jim called out again, followed by Susan.

'Say, Pete, you still coming?' she asked as she climbed the outside stairs. 'We're fixing to go, like, now.'

'You're going to the demo?' Brad asked.

'Yeah, I thought I told you yesterday.'

Brad sighed.

Susan put her head around the kitchen door.

'Almost ready,' Pete told her, as he scavenged in his pockets. 'Oh, not got that much bread, though, only a few pennies.'

'No worries, you won't need any.'

'And I'm wearing the same clothes as last night,' he said, although in all truth he was enjoying sudden bursts of Will's lingering odour and the tingling it still caused his body.

'They're perfect, you look great, ready then?'

'Yes, I guess,' Pete said, looking at Brad. Brad smiled lamely and Pete, imagining that he'd trashed the progress they'd made, felt mortified. When he got back from the demo, they'd talk, get to the bottom of it. Maybe he should find somewhere else to crash for the rest of his time in California.

'See you later,' he said, as he followed Susan down the outside stairway.

'Say, what's up with Brad? I thought you guys were getting on better,' Susan said, once they were on the pavement.

'I'm not quite sure. I did something that upset him, I think, something really dumb. I slept with his friend Will last night.'

'You didn't!'

'Well, Will said there's nothing going on with him, but the thing is, Susan, I might need somewhere else to crash.'

'That's cool.'

They joined Jim on the pavement and the three of them, linking arms, started up the street.

A crowd of people was moving the same direction. Jim conjured up some reefer and, with one hit, everything became very dreamlike to Pete and he felt more as if he were going to a festival rather than a demo. Once they'd crossed the campus, their group merged with others coming from different directions. It became a throng and once out through the main gates Pete felt as if he were being propelled along by a superhuman surge. Even more protesters joined in: people walking forward and upright, resolute and with purpose, thousands of them. The sense of solidarity was electrifying.

Although close to the park, they were unable to see it as the crowd had spilt out onto all four roads that formed its perimeters. It was quite unlike any march Pete had taken part in before. But it also seemed to him that, in an obtuse way, it was like Berkeley on a normal day, as all the same old serious politicos were evident, rubbing shoulders with familiar hassling street folk; indeed, he recognised quite a few characters from Telegraph Avenue, he'd seen playing music or rapping, chanting and clowning. There were even preachers to be seen, making waves through the crowd. Numerous placards were held aloft as several different segments of society came together there while others were hanging out of the windows of nearby buildings and cheering the crowd on. Did they all have a mutual reason or separate agendas, he wondered?

Looking up, Susan was sure that she'd spotted some armed fuzz up on one of the roofs.

'Hey, Susan, you know what? I clean forgot my camera!'

'Probably for the best.'

'This is more than about the park, surely?' Pete said.

'You bet,' said Jim.

'It's about life, the state of this earth, and freeing ourselves from all that is bad, corrupt and polluting. But, pre-eminently, it is a plea for peace, a plea to those in power to find a way to settle differences without course to violence and, most importantly, it is a protest against the futile war which is continually and increasingly dividing our nation at a terrifying cost; yes, ultimately, it is about the horrors of 'Nam and the daily tragic loss,' Susan said, passionately.

The great swaying mass of people was now roaring. Pete linked arms with Susan and Jim as, increasingly wedged in, he was losing his footing. He had no idea what was happening over that circular horizon of heads but quite suddenly on the street to north side of the lot, the crowd began to part. A tremendous cheer went up, car horns hooted, whistles were blown; then there came a lone, distant shout: 'It's the Panthers. Fucking far out, the Black Panthers.'

This news was relayed through the crowd and repeated over again, gradually increasing in volume as it echoed down to where he, Jim and Susan were standing. And with it, a great sense of camaraderie came seeping through the throng of people as the cheering got even louder. As Pete started to hear the sound of the Panthers' vehicles, Susan nudged him, finger pointing, and he saw through the parting crowd some Volkswagen Beetles coming into view.

The crowd's cheers increased even more, but then, as

the VWs drew closer to them and the Panthers passed by, the predominately white crowd went silent. Was it through reverence or fear, Pete wondered? The Panthers drove past in strict formation, black-bereted, faces immobile, looking straight ahead, eyes hidden behind dark shades. They were the business; they gave nothing away and looked like they'd take no shit from nobody. In an exquisite piece of choreography, one vehicle led followed by the others two abreast in strict formation, in perfect timing. The crowd parted like the Red Sea for them, but once they passed, it quickly conjoined.

It was as if the exit of the Panthers was a catalyst for things to get livelier, for whatever their purpose was in driving through like that, it certainly did rattle the cops, who weren't that evident up until then. It also fired up the crowd, who, remembering the reason why they were there, started pushing towards the park. The police evidently were trying to push them back, which caused more violent pushing. Some started panicking.

Susan said that the only police evident up until then were the local Berkeley ones, and that they, in the scale of things, were not considered the worst, but a shout then went up, repeated down the lines.

'The Blue Meanies!'

'Blue Meanies? What?' Pete asked.

'The Oakland police – they mean business,' Jim told him.

Now the crowd, in front of them, surged backwards while those behind still pressed forward, causing the three of them to be suddenly crushed together. Then a noise like gunfire could be heard and smoke was seen rising above the human swell.

'Crikey,' Pete exclaimed, as he lost his footing and started to fall back against someone behind him. It was beginning to be scary. He hadn't been prepared for this.

'Yeah, man, this is getting serious,' Susan said.

Something suddenly happened and it really kicked off. All around them was havoc, fear and confusion as people were fleeing past them with terror in their eyes, shoving, yelling out in extreme agitation. Again, the sound of gunfire was heard, quickly followed by more shrouds of smoke. What kind of gunfire, Pete didn't know. Live bullets or just dummies, or just the sound of tear-gas canisters being fired into the crowd? Smoke enveloped them, obscuring the blue sky above. A strange stench filled their nostrils as the pungent cloud floated over and about, overtaking them. In this confusing mêlée as they were pushed backwards, Susan and Pete got separated from Jim and had to hold on to each other for safety.

The strangest thing was, Pete thought as they were retreating, they'd not even seen any cops or knew from which direction they were coming. The toxic smoke made it difficult for them to interpret the hazy images about them, but then a girl bumped into them, blood pouring down her face. She was followed by a stream of walking wounded, all bleeding, bruised and limping.

Another cloud of pernicious smoke now descended and, completely unable to see in this mass of fleeing, frightened people, Pete lost hold of Susan and began to choke. Gasping for breath, his eyes started smarting and stung intensely as he tried to find his direction.

'Susan, I can't see. Where are you?'

'Me neither. I'm here,' Susan replied as their hands reached out to one another. 'It's frigging tear gas, man. Those fucking bastards, they just fired some canisters into the crowd again. We got to get out of here. Come, take hold of me.'

Still choking, Pete reached out for her, put his arm around her shoulders, and together they started to blindly run away. A passer-by, noticing how they were affected by the tear gas, handed them a rag with vinegar on it.

'Hey, man, douse this on your face, take care of the eyes, though. It'll sting real bad, but it's a good antidote,' he said.

It did sting, excruciatingly so, particularly as Pete's face was sunburnt. But things gradually became clearer for them both, although the nauseous stench remained.

As they gradually got further away from the action, the crowd thinned out, it was calmer and the effects of tear gas was wearing off. Now, with vision restored, they looked around and realised that they were further away from the core of the demo than they realised. Disparaged by the developments, they made a decision to split and make their way back home through the campus. Nothing was going to be achieved now by staying, Susan told him, there was no point staying around to be a useless statistic.

Pete stayed mute, internalised by an experience which he found to be in a different league to any protest he'd been on before. He was shocked by the casualties. And all because some people had made a beautiful park out of a wasteland and the authorities didn't dig it.

Reaching the campus gate, they found it eerily quiet. There was no traffic noise whatsoever, yet bizarrely enough amid all the madness they came across an open café. Inside people were eating hamburgers and French fries, drinking Coke and root beer, as if nothing of any significance was happening outside at all.

'Are you hungry?' Susan asked him.

'Famished, I've not eaten since last night, but I've got no bread, well, only sixty-nine cents. I was going to cash a travellers' cheque yesterday but clean forgot.'

'That's okay, go and grab that table there by the window, and I'll order cheeseburger and fries, right?'

'Yeah, please,' Pete said, making for the table.

His attention was diverted by a tap on the window. A face was pressed up to it. Uncertain of who it was, he looked away, and when he looked again, the face was gone. Then he felt a tap on his shoulder.

'Hey, wow, far out! I'm so glad I ran into you again. How you doing? Remember me? I'm about to hitch down to Big Sur, wanna come with me? It'll be fantabulous on a day like this, say you will?'

Pete looked up from the table and saw, bearing down on him, the dilated pupils of Leah, the spaced-out chick he'd met in the Rose Garden. She sat down at the table next to him, evidently quite oblivious to what was going on around her, despite the many agitated, injured people still arriving at the campus gates.

Susan returned with the food and sat down beside him. Before Pete could introduce Leah to her, she leaned over to Susan.

'You're sure the both of you don't wanna hitch down to Big Sur with me?'

'Nice thought,' Susan said, laughing. 'But I don't think so, not today.'

Whether Leah actually heard her or not was difficult to determine, for she was soon floating out of the café in joyous oblivion, her bundle tied onto the stick, slung over her right shoulder, with its bell jingling incessantly. Pete and Susan watched her wafting away. As she passed through the exit, Pete felt another tap on his shoulder.

'Say, what she want with you?'

Pete turned round and, after a double-take, saw a six-foot-tall, slightly overweight drag queen on roller skates, wearing a nurse's uniform, leaning over him. He was about to reply, but the drag queen continued, 'No, don't tell me, I know. She asked you to hitch with her to Big Sur, right?'

'Why, yes,' Pete replied, while Susan firstly looked up in disbelief before a flush of admiration came to her face.

'Well, you only have to be like the trillionth person she's asked today. Oh, is that a friend of yours waving over by the door? She now seems to be asking him.'

They looked up towards the door. Jim was evidently declining Leah's invitation, his eyebrows raised with an exaggerated earnestness. As he detached himself and walked over to join them, the drag queen, blowing a tin whistle, skated off towards the door and outside onto the pavement, parting the crowd.

'Make way, make way, emergency, emergency, coming through,' she shouted as she skated off.

'Right on, sister,' Susan called out, as they watched her disappear from view.

'So what happened to you, Jim? You're okay? Were you tear-gassed like us?' asked Pete.

'Luckily, no,' he replied. 'I just got bunched up and ended up having to take a long route to get back on campus. I imagined you might've decided to go home, but I thought I'd scout around first. You know, this demonstration is getting really heavy now. There seems to be a core hellbent on taunting the pigs, and for the Blue Meanies, you know, the more heads they bloody, the more freaks they arrest, the happier they'll be. It seems they've definitely got scores to settle.'

After they'd finished eating, Susan decided to go check on the dogs.

'I'll take them for a walk later when it's all died down,' she said as they got up to leave.

Pete and Jim followed her out, intending to accompany her, but halfway across the campus, Jim, quite out of the blue, asked Pete if he wanted to go with him to check out a new motorcycle shop that had recently opened up a few blocks away. Pete found it a strange thing to do that particular day, but since he'd been in California, he'd got used to this kind of spontaneous weirdness. So, leaving Susan, they made their way the few blocks to the shop. It was closed, but they lingered, enthusing about the big Harleys, the Choppers and BMWs which teased them from the other side of the plate-glass window. As they turned at last, intent on making for home, Pete noticed that the shop was facing what looked like a temporary parking lot.

'Oh, so was the park like that originally?' Pete asked.

'I guess so,' Jim replied. 'I wonder what plans some dodgy real-estate firm has for this.'

Pete was about to further quiz Jim, but any chance of conversation was abruptly interrupted by sudden loud bursts of gunfire coming from around the corner of a building the far side of the vacant lot. This ear-piercing assault was soon followed up by a view of a stream of people fleeing around the building away from the direction of the noise. Terrified, they began to sprint straight across the lot. One of them gesticulated at Jim and Pete as he went by them and no sooner than the last of the fugitives were around the next corner, a group of police appeared in pursuit, firing both guns and tear gas as they went. It was evident the police were heading straight towards Jim and him.

'Holy shit, man, we gotta get out of here,' Jim shouted.

They looked at each other for an instant, not knowing which way to take.

'Follow me, run, quick,' Jim said.

They sped down to the bottom of the road, their chests tight to bursting, adrenaline seeping through their bodies, inadvertently getting caught up in the fleeing crowd. And by that crowd, they were propelled right at the next corner and left down along the block. Halfway down the street, needing to draw breath and thinking that they were out of danger, they stopped. But they quickly became immersed in the noise of wailing, deafening sirens, as, as if from nowhere, police cars, blue lights flashing, converged on them from every direction.

They were surrounded.

'Hey, get the one in the blue shirt, that one with the slit eyes, that's the motherfucker.'

Pete wondered to whom they referring when the next thing he knew two cops grabbed him and twisted his arms up behind his back.

'We got you now, boy,' one of them growled.

His colleague proceeded to tie some plastic flex tightly around Pete's wrists. It dug into his flesh and, while Pete was being roughly searched by that one cop, the other proceeded to take out his billy club and, after slapping it on his hand, passed it through Pete's legs and, holding both ends, lifted him up on it so he was barely on tiptoes. The pain in his scrotum was excruciating and now, sick with fear and pain, Pete let out a scream. Everything became bleary and the sounds around him became one as he struggled to regain his composure. For a moment he imagined Jim shouting to him before Leah's face flashed across his mind.

'You should've gone to Big Sur,' a voice inside was saying to him.

Then everything seemed to go into slow motion, and he started to feel faint and passed out.

After being bundled into a windowless paddy wagon together with other arrested, Pete'd been taken to be processed. That formality now over, dazed, he sat on a wooden bench. What was happening? He'd no idea where he was; California had suddenly become a dark, dangerous place. As well as still experiencing the effects of tear gas, internally he was in turmoil, yet trying his utmost to mask any physical manifestation of being in that state.

He raised his head and looked around.

Washington, a guy whose hair reached his waist and was finished being processed, now sat down beside him. He wore granny glasses and his sole item of clothing was mauve women's panties. He'd not betrayed an inch of vulnerability during his process. Though the officers needled him, derided him something chronic, he remained stoic. *An inspiration*, Pete thought as he turned to ask where they were.

'The Berkeley Police Department,' Washington replied. 'So what trumped-up charge have they got you on?'

'Assault on a police officer with a deadly weapon,' Pete replied, hesitantly, not quite believing it. A mistake surely had been made and he'd soon be let go.

'Jeez, man, so what you do?'

'Nothing.'

'Hum, they just grabbed you. I thought as much.'

'What about you?' Pete asked.

'For,' Washington answered, with deliberation, his eyes scanning down at his near-nakedness, 'being myself, I guess. It's usually that.'

Pete had watched the hard time given to Washington when processed. Of course, dressed as he was, Washington was a dead cert for arrest, but it really kicked off when they asked his name.

'Surname first,' the officer had barked.

'Fuck,' Washington replied loudly; the room went quiet.

'Don't you go using that language with me – now tell me what your name is.'

'Fuck.'

'Enough of the funny stuff; now tell me your name.'

'Fuck,' Washington repeated, for the third time.

The officer's face grew red with anger. It looked like he was going to get decked yet Washington calmly produced his ID from a small cloth shoulder bag and handed it to the officer.

'Fuck's my given name, sir,' he emphatically stated. 'Please look at my driving licence, sir. Washington Fuck's clearly printed on it.'

A group of officers now gravitated towards what they evidently considered to be the freak of freaks, their faces distorted with a mixture of hate, disgust intermingled with traces of lust.

'So now,' the processing officer continued, unwilling to repeat Washington's legal name, 'your profession?'

'Sexual revolutionary.'

'Shit, whatever next, motherfucker?'

The cop had enough. He quickly sped through the

processing. Washington's strip-search certainly didn't take too long.

Pete's processing – the aggressive questioning, jibed comments and utter reluctance to believe his story – seemed Kafkaesque. There was scant acknowledgement of him being a foreigner; the cops acted like they didn't want to know. When it came to being strip-searched, he felt a severe stab of self-consciousness, remembering, while unzipping his jeans, he was wearing no underpants. This detail didn't go unnoticed, eliciting predictable comments, and there seemed to be more than an element of perversion in the cop's behaviour when carrying it out. His possessions were taken away from him; not that they were much, just his sixty-nine cents, gold ring and a Tissot watch which Zénaïde had bought him on the ferry for his eighteenth birthday, on her way back from visiting family in France.

'So what happens now?' Pete asked Washington, after a moment of silence.

'Oh, they string it out. Relax,' Washington replied, closing his eyes.

Relax, thought Pete, but how could he with his brain buzzing so? Too many questions were ricocheting around it. Like, *Why's this happening to me?* He'd not done anything wrong yet he was being treated like he was Charlie Manson. He looked around him. He was just one of many. Arrested for what, though? What would happen now? How long had been he been there? He'd lost all sense of time. How he wished he was away from that hot, airless, windowless room.

But it was the charge that shocked him, freaked him out. When he meekly enquired about it, he was snarlingly told he could go down for years, life even, as it was like attempted murder. But whose murder? No name was ventured. When he asked what the deadly weapon was, he was ignored. But they'd taken no knife from him; like, had he a gun? Yet when he denied it, the cops got so riled that he became fearful. More than once when alone in a corridor, taken by a cop from A to B, he thought he was for it, about to get a beating.

Didn't he have the right of a telephone call? Yet it wasn't mentioned, and in any case, he had no numbers, and try as he might, he couldn't remember Brad's. But if he had, maybe Brad would've still been pissed off with him.

After he'd arrived in the place, his eyes scouted around for Jim, but Jim wasn't there. Perhaps he wasn't arrested then, got away in the confusion. Jim would know what to do, find a solicitor or a legal aid centre or some type of organisation that could help. Do whatever was necessary to get him out because it was just all a big mistake, surely someone would realise that soon and he'd be released. For a while this thought kept his spirits up. But as the hours went by, he started to lose hope. He began to wonder what was happening back at Brad's, at Susan and Jim's. Were they all sitting around deciding what to do? Hopefully they were. But then he suddenly thought that Jim had been arrested too, but taken to another police station, and Susan would therefore think they were still looking at motorbikes. Or gone someplace else, maybe hitched into the city or even to Big Sur.

His grandfather, he hoped that Brad wouldn't phone him. He'd be mortified about the charge, and other than the fact there'd be very little that he could do, Pete didn't want him worried. Besides, he wouldn't understand. He was of the generation who believed that if the police arrested someone, there was usually a good reason. Thinking of his grandfather drew Pete's thoughts circling around those two sets of cliffs and the swirling opal between them. How he wished that he was there now, high up on the cliffs, walking in the warm moist west wind, blowing away all the nonsense.

'You're British, right?' Washington asked.

'Yes,' Pete replied.

'Well, you should get to see your consul. It's your right. And I guess they've not told you about the public defender either. Excuse me, sir, this guy is British. He needs to see his consul and the public defender,' Washington called out to a passing cop.

He was initially ignored, but despite the aggressive undertones, Washington persisted, and a desk sergeant, less aggressive than his other colleagues, came over to explain to Pete that the consul would be informed and he would see the public defender in due course.

'It's Saturday, the weekend, you know,' he said, sighing like he had the weight of the world on his shoulders. 'You won't be going to court until Monday.'

'You mean they're going to keep us here all weekend,' Pete asked Washington once the officer went away.

'You bet they are,' Washington replied, laughing.

After waiting hours, long after the last prisoner was processed, they were led in single file through to the cells for the night. No chance of privacy here: seatless toilets in full view, all open to see. Initially assigned to one on his own, Pete's sense of isolation increased, and, sitting on the bottom bunk and looking out on the windowless space surrounding him, all he saw were hard lines and cold metal. He felt like a fly caught up in a spider's web, a web of metal mesh and bars, steel doors, and hate.

After half an hour, there was some clanging: keys jangling as the opposite door from the one they'd entered opened. A warder entered and they were made to line up and file into an eating area. This room had barred windows. Outside it was pitch black. Food was served. It was disgusting, but all the same, he ate.

That first night was the worst; his skin was sore from sunburn, tear gas and vinegar, but with neither soap nor towel, he was unable to soothe his face. And as for a toothbrush! He lay back, but, his thoughts being exceedingly active despite extreme tiredness, sleep evaded him. He sat back up, observing those around him.

His companions were an assorted bunch, appearing to come from many different walks of life. But now they were united by a common feeling of injustice, a sense of oppression. From conversations he heard, it seemed what was a rude shock for some was commonplace for others. What charges were levelled at most he didn't know, but he did wonder how many, like his, were trumped up. Because it seemed many had just been nabbed for being in the wrong place at the wrong time; many, like him, seemed completely baffled as to why they were there, having been arrested for no apparent reason other than being in close proximity to the demo. A black man on his way to work was arrested for jaywalking as he was crossing a road. Others, to be true, were charged with more serious crimes, like the guy in the cell opposite Pete's, only three feet tall, who walked with the aid of crutches. A real live street character he was; for what he lacked in stature, he certainly made up with bravado, as he was arrested attempting to hook out a rifle, with one of his crutches, from the back of an empty police car.

Later, as Pete was nearly asleep, a new prisoner was put in his cell. He was shortish with shoulder-length curly brown hair and wild, staring eyes, a tattoo on his forehead and bore an uncanny resemblance to Charlie Manson. On the bunk below, Pete could hear him having a conversation with himself. It was disconcerting and his spirit was not healed by slumber.

The next morning Pete met with the public defender. He was sympathetic, although the shrug of his shoulders, once they'd been over the circumstances of Pete's arrest, said it all. For by going through the whole thing step by step, what he was doing before he was arrested, the actual arrest and the ensuing events, Pete began to realise for the first time how the facts could be interpreted in a courtroom, and he started to feel increasingly desperate.

When he asked what the deadly weapon was, the public defender told him it was a rock.

'A rock? But there were no rocks anywhere about,' he exclaimed, flabbergasted, as his mind pictured boulders in the desert.

'A rock doesn't have to be that big in legal parlance,' the public defender explained. 'It can be the size of a stone or a pebble.'

'But Jim was with me. He could testify for me. You could get in touch with him and Susan, his sister, or Brad, who I'm staying with.'

'I believe they've been trying to contact me; at least, I had a message from someone called Jim who I've got to get back to. But the problem is that it will be Jim's word against that of two cops, and they probably never saw him and could deny that he was there. Was anybody else there?'

'Loads of people, but they were all fleeing. It all happened so fast. I didn't know any of them. The crowd was frantic. It's all hazy.'

'That could be tricky, as the prosecutor will claim to have a clear-cut case. I'll get hold of Jim. However, the most important thing is to get you out on bail, and to do that you must plead innocent, and then bail will be fixed, and a date for a future arraignment set.'

'When you see Jim, can you ask him to tell Brad not to telephone my granddad? I'd really appreciate it. If they need to call someone back home, tell them to call Mel.'

When Pete got back from this meeting, he found to his relief that his cellmate no longer there. But as he got up onto his bunk, was just about to lie back and shut his eyes, a voice called out to him.

'Hey, Pete, man, be careful where you lie down,' the little man in the cell opposite said.

'Why?'

'Coz they just took crazy guy to get deloused. There'll be crabs and lice jumping all over the place up in there. A real circus of them. Jeez, that dude got so much hair, those crabs must have thought they gone to lice heaven.'

The little man chuckled as he slapped an imaginary louse while Pete, still suffering from the effects of gas and vinegar and feeling increasingly grubby, started to uncontrollably itch all over. Any chance of rest was thwarted.

Later in the afternoon Pete was taken by a warder to a windowless room the size of a broom cupboard and left locked up in there alone. He got scared, thinking the worst, but a few minutes later, a man in a blue blazer with gold buttons came in. He was the British consul. Pete was initially suspicious of him. Wouldn't he be of the establishment and assume that Pete was guilty?

However, to his surprise, he found the consul sympathetic, enlightened. Sadly, he didn't hold out much hope for Pete. He'd dealt with similar cases and reminded Pete of Anne Kerr, the British MP beaten up by the police outside the Democratic Convention in Chicago. The high-handedness, the bias of the police, was well-known, he told Pete, and he could only but hope.

This interview gave Pete little encouragement. Again, back in his cell Pete lay on his bunk, staring at the ceiling. Would he ever get out? His state of mind wasn't helped by a prison warder for whom taunting was evidently a blood sport. For when he ordered Pete to state the charge against him, he informed him the crime of assault on a police officer with a deadly weapon was an extremely serious crime and Pete was sure to get life. With that in mind, Pete's sleep that night was restless and he awoke several times in a profuse sweat, from a nightmare in which he was running around and around in circles, unable to stop.

Monday morning arrived; the weekend's nightmare over, a new one was about to start. Pete was feeling ultra-nervous about his appearance in court. After an ill-tasting breakfast, they were all locked up in the eating area. Through the bars over the windows he could see it was bright, sunny day. He tried to conjure up the fragrances of the blooms in the Rose Garden because the fragrances inside were now most unpleasant; most of the prisoners badly stank, were grossly dishevelled with varying degrees of six o'clock shadow.

'Of course it's all a ploy. Keeping us like this is,' Washington Fuck said. 'That way we will be even more repugnant to the judge and the prosecutors.'

A number of officers entered the room and made everybody line up and marched them back to the processing area. They were issued with their confiscated possessions and made to line up in twos. While this was happening, one of the cops them noticed that Washington, still only clad in his purple panties, had draped himself in a prison blanket,

'You can't take that with you. That's police property,' the cop snarled, snatching the blanket away. 'Head of the line for you, and you, that freak there.'

He was referring to Pete's crazy cellmate. With Washington and the crazy cellmate heading the line, the prisoners waited in silence for several minutes until two more cops entered carrying two clanging long chains with manacles on them. Pete watched, astonished, as they were manacled together in pairs. After the final handcuffs were fixed on the last pair of prisoners, they were led downstairs by two cops to a backdoor of the police station and ordered to march across a small quadrant of grass to the nearby courthouse. Being adjacent to a busy pavement and an even busier road full of cars with drivers on their way to work, Pete, feeling painfully self-conscious, looked straight ahead. He didn't like to imagine what bystanders might think.

However, he soon realised the crowd was laughing. Not at them but with them, as Washington and his companion had started to sing a rousing chorus of chain gang dirges in a parody of some long-forgotten, bad Hollywood movie. As much as the officers tried to stop it, both prisoners and the public on the pavement, whose numbers increasingly grew drawn to this strange procession led by a weird man with waist-length hair, granny glasses and only wearing the skimpiest pair of women's panties, burst out into loud, appreciative applause. The cops, being exposed to what clearly amounted to extreme ridicule, were at a loss as to how to control the situation, and their tight, bloodless lips curled up as they grimaced in contempt, their billy clubs twitching in their hands.

Arriving at the backdoor of the courthouse, the prisoners were herded inside and up a narrow staircase to another small, windowless room. Their manacles were removed. Around fifty people crammed in there already, no doubt shipped in from other penile institutions.

How the system worked was a complete mystery to Pete. There was no list and names seemed to be just called out at random. And what he certainly hadn't expected was to be incarcerated in that small, stuffy room, till evening, without food and water.

It was an eternity until he was called. He gingerly walked down the staircase between two officers. Stifled, desperately needing fresh air and itching, aware of his body odour, his hair was unkempt, his face stubbly, while throat and mouth felt constricted, dry.

On entering the courtroom, the usher directed him to the dock.

It was only then that he dared to lift his head and saw Jim and Susan in the throng. He was relieved to see them and then there was Brad, with Will next to him.

They all were smiling. It was the first warmth he'd felt for three days.

Obviously discounting Perry Mason or Ironside, his experience of the American legal system was nil, his knowledge of English one not much better, so he was ill prepared for what lay ahead and found it plain confusing.

When asked he pleaded not guilty. Then the public prosecutor called his first witness. This was the victim of Pete's alleged deadly assault and he watched as the police officer, a complete stranger to him, took the stand.

'Do you recognise the defendant?' the public prosecutor asked him.

'I most certainly do sir. He was the one who threw a rock at me.'

'And how can you identify him?'

'By his blue shirt, sir. The one he's still wearing.'

It seemed the whole case was to be decided by Pete's blue shirt. Scant detail was paid to the time and place of arrest or from where the offending projectile was thrown. No rock was produced as evidence.

Pete looked over to the judge. Surely he must have known that the kind of blue shirt which Pete wore, bought a few days before, was commonplace, was a type worn by countless male and female students on the campus, indeed was a type of shirt worn by the majority of workers in America, was in fact the origin behind the term *blue-collar worker*.

The arresting officer was then called to take the stand, completely corroborating his colleague's story. Pete recognised him only too well; his scrotum still felt sore from the man's sadistic actions.

'So where did you first see the prisoner?' the public prosecutor asked him.

'I first saw him running across a vacant lot where we were dispersing protesters.'

'And what did he do then?'

'As he got to the corner before he turned, he bent down, picked up a large rock and threw with considerable force at Police Officer O'Donnell, who was near me. Boy, can he throw! It hit him right in the chest. I hate to think what would have happened if it hit his head, sir.'

Pete was stupefied to hear of this veritable sporting achievement. His throwing action had always been crap. He also found it strange that the first officer was not required to go into any injuries he sustained. The two police officers exchanged glances after the second one stood down, as if to say they'd got it in the bag.

But now, it was the turn of the public defender, and Pete was taken aback by his impassioned plea. He asked the judge that the proceedings be adjourned and bail be set, explaining to his honour that he had serious reservations about the charge and that this was a tragic case of mistaken identity.

'I truly believe this young man is innocent,' he declared.

The judge ruled that the case be adjourned until the following next day, setting bail at five thousand dollars.

On hearing this Pete's heart sunk. What? Five thousand dollars?

'Outrageous,' Susan shouted.

She was promptly told by the judge that she would be removed from court if she didn't stay quiet.

Where was he going to find an amount of money like that, he thought? It was the price of a substantial house back home; it was a to-be-dreamed-of annual salary. Even when the public defender came over to quietly inform him how the bail system worked, that if a defendant could raise ten per cent of the bail, a bail bondsman would pay the rest, Pete just gasped. For ten per cent was five hundred dollars.

But there came another hitch, for as he was on his way out of the courtroom a colleague of the public defender came up and explained to him that, even if he could raise the five hundred dollars, he would be lucky to find a bail bondsman who would touch him.

'You're an alien, you see,' he said.

As Pete was escorted back up the staircase to the upstairs room, freedom, which seemed, a few minutes ago, within his grasp, fast slipped away. He must remain on remand.

But the worst was yet to come as he was soon informed by a cop that he wasn't going back to the police station that night but would be taken to Santa Rita Rehabilitation Centre in Almeida County.

Santa Rita, that name sounded familiar. Where had he heard it?

As he stared around that stuffy, windowless room, he noticed that there were fewer prisoners there, and that those who remained were mainly black or Chicanos; Washington Fuck was gone. Then it dawned on him how he'd come across the name Santa Rita before, that the words *Fuck Santa Rita* had been a slogan of which he took a photo. He also wondered, as he scrutinised his fellow detainees, whether the true colours of the stars and stripes now were really making themselves be known.

Another journey into the unknown, lasting six hours, now commenced for him, as he and the other remaining prisoners were led back down the staircase to waiting blacked-out paddy wagons. After an hour, the wagon drew to a halt and, once backed up to a doorway, the prisoners got out and were made to walk in single file down a mesh corridor and into a room subdivided by mazes of mesh and heavy wire netting, reminding Pete of an animal market. Guarded by cops who'd accompanied them in the paddy wagon, they stood there for ages. Finally, some prison staff entered, sat down at the desks and, like an airport, the place came alive.

They were ordered to file past the desks, where their possessions were checked in. Pete again was required to sign for sixty-nine cents, his gold ring and the watch. They then were moved to another area, again partitioned by mesh, and waited. More warders appeared, making them strip, and, with buttocks required to be widely parted, they were searched again. Cardboard boxes were provided for clothes, after which they were left in a state of near-nudity for over half an hour, Pete, still without underpants, being completely naked, feeling ultra-vulnerable, a fact which caused the guards to take a perverse delight until he was eventually issued with a pair of tan boots and some orange overalls with Santa Rita Rehabilitation Centre emblazoned in big, bold, black letters on the back.

They were required to be processed over again. By now, it was nearly midnight, but still it continued. He could hardly remain upright. The penultimate line of the evening was for food, which came in the form of a sandwich made of a thick white bread the texture of cotton wool, with a filling of margarine and spam. Being ravenous, he could only but devour it. Back into single file, they were escorted by three warders with torches outside along a confusing warren of mesh corridors to some wooden huts. The door of one was unlocked, they were ushered into a long dark dormitory and told to find the nearest available bunk. Allowed no lighting, they were greeted by the groans and swearwords of woken inmates as they all muddled their way through the darkness until each one of them was settled in a free berth.

Locating a top bunk halfway up, Pete clumsily clambered up. Keeping on his orange overalls because of his lack of clothing underneath, he took off the boots to use as an impromptu pillow. Despite them being hard, he was soon fast asleep.

'Time to get up, you sons of bitches, I say, get up, motherfuckers.'

Pete awoke, raised his head and looked around. Although he couldn't make out much because no lights were on, he remembered where he was and his heart sank as his eyes took in the outline of the small, barred window opposite his bunk.

It was pitch black outside, no moon shadows whatsoever. He quietly groaned and lay back, again wishing this continuous nightmare was just only a dream. A pang of despair came over him as the aggressive shouting recommenced, soon to be complemented with some heavy banging on metal. Shocked right out of his slumber now, he felt he'd hardly slept at all.

'I won't say it again. Get up, you trash, you bunch of red commie bastards. It's time for the courthouse. I said, now.'

The voice now rose to an ear-piercing crescendo.

Now terrified, Pete scrambled down from the bunk and followed the other cellmates filing through a doorway at the end of the long dormitory. He found himself in a dimly lit, small, sordid bathroom. His eyes fixed on a couple of cracked washbasins and a rusty shower. A shower, yes, how he craved one, but the screws' voices were becoming even more menacing now, and with everybody frantic in there, pushing and elbowing each other out of the way, he had only time to splash some water over his face and cup up some dribbles into the palms of his hands in a feeble attempt to rinse out the acrid taste from his mouth. Without soap and toothpaste for over three days now, without hardly any water to drink, and painfully constipated, he was in a bad state.

But going back to his bunk and dragging on the ill-fitting boots, he concentrated his thoughts on the world outside, visualising those two sets of cliffs and that opal swell as he hurried to join the others filing out of the hut and beginning to walk down the narrow, mesh-enclosed outside corridor.

Outside, he could see an inkling of red in the eastern sky above the one-storey hut and, by this dawn's early light, began to make out the layout around him. His hut, one of four set around a quadrangle, was sealed off by a wall of mesh, while another double wall of mesh over twelve feet in height on the inside, fenced in the corridor, separated the huts from an open space with a hard dirt surface, presumably an exercising area.

Continuing to follow the line of sleepy, stumbling prisoners, he turned the first corner of the quadrangle. A lone screw was lounging a couple of yards further up with one foot crossed over the other, supporting himself against the wooden wall of the hut. As Pete passed, he pulled him to one side.

'So you, boy, tell me, why you are here? What you done?'

'What?' Pete asked, blinking with uncertainty.

'I said, motherfucker, why are you here? What have you done?'

'Nothing,' Pete said.

'Nothing, boy?'

The officer's menacing, staccato reply came as quick as machine gunfire at him, causing him to sense danger. As he looked up, he saw two cold grey eyes set in a twisted bulldog face, staring at him, oozing hate, contempt. This officer, his belly overhanging his trousers, now roughly manhandled Pete into a position faced up against to the weatherboard wall, making him stand aside while others continued to file by.

'Nothing, boy, now you know you ain't telling the truth. You wouldn't be here if you ain't done nothing. Now, motherfucker, you better tell me why you are here one more time. I want the truth this time. What you charged with?'

The officer's voice resonated around him, as those still filing past understandably lowered their eyes, terrified that a chance look and they'd be hauled over alongside Pete.

'Assault on a police officer with a deadly weapon,' said Pete quietly.

The sound of those words as they rolled off his tongue felt as acrid as the taste in his mouth.

'Louder, boy, I can't hear you.'

'Assault on a police officer with a deadly weapon.'

'Assault on a police officer with a deadly weapon what, boy? I need some respect now.'

The prison officer began to look really menacing now. His hands started to caress his billy club as he rolled it around in his palms. Pete was stumped for a moment, but then he realised what was missing: the word sir.

'Assault on a police officer with a deadly weapon, sir.'

'That's better, boy. And for your information, assault on a police officer with a deadly weapon is not nothing. Do you hear me? It is one helluva serious crime and you *will* go down for it. Be sure of that, boy. And for a long, long time too.'

The officer continued agitating his billy club in a provocative way, like it was his full intention to make Pete sweat. For a moment he thought it was going to come crashing down on his head.

'Now get a move on, you piece of shit,' he barked, suddenly losing interest.

With stomach churning, Pete hurried to catch up the line of prisoners. As he followed them into a dining area, he looked down at his hands and noticed they were trembling.

His attention was now diverted by the sheer amount of people in the dining area. Were that many arrested during the demo? But taking a closer look told him no, as he realised that before him was a good cross-section of the great American dispossessed, many who looked like they'd walked straight out of a Steinbeck or Kerouac novel, been prototype characters in the lyrics of Woody Guthrie or Robert Johnson tunes. But could that many people be going to court that day, he wondered, as he took his place in the queue for breakfast?

Since the encounter with the warder, that numb feeling had come back, and although he'd hardly eaten for over three days now, he didn't feel hungry. He felt even less so when he saw what was on offer. His stomach churned.

'Hey, dude, how you doing? You okay? I saw what happened back there.'

He turned to see behind him a tall thin guy, with a very dark complexion and an Afro hairstyle, whom he recognised from the paddy wagon ride the night before.

'Yeah, I was beginning to...' answered Pete, but then, suddenly, feeling reticent to admit how scared he was, his voice trailed off.

'It's okay, brother, I hear you. Say, now where you from? I can tell by your accent you're not American.'

'England,' he replied.

'Cool, man, far out. I'd sure like to visit London, and Europe. Say, I'm Henry Abercrombie.'

'I'm Pete Jones.'

'Give me five!'

Pete's response was embarrassingly clumsy, but Henry flashed a smile at him.

'You'll learn.'

'Hey, you two lovebirds over there, get a move on,' a screw shouted at them.

Henry looked at Pete.

The expression he wore said just ignore it as the two of them picked up their now-filled trays and carried them to a nearby long table. Sitting down at a bench, they started to eat.

'This is rank,' Henry said, pushing away his tray and then, looking at Pete, continued, 'So, Pete, tell me, how long you been in California?'

'Five weeks, but it seems like a lifetime,' he said, laughing. 'Yeah, about five weeks, I guess.'

'You enjoying yourself?' Henry asked him, grinning.

'Well, I was.'

And, after a momentary lock of their eyes, they both burst out laughing.

'Sure, man!' Henry retorted, his eyes looking up to the ceiling before he gave Pete another five. Pete's response was better this time.

It was the first time since his arrest that Pete had felt any release from the tremendous tension inside. And somehow, a new kind of perspective emerged for him, as he recalled that it was true, that he'd been having a great time, that it'd been such a great trip up until the moment of his arrest, regardless of Brad. For up until his arrest, he'd been starting to feel that he could actually be himself for the first time in his adult life, and for a moment, in that grey, desolate prison environment, the sunshine, those pearly shores streaked with foam, came to the fore in his imagination and he forgot where he was.

'Hey, you there!'

Pete was bought back to the real world by a screw barking at him to take his tray back to the counter.

'Hey, you know, you better do what he say now,' said Henry whimsically, as they deposited their trays. 'Stick with me, little brother, and you'll be fine.'

They joined another queue forming by the exit.

Pete sighed. 'I hope I'll get bail today,' he said.

'So you have got some people taking care of business for you on the outside?'

'What? Sorry?'

'Taking care of business, you know, lawyers, bail man.'

'Yeah, I think so.'

'You better know so,' retorted Henry.

'The trouble is, I'm an alien and the public defender said that bail bondsmen usually don't touch aliens, and my bail's set at five thousand dollars.'

Henry shook his head. 'Shucks, five thousand! What jokers! And you, an alien, whatever next, so what planet you s'pose ta come from then, Pete?'

Pete laughed as his thoughts went back to what Henry had previously said about lawyers and wondered whether the public defender managed to speak to Brad, Susan or Jim.

The queue started to move off and he followed Henry out of the dining area, and they joined another queue to be issued with their clothes and possessions. Then they were required to sign for their valuables, hand back the orange overalls and boots, after which they got dressed in their own cloths and, again negotiating the perplexing system of mesh divisions, which in the light of day reminded Pete of a cattle market, joined another queue waiting to climb up into the blacked-out paddy wagons, which would take them back to the courthouse.

It was completely light outside by now, another sunny Californian morning. As he climbed into the paddy wagon, despite being surrounded by people, Pete felt very alone. He was far away from home, and in an attempt to stem a flow of negative thoughts, he tried to think of all the different colours Zénaïde and he would claim they'd seen in the opal sea. But it didn't help; he could only imagine it grey, murky and tempestuous; he just desperately wished he was back there beside it. It dawned on him that while using the same language as his own, most people he'd come across since he'd been incarcerated, warders and prisoners alike, didn't seem to get his drift, certainly made no attempt to understand him despite sharing a common language. Still, Henry was an exception. But as he sat there, what was the rudest shock for him was the realisation that his word was doubted, that he wasn't believed when he told the truth,

But did the actual truth have any bearing on events? Wasn't he, like many others, deemed guilty as charged even before a trial had taken place? Because in reality, his crime had nothing to do with whether or not a rock was thrown, but more the threat that people like him were perceived to be. Yes, they wanted to do things differently, held alternative views, had different sexual orientations and wished for a more just, fairer world. He began to realise that he and those like him disturbed the certainty, the reality of the world of straight people, of the money people, as they constantly questioned it, and it was so obvious that his worldview they definitely cared not to see, let alone try to understand.

'Hey, Pete, man, hello, Henry to Pete, come in, alien.'

He looked up, confused.

'Pete, time to get out, you been napping? You choose your time!'

Henry's laugh anchored him back to the present and he looked up. They'd already reached the courthouse. The doors of the paddy wagon were opened and he got up and followed Henry out of the vehicle.

Except for lack of chains, his entry into the courthouse was a repeat process of the previous morning and he was soon again in the same windowless, stuffy room. This time as he looked around, there was no one he recognised. Evidently all those with whom he was locked up in the police station over the weekend, got bail or were already convicted. He sat down on the floor in a corner, shy to join Henry, who was seated in the midst of a group of other black men.

However, Henry called him over and he joined them but found it hard to follow the ensuing conversation as they all talked too fast for him. He found that they used words of which he either didn't know the meaning or words he knew but that were used in some different, hip context. But they were kind to him and gradually drew him into their conversation, initially enquiring about his home and about the people, fashions and the music there. Swinging London's supposed reputation was not lost on them.

'Say, you all remembered those plastic Beatle wigs,' Henry asked the others. 'My mom bought me one once for Christmas.'

'Oh yeah, they were kinda weird,' Pete injected, recalling an advert for them in *Melody Maker*.

They all laughed. This light, amicable banter grounded Pete, but still, underneath the mirth, he was churning up inside, praying that he'd get bail or better still that someone would recognise that it had all just been one big mistake.

Just like the day before, they waited an eternity and the room became increasingly hot, allowing Pete's memory to recall stories of mistrials, horrendous miscarriages of justice.

He had no idea of the time when he was eventually called, but it must have been late afternoon. Once in the courtroom, he noticed Brad, Susan and Jim seated together near the front but no Will. He wished that he'd been able to talk to the public defender before so he was briefed about the proceedings. Lacking understanding of the process made him feel removed from them as he stood in that dock, especially as this time, he wasn't required to speak.

'Your Honour,' now the public defender was speaking, 'yes, Your Honour, of all the defendants caught up arrested in this demonstration, I sincerely do believe that this defendant is telling the truth. I am convinced of his innocence. I do strongly feel that the bail should be lowered.'

'Right on,' Susan chipped in, enthusiastically.

The judge gave her withering look, which quickly silenced her.

He thanked the public defender and, after leaning over to have some words with a court official, he announced he would lower bail to two thousand dollars and set a date for a new arraignment for three weeks hence.

Now, Pete thought, surely a bail bondsman would now take him on. He was going to be out in no time. As he walked back out of the courtroom, he couldn't see Brad's reaction, but Susan was widely grinning while Jim gave him a thumbs-up.

However, back in the stuffy, windowless room, thirsty and hungry, he waited and waited. Was it the paperwork? Starting to feel extremely agitated, he went over and sat next to a shut-eyed Henry, who, unlike his friends whose cases had been heard, was still waiting.

'They really string things out here, don't they?' Pete said to him.

'Ain't that the truth? Now that's something they really excel in.'

'You know, I was wondering. Do they always get people up early in the prison to get here? Why do they do that?'

'They like to try to wear you down, you know,' Henry replied, sighing. 'But don't let them get to you, little brother, I seen it all before. Don't matter what you do, don't matter what you don't either, they's always coming at you. Shit, just evil and nasty, that's what they are.'

His voice was becoming animated.

'Always stirring things, they are. They just don't know how to stop. Still, it don't pay to get wound up by it.'

His voice got calmer again as he said that last sentence.

'Because whenever I start getting mad, I remind myself what my mom told me a long time ago. She said, "Henry, don't let them upset you, chil', don't let them get to you. It'll make you too angry and, Henry, you don't want to be full of hate like them. They ain't worth it. You're too precious for that. Never let hate destroy you." She's so right, you know, you just don't let them get to you, you know that. Believe me.'

They were both silent for some time.

'Yeah, *keep the faith*. Now that's what you have to do,' Henry said, quietly. '*Keep the faith.*'

And these words planted once again a glimmer of hope in Pete.

'Well, I should be out of here once they sort out the bail,' he said, just as Henry was finally called to go down to court.

'That's right, Pete, you will. Take care now, remember what I said. *Keep the faith*, Pete, yeah?'

'Good luck, Henry. *Keep the faith*,' Pete called out, as he watched Henry's departing silhouette.

Suddenly realising he'd mainly talked about himself made him feel mortified. He'd never even asked Henry with what he was charged. Would he ever see the guy again? They hadn't said a proper goodbye. He should've thanked him. He felt he was a bad person.

Only a few prisoners left now, the room had been gradually emptying as people went down and not returned. *Can't be long now*, he thought. But after an hour, he started to worry because it was apparent the day's cases were concluded; only remand prisoners still remained in the room. He asked a warder what the holdup was but was just given an icy stare.

Worn down by the length and stresses of the day, Pete closed his eyes. He tried willing an officer to come back into the room and tell him he was free to go. Three of them eventually came and started to herd him and the remaining prisoners down the stairway to the waiting paddy wagons. Pete stood his ground and refused to get in.

'But I've got bail,' he protested.

'Like shit you have, fag, you're an alien. A bail bondsman won't touch you,' the screw said, manhandling Pete towards the wagon. 'Now you better get in that there wagon, you hear me, boy.'

'Excuse me?' Pete, once inside, asked of one of the prisoners. 'Do you know where are we going now?'

'Back to Santa Rita, where else?'

And thus the dark, ominous route of the previous evening was retraced; the routine was almost familiar to him now and as the prisoners who he was with were evidently to be enmeshed there under the watch of the warders' eyes for the foreseeable future, they were paid scant attention. No one even bothered to verbally abuse them while they were being processed, which was undertaken with great speed. He was issued with an even worse pair of boots, narrower than the previous ones. As he felt them pinching his toes, he realised the screws had plenty of time to draw things out now.

Hijacked by despair, feeling he was sinking into a quagmire, he was escorted back to that same hut in which he slept the previous night. The screws ignored any questions he asked.

So was he to go back to court the next day? A terrifying thought now came to him. Perhaps he would be kept there for the next three weeks, up until the date of the arraignment. And then he wondered that if he was going to kept inside up to the arraignment, that, as he'd pleaded not guilty, he would be kept there after it, up until the time he went before a jury. A Catch-22 situation because if he'd pleaded guilty to speed up the process, he'd be given a gaol sentence anyway and be locked up for years. He'd never get home. The expansive world in which he'd so recently arrived had badly shrunk.

Back in the hut, there was a Bible on a table. He recalled reading some novel about a character opening the Bible on a random page and acting on the advice on that page. He hadn't much been to church – neither Zénaïde nor Albert had time for organised religion – but in his numb desperation, and with loneliness welling up inside him, he decided to try it.

He closed his eyes and randomly opened it. What would Isaiah or Elijah have to say to him? Would there be a message from Moses, Elisha or Joshua about his enemies being smitten? But no, he only found Christ biding him to turn the other cheek. The Psalms, with their poetry, were soothing, lyrical, but how, when incarcerated, could he go up unto the hills to find his strength? His despondency just grew, an ogre inside him gnawing away. He returned to his bunk, clambered up and closed his eyes, but nothing went away. With eyes closed, it just seemed worse.

'Hey, Pete, man, are you sleeping?'

Startled, he looked down from the bunk. It was Henry.

'Hey, Pete, you didn't get no bail. Sure is a bitch, shit!'

'Yeah, and nobody will tell me what's happening, but what about you?'

'Tomorrow I'll be out; they're going to drop the charges. The pig who falsely arrested me will be squirming, I'm sure, but he'll live to do the same another day. You know, my friend, justice is very fluid in this country. It can run through your hands like water and quickly get mixed up with the dirt beneath your feet. There's one kind of justice for some folks and another kind for others, that's the good old US of A for you. And you, my brother, you just learnt what justice for the others is like. Us black folks, we used to it – we get marked out early on.'

'Yes, there was a lot back home on TV about discrimination and injustice here, documentaries about civil rights and things,' Pete said, feeling out of his depth.

But he'd always been aware how a significant segment of the American population was treated, what they had been, were still often subjected to, and recognised his four days in a gaol here didn't amount to much in the scale of things, and he felt ill prepared, too ignorant about it to discuss it.

'I hear you. Say, listen, once I was old enough, I soon got into trouble and it been carrying on ever since. No reason but for my colour, for living the wrong side of town. You know the place where I originally came from, it's what they call a border state, in the south, well, we had curfew there. Meant that nobody under the age of eighteen supposed to be out after ten at night without an adult member of their family. You know, sometimes in the summer when I was a little boy, my step-uncle would take me fishing. We just loved to go catch some real fine river fish for my mom to fry up for us, crisp and crunchy. Sitting there, as it gradually grew dark my uncle would light an oil lamp, and we'd have some pieces of fried chicken, a flask of refreshing iced tea or some soda pop. Anyway, one time when we come back later than usual, it had been such a magical evening, and then my uncle's car done broke down. A patrol car comes by eventually, at last; help, we thought. But they arrested my uncle and me, and took us down the precinct. Breaking the curfew, we were, as we weren't related, didn't have the same blood. Got released in the end, but…'

Henry's conversation tailed off and he was suddenly deep in thought as if he was back in that border state. Pete was quiet too, not knowing what to say, so astounded was he by this revelation, his troubles having dwindled to a ridiculous insignificance as he listened. It was like institutionalised terrorism.

'So have you been in gaol since then?' Pete asked Henry after a poignant silence.

'Hell yes,' replied Henry. 'When I was sixteen, on a trumped-up statutory rape charge.'

'What's that?'

'Well, I was seeing this girl, we were real sweet on each other, you see. She was fifteen and I sixteen, and I get her pregnant. Someone who didn't like me much got mad and snitched, and I get arrested.'

'But that wasn't rape surely?'

'Hell no, but don't make any difference, with her being underage. I's sent to gaol for three years. She didn't want to press charges. But she was sent away to live with an aunt up in Baltimore. I never saw her again, never knew what happened to the baby either.'

'But that's outrageous,' Pete said.

He recalled Nicknick's acrimonious situation, the time she got pregnant, and how things were resolved then. But this was so twisted; again he was lost for words.

After another period of silence, Henry suggested with a broad grin on his face that they went outside to catch the last rays of the sun. Once outside, Pete realised that it was the first time he'd been in daylight for four days. The lowering sun was still warm and felt soothing on his grimy, sore skin. He stunk badly now and he knew that soon he would have to source soap and a towel, but at that moment, he was past caring. He just wanted to be still.

Some of Henry's mates out there were playing a card game and called the two of them over to join them. Henry did, but Pete declined; he was crap at cards. He absentmindedly observed as they went about their game while his mind buzzed about Henry's revelations.

A debate ensued, a heavy rap, about whether it was better to convert to Islam and join the black Muslims or enlist with the Panthers. One guy wanted to become a Marxist like Angela and claim political asylum in Cuba; another talked about going to Sweden or Canada to dodge the draft.

Listening to them all, it was like a crash course for Pete in the realities of the caste system in the land of the free, and how citizens of a country, when denied proper citizenship and made not to feel like they belong, can feel the need to look elsewhere. Citizens were naturally expected to love their country, respect the flag and sing the national anthem, but how could they take any pride in those things if they were denied rights, treated as second-class citizens, had no sense of belonging? How could they believe in a country when the law was there not to protect them but to control them?

'Hey, Pete, Pete, man, alien! You being called,' Henry called out to him.

'Peter Jones, Peter Jones, where is that English boy? Don't he want to get out here?'

Pete jumped at the sound of his name.

'Hey, man, that screw's calling for you. You better get up and go to him, over there by the fence,' Henry said.

Pete looked up and, beyond Henry and his mates, saw a warder peering through the mesh fence, looking in his direction.

'Peter Jones,' the warder called out, again.

Pete walked over to the fence.

'So you Peter Jones then?'

Pete nodded.

'Well, your friends are here to take you home, you got bail. So come on, make a move if you want to get outta here, that way.'

The screw pointed to a gate in the mesh which Pete had not noticed before.

'Err, what… sorry?' Pete said.

He couldn't quite believe it. It was a wind-up, right? But as his eyes looked past the guard and beyond the exit in the mesh fence, he saw Brad, Susan and Jim. They clocked him at the same time and beamed through the mesh at him.

'You got bail at last. We went to see the judge. We nearly didn't make it today, but you're free to go,' Susan shouted.

'Cut that schmaltzy crap,' the guard barked over his shoulder. 'You, go get anything you got in the hut and then follow me to get your other possessions. As far as I'm concerned, the sooner your red commie ass is out of here the better.'

Pete had nothing inside, but he went back into the hut.

Henry followed him.

'Wow, man, I'm really glad for you. I guess it's goodbye, then,' he said, and then hugged Pete, after which he raised his fist in a clenched salute.

'Remember, *keep the faith*,' he said.

'I will. And listen, thanks for everything, you got me through, goodbye.'

They smiled at each other.

Outside, the screw was shouting to get a move on. As he passed through the door, the thought passed through his mind that they should exchange addresses, but he had no pen or paper. He also was shy.

'Hey, buddy, just one thing,' Henry said. 'Your boots are bigger than mine, right? I need to swap. These ones are too small, they hurt me.'

'Sure. Okay.'

Despite the screw hollering, Pete took off his boots and exchanged with Henry. Try as he might, there was no way he could fit into Henry's, so he just slipped his toes and the front of his feet in them, walking, sort of dragging them across the dirt.

'Jesus, you fruit, get a move on.'

The poker game was still taking place and the players all looked up as he passed them, whistling, calling out goodbye and asking of him imaginary favours.

'Bye, say, now I don't want to see you here no more, you know that, don't you?' Henry called out, as he leant up against the doorway while Pete passed through the gate in the mesh.

Pete turned, one more time, and waved.

'Cut the crap, don't you want to leave here? Now follow me, won't you? And, hey, you three,' the guard said, right narked by now, addressing Brad, Susan and Jim. 'You go back to where you parked. You ain't supposed to be here.'

They beat a hasty retreat while Pete followed the screw. Once in the processing area, the warders grudgingly went about the task of returning his clothes and possessions. They contrived to be very thorough. Pete couldn't care a fig because he now knew he was going and, strangely, because he was going, he was almost beginning to feel sorry for them.

Once dressed, he was ushered out through a door into a parking lot. Blinded by the setting sun, he blinked for a few seconds before making out the silhouettes of Susan, Jim and

Brad coming towards him. They fell onto him, corralling him in a giant hug before they all piled into Jim's beat-up Oldsmobile, Jim in the driving seat with Pete besides him, Susan and Brad up back. Negotiating the final security checks on the prison's perimeter was tense for Pete, but in no time, they were speeding off down the dusty road to the highway towards Berkeley.

'So what happened then?' he asked. 'How come I finally got bail?'

'He's a good man, that public defender,' said Jim. 'After today's hearing, when we found out a bail bondsman still wouldn't touch you, we went to see him. We all went to the judge with him and he pleaded for your bail to be reduced to $200 in cash, and the judge agreed. Wow, man, we got to the bank before it closed and got back to the clerk of the court just in time. He issued us with the order for your release, and hey, man, here we are. Thought it was going to have to be tomorrow for a while, but… hey, dude, we got here just in time.'

He then slapped Pete's thigh in a friendly manner, but the sudden physical contact made Pete flinch.

'So,' Susan said, leaning over the front seat, ruffling his hair, 'you're a free man, Pete.'

'That's right, Booby, you are,' added Brad.

'Yes, I suppose I am,' Pete said.

'Boy, did you have me worried, though,' Brad continued.

Pete remained quiet for the rest of the journey and the other three seemed to cotton on that he didn't want to talk much. He felt kind of choked, yet impatient to cleanse away the events of the last four days, and he was aware he and Brad hadn't talked since the night he'd spent with Will.

When they eventually reached Brad's, first thing he rushed to the bathroom, but it was already occupied. But when Angel Dust came out, as Pete ran in, he heard him telling Brad somebody called for him: his German friend, he thought it was, but he wasn't too sure, as the line was bad and the guy left neither name nor message.

During the days following his release, whenever Pete left Brad's alone, it was with great trepidation. Try as he might, he couldn't stop feeling paranoid. Consequently, every time a cop car cruised along the street, thinking he was about to be nabbed again, he froze inside. Fear welled up and he started to shake as irrational thoughts filled his brain.

What if his bail was revoked and they were coming to take him back to Santa Rita? But he stood his ground, when they checked him out as they drove by, despite wanting to flee back inside the apartment and jump into the shower or take cover elsewhere. He only allowed the feeling to take hold once he knew that they were off the radar. He mentioned all this when visiting Susan.

'Well, you know, Pete,' she said, with a face full of sympathy, 'it's natural. You're most likely traumatised.'

'Traumatised?'

'Yes, like your body's in shock. It's like you've been violated. You know, it has to work its way out, somehow.'

'Oh,' he replied, as he considered what she said. Traumatised was a word with which he was unfamiliar.

'I'm sure that you'll feel better in a few more days,' she said. 'Try and get some more rest. Let's smoke a doobie and I'll make some camomile tea.'

'The thing is, Susan, I am really confused by it all now. Like, what I should do.'

Jim came back in at that moment and joined in the conversation. 'Maybe you should wait until you go to the arraignment. See what happens there,' he said.

There was just over two weeks to wait for the arraignment. His ticket home was valid until a couple of weeks after that. During a meeting two days after he was released, the public defender told him that the arraignment was a mere formality and that his case would be, most probably, adjourned for six months. This knowledge caused him a dilemma, as he realised that if he stayed that long, he would overstay his visa and, if he lost the case, might risk imprisonment at the end of it, particularly if no witnesses came forward.

However, since his release, despite his paranoia, his gut feeling was to stay and fight to prove his innocence, partly because it had become stark clear to him that if he did leave before the case came to court, he'd have jumped bail and most likely would never be able to return to America. In addition, he felt that, to the authorities, such an action would be like admission of guilt. He was enjoying being in California big time. He felt he was just only really getting to know the place and gradually, after a few days of freedom, the excitement of being there was coming back to him.

'Yeah, Pete, wait till after the arraignment before deciding. You've got bail. There's no reason why they should rearrest you. Like, they have bigger fish to fry and also there's a slight chance charges could be dropped then,' Susan said.

'Oh, I almost forgot,' Jim now said. 'The public defender called here just before I split while you and Susan were out.

He'd been contacted by the consul, who wants to speak with you. The number's here. You can call him now if you like.'

Pete dialled the consul's number. It turned out the consul was just checking he was okay. There was no further advice or support. Pete was on his own.

He was relieved nobody had telephoned Albert when he was inside, but apparently Brad tried to call Mel at the library and left a message but there'd been no reply. Pete really missed Mel, often drawing comfort from imagining her furrowed-up brow as she sympathetically listened to him. He also tried to speculate what she would advise him to do, for there was also the question of the bail money. He somehow had to pay Brad back, although the latter said there was no rush. But Pete, after calling the consul, went by a post office, bought an aerogramme and, that night, wrote to Mel asking her if Baz could lend him the two hundred dollars to pay his bail. He posted it down on Shattuck Avenue early next morning, when few people were about.

Since getting back from Santa Rita, things were easier with Brad. He termed his jealousy over Will 'retarded' behaviour. Yet Pete's feelings about him were still confused. He still liked him, but somehow, the sparkle, that great attraction which had erupted the previous summer, had fizzled out, and he now wondered whether, although he had thought he was in love back then, perhaps it had all been infatuation. Maybe he'd been just simplistic about it all.

Still, that did not prevent him from accepting Brad's offer of exchanging the sofa for half of Brad's big double waterbed. It was the ultimate in luxury but he kept to his half, though. Somehow, the idea of having sex with Brad, or even just touching him, was no longer appealing. He wondered if now he had an aversion to people touching him; for a start, he still felt dirty. In the Bancroft library he read up about something called haphephobia. He hoped he wasn't developing that.

How he savoured that waterbed, often staying in it late into the morning after Brad had gone to the campus. But once, in that strange moment between being asleep and awake, when dreaming and reality become momentarily entwined, he dreamt he was back in Santa Rita searching for Henry: Henry, in whose company he felt safe in a way he'd not experienced since being a small child with his grandfather and Zénaïde. But Henry was not to be found and Pete woke up sweating, disturbed, until he recognised the familiar surroundings of Brad's apartment.

It was on a morning when Brad did not have to go anywhere and stayed in bed that he opened up to Pete in a way like he had not since the previous summer.

'Hey, I'm really sorry all this shit has happened to you. I feel responsible.'

'Well,' said Pete, 'it's hardly your fault. I was just in the wrong place at the wrong time.'

'Yeah, but, you know, maybe I created bad vibes that were a catalyst. I can do that. I dunno why, but sometimes I shower people with my own shit.'

'But, Brad, you weren't even around. I hardly saw you during the days leading up to my arrest.'

'Yes, exactly, Pete, because you were keeping out of my way. If I'd been honest with you from the start, maybe it wouldn't have happened.'

'Mémé used to say to Nicknick and me when we were little that there's always a maybe, but it's not worth dwelling on. It's now that is important; maybe's a waste of energy.'

'Yeah, but I guess I'm trying to say I treated you badly. You know, I didn't mean to lead you on. Things kinda got out of control. You know, that time last year was special. I'll always remember it.'

'Me too, I've been thinking, and perhaps I have been—'

'No, let me finish. I want to explain. You know, I found it so easy with you last year. Before meeting you, I was scared to commit, not for fear of rejection but loss. But being in Europe made feel like I was another person. I felt free, lost my hang-ups. But when I got back to America, it was like my old hang-ups reclaimed me as fast as I'd reclaimed my baggage from the carousal. You know, I never talked much about my family.'

'Well, I'd noticed, but then I thought maybe it was because I talked too much about mine. But it did seem strange. It was like you just cut off when I brought up the subject.'

'Well, that's because I don't speak to them much. My family's from New England, you know, and been there for generations, since just after the *Mayflower*. Bradford Lowell Brewster, I was christened, like many of my male forebears before me. I was expected to be something I could never be. I could never, nor did I want to carry on the family traditions. Like, follow my father into his business or produce sons to carry on the family name. But you know, from an early age, I was made to feel that I should. That it was somehow my duty.'

Pete remained silent.

'You know, I always kinda knew I was gay.'

'Me too,' Pete said.

'But you know, when I was younger, a teenager, I just denied it. I used to date girls who I, now looking back, treated badly. But things kinda came to a head when we went on vacation with another family: my dad's friends from way back who I'd not met before, as they were in the diplomatic, so always on the move. It was just the two families, together in a rented house near a sandy beach, onto which the roaring waves of the Atlantic crashed. They had kids that were the same age as my sister and me. After a few days in their company, it became obvious to me that the son, Joel, was gay, and I opened up to him. We would go off together on our bikes and muck around in the dunes. I got really fond of him. He sure was a crazy boy, very special, talented but always fooling, fearless. But somehow, one day during our vacation, his parents found out he was *queer.'*

Brad waved his two forefingers to indicate the parentheses.

'Of course, they didn't know about me, but he'd been seen going somewhere. Some friend of theirs saw him going into a gay bar or someplace, and later, he came out drunk, got picked up by the cops and taken in on a charge like importuning. Well, the shit hit the fan. His folks dragged him off to a psychiatrist, had him sectioned. He was even given electric shock treatment to cure him, Pete. Imagine that! When I saw him a few months later, he seemed weird, like he was broken, vacant. He didn't even recognise me and jumped when I got close up. It broke my heart because I realised I loved him and done nothing to help him because I was too much of a coward, because I couldn't own up to what I was.'

Pete could see tears forming in Brad's eyes now.

'But what could you have done?' Pete asked him.

'I don't know. We could have run away together. Come to California. We both talked about it that summer. But it was too late. He committed suicide two months after I saw him last. Broke into the gun cupboard in his dad's den, took out a shotgun, shot himself in the temple.'

'Brad, but that's terrible. I'm really sorry, I don't know what to say...' said Pete.

'I lost it at his funeral. It was all so phoney. Everything ironed over, the real facts not mentioned. I'd had enough. And a few days afterwards, I got mad, told my folks I was gay and asked them what they were going to do about it because I knew what I was gonna do. Get the fuck out of there.'

After Brad finished his story, they stayed silent for some time. Pete had never seen such pain on his face before.

'That's so heavy, Brad. I never imagined anything like that had happened to you. I wish there was something I could do,' Pete said after a few minutes.

'No need, Doll,' Brad said, in Baz's accent.

They laughed. The poignancy of the moment had passed.

'Boy, you know, it was the best thing I ever did,' he continued, after a while. 'Get away from there, but losing Joel like that did make me scared about getting close to someone again. I was so afraid I'd lose them. Until you came along, that is. You know, when I left London, you were the only one. I was totally sincere; I was certain about my feelings, although I admit I was a little wary of the idea of setting up house with someone. And since you arrived here, I have thought about this, really tormented myself trying to work it all out as to whether I was just using you in London, but I am pretty sure I wasn't. Of course, that postal strike didn't help, and, like, I'm the worst letter-writer. But the thing is, something happened in Frankfurt; it just knocked me off my feet, Pete. You see, I found someone in those last few days there. He's just so amazing. I feel so guilty because the guy in Frankfurt...'

'Oh, was he the one that Angel Dust mentioned before I left for the desert? I did wonder,' Pete said.

Brad looked confused for a moment. 'Er... yes, that's right. You know, I feel like making some coffee. You want some granola and banana too?'

'Yummy, thank you.'

Brad got up to go to the kitchen. Soon, the smell of brewing coffee soon started to waft through to the bedroom, lulling Pete into a reverie. He lay back. Now, things seemed to be making sense. When Brad came back with the coffee and bowls of granola, Pete was just going to ask Brad more about the mystery German when the phone rang. Brad went to answer it.

'Hey, Pete,' said Brad when he came back. 'It was Susan calling. Want to go wine-tasting in the Napa Valley? I said yes. I said we'd be down there in half an hour.'

The date of the arraignment arrived with alarming speed. As the day drew nearer, Pete became increasingly nervous, but underneath he was glad; he wanted it over.

The day before, he was alone in Brad's flat as Brad was out and Angel Dust, whose work Pete had found out was to do with computers, was off at some convention. He was in bed reading a fascinating booklet about the Kiowa Indians, which he'd picked up at the Museum of Anthropology. Just as he sat up to take a sip of coffee, the telephone rang. He put down the booklet and got out of bed to answer it.

'Hello, hello?'

The line was scratchy, and it was like no one was on the other end. However, as he was just about to replace it in the cradle, he heard a faint voice.

'Pete, is that you?'

'Mel?'

'Yes, Pete, it's Mel. Oh, Pete, I've got hold of you at last. I tried that many times, but you know, what with the time difference, it's difficult. It's the wee hours here. I stayed up late especially, to call you. I had to walk down to Whitechapel to find a phone that's working. The call's free, though, you know our friend at the International Exchange? How are you? We've been so worried about you.'

'You got my letter then? I know Brad called you, but I didn't think he said anything. Like, what happened.'

'Oh yes, we got the letter, but someone left a message at the library first. I imagined it could have been Brad, but he didn't say anything. No, Baz called… before we got the letter… found out from… Brad said…'

The line started to insanely crackle now and he could only make out certain words.

'What's that, Mel? I can't hear you. Hang on. Oh, that's better.'

'Yes, it's horrendous, unbelievable. Are you alright?'

The line began to crackle, even more violently, causing Pete to move the receiver away from his ear for an instant.

'Mel? Mel? Are you still there?' he said after a moment. 'This line is—'

'Yes, still here. Anyway, I thought I better call you. Nicola called me.'

'You're breaking up again.'

Mel evidently was trying to speak very slowly and clearly. 'Oh, thank god. I can hear you now,' she said.

'What's that you said about Nicknick?'

'Yes, Nicola rang me at the library. She was worried about your grandfather.'

Pete's heart jumped a beat. 'He's not ill, is he?'

The line now became mysteriously clear.

'No, he's fine. I called him immediately. It was a nasty bug that was going around apparently, the doctor said. In any case, at the time, Baz and I were about to drive down to the ferry to go to Belgium, to get some spare parts for the barge, so we called in on him on the way. He was much better. We took him out for a drive and had tea at that Doll's House

Tearoom place up that little valley. I can tell he's missing you, though. He doesn't say it, but he did say he doesn't understand why you're over there, says you ought to get a proper job, you know. His roses are incredible this summer. There's no need to worry, but I just thought I should let you know. Pete, when are you coming back?'

'Soon,' Pete said, firmly.

He knew his grandfather and knew how he could put on a show for people. He felt he had the sign he was waiting for and he should return.

'Yes, one day next week, maybe Wednesday,' he continued. 'The arraignment is tomorrow and the public defender has told me the case will be adjourned for six months. There's no point staying, although I'll have to jump bail. There's no other way.'

'How's it going with Brad?' asked Mel.

'It's not.'

'What? I can't believe it. What happened?' Mel sounded shocked.

'Nothing. It never happened. It turns out he met someone else when he was in Germany before he flew back. To begin with I couldn't get my head around it, but now, well, you know, maybe it just wasn't meant to be. Oh, Mel, did you ask Baz if he can lend me eighty pounds? That's about two hundred dollars, I reckon, you know, to repay Brad my bail money.'

'I think he has…'

The line recommenced crackling.

'What's that you say? He will? The line's gone bad again.'

'Let us know what time your flight gets in? We'll drive up and meet you. I got some time owing.'

'Mel, what did you say about the money?'

But there was no reply from Mel and he could only hear a series of clicks, and then, another voice was heard, saying the receiver on the other end of the line had been replaced.

A gust of wind blew into the living room from the open kitchen door and Pete shivered; his naked body started to get goose bumps. He located a tee-shirt and his loons and put them on quickly before going into the kitchen and brewing some fresh coffee. The coffee made, he went back to the bedroom and sat up in bed drinking it while musing about what Mel had said. He was confused; still, he'd be home in a week and see how his grandfather was for himself. And it sounded like Baz would lend him the money, so that was a relief.

He took up the booklet about the Kiowa Indians again and was quickly away with the braves, medicine men and squaws in their battle for survival against the forked tongues. Consequently, he stayed in bed all day, only getting up to answer the phone from Brad saying he wouldn't be back till late, but he told Pete that he'd be there to go to court with him. However, Brad didn't come back at all and Pete spent a restless night unable to drop off until the early hours and, when he eventually awoke, felt exhausted.

It was day zero, the arraignment was set for two-thirty and Pete started to feel increasingly nervous, and the thought that it would all be over by the end of the day was no consolation. Too nervous to eat, he ended up sitting on the outside stairs, chain-smoking and drinking black coffee. The summer was getting hot now, and as he sat shrouded by the shadows of the rustling leaves of a tall elm in Brad's backyard, he contemplated how time seems so strung out when waiting for something. Attempting to scupper this elasticity of the time, he went back into the apartment and methodically paced himself while he shaved and showered. After he was dry, he chose the clothes to wear with the utmost of care, laying them out on the bed with a precision he'd learnt from his grandfather.

He dressed slowly. He borrowed a sombre tie from Jim a couple of days before, and Brad lent him an old preppy sports jacket. His most drastic measure involved his hair, as he brushed it back, severely combing in a side parting while tying the excess into a ponytail so from the front it had the appearance of being short. Once ready, he sat on the sofa in the living room, his thoughts going back to the cliffs back home, the opal swell between them and that first ever crossing he made with Zénaïde. How long he remained in that state he couldn't say before the sound of Jim's voice reverberated through the kitchen door from up the outside stairs.

'Hey, Pete, time to go!' he shouted.

'Okay, I'm ready,' he replied, suddenly realising Brad hadn't returned.

Now there was a tap on the outside door and he looked up to see Susan standing there. He didn't recognise her at first. She was completely transformed. She looked like a high-powered secretary.

'Ting,' she exclaimed. 'You ready? Wow, don't you look smart, straight or what. Say, where's Brad?'

'He said he'd meet us there,' Pete said.

He didn't know why he felt he had to lie.

'Well, Jim's already in the car. Come, let's go.'

The moment Pete stepped out onto the steps, his numbness intensified as a long-ago feeling of desertion, of that time when he was reclaimed by his own father, rose to the surface. But this time, it wasn't Guy Fawkes' Night, and he couldn't run away, sneak on the train and arrive back at Albert and Zénaïde's in time to go to the fireworks. He took a deep breath and started to walk down to join Jim, who was revving up the car. Jim opened the passenger door for him while Susan clambered up behind.

The drive to the courthouse didn't take long and they were there with plenty of time to spare. Coincidently, Brad arrived there at the same time on a borrowed cycle just as Pete had to attend a brief meeting with the public defender. Afterwards they sat silently on a long hard bench outside the courtroom waiting to be called. There, the battle started up inside Pete and he felt again torn, having doubts about his earlier decision to leave. He should stay and fight, strike a blow for justice and freedom, but then, wouldn't he sacrifice Albert to this cause? Besides, without any plausible witnesses, how could he fight?

He wondered what Albert would've done in such a situation, what he'd advise him to do; Albert, who twice had fought for justice and freedom; Albert, who was occasionally heard to comment, 'And for what?' But surely it had to have been for something; it wasn't in vain?

As he sat there, the sound of Zénaïde's voice came suddenly to the forefront of his mind. It was the first time he could recall hearing it with such clarity since her death, eliciting a strong childhood memory of her bending over him as she kissed him goodnight.

'*Tu dois revenir, mon enfant, parce qu'Albert a besoin de toi. Il faut que tu en ailles. Laisses toi la bataille pour un autre jour.*'

She was telling him to return home; the fight would be won another day. More practically, as he considered his situation, he recognised that his bread was running out and innocence was expensive to maintain in this sixty-eight-million-dollar democracy where cash was king and without it, a person nothing.

The courtroom, once inside, seemed a long way from Santa Rita. Perhaps it was because he was wearing *respectable* clothes, but he found the treatment metered out to him by court officials and police discernibly different. The arraignment itself only took a few minutes, just a rubber-stamping, really. His plea of innocence repeated, his terms of bail reconfirmed and a date was set for him to go before a jury in the following December.

They came out blinking in the sunlight, and as their eyes adjusted from being in the sombre, magisterial environment, a feeling of relief ran through Pete. It was over for him, even if it wasn't for his incarcerators and tormentors.

Brad announced that he had errands to run and had to return the bike, so he quickly split. Disappointed, Pete wondered if he wasn't trying to avoid him and, thinking back to Mel's fragmented telephone conversation of the day, his mind reignited with confusion.

'Let's go for a drink,' he suggested. 'A sort of celebration, you know, and I need to tell you all something. I'm going home next week. I decided.'

'In that case, why not?' said Jim.

'Yeah, let's go across to San Francisco,' said Susan.

They climbed into the car and, in no time, they were over the Bay Bridge and in the city and tumbling into a nondescript little bar of Jim's liking.

On returning, Pete ran into Will at the top of the steps on his way out. He hadn't seen him since that his first time in court and felt nervous about the encounter. He needn't have, though.

'Hey, Pete, how you doing, man? Brad told me about the arraignment,' Will said, beaming at him.

'Well, to your first question, I'm somewhat pissed. I don't mean pissed off, that is,' he replied, getting confused. 'I mean, I'm a little drunk as I went to the city with Jim and Susan to a bar. And two, I'm really glad the arraignment's over.'

'Yeah, so what will you do now?'

'Go home, I must. I could end up in gaol in six months' time and I don't think it's worth waiting hanging around for that. Besides, I've not got the bread to stay.'

'Oh, shame! Well, man…' Will said, leaning over to hug him and planting a lingering kiss on Pete's mouth. 'Okay then, cheerio. Isn't that what you Brits say?'

He moved off down the steps.

'We could just say *au revoir*,' replied Pete, although his gut feeling told him that it was an *adieu*.

It was Connie who called the doctor when Albert was ill. It seemed he'd recovered, but something she couldn't quite put her finger on made her still concerned about him, so she and Nicola decided one of them should check up on him every day.

Being almost midsummer and therefore light, she woke around six thirty. Sitting up in bed, she suddenly realised she'd forgotten to go the day before. Ernie's sudden arrival at teatime, and his and Nicola's acrimonious exchanges, had distracted her, as did her ensuing conversation with her daughter.

'He's not gonna change, Mum,' Nicola'd told her. 'I thought I could change him, but I was a daft cow for thinking that. And besides, Mum, I don't want Darren growing up a villain, and he'd have no chance staying around Ernie and his brothers. I know his constant questions are a pain, but he is clever, Mum, he could go far.'

Perhaps he could, she thought, and lay back down again.

It was only when she went downstairs half an hour later, after washing and dressing, to make herself a pot of tea that she realised that she couldn't hear Albert's radio which, because of his growing deafness, was usually turned up loud. She went into her front garden, but she couldn't hear it from there either. He was normally up by this time, yet his curtains were still drawn. She went through her gate and up to his front door. She knocked and waited.

'Mr Jones,' she called out. 'It's me, Mrs Strachan.'

However, getting no answer, she went back and woke Nicola.

'I'm worried about Mr Jones. I can't hear his radio, and the curtains are still drawn. I went round the front, Nicky. I knocked, but there was no reply. Can you go around the back?'

A protesting Nicola, putting on a large jumper over her nightie and slipping her feet into her flip-flops, trundled downstairs and was quickly through the gap in the hedge and down Albert's garden path. Once by his kitchen door, she knocked gently, but there was no reply. She knocked again more loudly and called out his name.

'Mr Jones, Mr Jones?'

'Well, Nicky?' asked Connie, now the other side of the hedge.

'Shush, Mum, I think I can hear a noise like a groan.'

Pressing her nose up to the kitchen window, she peered in. The room appeared to be empty, but as her eyes panned round it, she saw, poking out from the side of the kitchen table, a slippered foot. Fear engulfed her as she came to an instantaneous realisation that Albert must be lying out of view, on the floor the other side of the table.

'Mr Jones, it's Nicola, are you alright?' she called out, tapping on the window.

There was no reply; the foot didn't move.

'Nicky, what can you see?' Connie asked.

Nicola turned around towards her mother and Connie became greatly alarmed by her expression.

'Mum, you better ring for an ambulance.'

'What is it, Nicola? What's happened?'

'Just call an ambulance, Mum. I'm gonna break in.'

Connie, Nicola and Darren, all still in shock, watched the wailing ambulance with Albert inside turn the corner at the bottom of the street where the dairy had been.

'We better get hold of Pete, but how?' said Nicola,

'Phone that Melanie again,' Connie said. 'She'll know. The library that she works at will be open by nine o'clock.'

It was Pete's last evening in California. Earlier, around four-thirty, Susan invited him for a farewell meal. It was early because Jim had an evening class and Susan work at seven. Brad was also invited but had some prior arrangement, about which he was vague. It was great meal, certainly Brad's loss: a dish with chickpeas, mushrooms and apricots being the main ingredients – a Moroccan dish, Susan said – accompanied by brown rice and a mixed salad. For afters, there was apple pie and the most delicious chocolate-chip ice cream from the parlour up the hill and, naturally, Susan made some brownies.

'Pete, how you planning to get to the airport?' Jim asked him, as they were leaving the apartment.

'I'm going to take the bus.'

'No way,' said Jim, emphatically. 'It's at eleven thirty right, your flight? We're not working. We'll take you, right, sis, okay with you?'

'Absolutely,' said Susan. 'Then we can say a proper goodbye.'

'Well, if you are sure that's—'

'Of course it's alright, Pete,' said Susan, interrupting him. 'It's the least we can do. So what are you going to do now?'

'Oh, I don't know, I gotta call some friends in the city, you know, I'll see.'

'We'll call by for you about nine in the morning. That should give us enough time,' said Jim, now in the car, leaning over from the driver's seat to unlock the door for his sister. 'Hey, jump in, sis! I don't wanna be late this evening. Bye now.'

'Bye, and thanks for the meal. It was… scrumptious,' said Pete, waving from the bottom of the steps.

After watching the car disappearing up the road, he started to climb the steps, but once alone in Brad's apartment, he found himself at a loss as to what to do. Angel Dust was elsewhere, his packing was taken care of and he didn't feel like reading as his mind was very much on his return journey. He was feeling nervous about it, particularly about the changeover in New York, going through immigration. He started to pace around the living room. *Yes, Brad would've enjoyed that meal*, he thought as he moved outside to sit on the top step and, immersed in a pleasant evening breeze, smoke a cigarette. He'd imagined for his last night that he and Brad would've gone out for a drink or to dance.

Once his cigarette was finished, he went back inside. The telephone rang, making him jump out of his skin, but it went dead when he answered it. However, its ringing made him remember that he'd planned to call Kurt and Gene. He'd had no contact with them since he got back from the trip to the desert. He scrounged around in Baz's Pan Am bag looking for the flyer they'd written down their number on. However, they weren't there when he got through.

'Oh no, man, they've gone away. Say, is that the English guy? Pete? Who visited that time? This is Dennis. Remember me?'

'Oh yeah, hi, Dennis, how are you?'

'Groovy, man, now you're not gonna believe this. But Kurt and Gene went down to Southern California and while there they got invited to some Hollywood big-shot's party and you know what, he's only gone and taken them to his place down in Mexico. All expenses paid. Wow, man, imagine, all that peyote they'll be getting. So what have you been doing lately, Pete?'

'Well,' Pete said, hesitantly, 'I've kinda been away myself on an all-expenses-paid trip too.'

'Cool! Where's that?'

'Santa Rita.'

'Where's that? Never heard of it, is it one of the small pretty towns up on the coast, Marin County, somewhere? Hey, Pete, baby, I'm real sorry, but I have to go. Someone's at the door. Maybe I'll get lucky and it's some trade. Listen, call again soon,' Dennis said.

'Well, I'm catching—'

He never finished his sentence as the line went dead.

He could no longer stay in the apartment; he had to go out. Soon he was strolling up the hill. The leaves on overhead trees were rustling in the slight breeze, and as he momentarily looked back behind him, he realised the sun would soon set. His body felt light, his limbs relaxed, one of those rare moments when everything seemed to work properly, like you're walking on air. He realised he was going towards the Rose Garden and with that realisation came a desire to experience the sunset there. Aware that the sun would not wait, he increased his speed. As he climbed the hill, he became fascinated by all the sounds coming from the houses that he passed, the sounds of people chatting softly while sitting on their stoops or talking loud in excited voices coming through the wide-open windows. There was an eclectic miscellany of music, the obvious aromas too, yet weirdly he felt alone on the street.

Reaching the Rose Garden, he was drawn to the bush that so affected Leah, the jingle-jangle girl. He gazed at it for some time, thinking of his grandfather. Yes, its blooms were supremely beautiful. Looking up, he saw the sun was now ready to dive and chose what he thought was the best place to view this clip of celestial cinema. What a fabulous show, this glorious, technicoloured panorama stretching out across the sky before him was! He lowered his eyes from its intensity and saw below a sparkling San Francisco with flickering reflections from moving cars and glinting glass of skyscrapers as they caught the last rays. Then his gaze took in the Golden Gate and Marin County with Mount Tam rising majestically above it while within the perpetual motion of the bay, Alcatraz, in all its eerie isolation, was surrounded by ships and boats with their foamy trails, the specks of port and starboard lights now just becoming visible.

Encompassed by this magic, it was simple to understand how so many people who visited the Bay area for a week ended up there a lifetime. He might have easily, had things been different.

Things? The consequences of jumping bail again dawned on him. By the end of tomorrow, he'd be wanted, an outlaw, all because of a trumped-up charge. Would he never be able to return to this beautiful place? He looked up. The sun was gone; it was becoming dark; only a few red streaks could be seen low down in the western sky. Time to go. He stopped by Leah's rose bush for one final look and picked a bloom, sticking it in his shirt buttonhole, something he always remembered Albert doing. He suddenly felt his grandfather's presence strongly. He shivered.

There was no moon that night, and in the growing darkness, he found himself lost and to get out, started to scale part of the perimeter fence. Hoisting himself up, he was just dropping down to the pavement on the other side when he was blinded by a torch. He lost his footing and went crashing to the ground, landing heavily on his ankle. Looking up, he could just make out the silhouettes of two cops standing over him and, beyond them, their squad car parked across the road. The torch was still pointed right in his face as he struggled to get to feet.

'I swear that's one of the fuckers from the courthouse.'

And a hand came towards him and, with considerable force, pushed his shoulder, and he tumbled down on the ground as the rose fell before his eyes. The cop crushed it underfoot.

'Yeah, and he's some kind of fruit by the looks of it,' the second cop said.

'Hey, hippy trash, on your feet.'

But as Pete started to get up, he was violently pushed again by the first, the larger of the two, and fell to the ground.

'Is he drunk? Or we got a freak here that's out of its head on narcotics? Now what do you think?' his assailant asked his companion.

Pete's face was in line with a large, extended belly. As he struggled back onto his feet, his gaze met the man's eyes. They had a crazy look to them. He had no chance to deflect when the billy club came crashing into his right side. He crumpled up under its impact and fell, yelling, to the ground. A boot went in just as he was curling up.

'Filthy fag,' the voice, above him, bawled.

'Hey, Moe, that's enough, come, leave the motherfucker be now,' the second cop said, anxiously. 'Moe, they're radioing us.'

Pete heard a tinny radio sound coming from their squad car, and as he looked up from his near-foetal position on the dirt, he watched the second cop go to respond to it.

'Okay, Moe, let's go. There's a break-in near the campus,' he cried.

Moe looked down at Pete and, unable to resist, put the boot in once more, before swaggering back to the car. Its engine was now running, the accelerator revving up; once Moe was inside, it sped off.

Pete slowly sat up on his haunches, dropping his head in between his knees and hugging it. He remained like that for some time. Looking up, he glimpsed the Rose Garden gates and started to limp towards them. His ankle was painful and swelling. He had only one thought now: the route to the airport and getting on that plane. When he reached Brad's, he would get his bags, hitch there if he didn't have enough money for a cab; yes, he'd sleep in the terminal building.

He started to walk down the hill. He hurt badly. Halfway back, he saw a car driving up the hill towards him and started to panic. Was it the cops again? He tried to merge into the shadows of a tall tree on the pavement. The car came closer and drew to a halt. As he covered his head with his hands in some lame attempt at self-protection, he heard the door open and close. They must've returned. He froze. Footsteps got closer.

'Say, Pete?' he heard a voice call out. 'Is that you?'

Who was calling his name? It wasn't the cops, but who on earth, on that dark side of a deserted street on the other side of the world from those cliffs and that opal swell, knew his name?

'It *is* you. Say, you alright, dude? What's happened, man?'

He was shit scared now.

'Hey, Pete, man, remember me? It's Henry, Henry Abercrombie, remember, from Santa Rita?'

Pete looked up. He instantly recognised Henry's face.

'Henry, how on earth?' he said, in a barely audible voice.

He was unable to finish the sentence he was so choked up.

'Hey, Pete, what they done to you? Who did this to you, man?'

'Cops,' he muttered though his sobs.

'The cops, I knew it was. We saw a squad car driving off down the road with two evil-looking faces inside as we came up here. Where are you hurt?'

Pete's response was to lose himself in uncontrollable tears.

'It's okay, buddy, just go ahead, let it out.'

Henry turned to his companion.

'Hey, Buster, this is the English dude I's telling you of, remember? Look like the pigs done beat him real good this time. Come. Let's take him to my mom's. She'll tend to him. She should be back from the hospital by now.'

Laverne Jefferson was seated in her porch appreciating the cool, smoky blue night. She'd just got home after her shift at the hospital. Her feet were sore so, kicking off her shoes, she placed them on a small stool in front of her.

There was no cloud cover and no moon, which caused the stars in the sky above her to be bright, twinkling and plentiful. She leant back to observe them. This was something she often did, as it both relaxed her and fed her imagination, causing sweet thoughts to trickle through her mind, inspiring her and preparing her for the next day, when the next full flash of daylight around her would again flush out the world's true colours. For she was a woman who had seen many bad things in her life, so bad they'd be hard for someone to invent, but she'd always kept her faith in God and never allowed herself to feel hate for the perpetrators of those bad actions, and only tried to see good in her fellow human beings. Some of her friends thought her head was too much in the clouds, but better in the clouds than in the sand like an ostrich, she always argued.

She believed that in the clouds there was a better place, a place she would go to one day, where she would be free from all the iniquity which surrounded her and plagued the world, a place where nobody would be denied and all people would be equal. Where, unlike on Earth, nobody would go without.

Yes, everybody would be healed, she liked to believe, and costly treatments and medicine would not be only available to the rich.

The strength of this feeling had been determined long before by what had happened to her sister. Tears could still come to her eyes when she thought of her. For what happened to her sister, her beautiful big sister to whom she'd always looked up, who protected her, was like a second mother to her, was what made Laverne decide to become a nurse.

It was all a hazy memory. She'd been so young when her sister was suddenly taken ill, so she was never quite certain whether the memory of it all was hers or gotten from others. But what she did know was that her sister never should have died. But she had, and she'd died because she was refused entry to a hospital, not because of any lack of money but because it was a whites-only hospital. There was one that admitted blacks, her parents were told, but it happened to be miles away; in fact, too far, as it turned out, for as her parents stood pleading at the hospital gates and were threatened with the police, her sister, there and then, just faded away in front of their eyes.

Things didn't get better after her two eldest brothers came back from fighting for their country against the evils of fascism. And once that war had been won, the country was alerted to another evil: that of communism. What she found strange was that nobody ever seemed to equate those evils with the ones carried out against her own people. Were they blind that they were unable to recognise how the wealth of the nation was built on the backs of the dispossessed and disenfranchised? That liberty had for four hundred years been denied to a significant many?

Now her children told her of evil dictators, who oppressed their own people, in the pockets of US companies, and supported by the CIA in Asia, Africa and South America. And this terrible war, Vietnam, it was devouring too many. All this saddened her because she loved her country, for she was an American and a patriot.

Life was better in California than back home in the South, she had to concede, but with desegregation had come exposure for the children, things from which they'd been protected before until they were of age to understand them. Here in the outside world, perhaps the barbed comments were more stunted, but she knew how to read what a face was saying.

Still, things were changing. When she was a child and her family made visits to relatives and friends in neighbouring states, visits that required a lengthy journey, her daddy would not stop except for gas until they arrived at their destination, while her mother made sure that they had all the food and drink they needed with them for the journey. No one took any chances in those days. One crazy cracker on the road and your life was in their hands. Strangely, though, those journeys she always warmly remembered, because tucked up under those warm covers in the back of her daddy's car, she felt safe. She could still conjure up the aroma, the taste of her mama's shoeboxes packed full of freshly fried chicken, hard-boiled double-yoked eggs and the thirst-quenching freshly made root beer or lemonade.

The sound of a vehicle caused her to look up from her reveries.

A car was turning into the unmade road; its slight skidding caused a cloud of dust to rise from the dry dirt and gravel on its surface. Was that Henry, she wondered?

He should be due back from his drama class by now. Yes, it was, and in what looked like Buster's car. She always let out a silent sigh of relief when her children got home safely. The car drew alongside her porch – yes, it was Henry. She smiled. Her heart lit up. Although she would have never admitted it to anyone, Henry was her favourite of all her five children.

'Hello, oh, Jesus, fucking hell, can you hear me, is that Kensington Library?'

'Yes, how can I help you?' said Mel.

She was somewhat perturbed by the voice at the other end of the line. It was so coarse but strangely familiar.

'Is Mel there?'

'Mel speaking, oh, it's you, Nicola?'

'Yeah, me.'

'What a surprise? I thought I recognised your voice.'

'Mel, I've been trying to get through for fucking ages. I think some old biddy put the phone down on me earlier, the cow. The thing is that we need to get hold of Pete. Something really bad's happened. His granddad's been taken sick. He's in the hospital.'

'Oh no, how terrible, what's wrong with him?'

'We don't know yet, maybe a stroke. He's conscious now, but it's like he doesn't recognise anybody. We found him like that yesterday morning. Are you able to get hold of Pete?'

'Well, he's due back the day after tomorrow actually. Baz and I plan to drive up to Manchester this evening as Baz has got some biz up there and we'll stay over and pick him up. Listen, I'll try and call him. It's a bit difficult from the library, but I got a friend who works for the international telephone exchange.'

'Listen, Mel, tell him not to worry.'

'I will, and I'll get Baz to drive him down there. What's the name of the hospital they've taken him to?'

'They said he'll be going to Stockfield in the next day or so.'

'What kind of hospital is that?'

'It's a geriatric hospital, Mel.'

'Oh, I see,' said Mel, then, lowering her voice to a whisper, she continued, 'Nicola, I got some bad news too. Pete was arrested in California.'

'Naw, you gotta be fucking joking,' exclaimed Nicola. 'What, Pete? You're having me on.'

'No, it's true, he was on some demonstration. You know, those pigs there are diabolical. It sounded like they just grabbed anybody they could. I don't know too much about it. Listen, I got your mum's number. The head librarian here is a right Hitler. She's spotted me and is coming over to have a go, no doubt. Love to your mum and Darren.'

And with that Mel promptly placed receiver back in its cradle.

During her elevenses break, Mel sneaked out and found a phone box on Kensington High Street. She dialled the friend who worked in the international exchange. She was lucky. He was there, and once she'd given him the number, he told her to hang up and wait for his return call. Her wait in the box made her nervous as an elderly man outside started to mutter, and despite her opening the door to tell him that she was waiting for the operator to call her back, he displayed much annoyance. Consequently, she nearly jumped out of her skin when the phone started ringing.

'Hello,' she said. 'Is that Brad? It's Mel.'

'Mel, is that you? Yes, it's me,' a breathless voice replied.

'Sorry, I just ran up the steps to get to the phone in time. Mel?'

'Brad, it is you?'

'Yes, Mel, it's me. How are you?'

'Well, I was alright till Baz told me all about it, about Pete and everything.'

Brad did not reply immediately. The line was crackling and their voices were reverberating and echoing over each other and he was unsure as to what Mel had meant.

'Baz told you? What? I didn't quite hear,' he enquired.

'About Pete's arrest, is he there?'

'No, he's not back yet. I'm not sure where he is. I know he went to dinner downstairs earlier. I've only just got home.'

'I know I'll see him in a couple of days, but I just had a call from Nicola. It's all rather worrying as his grandfather is in hospital. Sounds pretty serious. Can you tell him about it and also tell him we'll meet him at the airport?'

'Oh, that's too bad, sure, but not too serious, okay, of course I'll tell Pete,' said Brad.

The phone suddenly went dead and Mel wasn't sure whether Brad had put it down or whether she was cut off. She was perplexed as she'd wanted to ask Brad more about Pete's arrest. Her brow knitted up in frustration as she put down the phone. Leaving the telephone box, she smiled at and profusely apologised to the old man and made her way back to the library.

'You're late,' said the Dragon Librarian as Mel squeezed herself in behind the counter. 'We've had a rush. I could have done with you here. You know, I do despair of you, Melanie. You'll never make a proper librarian.'

'Like you, Miss McPherson. God, I hope not,' Mel said, under her breath.

'Good evening, Miss Jefferson.'

'Why, good evening, Buster. So how are you?'

Laverne Jefferson drew out every word whenever she enquired after someone's health, especially the last. It had the effect of making the person she was addressing feel like they were her only *you* in the world.

'I am fine, Miss Jefferson. And how are you?' replied Buster, with a slight bow of his head.

'Well, after a shift at the hospital and at my age, I can't complain,' she answered, flashing Buster with such a smile that it gave him a sudden insight into what a pretty young girl she'd once been.

'Why, Buster? Who that white boy getting out the car wit' Henry?'

'He called Pete, Miss Jefferson, the English boy Henry met when he was—'

'Oh yes, I remember now.'

She intentionally cut Buster off as the very mention of gaol was abhorrent to her. She was relieved the case against Henry was dismissed, trumped up as it was, and happy that he was left with no further blemish on his character. She raised all her children to tell the truth, despite all the lies surrounding them, and to respect other human beings, regardless of who they were, but it had been a hard fight for her because of many external pressures.

She found young folks these days were sorely tempted, and perhaps gave in more easily to temptation, partly, she often wondered, because there seemed to be more for them to be tempted by. Why, even just now, she'd heard through a member of her church that the mafia were starting to peddle hard drugs big time in the Bay Area, targeting black youth; caught between the mob, gangs and the cops, it seemed they were now.

She'd been young once and liked to enjoy herself, had loved to dance and stay out all night long, and knew how easy it was for someone to lose themselves without care, to get hooked, get a habit. She'd seen it and seen people who profited from the pushing too, seen how they had no scruples whatsoever. She saw it all in Kansas City when, as a young girl starting out in life, she got a job cleaning in a jazz club frequented by the local mob boss.

He took a real shine to her, developed an obsession about her. It chilled her to the bone because she'd heard such things about him. So scared she was that she quickly got the bus out of town and settled in Chicago, and that was where she met Henry's father. They fell in love, married and went back down South. They had a good life together but sadly he died young. She only moved to California after she was widowed for a second time. They took the bus the entire way.

She watched as Henry led Pete up the stoop of her wooden one-storey house and introduced him to her. She greeted him warmly with a hug, noting his flinching. She liked what she heard from Henry about him, but as Pete came within the bright light of her living room, Laverne noticed he was injured.

'You been in a fight?' she asked him, severely.

Pete started to stutter a reply, but Henry came to his rescue, explaining how Buster and he came across him by the side of the road trying to make his way back to where he was staying.

'The cops did it, Mother.'

Laverne frowned.

'He didn't want to see no doctor, Mother. I don't think there's anything broken, but perhaps you can check him over.'

Laverne let out a heavy sigh and then started to take charge. Henry, she asked to fetch her first aid box, get some disinfectant and boil some water, while she began to examine Pete's ankle, shoulder and then the bruise on his side. She confirmed what her son said and, once he'd returned with what she'd requested, gently started to bathe and clean Pete's cuts and grazes, after which she administered some healing balm to his bruises.

'You all hungry?' Laverne asked them from the kitchen once she was finished and had put away her first aid kit. 'I got fried chicken, some potato salad, or macaroni cheese, okra… now let's see. Ooh, it was a good thing I called in at the store after work.'

'I'm real hungry,' said Buster.

'You's always hungry,' said Henry. 'How about you, Pete?'

Was he hungry? He wasn't sure. He was still in a state of shock, although the warm environment to which he'd been led was already creating a marked distance from his earlier experiences. But, thinking he was imposing on Henry and his family, he suggested he should go back to Brad's because of having to take the plane in the morning.

Laverne was having none of it, insisting that at least he ate before he left. And the table was laid and, once the food was brought in, the smell of it really cranked up Pete's appetite. Ushered to the table, he took his place. Once everybody was served, Pete's hand was just about to reach for the fork when he noticed that Laverne, Henry and Buster's heads were bowed.

'Say now who's going say grace? Perhaps our guest would like to?' Laverne asked Pete, smiling.

Pete quickly drew back his hand and put it on his lap as his mind went suddenly blank and a feeling of shame washed over him. Saying grace was not something that Albert and Zénaïde had done at meal times when he was growing up. They kept their thanks for when they were in places like their orchard or during visits to the wild strawberry wood. So as he racked his brain, feeling awkward, he heard the silence loudly all around him for what seemed like the longest time. But then came inspiration as a far-ago voice rang in his memory, the voice of Zénaïde's cousin Marie-Thérèse, the only true Catholic of *la famille Collin*, saying grace in the dining room of the house by the dunes where he went often as a child. How he and his cousins Françoise and Jean-Luc used to mimic her! Of course, it was in French. After he'd finished, Laverne lifted up her head slowly and smiled at Pete.

'Well, that sure was pretty, but what does it mean?' she asked. 'Oh, please get started.'

As the four of them picked up their knives and forks and began to eat, Pete told them about Zénaïde and about her raising him, her being French and how he remembered the grace from when he was a boy on a visit to relatives in France and translated it for them.

'Well, I say,' exclaimed Laverne. 'Just wait till I tell Miss Maxine about this. She's a lady from my church. I can't wait to tell her I had a handsome young gentleman from Europe come up here in my house, and he say grace in the French language. I hope you like the food, Peter?'

'Oh yes, it's delicious.'

He definitely had an appetite, now. He felt he was eating away not only the memory of the previous few hours, but the utter confusion in him caused by his arrest and the disappointment of things not working out with Brad.

More still, despite being in a strange place, he felt he was in familiar surroundings. He couldn't put his finger on it, but it was like he was home again in the house under the downs or the house by the dunes. Back in an environment of loving, tranquillity, something that he'd missed for over two years now since Zénaïde's sudden death.

As they all exchanged family anecdotes and sat about laughing in tremendous harmony, he became excited about seeing his grandfather again and visualised telling him of his adventures, leaving nothing out. He would not lie to Albert. He would be straight with him about his sexuality. The old man, he felt, would be philosophical about it, he was sure of that, and he'd be bound to have some appropriately ancient saying. Yes, when he got back to Manchester, the first thing he would do would be to hitch back home. Yes, in fact, he would go back and live with Albert, get his work together, develop his new ideas, renovate his old darkroom in the shed. Yes, it would work out somehow.

From the welcome table, they moved over to the upright piano on the opposite side of Laverne's parlour. Laverne played a few songs, some jazz standards, a couple of gospel tunes, which Henry and Buster joined in with. When she finished, she turned to Pete, enquiring if he could play.

'Well, I took lessons when young, but—'

'Play something then,' she said, with a coaxing smile.

'I don't know if I can remember anything. I used to read music. I'm no good at playing by ear,' Pete replied, nervously.

'But you must remember something,' Henry said.

'Well,' Peter replied, sitting down on the chair in front of the piano, 'I do sort of remember this one.'

He proceeded to thump out while singing in a somewhat faltering voice the first verse and chorus of 'Plaisir d'amour'. The applause that he got afterwards he felt was unmerited.

Because he was now very aware that it was late, he asked Henry if he had a number for a cab. However, Laverne and Henry insisted he slept there. A compact sofa bed beneath the wall, on which there was a richly woven portrait of Dr Martin Luther King about the size of a Muslim prayer rug, was rolled out to the middle of the floor. Bedding was conjured up, and under Dr King's watchful eyes, Pete soon fell into a deep, restful slumber.

The next morning, after a filling breakfast, Henry and Buster insisted on driving Pete back to Brad's. Pete thanked Laverne, who enfolded him in her arms as she said goodbye. She could be seen waving from her porch, watching the car as it made its way down the dirt road until it was out of view.

'It's the turning on the right just after Harry Ramsden's and then up two blocks,' Pete told Buster as they came up Shattuck Avenue. Buster swung the car over into the inside lane, and with the lights luckily being green he swiftly turned into Brad's street and started to cruise up the hill.

'Yeah, here on the left, that's it.'

The car drew to a halt alongside the pavement in front of the apartment.

'Wow, well,' said Pete. 'You know, thank you both for everything, thank you, I don't know what I would've done.'

'Hey, Pete, that's cool, it's nothing. Listen, what's your address? You never know, man,' said Henry.

'I'll give you my grandfather's address.'

Henry found a ballpoint and they exchanged addresses and numbers. The parting was poignant as Pete felt quite melancholy at the prospect of leaving Henry just as he was getting to know him.

'Hey, Pete, remember now what I say, keep the faith,' Henry said, once they'd said their goodbyes. Buster turned the engine back on, started off up the hill while Pete remained motionless on the pavement, watching the car as it disappeared.

'Oh, there you are, Pete. I was just coming up to get you.'

Pete turned to see Jim just coming out of his apartment.

As Pete walked toward him he noticed that he was limping.

'Say, Pete, what happened?'

'Long story, I'll tell you on the way to the airport. Are you ready to go?'

'More or less, Susan's just out of the shower.'

'Okay, I'll go up, get my clobber and be right back,' Pete said.

He turned in the direction of the outside staircase and, as he did, looked up at the apartment and saw Brad draw away from his bedroom window. When he got inside, Brad was in the kitchen in the process of brewing some coffee.

'Who were those guys in the car?' he asked in a suspicious tone.

'Henry, you know, I told you about him. He's was in Santa Rita. And his friend Buster. I was over his mum's house.'

'You didn't say he was black.'

Pete looked at him and smiled.

'Listen, Jim's waiting. We'll have to say goodbye,' he said.

They hugged, both knowing there was so much left unsaid.

'You know, it has been great, it really has, despite, you know… thank you, Brad,' Pete said.

'You know, I'm sorry if I—'

'Don't be.'

'Maybe see you in London next year?'

Pete was thrown by this. He smiled and nodded. Jim was hooting by now so, picking up his bags, his jacket and swinging them over his shoulder, he gave Brad one last hug and then hurried out the door. Loading his baggage into the trunk of Jim's car he slipped in the front passenger's seat beside him. He turned to greet Susan in the back. She beamed back at him and handed him a doobie. Jim started to ease out from between two tightly parked cars and then, as he was getting to ready to accelerate, there was a sudden knocking on Pete's window. He looked around and, seeing Brad, rolled down the window.

'Pete, I forgot to tell you, but Mel called up last night. I think she said they'll meet you at the airport and, oh yes, apparently your grandfather is ill. But it's not serious.'

'Pete, Pete, coo-ee. We're over here,' Mel cried out.

'Melanie, he'll see you soon enough, behave, won't you?' Baz snapped. He was easily embarrassed by Mel's spontaneous behaviour, the way that she always showed what she felt.

'Don't be so stroppy, Baz. Coo-ee, Pete?'

'Tone it down, Melanie, won't you, for Christ's sake, people are watching us.'

They were, but not because of her voice or even her jumping up and down. Many were doing exactly the same as they tried to catch the attention of those they were meeting as the crowd of weary travellers began to emerge from through customs. No, the attention she drew to herself was caused by her brightly coloured, embroidered Afghan wedding dress which Baz had bought her on a recent trip. Quite oblivious to all this scrutiny, Mel, smiling and with furrowed brow, excitedly ran over and extracted Pete, like a piece of a luggage from the carousal, from being swept to the exit by a group of loud, tartan-trousered American golfers who were asking, anyone and everyone how far it was to the Royal Liverpool Golf Course.

There had been no mishaps on the flights or during the stopover. No sinister-looking, dark-shaded-eyed agents poked up their heads over the potted plants or cacti in the airport lounge and tried to apprehend Pete while he was making his escape from those pearly shores streaked with foam. Yet once high above the Atlantic, a sense of relief flowed through him and, excited about arriving home as well as being confused about Brad's parting shot, he was unable to read, to concentrate on anything or sleep, so he just sat back and scrutinised the beauty of the heavens.

'Hi, Mel, I wasn't sure if you were coming,' he said, after receiving an extended hug from her. 'I was thinking that I'd have to hitch or something. Is Baz here?'

Baz moved up behind him.

'Of course, you dozy cunt,' he said.

'Oh, am I glad to see you, Pete, and relieved to know you're safe,' Mel said, once she'd let him out of her grasp. 'Wow, you look so tanned – in fact, you look really well.'

'It's the sun, cycling and the outdoor life.'

'But, Pete, why are you limping? And how did you get those bruises?'

'Long story, I'll tell you later.'

They started to make their way to the car park. As they came out of the terminal building, Pete clocked the difference in the quality of the light. After countless days of Californian sunshine, the sky seemed so different, opaque, a monotonous grey colour, dull yet luminous and causing him to screw up his eyes and squint. Once in the car park, he stood still for an instant, taken aback by the familiar sight of the VW bus as it brought back so many memories. Baz slid open the door and started to haul Pete's luggage inside.

'Oh, shit, Baz, you know what?' Pete said. 'I've left your Pan Am bag at Brad's. I'm really sorry. It was too late when I realised it in the car to the airport. If we'd have gone back I'd have missed the plane.'

'No worries, mate,' replied Baz, winking.

They all clambered up onto the front seat. Baz wheeled the van out of the car park and they were soon driving south.

'Mel, I'm a bit confused,' Pete said, after a period of silence. 'Just as I was leaving Brad told me that you called saying that my grandfather was ill? But he said it wasn't serious. Is it the same bug?'

'No, Pete, it's not. I actually told him the opposite,' said Mel.

'What? I didn't think I misheard him, but we were in a rush so—'

'But, Pete, don't worry. I rang Mrs Strachan before we left and she'd just been to visit him in the hospital and—'

'Hospital?' Pete was suddenly confused. 'But Brad never said—'

'He's alright, Pete. As I said, I spoke to Mrs Strachan and Nicola. They said he's stable, but it's early days yet. Apparently he's had some kind of stroke and needs lots of rest. But it doesn't seem to be life-threatening. That's all she knew. We're going to drive you down there now. Right, Baz?'

'Yes, Doll.'

'Are you sure? I could get the train,' suggested Pete.

'No, we'll take you. You get some rest. There's a pillow and sleeping bag in the back.'

'Yeah, I think I might, but first, Baz, I do need to ask you a favour. You're not able to lend me eighty quid so I can pay back Brad the bail money? I'll give it back as soon as I get a job.'

'No sweat. See it as done. In fact, it is done.'

'What?'

'Didn't Brad tell you?'

'No.'

'Oh, maybe it came through after you left.'

'No, it was before, surely,' Mel interjected. 'Yeah, you know, Pete, I said when I called that Brad left a message at Tiny's after you were arrested and Baz called—'

'Oh, that's what you were saying? It's really weird. He didn't tell me. How come he had Tiny's number?'

'I gave it him,' said Baz. 'When we drove to Frankfurt last year, I thought that if he wanted to get in touch… you know… Tiny's like my telephone service.'

Pete was too tired to enquire further. He yawned.

'Pete, get in the back. Get some shut-eye,' Mel suggested.

'Well, thanks, Baz. You'll get the bread back, I promise. Yeah, I think I'll sleep now.'

He climbed over the front seat, rolling onto the sleeping bag as he heard Mel say, 'But, Baz, I thought you only called Brad once. Now I'm confused as well.'

'Oh, Mel, whatever, don't get your knickers in a twist – once, twice, what does it matter, Doll?'

'Can we go straight to the hospital?' Pete asked, but before Mel's reply came he was fast asleep.

The only time Pete opened his eyes, he found he'd been sweating and they were in London driving down Park Lane, but he went straight back to sleep and didn't awake again until they arrived.

PART THREE

Dans L'opale de Toute L'immensité

As they walked up the ward, the stench, which hit them when entering, grew even stronger. Mel's brow furrowed up with disdain; even Baz seemed perturbed.

'Jesus, don't they fucking clean this gaff or what?' he said.

The stench was a combination of urine and faeces laced with disinfectant. Halfway up the ward, Mel started to cry.

'How can human beings be treated like this?' she said through sobs. 'I expected a Nightingale ward but not to go back to Victorian times too.'

Pete was speechless. The ward was vast. There were at least fifty beds, each occupied by an old man, some looking already expired. A cacophony of snores, groans and yells echoed around them, words repeated like a stylus stuck in the groove.

'Help me, somebody help me?' one shouted out.

Mel stopped in her tracks, her initial reaction to start towards him, but turning around to see whether help was coming from another source, she caught the eye of the male nurse whom they had met on their arrival in the ward and directed them to Albert's bed.

'Don't bother, deary. That one shouts all the time,' he bellowed out.

On reaching Albert's bed, Pete was shocked to find his condition worse than he'd imagined. Seemingly lifeless, face sunken, his teeth were displayed on the bedside cabinet for the world to see. He was almost unrecognisable, this old, shrunken man propped up by pillows supported by a metal frame wearing a soiled bib. Some device seemed to be holding the blankets up over his legs and feet, its sheer size making him seemed tiny, submerged. Pete had never seen his grandfather look vulnerable before. But his gaze then took in the familiar shock of thick, white hair and the prominent nose, those features that were a beacon to him as a child, and a sense of normality returned. He drew up a chair to the bed; Baz and Mel stood behind him. They'd seen Albert the previous month. No way was this the man who'd regaled them with stories and jokes when they'd so recently visited that tearoom together.

'Granddad, it's Peter,' Pete said, leaning over and taking the old man's hand.

Albert didn't respond. Despite his eyes being open, he displayed no recognition of his grandson.

'Granddad, it's Peter,' he said, this time a little louder. 'And here's Mel and Baz.'

As he drew up his chair nearer to the bed, he inadvertently let go of Albert's hand, causing it to flop over the edge of one of the metal bed-guards. Alarmed, he took Albert's hand again in his and stroked it.

'I'm here now, Granddad, and I'll stay, and you know what? You're going to get better.'

He started to feel a slight pressure coming from Albert's hand as he looked up into those dark brown eyes, and for an instant he felt he saw traces of that familiar twinkle. Yes, Albert did know he was there. A feeling of hope rose up in him. Mel saw it too and nodded. Pete looked up at Albert once more, their eyes met and this time he was convinced there was recognition.

'I'll have to ask you to leave,' said a voice loudly behind them, causing Pete to jump. Baz began to remonstrate with him, but Pete acquiesced and, pressing Albert's hand, leant over and kissed his forehead.

'I'll return tomorrow, Granddad,' he said. 'No, Baz, let's go.'

Walking back down the aisle through the geriatric chorus, he suddenly felt exhausted. So much had happened in the course of the last forty-eight hours. It was a relief to get outside, away from the stench, and breathe in the fresh air coming from off the Opal Causeway.

'You know, Mel,' he said, as Baz strode off to unlock the van door, 'it is so weird how communication can suddenly be cut, just like that. Like, being in Santa Rita, I was stuck there for three days without being able to contact anybody, hemmed in by both a physical and invisible wall. Yes, that was just weird, you're so powerless, but that someone can become a prisoner within themselves, is no longer able to talk and you've no idea whether they can think, well, that never occurred to me before. Mémé just died talking and, sad as it was, there was time to say goodbye, but with my granddad, it is like he is neither here nor there. What kind of world is he in now?'

The following day, after waving off Baz and Mel, he went over to Connie's. Darren opened the door. He was overjoyed to see Pete. Besides him was a little puppy, a new addition to his menagerie of two gerbils and the goldfish.

'He's a present from my dad. He's called Apollo, after the space mission,' he said.

Apollo was a curious-looking mutt. It was difficult to work out his scrambled pedigree.

'Yeah, and Mum went ballistic when we turned up with him,' said Nicola, appearing behind Darren. 'But she eventually relented when Darren promised he'd clean up after him. Hey, great to see you. I missed you. We've been worried. Here, give us a hug.'

Connie now came into the hallway.

'Hello, Peter. I didn't knock earlier,' she said. 'I thought I'd better let you sleep.'

'I was probably awake, Mrs Strachan. I woke up early. Jetlag,' said Pete. 'Besides, I had to see Mel and Baz off.'

'Oh, they gone back to London already?' Nicola asked. 'I'd have liked to have seen them.'

'Sorry, Nicknick, Mel said to say hi and hopes to see you soon.'

'You had breakfast?' Connie asked.

'No.'

'Well, come into the kitchen, we're about to have ours.'

During breakfast Connie and Nicola told Pete how they found Albert on the kitchen floor.

'I worried about him after he came down with that virus,' Connie said.

'The thing is, Mrs Strachan, I don't even understand what exactly is wrong with him. There was nobody at the hospital to ask, well, only an orderly and an unfriendly nurse.'

'Oh, him, he's fucking useless. And nasty with it,' Nicola said, while the expression on her mother's face complemented that sentiment.

'Very unpleasant, he was, and unhelpful when we visited after Mr Jones was moved there. You'll have to find a doctor, consultant, they call them, to ask,' Connie said. 'The name should be written above his bed. Maybe if you went up earlier when they're doing their rounds, you'd find someone to talk to. They said it were something to do with the arteries leading to his brain.'

Despite being jetlagged, Pete determined, as soon as he finished breakfast, to go to the hospital. It was a long journey, two buses, and there was a fair wait between them. Waiting at the second bus stop, he became disheartened, but once on the second bus and up on the top deck, he could see the sea far below, their Opal Causeway – his, Albert's and Zénaïde's – and it raised his spirits, strengthened his resolve.

But alas, there was neither doctor nor consultant with whom he could discuss Albert's condition that day, and it was only a week later that a consultant telephoned him. But the conversation confused more than clarified things. Albert's condition was called cerebral arteriosclerosis; apparently the arteries in the brain were blocked, causing a number of small strokes and dementia. Pete was at a loss to understand it. Why was Albert no longer able to use his limbs or unable to talk, he asked?

'Perhaps he'll make progress; he could get better, walk and talk again, but on the other hand, maybe he might not,' the consultant said, in such a way that Pete could imagine him shrugging his shoulders.

Not long after that, when visiting his grandfather one afternoon, a nurse whom Pete hadn't seen before told him in a quite brutal manner that he didn't think the old man was long for this world. The tea trolley was on its way round at the time and, at the sound of it, Albert stirred, his movements becoming quite animated. Pete raised him up on the pillows, fed him cake and helped him drink his tea while the nurse looked on astounded.

You don't know him, thought Pete, as he removed crumbs from Albert's chest. Their eyes met and Pete knew Albert recognised him. It seemed as if he were about to say something as his lips started to move. However, nothing audible came, and after that great effort, he sank into the mattress as if exhausted, eyes glazed, small and wizened again.

However, after Pete got up to leave and was half down the aisle, he heard Albert swearing. He rushed back to the side of the bed, but by that time, Albert had retreated. The nurse wasn't impressed by this outburst, but what Pete didn't realise till some time later was that Albert was prone to having shouting fits, bellowing out swearwords Pete never heard him utter before.

Was he was trying to kickstart himself, Pete wondered? Because when he'd witnessed for the first time one of these outbursts, he could see the frustration in the old man, like as if he was angry with himself for not being able to form words or use his limbs. However, there were other times when Pete visited and the old man, with dribble running from the corner of his mouth, was morosely silent, like at death's door, his breathing laboured. It was only later that Pete discovered he was sedated with largactil. Pete became increasingly unhappy with his care but didn't know what to do about it. It was Connie who suggested to go and speak to Albert's GP.

'He's a nice man,' she said. 'He has time for people.'

Pete hadn't visited the surgery for some years. Dr Crammond had been his doctor as a child and he always remembered those soothing hands examining him when he had some childhood ailment. Not only sympathetic and understanding about Albert's condition, but also of the predicament in which Pete now found himself too, he was also more forthcoming than anybody at Stockfield. He patiently explained, and in lay terms too. But Dr Crammond's explanation caused the grim reality of Albert's condition to hit Pete and he began to realise there was little chance of improvement. But how long his near-vegetable-like existence would last, Dr Crammond couldn't say.

'Obviously I can't use this as a diagnosis, but I truly do believe that Albert's condition is caused by a broken heart,' he said.

He'd treated Zénaïde in her last days and knew of the couple's devotion to each other.

In the autumn, Pete took the ferry across the Opal Causeway to attend a funeral. Germaine, Zénaïde's niece, had telephoned to tell him of the death of Solange, their elderly cousin and sister of Marie-Thérèse. This news brought back memories of joyful days of childhood shared with his cousins, either spent in the house by the dunes during the summer holidays, or in the house under the Downs.

For him and his cousins, and for Nicola too, both the unusually tall Solange and the diminutive Marie-Thérèse always seemed young. Solange was constantly singing and both sisters played with them on the beach, made sandcastles and swam, activities which the other adults copped out of. And it was in their apartment, on the *rue Bonaparte*, on the *rive gauche*, full of interesting books, pictures and other beautiful artefacts, where Pete decided to go to art school.

It was an exceptionally fine St Luke's summer's day on which he travelled, and as the ferry glided across the calm, flat sea, with countless seagulls pursuing its foamy trail, Pete recalled that first ever crossing with Zénaïde, on their way to visit her sick mother, and how she pointed out to him all the tones and hues in the water surrounding them, comparing them to her opal brooch. She'd also recounted stories of ancient seafarers such as Jean Bart, Eustace the Monk and the Sea Beggars. Then there had been a cool wind, and they sat, to get away from it, close to the funnel, attracted by the warmth coming from it. But now, the ferry was so much larger; the funnel no longer accessible.

As he watched Shakespeare Cliff disappear and kept a look out for Cap Gris Nez, it dawned on him that he'd not visited *L'Hexagone* since Zénaïde's death. Had he been avoiding the land of Marianne because of it? Had he inadvertently blamed the country for her death? For it'd been at Vence, in Matisse's chapel, where she first was taken ill, and that journey back held painful memories for him. Had that experience propelled him on a furtive search for something different and had subsequently taken him far, far beyond?

But he found it was like coming home when he got there. They were all there: Marie-Thérèse, Germaine, her parents Uncle Gaston and Aunt Ghislaine, divorced for nearly twenty years yet still not talking, Germaine's husband Jean-Daniel and children, Françoise and Jean-Luc. Jean-Luc was halfway through his doctorate in philosophy at Nanterre, while Françoise, it turned out, had just returned from teaching in Rufisque, a town in Senegal, but she was planning to go back there to work as a sound engineer with local musicians. Her stories and photographs were fascinating, and for a moment, remaining in France tempted him, but after two days, with Germaine promising to come and visit Albert very soon, it was back to his duty.

It was on the crossing back that he decided on his new project, a photographic study of the Opal Causeway. Of course, his subjects wouldn't solely be human like the work of Chauncey Hare, but who was it that said *Environments inhabit us?* He needed to seriously consider the themes, but the thought of it excited him.

The day after his return, when he visited Albert, he told him in great detail all about the visit, conveying the warm greetings from the family. Albert was now managing to say a few words, although disjointed, and Pete never quite knew what the old man took in, but on the return voyage, he decided to broach the subject of his sexuality. And on that day, Albert seemed quite lucid, so the moment seemed right.

'Granddad, I have to tell you something. I like men, I'm gay,' he said, inwardly cursing his clumsiness. 'You know, what your generation would've called queer... or pansy.'

Albert's eyes seemed distant for a second, but there then came a flicker of recognition, an understanding. He struggled to speak: 'I... I... I know. Z... Z... Zinny... told me. I... I... I... know.'

'But when?' he asked, gobsmacked.

'A... A... After... visit... when she fell... visit to ch... ch... chapel. Said sh... sh... she known for a l... l... long time.'

'She knew?'

'Yes... s, you s... s... see, first husband was...'

Albert's flow was interrupted by coughing. Pete lifted him up and, pumping up the pillows behind him, got a spittoon from the bedside cabinet and leant the old man over it. When he was finished, Albert sank back on the pillow, exhausted and looking confused. It was gone, that sudden clarity, and a blank look was again on his face.

'Granddad, I do love you,' Pete said, leaning over to kiss the old man's forehead.

Albert's right hand reached out and, with a force that Pete thought he'd long lost, tightly grabbed his grandson's left hand. And then he promptly fell asleep. It was only with great difficulty that, five minutes later, Pete was able to extricate his hand.

Germaine was good to her promise and visited for *La Toussaint*, All Saints' Day, bringing with her Marie-Thérèse, Françoise and Jean-Luc. They stayed until the day after Bonfire Night, making two visits to Albert.

His face beamed on seeing them. Pete wondered whether he thought Germaine was Zénaïde, for, as Connie remarked, she'd become more like her aunt as she got older. Pete found it uncanny; he'd never seen the resemblance when Zénaïde was living, but Germaine now seemed a dead ringer for her; her mannerisms, the line of the neck were the same. She was wearing the opal brooch which Zénaïde had left her in her will.

Nicola was well chuffed to see Françoise again and they paired off as they had when children, secreting themselves in corners chatting away.

The day before Bonfire Night Connie suggested they go to Canterbury. She liked to shop there and, with Christmas was coming up, she had a list. So after walking a sulky Darren to school, the seven of them made their way down to the bus station.

Once in the city, Pete and Jean-Luc, having no wish to shop, left Connie, Marie-Thérèse, Germaine and the girls to wander down St Peter's Street to Lefèvre's.

They themselves were determined to be drawn into antiquity, and after walking slowly along the old town walls while Jean-Luc explained some of the complicated theories which abounded in his *philo* studies and Pete told his cousin of his experiences in California, Bell Harry Tower suddenly beckoned them and they ended up in the cathedral.

Neither of them had visited the Gothic giant since childhood and they walked around the building awestruck by it. The organ was thundering out as they walked along the central aisle in the nave and Pete was transfixed by the ambience. He felt as if it was the first time he'd visited the cathedral, marvelling at the inspirational symmetry, the beauty of both the stain glass and carving. As he passed ancient tombs with inscriptions of names that could be either of French or English origin, he thought back to a time when the sea was less of a barrier, which naturally made him think of Albert and Zénaïde.

It was at the martyrdom that he decided. As a child, he'd spent much time longingly staring across the Opal Causeway. After Zénaïde's death, for some reason, he couldn't look across, averted his eyes while he found himself drawn to, and distracted by, other far-off places like America, a country which he now wondered was not hurtling itself towards spontaneous combustion. No, it was time to cross over the Opal Causeway again; it all made such sense. He desired, at least for the time being, a different, non-Anglo-Saxon way of expression, to be freed of Anglo-Saxon prejudices. Yes, when he was able, he would live in France, he vowed.

During her visit, he wanted to ask Germaine about Zénaïde's first husband – what his grandfather said had made him curious – but the opportunity didn't arise. There was an opportunity when alone with Marie-Thérèse, for she would have known, but he didn't even consider broaching the subject with her as she liked to talk about the niceties of life. For her, distasteful or deemed-to-be private topics were brushed under the carpet and kept there. However, he did talk to Françoise and Jean-Luc about his Opal Causeway project. They were well into it.

'You know, Petey,' said Françoise, 'you should have a soundtrack.'

'Soundtrack?'

'But yes. It would enhance it. I am up for it; you know, sounds associated with being on or by the sea. I could do some recordings our side and then come over to you for a few days. I got time before I return to Senegal next year. It'll be cool, doncha think?'

'Wow, yes.'

Waving them off from the Prince of Wales pier, Pete felt sad. Their departure left him feeling fretful about the future. As he reclaimed the empty house, he wondered, despite Françoise's enthusiasm, whether he'd be able to get his project off the ground. Would he still be able to tap that inspiration he'd had in California? Because one thing was certain, he would stay near to Albert, endeavouring to visit him every day. For as long as it took, he would see it out. But he became increasingly concerned by the fact that he now had little money. He still owed Baz eighty quid. He would have to get a job. But therein lay a dilemma. Visiting times were afternoon only. If he worked nine-to-five, he'd only have the weekends for visiting. But he couldn't leave the old man alone for five consecutive days in that place. He'd be failing in his duties. In any case the Sunday bus service was abysmal while Albert's old Austin Seven, though in the garage, was apparently irreparable, even if he could've afforded it.

It was Nicola who came up with a solution. They were sitting down on the shingle beach one afternoon in late November, taking in a rare burst of sunshine while lamenting the line of plastic cups washed ashore which they knew were part of the refuse cast overboard from ferries, now china cups no longer were used.

'You know, Petey,' she said.

'I know what, Nicknick?'

'I was thinking, why don't you get a job with the mail? A postie, you're bound to get one this time of year; they might keep you on after Christmas. You start early, finish by dinnertime. That gives you afternoons free, you visit Granddad, and what's more...' she grinned at this point, '...they'll give you a fucking bike and you can use it to get up to the hospital.'

'Nicknick, that's a fantastic idea!'

And that was exactly what he did, and it allowed him to go and visit Albert nearly every day, staying for the full two hours without worrying that he would miss the bus.

One reason why he felt he should regularly see Albert, was to check he was getting proper care. A few times he'd found his grandfather in a soggy condition or worse, and it seemed some of the hospital staff were happy for him to be there doing stuff as they were understaffed. He also worried the old man wasn't properly fed. He started to take in tasty morsels to tempt his grandfather: pieces of fruit and little cakes, pies and jellies, and fish paste sandwiches with the crust cut away. He soon found himself often helping to feed other patients. Most staff were grateful to him, but others, like the nurse who'd been on that first day, were resentful.

It was Connie who advised him to lookout for bedsores. Bedsores, she said, were a sign of bad nursing, could become gangrenous. He imagined the nursing staff turned Albert at regular intervals when he wasn't there, but he decided to do himself, all the same, checking for any tell-tale signs. He was reticent at first to do something so intimate to his grandfather, but this procedure, as well as putting him on a bedpan and holding a bottle in the right place for him to urinate, soon became a regular part of his visits: normal and necessary.

Gradually, Pete's daily routine started to level out. He resurrected his makeshift darkroom which he'd first used a teenager in the garden shed and really got down to his Opal Causeway project. He was having that many ideas that, if he didn't make notes, he could easily forget them. He planned to create a circular panorama portraying the 360-degree horizon of the Opal Causeway as shot from somewhere in the middle – well, more or less. Nicola had a fisherman friend who'd take them out. He *would* call it *Environments inhabit us*. After rummaging around in a few tucked-away boxes, he'd located an old *Cinéma* magazine from *Octobre 1961* and found the quote in an interview with filmmaker Agnès Varda. Maybe she'd even come! Now that was a thought!

Shingle-patterned lino, a kitsch element, yeah, why not, would be on the floor while beyond the circle he envisaged mounted on the surrounding walls seven large photographs recording the variant colours of the sea. But the viewer would first be greeted on entry to lead into the exhibition by small polaroid, instamatic and black and white prints, prints depicting the peoples and flora and fauna of the shorelines, examples of pollution too. And then there were the golden Goodwin Sands, the lighthouses and ships, and the wrecks, because the Opal Causeway was, for the less fortunate over time, a graveyard. He also thought of including images demonstrating the mirror image further inland by photographing the little valleys of the Stour and the Nailbourne, the Aa and the Course. But the most important thing was to emphasise colours, the opalescence.

The central idea, he realised, was influenced by a visit to the ICA a few years previously to see Mark Boyle's *Journey to the Surface of the Earth*. But Boyle was originally a sculptor, and his resin reliefs, developed with his wife Joan Hills, cast from randomly chosen sections of the earth's surface, questioned the boundaries between sculpture, painting and performance. So really coming from a different base, yet what he recalled of the central piece was that the viewers entered into a circular space and lay down on cushions watching a film of waves crashing all around them while a soundtrack recorded the sounds of the sea as it came to shore. But that was any sea, every sea, not the Opal Causeway, and Pete's images wouldn't be moving.

But development of these ideas came to a halt one day in the spring, when Darren pleaded with him to take some shots of him with Apollo, now known as Mr Polly. He wasn't really too keen, but Darren was thrilled with the first print once developed.

'You know what, Petey?' he said. 'Can we do another now or very soon, this time with Sputnik and Telstar? And Gemini as well? Please!'

Pete initially baulked at this. The gerbils would be bad enough, but taking a photograph of a goldfish! But Darren was so persuasive that in the end he agreed. And it was Darren's perseverance that was responsible in gaining the first major recognition for Pete of his work.

He entered one of the photographs into a competition: a photograph of Darren sitting next to Mr Polly, with his head leant up against the dog's, while holding Sputnik and Telstar in either hand. Mr Polly, with tongue out and teeth slightly bared, looking as if he could wolf down the two gerbils in one gulp, all looking strangely distorted as the photo was taken through the fish tank in which Gemini was obliviously swimming past their noses.

This photograph won first prize. And as a result of this Pete was invited up to London the following September, for the presentation, to receive a cheque for fifty pounds.

Pete invited Nicola and Darren to the presentation. Darren was over the moon about going but, when told Mr Polly couldn't, burst into tears. Still, he'd be off school and they planned to make a day of it, starting with a picnic with Mel in Holland Park, after which Pete would take him to the Science Museum while Nicola shopped for clothes in High Street Ken. The presentation was to be held in a gallery somewhere between Charing Cross and Covent Garden. They were to be there for six-thirty and it all kicked off at seven.

Darren was that excited once on the train that he must have run a marathon up and down its twelve coaches. Now in the park, while Darren was in pursuit of a peacock and Nicola in pursuit of him, Mel leant over to Pete asking if he'd heard from Brad.

'No, not for nearly a year. I think it was around the time I paid back Baz the money just after Christmas,' he replied.

He found it uncanny she asked him but surmised that perhaps she'd the same memory of that afternoon, two years before, they'd spent in the park together. In fact, over the first few months after his return, he received a couple of letters from Brad, but somehow, communication fizzled out; he couldn't recall who stopped writing first. But it wasn't a conscious decision on his part not to write; it was just that, being caught up with his grandfather's needs, he'd found Brad rarely on his mind. He still heard from Susan, though.

He found his visit to California and events that occurred there had taken on a dreamlike quality. But yet, amongst the stronger images he retained from the trip was of that evening in Laverne Jefferson's house. He'd sent her a card when he got back and she'd replied with a long, newsy letter full of the word *smile* in brackets, and continued to send him cards. He would send her one at Christmas. He often wondered how things worked out for Henry. He hoped he hadn't been drafted.

'Pete, I've got something to tell you,' Mel now whispered.

'What?' he enquired.

'Not now, after the presentation,' she replied.

'Is Baz coming tonight?'

'"Wouldn't miss it for the world, Doll," he said. I've arranged to meet him there.'

After visiting the museum, Pete and Darren met Nicola in the café in Kensington Market. She'd bought a top from Biba, and a pair of hot pants from a nearby stall where she'd changed. She was all made up and looked stunning.

'Wow, Nicknick! We'll have to make a move. The congestion outside looks chronic and we've got to go to Charing Cross first,' he said, as the gallery owner had requested Pete bring up his portfolio and, not wanting to lug it all around with him, he'd left it in left luggage at the station.

They consequently arrived at the gallery with little time to spare and found an anxious gallery owner pacing up and down on the pavement outside. His eyes lit up when he saw Pete approaching, but they narrowed again when he realised Nicola and Darren were with him.

'Oh, thank god, Peter Jones? You're here at last,' he said, extending his hand to Pete while hustling him up the steps into the gallery. 'I'm Alain Steiner. Did you have problems finding the place? I never realised you were married.'

'No… I mean… Yes, I am Peter Jones, that is, no, sorry I'm late, but the traffic was bad,' Pete said, shaking his hand. 'And no, I am not married. This is my friend Nicola.'

Alain Steiner, having halted by the reception area, raised his eyebrows and nodded.

'And this young man is Darren, who perhaps you recognise from the photograph?'

Darren beamed from ear to ear as his little face tilted up in the direction of the gallery owner.

'Oh yes, of course, now I see,' Alain replied, giving Darren an almost disdainful look like he was scrutinising him through a magnifying glass. Whether the lack of a goldfish bowl in front of him to distort his face played any part in this reaction was difficult to say. In any case Darren, with eyes darting all over the place, was so excited and, oblivious to any unkind vibe, continued to smile like he imagined a star of his calibre should.

Alain began to get unexpectedly agitated.

'Now, Peter, it's a good thing you didn't arrive any later. I need to have a private word with you about the procedure and introduce you to the competition organisers before it kicks off, and our sponsor, of course. Very important, that, I cannot stress it enough. I see you got your portfolio too. Jolly good, would you be so good as to leave it in reception for now?'

Pete turned around to the counter. The girl behind it, whose application of mascara rivalled Nicola's, smiled as she came round and took his folder from him.

'Don't worry; it will be safe with Evelynne. Now will you come this way?' Alain said, and pirouetting around, took Pete by the arm, leading across the gallery to an office.

'Mum, what's a procedure?' asked Darren.

'Fucked if I know. Oh, look, there's Mel, thank God, am I pleased to see you, girl.'

Mel was walking up the steps to the gallery, her brow earnestly scanning around.

'Oh, there you are, you two,' she said. 'So tell me about the market and the museum – did you have a good time, Darren?'

As Darren regaled Mel with the events of the afternoon, they made their way into the space. At the end of the long narrow gallery was a trestle table, covered with a white table cloth, laden with rows of glasses of both red and white wine and orange juice. A number of people who passed them at the entrance were congregating around the table, already with wine glasses in their hands.

Darren spotted the prize-winning print and rushed over to view it while Nicola and Mel looked across the room for Pete. As Darren returned to them, countless eyes bore down upon them as his face began to be recognised and people started to whisper and point him out. Something in the atmosphere rendered Nicola strangely shy, and she turned to Mel.

'Expect you're use to this type of thing, Mel.'

'Not really.'

But Darren felt none of the constrictions of his mother and was soon buzzing around the gallery talking to all and sundry, exploring it as if it was a land recently discovered, ripe for plunder. He found a laden buffet table and, rushing back to his mum and Mel, dragged them over to it. Nicola, who had not eaten since being in the park, immediately took full advantage of the spread. Mel was demurer about her consumption.

The gallery now packed, a bell sounded and they watched Alain Steiner, together with Pete, the second and third prize winners, and four highly commended competitors, together with a large, heavy-set man with a bushy beard who resembled the actor James Robertson Justice and who, they later learnt, was the sponsor, get up on a dais at the end of the gallery.

Alain Steiner called for silence, which he immediately started to fill, but after his complicated, waffling build-up, the actual presentation was a quick affair; Pete, after saying a few brief words, was relieved to get it over.

He had a strong impression of his grandparents during the presentation. How he wished they could have been there. He wondered what they would have made of it. He planned to visit Albert the next day after his shift and tell him all about it.

However, if Pete thought his contribution to the evening was finished, he was mistaken, for suddenly a surge of people gathered around him and offered their congratulations. After a while, desperately looking for a way to extradite himself from the mêlée, he saw Mel at the edge of the group trying to catch his attention.

'Oh, excuse me, there's one of my friends. I need to speak with her. Please excuse me. It's just I think she has to leave,' he mumbled to the sea of faces, whose eyes swivelled around in unison and fixed on Mel's face, which instantly reddened. Gliding away with her across the shiny wooden floor, the two of them ended up in the reception area.

'Mel, thank god you came when you did. You saved me, so many questions!'

'But, Pete, it's great, I'm really pleased for you. You're a great success; you deserve it,' Mel said.

'Thanks, Mel, so no Baz?'

'No, I don't know where he is, but you know Baz.'

'What was it you were you going to say in the park, Mel?'

'Well, there were two things actually. Come over here by the entrance where it's quieter.'

As they passed through the vestibule and stopped at the top of the steps at the gallery's entrance, Mel's look became serious. They started to walk down the steps and onto the pavement. There was a slight drizzle now and the air cooler, pleasant on the face, grounding.

'Yes, well, it was two things,' Mel said, slowly. 'Firstly, I, or rather we, got a letter from Brad and…' She stopped in mid-sentence, trying to gauge Pete's reaction.

'Well, yes?' Pete said, taken aback.

'It was a nice letter. I was surprised to get it. It came out of the blue. Of course, Baz had called him that time about your bail and I spoke to him around then, but we've had no contact since. From what he wrote, I did get the impression that he was afraid to write to you after all this time, said he felt guilty about it. But you know what? He's coming over soon. He's finished his degree and landed a job as a correspondent for some English-language newspaper in Europe, based in Germany. Sounds fantastic, but as he is passing through London on his way there, he thought we all should know. Actually, he asked to stay on the barge.'

'Well, it will be good to see him…' Pete said.

But would it be good to see him, he wondered? He wasn't

too convinced that it would be, as it dawned on him that for him, there was so much was unresolved with Brad, masked as it was by his current situation. Did he really want to deal with it now after such a length of time? Awaken sleeping dogs?

Mel sensed his turmoil and, very naturally reaching out, hugged him.

'You don't have to see him, you know,' she said.

'That's true,' Pete replied, suddenly finding it difficult to get his head around it.

He felt so confused that a mashed-up feeling started to gnaw the pit of his belly.

'And the second, Mel, what else were you going to say?' he asked, after a brief silence.

'Well, I haven't told anybody else yet, promise you won't say anything, but I—'

What she was about to divulge didn't get spilt as Alain Steiner bore down on them and, quite ignoring Mel, elbowed Pete into another direction to another round of turgid ear-bashing.

'There are some people over there who are absolutely dying to meet you, dear boy,' he said. 'They are extremely interested in your work and want to see more. You did bring your portfolio, didn't you? Oh yes, of course you did. Silly me! One of them puts on exhibitions here and in France. You never know your luck, dear boy.'

As if luck has anything to do with it, thought Mel, as Pete was whisked away from her. She was desperate to tell him something. Looking around forlornly, she spotted Darren helping himself to some wine and went over to sweetly scold him as Nicola was nowhere to be seen.

As Pete was being led over to the group of people who Alain told him wished to meet him, he noticed Nicola in the far corner. Her unnatural shyness now cured by a few glasses of wine, she appeared to be surrounded by a group of her own admirers, quite milking it. The fat sponsor seemed to be particularly taken by her, gradually and skilfully edging her to a place in the room where he alone could have her fullest attention.

Creepy or what? thought Nicola. However, although or rather because he repelled her, she was always up for a laugh.

'So, my dear, hope you don't mind me asking, are you married to our photographer?' the fat sponsor asked her.

'I don't mind you asking.'

'Sorry?' The fat sponsor raised his busy eyebrows.

'I said, I don't mind you asking. No, I'm not; we live next door to each other.'

'Oh, how simply super, what a wonderful arrangement!'

'Listen, he's not my fella if that's what you think,' said Nicola, laughing, her eyes now intently on him, wondering how he could possibly know whether it was super or not.

'So, my dear, go in for hot pants, do you?' the fat sponsor asked, his eyes perversely scanning her body.

Nicola chose to ignore this comment, though she did let a small, encouraging smile come to her lips. The fat sponsor now looked her over in puppy-dog fashion, but she remained silent.

'So, my dear,' the fat sponsor persisted, 'is your husband here then?'

'What's it to you, mate? Anyway, I ain't got a bleeding husband.'

This wasn't exactly true as although she'd taken out divorce proceedings against Ernie, it wasn't yet final.

'Oh, did you have one?'

'Listen, mate, two things, right,' said Nicola, now thoroughly pissed off. 'One, it ain't none of your fucking business whether I have or not, and two, why would I want one, in any case? They're fucking useless.'

'Oh, but that is your child?' he continued, pointing to Darren, who was just passing with Mel hot on his heels, now somewhat shocked by the vehemence of her reply.

'So what?' said Nicola.

In his intoxicated state, the fat sponsor, ultra-intrigued, with lust oozing out of every pore, seeing this feisty, very desirable young woman, with no husband but with a child, only imagined one thing. She was an easy catch.

'Well, I must say,' he continued, 'you seemed like a high-spirited young thing.'

'I'm not a bleeding racehorse, you know,' retorted Nicola.

By this time, she was leaning up against a wall, with the fat sponsor seeming to be intent on cornering her in. But she's been in similar dodgy situations before and excelled in fighting her way out of them.

The fat sponsor, now drooling, smiled at her, while feasting his eyes up and down her body. She smiled at him. Anybody watching who knew Nicola would have recognised such a smile as a warning light, but he only thought it a come-on. He raised his eyebrows and winked. Nicola could hardly stop herself from laughing.

Jesus, is he a wanker or what? she thought. Like, did he really think that she fancied him? Any man assuming that made her angry, and when angry, she went in for the kill. She moved back further into the corner which the fat sponsor took as a sign to get closer.

'So, my dear, what is it you do?'

'Do? Ain't it obvious?' she said, heaving up her breasts.

The bushy eyebrows were raised once again. 'Oh, I see.'

The fat sponsor was now aroused, a fact not unrecognised by Nicola.

'Perhaps you would care to join me for a little light supper afterwards.'

Nicola smiled again.

'And then afterwards we could…'

His hand now moved with uncontrolled swiftness towards her crotch.

'I don't think so, mate. I am a mother actually; I got a kid to take home and get to bed. He's got school tomorrow, you dirty ratbag.'

And giving him the onceover, noticing he was even more aroused, she pushed him away and, casting her eyes around the gallery to make sure she wouldn't be detected, quickly brought up her knee with some considerable force right in between his legs, and while the fat sponsor stifled his cries of pain, she split.

On the other side of the gallery, caught up in the midst of a group of people, Pete looked anxiously at his watch. It was getting late and they needed to get the ten o'clock train. For as well as Darren having to go to school in the morning, he realised he wasn't going to get that much sleep because of his early start, and besides, tired or not, he was determined to cycle to the hospital after work. He looked over Alain Steiner's shoulder across the room and noticed Mel and Darren approaching.

'Where's your mum, Darren? We really got to go now else we'll miss the train.'

'Oh, do you?' intoned Alain. 'What a pity? You could always…—'

'Work tomorrow, I'm afraid.'

'So are you going now then?' Mel asked him.

'Have to, oh, shit, we never finished our talk, Mel. I clean forgot. Sorry.' He went over, hugged her. 'But I tell you what, I'll try and telephone you tomorrow, around dinnertime. Anyway, I may be up again soon to see this gallery owner that Alain introduced me to.'

Just then, Nicola appeared. She was laughing; her lips were curled up in a wicked curve.

'Hey, Nicknick, we should dash if we want to make the train, so what's the joke?'

'Tell you later, Petey.'

Pete turned to say goodbye to Alain Steiner, and after embracing Mel, he, Nicola and Darren tumbled out of the gallery. They just managed to make the ten o'clock. Darren was asleep before the train was over the Thames, Nicola quickly followed suit, but Pete, in a reflective mood, his head buzzing, took a card from out of his pocket.

It was the card of the man to whom Alain had introduced him, and who'd expressed an interest in mounting an exhibition of his work after he'd told him of the Opal Causeway project. He looked at it for some considerable time. It conjured up a whole new scenario for him; suddenly doors appeared to have been unlocked. It was only when the train was speeding through the long tunnel between Orpington and Sevenoaks that he finally returned it to his pocket. On it was printed the name Anton de Grande, who owned two galleries, specialising in photography and multimedia work. One was somewhere near King's Cross and the other in Paris on Rue St André des Arts. He closed his eyes, was across the Opal Causeway and could smell France. He thought of his grandparents for a second, but before the train reached the other end of the tunnel, he too was asleep.

Mel felt despondent as she watched Pete, Nicola and Darren dashing away down the road. She had much on her mind, had wanted to open up to someone. She also wasn't looking forward to the trek back to *De Mooie Marieke*. At that time of night, it could take ages depending on whether tube and buses were synchronised. She started walking towards the tube, but when she reached the Strand, she decided that she'd take a taxi. After hailing a couple which were going in the opposite direction and were evidently intent on carrying on doing so, a black cab screeched to a halt and she got in.

The driver didn't give her a chance to dwell much on her thoughts during the journey as he incessantly chatted. But in the silences, when the geezer wasn't regaling her about his holiday in Benidorm, she thought about Pete and how he had become her closest confidant ever since their time in Manchester. How she would give anything to have a good rap with him now. She worried about him too because of the situation with his grandfather. It disturbed her that Brad had written to Baz, not to him, and hoped Pete wouldn't feel hurt, left out. His thing for Brad had been deep. Of course, she and Baz were friends with Brad, and Baz, when he'd arrived back that time after dropping off Brad in Frankfurt, seemed to have nothing but good to say about him. But that was the funny thing about Baz, you got these real about-turns from him. She sighed loudly.

'You alright, my darlin'?' the cabbie asked.

'Oh yes,' she lied. 'I'm just tired. Oh, here we are. Could you drop me there by the entrance to the dock? Yes, just there. Please.'

The cabbie swung his vehicle around, stopping in front of the entrance. 'This do you, love?'

'Yes, fine, how much is it?' Mel asked.

The cabbie named his fare, she paid and then, opening the door, she stepped out onto the pavement. There was still a light drizzle, but it was one that she appreciated. As she watched the cab drive off, she also appreciated the complete silence in this part of London. It was hard to imagine it had been a busy community, choc-a-bloc with people day and night, unloading all sorts of goods and commodities from ships which docked there from the four corners of the earth. She sat down on a stone block, the function of which had been to protect the gates of the wheel hubs of wagons as they turned into the dock. She wasn't ready to go back to the barge yet. She had something to tell Baz and was apprehensive about the way she should disclose it to him. She just had no idea how he would take it. Hazel, and the women in her group, told her that it was all down to her, her decision alone, that Baz didn't have any part in the equation. *It's your body, Melanie, your decision, ultimately,* they said. But being the person she was, she wasn't yet convinced. The thing was that she hadn't come on for two months now and usually her periods were like clockwork. A child, she was now pretty certain, she was going to have, and what's more, she wanted it. A few of her friends had had abortions; sometimes it was of their own choice, but often it was because boyfriends bullied them into it or because parents threatened to cut them off forever.

As she sat there, the moon came out from behind a cloud, the drizzle dwindled and she began to have second thoughts, wondering what the urgency was. She should delay telling Baz. Until at least she knew it had really taken, was confirmed by a doctor. But that was a silly approach, as she was pregnant, totally convinced of it, as her body was feeling different. Going through the gate towards the barge, her mind changed as to what to do a thousand times. But once she was almost there, just as she walked round the corner and saw the barge glinting in the waxing moonlight, she decided that she would tell him.

Taking care not to trip over the cable that Baz had fixed up to the dock's electric supply, every night, once certain that the place was deserted, she now walked purposely towards the barge. *No time like the present,* she thought, stepping across the precariously placed planks which formed the gangplank from the quay to the vessel.

'Baz, I'm back. Baz?' she cried out, as she negotiated the hatch. 'Baz, are you there? It was great. You should have come. Everybody thought Pete's photo was fantastic and there was a gallery owner there who apparently was really, really interested. From France, I think. So he might get an exhibition.'

As she walked through the large hold area into the forward cabin with her eyes lowered, she espied Baz's Pan Am bag laying opened on a chair, but before she could think how it got there, she heard an unfamiliar voice.

'Well, now, why, isn't that far out about Pete?'

The accent sounded American. She looked up and saw Brad smiling at her.

'Brad! Wow, I knew you were planning to come, but I didn't expect you…'

She stood there perplexed because this unforeseen alteration to her great scheme of things, of coming right out to Baz with her news, quite threw her off course.

'Well, don't I get a hug?' said Brad, as he came towards her with his arms outstretched.

'Of course,' she replied, moving towards him. 'I was so lost, deep in my thoughts. You really took me by surprise, hey, good to see you.'

And she genuinely felt that, as that brief time over two years before, during her last days in the squat before moving to the barge, as they all watched summer turning into autumn together, held very special memories for her, and Brad was part of those. It just saddened her that it hadn't worked out for Pete and Brad because it was their coming together that made that time possible and so special.

'So where's Baz?' she asked.

'Taking a shower, I guess.'

'Oh, that's unusual.'

'What to have a shower?'

'No, just for him to have one at this time,' she said, recalling how sometimes she had to plead with him to have one because of his unpleasant smegma.

'I expect he wanted to be all clean, spruced up for you. Ain't you the lucky girl?'

'Yes, I suppose I am,' Mel said, masking her utter bewilderment by this sudden change of habit.

'Hello, Doll, how's tricks?' said Baz, coming into the cabin and positioning himself by the hot stove to finished off drying. He was just wrapped in a towel. This intimacy in front of a stranger was unusual for him and embarrassed Mel, but Baz seemed to have a lightness about him.

'So it was good, the presentation?' he asked her.

'Yes, they were all good, all the entrants,' she replied. 'But that photo Pete took of Darren and his pets is just amazing. Darren and Nicknick came up as well. Nicknick…'

Her voice trailed off as she thought of Nicola. She'd surely have no reservations about telling Baz if she was in Mel's situation. There never was any beating about the bush with her. Mel wished sometimes that she could be more like her – well, perhaps Nicola without the overly aggressive streak. But the Nicola who seemed so scathing of the need to have other people's approval, the Nicola who was always ready to fight her way out when backed into a corner, definitely yes.

'What's that about Nicknick, Doll?'

'Oh, God, you should've seen her. She looked stunning. And got chatted up by some dirty old man, actually, the gallery's sponsor, and he started getting free with his hands and she had to knee him in the crotch to get away.'

'Ouch! Geez, that chick!' exclaimed Brad, remembering when they'd danced together, how she dealt with Ernie. Baz just grunted.

'So, Brad, what are your plans? How long are you here for?' Mel asked.

'Not long, a week or two. I've got some errands to run here and then I'm off to Germany to start my new job.'

'Will you have time to visit Pete?' Mel asked.

'I should like to, but it's not going to be that easy. I feel really bad about his grandfather and everything. But I guess it's the time getting down there. You know what your transport system's like.'

'If it makes it easier, I got an idea,' she said, while

rummaging in her bag; a book on organic gardening fell out as she was doing so. She quickly put it back inside.

'I'm invited to the party for the launch of this new women's magazine – they're a collective – by one of the women in my group. I know Pete's planning to come up for a meeting with the guy who's interested in his work. I could invite him. If we all go, you can meet up with him.'

'Yeah, that would be great.'

Mel yawned. It was past midnight now. She was dying for her bed. She left Baz and Brad to it, rapping away, drinking wine in front of the stove, listening to the Grateful Dead.

Oh well, there's time to tell him yet, she thought, as she fell asleep.

Some while later, as he and Baz started to play a game of chess, Brad remarked, 'I didn't know Mel was into gardening.'

'I didn't think she was, mate. Why you say that?'

Mel was feeling nauseous when Pete called the next day. He'd just finished work and, after lunch, planned to cycle up to the hospital. She didn't tell him of Brad's arrival and, as for the second thing she seemed eager to tell him the previous evening, it was of no consequence, she said. However, she did invite him to the magazine launch at the beginning of November.

He was pleased for another opportunity to visit London. It'd been great to be back in the buzzy metropolis, and maybe the invitation would give him more credibility with Anton de Grande, who, after finishing his conversation with Mel, he phoned to arrange a meeting. Excited by the result of this telephone call, Pete set out for the hospital.

Things seemed to be coming together at last. Yet he recognised his commitment to his grandfather was his prime priority; he wouldn't be able to just up sticks. Sometimes, when he felt really optimistic, he imagined his grandfather cured, out in the garden, tending his roses, but in reality, he knew there was no cure and things were destined to take their course. At present, though, it was like Albert was caught in a time warp.

Pete had started to detest the hospital even though he recognised it was no one there's fault that the care was so meagre. But why was it that someone, he thought, who had given so much for their country in two wars, sacrificed the years of their youth, was kept in such a place, forgotten and in such appalling conditions? No, he couldn't blame the nursing staff, although it had to be owed some were less than diligent; no, blame should be levelled much higher up, as the awful conclusion he'd come to over the past year was that the old men and women in that hospital were hardly considered much better than the slag heaps outside one of the local collieries: unwanted, useless, they were dumped there, to decay and dissolve until the weeds and scrub grew up over them.

During his shift that morning, Mel mentioning Brad's plan to move to Europe awoke dormant feelings and, thinking of it again, he weakened just as he began to negotiate the steepest part of the hill. Once at the top, he stopped to catch his breath, looking back over the Opal Causeway, he found it unusually blue for the time of year, the blue of the sea at Cagnes-sur-mer. But with passing clouds quickly blown over from the west, it soon became thickly opaque. Was a storm brewing, he wondered, as he scrutinised the sky in the west? It was becoming dark and gloomy; he was bound to get wet and blown about on his way back. Still, it was downhill all the way and he'd be able to freewheel in the more sheltered parts. Besides, he was never too concerned as he always enjoyed the storms from the west. They were warm and wet, revitalising, and made him feel totally part of the environment, often uncannily contriving to mirror his moods. The dry cold winds from the east, on the other hand, made him feel isolated.

He scanned the horizon and thought he could discern a fragment of the French coastline. Yes, France; he could see it; he wasn't in it, but he would be one day. Was it Cap Blanc Nez? His thoughts went back over the years to the house by the dunes, those golden sands and eating tartines filled with rich dark chocolate after an afternoon on the beach. From there, the White Cliffs always seemed immense, nearly always visible.

Albert was sleeping when he arrived. He didn't rouse the old man as his face looked so peaceful. After letting down the cage on the side of the bed, Pete got out note and sketch books from his rucksack and started to plan. While the old man quietly slumbered, he plotted more ideas for the exhibition. It was almost an hour before Albert opened his eyes and, on seeing Pete, a smile came to his face before confusion kicked in.

Pete sat him up, puffing up the pillows behind him, smoothing the sheets. He noticed a bruise on Albert's arm and went to ask one of the nursing staff about it. He was told Albert most likely hit himself on the metal bed frame, but Pete was not convinced. There had been bruises before, all unexplained.

'Granddad,' he said, sitting down again beside him. 'You'll never guess what. A gallery owner wants to put on an exhibition of my work. Isn't it wonderful? I went up to London yesterday with Nicknick and Darren.'

He then proceeded to recount all the details of the previous day's events. But did Albert take it in? Pete always believed he did; he had to.

'Anyway,' he said, 'if the exhibition's successful, maybe I'll earn a lot of bread, money and be able take you away from this place. Take you home where you belong. Look after you there. You'd like that, wouldn't you?'

Was that a glint in Albert's eyes? He'd often thought of bringing his grandfather home, but the practicalities of it seemed insurmountable. Yet he could dream. He was bought to his senses by the bell sounding, and as a melancholy feeling flowed through him, he kissed the old man on his forehead, pressed his hand and then went out into the wind and the rain.

The exhilaration of the downhill ride home uplifted him.

Pete was bowled over to find Françoise waiting for him outside the house. She'd driven over in Germaine's car with a lot of expensive-looking recording equipment.

'Yes, Anton de Grande, definitely someone to know. I well know the gallery in Rue St André Des Arts, ' she said, smiling when he told her of the tentative plans for an exhibition.

She played him the material she'd already made and the next day they wended their way in the car along the coast, stopping to record different sounds: of the tide over shingle, sand and breaking against the cliffs, of fishing rods being cast, of the resonance of chains and metal as a ferry cast off, foghorns, the cries of gulls and kittiwakes. The day after they went out with Nicola in her friend's fishing boat and Pete was able to take more shots for the panorama while Françoise continued with the soundscape. Once back home after eating fish and chips, Françoise again played her material to him, explaining how she planned to mix it. Pete became really excited by these developments. At last things seemed to be on track. Françoise had to be back the next day as she had work at the Château d'Hérouville studio and soon after was returning to Senegal but they arranged she'd drop off her finished tape for Anton in his gallery in Rue St André des Arts.

A week later Mel met Pete at Notting Hill underground. Pete got the tube there from Tower Hill, having walked across Tower Bridge from Anton de Grande's office, just off Shad Thames. He'd never visited that part of the city and was knocked out by the vast, empty warehouses and their strange sculptural, aerial walkways. The meeting with Anton went well; he felt Anton was someone whom he could trust. On the strength of work done so far on his new project – he'd even taken a small maquette – and the ideas, the concept, he was pencilled for an exhibition in his London gallery.

'I've got a slot late January because of a cancellation. Would you be ready by then?' asked Anton.

'Yes, I should be. I was planning to call it *Environments inhabit us*,' Pete told him.

'Ah, Agnès Varda, sounds good, I like it,' said Anton.

'You see,' he continued, 'these environments do inhabit me. I was raised in them, on them, taught to understand the duality, the mirror image. The central 360-degree panorama portrays a true horizon. Of course, for many a horizon might look like a straight line, but that's a false notion, a true horizon ultimately encircles.'

'Could you write something pertaining to your ideas for an introduction?'

'I have already,' said Pete, handing Anton an envelope.

Anton was very taken by the idea of Francoise's soundtrack and said he'd line up a set maker.

Waiting for Mel at the top of the escalators, Pete now felt exhilarated; his feverish activity paid off. He was really looking forward to the party; he'd not been to one for that long and, no doubt, interesting people would be there.

He was surprised when Mel materialised at the top of the escalator. She was dressed completely different. In a week, gone were the silk scarves, long flowing skirts and little dainty shoes; now she was wearing a pair of loose blue and white-striped, American-style dungarees like Susan's over a tee-shirt and on her feet a pair of Doc Marten's. The only item he recognised from before was that large pannier basket that accompanied her everywhere.

To kill time, they went to the pub in Bayswater Road. Pete hadn't been there since that incident with Brad. The atmosphere was quite changed from then, the staff neither hostile nor blinking an eyelid because of their dress. After getting their drinks, they found seats by the coal fire, glad of its warmth as it had been an unseasonably cold day.

'You know the last time we were here was with Brad. You remember we got thrown out.'

'Yes, I remember,' Mel said, dwelling on her words, as if she was about to add something more but then thought the better of it.

They remained silent, gazing into the leaping blue and orange flames of the fire.

'He might be there tonight, in fact, at the party,' she blurted out into the silence.

'Who?' Pete asked.

'Brad. He might be there.'

'At the party?'

'Yes, at the party. Listen, I didn't tell you on the phone, perhaps I should have and I'm sorry, and please don't be angry with me, but when I got home after seeing you at the gallery, Brad was there. I was really, really, shocked, hadn't realised he was due so soon. Baz didn't think it unusual. He's staying with us till he goes to Europe. He and Baz are as thick as thieves now and said they'd come to the party.'

Pete suddenly felt excluded. Why had Brad not wrote he was coming? But Brad was under no obligation to him and he wondered whether what had been vexing him about the whole sad, sorry affair was a feeling of failure. If only Brad had stayed in London after they met instead of going back; if only there'd not been a postal strike and the physical distance not been so great. If only, if only; just two little words which he knew could only be said in hindsight.

'Well, it'll be good to see him,' he said, haltingly.

After a silence, in which Mel looked at him with an investigative expression on her brow, he continued: 'Sure, I'm nervous about it. I never mentioned this before. But you know I told you when I got to California, Brad seemed to have completely changed towards me. Well, it turned out he'd met someone else.'

'Gosh, Pete, yes, I now remember you saying something like that when I called you that time. But I really didn't take it in and you didn't mention it again. That must have been terrible for you, especially if you had to meet the guy as you were staying at Brad's.'

'But I didn't meet him. That's the thing. And I don't know who he is. He said he was someone he'd met in Germany before returning home. I just wish he'd been straight with me about it before I left. Before I got my ticket, you know. I felt like such a wally. That boring stint at the catalogue company was for nothing, an utter waste of time.'

'Oh, Pete, I'm so sorry,' Mel said.

Suddenly, the floodgates opened, as the tensions of the last two years rose to the surface and Pete began to unburden himself in a way which he was quite unable to do with other friends. That was always the thing about Mel and their friendship, their ability to talk and express themselves to each other; and he suddenly found himself opening up in a way he'd not done since his return from California, particularly about Albert and how he hated seeing him in that hospital, about his fears for him there and about how he wished there was another way to look after him.

'You know, Mel, I'm lucky to have my work, both my photography and the post office, as when I work, I am more able to forget, forget about my grandfather's problems, forget about the hollow feeling inside. I'd thought I'd found a partner for life, but that dream's shattered. You know, I often thought lately that my loneliness was to do with feeling left out, some kind of residue, from that long-ago twilight world, when my real mother existed for me.'

'Do you actually remember her, Pete?'

'No, not really, well, only a sort of presence.'

'Do you really feel lonely?'

'Not when I'm busy,' he said.

He found Mel such an attentive listener and was always astounded how her concerned forehead reflected the rhythm of the words to which she was listening.

'But I guess it was loneliness that drew me to Brad. You

know, except for during the time in Santa Rita, and despite what went down with Brad, I never felt lonely in California, and meeting people, other guys there, was so natural. If they liked you they told you. They just came up to you in the street. They had no fear. Not like here. It wasn't like it was dirty or anything. They didn't talk all pervy. Here, it seems that gay men are sentenced to meeting people in public toilets.'

He started to feel level again. It would make no difference if Brad was going to be at the party, he had to look forward, move on, think of his plans. He looked up at Mel and then down to her basket. There was a book on organic gardening lying at the top of it.

'Mel, why have you got a book on organic gardening in your basket?' he asked.

And he remembered she'd something to tell him and, so far, it was he who had monopolised the conversation. She said on the phone that whatever she had wanted to tell him last week was unimportant. But was that Mel just putting others before herself? He began to feel bad and was just about to ask her what it was she had been going to tell him, when she leant forward towards him.

'This book was lent to me by Hazel. She's going to Wales to join a commune. They aim to be self-sufficient. She'll be there tonight, Pete. But you know, I've always been interested in gardening and I don't know if I want to stay in London forever. I've always dreamt of living in a beautiful cottage in the country ever since I was little.'

'Oh, I thought you were happy on the barge,' he said.

'It's not what I really dream of. Pete, the thing is that... I'm pregnant.'

Pete was stunned.

'When did you find out?'

'Last week.'

'Baz knows?'

'I had to build up my courage first, but he sort of seems pleased. Difficult to tell, you know Baz.'

'Well, what will you do?'

'I don't know yet. One thing, though, is I'm not sure if I want to have a toddler on the barge with nowhere to run about.'

'I take your point.'

'And, also, I haven't told anybody this…'

Mel was a little hesitant now.

'You see, I'm not really sure whether the baby's Baz's.'

This statement came like a thunderbolt. Mel and Baz's relationship had always seemed like rock solid to Pete. Yeah, Mel had to put up with a load of shit from Baz, but somehow, they always seemed to be able to reach an accommodation. And the idea Mel had an affair, or even more, a one-night stand, was a concept difficult to fathom.

'Not his?' Pete said.

'Well, I'm not sure but pretty certain.'

'So what will you do?'

'I don't know yet.'

'What about the father?'

'He was just a one-night stand, or rather a one-day one. Pure lust, I got the better of myself. It was when Baz was away in Belgium, Amsterdam or somewhere.'

'I'm amazed,' Pete said. 'Do I know him?'

'You met him once.'

Pete looked at her. Although he felt he shouldn't ask her, he'd become curious.

'You remember when we went up to that garage in Crouch End? To get a new tyre? You remember Tiny?'

'Tiny?' Pete said, incredulously.

'Yes, Tiny,' Mel said, now blushing. 'Baz had taken the bus up to the garage for a service before he left, Tiny brought it back and I invited him onto the barge for a cuppa. Well, when he started to walk across those planks, you know the ones which Baz erected in a Heath Robinson fashion as the gangplank, he slipped and fell into the dock. Oh, Pete, it looked so funny; it made me laugh. I felt awful afterwards.'

A broad grin now came on Mel's face and she giggled, recounting how Tiny, with his size twelve feet, slipped and went crashing down into the dock's murky waters. Then, realising that Tiny couldn't swim, she and a passer-by managed to haul him out. In shock, shivering badly, with water cascading out of his clothes, she led Tiny down to the hold, offered him some Dutch brandy and then helped him out of his wet clothes. Taking them, she placed them to dry on a clothes horse by the old cast-iron stove to the fore, and as she handed a towel to him, she tried, not very successfully, to avert her eyes because his tall, muscular body suddenly held a fascination for her. Noting this, Tiny became all smiles and furtive glances. Mel, who'd felt his kindness, his consideration for her before, was now overcome by his gentleness and smiled. But Tiny, the gentle giant, was not that subtle and, standing by the stove, she could tell that under his towel he was aroused.

'You know, he's a sweet man, a lovely person.'

'So will you tell him?'

'I don't know. I don't think so. Besides, I don't really know if it's his and I think he's married.'

'What about Baz?'

'Well, I don't know. He's been very secretive lately. You know I don't like to pry into his affairs. He's always got some pot boiling, some scheme afoot, but recently, he's been doing the weirdest of things. You know, the night that Brad arrived, when I got back from your presentation, he was having a shower. It is unheard of at that time of night. I told you about the fights with him over his... smegma?' Mel whispered, at this point.

'Anyway, I'm seriously thinking of making changes in my life. Miss McPherson is making my life hell and Hazel said the other day, why don't I move to Wales with her? But I don't know yet. I know it's decision time, but it's difficult to know what is the right thing to do.'

'Wales, wow! But would Baz go? He couldn't do much wheeling and dealing there.'

'I don't think I'd go with Baz.'

They remained silent while their eyes took in the fire. Pete looked at his watch.

'So what time does this party thing start then?'

'Right about now, I'd say.'

'Is it far?'

'No, it's in the squat near Vicarage Gate, where Hazel lives.'

There was a smattering of people when they arrived, mainly the women from the collective, the journalists, designers, editors involved in the launch. But Hazel was there and whisked Mel away to her room, leaving Pete standing in the kitchen, listening to but no way involved in the in-house talk. Feeling awkward precipitated him towards a bottle of cheap Spanish red wine.

The conversation was of the magazine, the first ever feminist magazine to be launched in the country. One of the women, short, slight and with cropped but thick dark curly hair, kept looking at him while she was speaking as if trying to include him in the conversation. Mel told him earlier how some women in the movement vowed never to speak to men; being gay absolutely making no difference. Although he could understand the point they were making, Pete was relieved when Mel and Hazel re-joined the fold.

'You're back! I thought you deserted me.'

'Would I do that? No, Hazel was filling me in about Wales,' Mel said.

Pete observed Mel interacting with the other woman in the room. He had never been with her in this type of environment and now saw a different Mel, a Mel more her own woman, assertive and confident, no longer acting like she was a man's appendage.

The doorbell rang. Pete flinched. But it wasn't Baz and Brad. The newcomers were a group of gay men, one of whom, Spencer, Pete knew of from articles in the underground press as being a speaker at those first GLF meetings two years previously. Over the following years, he'd made quite a name for himself in the underground magazine collective in which he was involved. He'd been taken to court once, under the obscene publications act, and in consequence had become a man much sought after by journalists for comments on gay liberation, the underground.

As the evening progressed, Pete began to feel anxious. Not only did his nervousness about seeing Brad increase, but he felt out of sync with everybody. Perhaps it was the wine and salty peanuts taking their toll on him, but in a quite different way, for while everybody seemed to be increasingly merry, he began to feel maudlin. And his thoughts went back to Albert and he started to feel guilty. He shouldn't be there at all.

Suddenly he found himself standing in the middle of the room, and although there were people talking all around him, he felt alone. His head spinning, he needed fresh air. Stumbling slightly, he passed through the door, down the staircase and sat down on the steps leading up to the house.

It was a lot warmer than earlier; the dry, cold air of the day was replaced by drizzle and a slight breeze. It refreshed him. Through the gaps in the fast-moving clouds, he could see the moon was almost full. Maybe the reason he felt the way he did was because he was affected by the moon's pull. Like if the moon was able to make the seas and oceans rise and fall, what could it do to the water content in a human body? Water made up sixty per cent of total body weight, so if that were the case, the moon had to hold sway on body rhythms. The realisation that his body and his thoughts were being manipulated by something external, something over which he had no control, was sobering.

As he sat there, he remembered something he'd put off doing, something that Connie suggested he do the previous winter.

'Have you written to your dad, Peter? He ought to know,' she'd said.

It was a shock to him to hear someone referring to his *dad*. Neither Albert nor he much heard from Georgy since he settled in Australia with his family. They were never much in the forefront of his mind. In all truth, he'd never thought of Georgy as his father. But he should write to him, as Albert was his father; Georgy had a right to know.

'Hey, you okay, Pete?'

Hazel's voice anchored him back to the present. Sitting down beside him, she lit up a cigarette and offered him one, which he refused.

'You know, just thinking about things.'

'Well, sounds like you got a lot to think about, Pete. Mel told me about your granddad and all you're going through. It must be hard. Not many people would do that. They'd be too into getting their kicks.'

'I can't leave him alone in that place,' Pete said.

He suddenly felt all choked up and tears started to form in his eyes. Hazel put her arm around his shoulders.

'I don't know why I am crying. I think it's suddenly being reminded how I could live, how I wanted to live. And...'

He hesitated for a short time, but seeing Hazel's big brown eyes encouraged him to continue.

'And I got really fucked up about this bloke, who's now reappeared on the scene. Long story, you know.'

'Oh yes, Brad. Mel told me about him turning up. Sounds like a snake to me and all he wanted was to slither up your jeans, like, you're better off without him.'

Pete suddenly burst out laughing – Brad, a slithering snake! Yes, he'd done a lot of slithering to get what he wanted when Pete thought about it. He laughed, his tears different this time. Before, he'd never have listened to anybody saying anything derogatory about Brad, but the way in which Hazel said it brought home for the first time that Brad had treated him shabbily.

'Thank you,' he said to her. 'I think I'm ready to go back inside. It's getting a bit chilly here.'

'Me too. Hey, let's go and have some fun, eh?' said Hazel, stubbing out her cigarette on the step and tossing the butt with great precision into a nearby open dustbin.

Once back in the party, Hazel got into a rap with Spencer about the GLF meetings. After attending that gay group in San Francisco, Pete planned, once home, to go the meetings, but like many of his plans, his plan was scuttled.

'The meetings are vast now.' Spencer told them. 'Just hundreds of people turning up. It's so exhilarating.'

'Yeah, but it's sad the women stopped going,' Hazel interjected, harshly.

She explained, because many men just used the meetings as a cruising ground and were behaving just like the men, whose behaviour women would no longer tolerate, the lesbians split off from the group. But Spencer claimed this segregation was organic, although Pete lamented such an evaporation of mutual solidarity.

'You can't expect people to change their behaviour overnight; the process isn't like being on the road to Damascus,' Spencer said. 'You must come to the meetings, Pete. They're held in a hall near Powis Square, Wednesday evenings at seven thirty, and afterwards people go to the Elgin. There's a large function room there, there's music and a deejay.'

The party was in full swing by now and many people, including Mel, had started to dance. She came running over and dragged Hazel to the middle of the floor; Spencer followed them, but Pete, spotting a seat in the corner, sat down watching. The clock on the wall opposite was telling him it was getting late, but he was unable to rouse himself to leave.

After Mel and Hazel finished dancing, Mel moved over towards him.

'You know, Pete,' said Mel, 'I shall have to go. Miss McPherson is on an early tomorrow, so I can't afford to be late for work. I can't do anything right for her. Don't know what's happened to Baz and Brad. I really thought they were coming. I'm sorry—'

'Don't be. I got a bit wound up earlier about it all, the apprehension thing, you know, but I had a good rap with Hazel. I really like her,' he said.

'So do I. Listen, I'm staying with Hazel tonight. What about you?' Mel asked.

'I think I'll stay bit longer. I still got time till the next train.'

'You'll be alright?'

'Yep.'

'Well, I'll phone soon,' she said, and leant over to kiss him.

After she and Hazel disappeared, Spencer and his friend came and sat on the sofa either side of Pete. His friend skinned up. He also had a bottle of vodka which he passed around freely. *Shame, this party's getting going and I have to leave,* Pete was thinking, just as a whole new crowd of people poured in, a lush representation of trendy and cool, their clothes flamboyant, making a thousand statements. The room was jumping, the volume pumped up and everybody was dancing, to James Brown, the Wailers and old soul classics.

Pete, Spencer and his friend were magically propelled upright and got into the groove. Of course, it was the toke on that joint that transformed Pete, made him feel like he again belonged. Brad and Baz went out the window as he started rapping with Spencer. He was enjoying himself in a way he hadn't for ages, so his train also went out the window and when he did finally get around to looking at the clock on the wall, he realised that he'd missed the last one.

'Oh shit!' he exclaimed.

'What's the matter?' Spencer asked.

They were now back sitting on the sofa and Spencer's leg was now touching his own, in an extremely provocative way, while his friend felt up Pete's other knee.

'Oh, I've gone and missed my train.'

'You got nowhere to stay then?'

'No, not really.'

'No problem, you can crash at ours.'

'Are you sure?' He'd been wondering whether he might crash where he was.

'Are you sure?' said Spencer, rubbing his knee and up the inside of his thigh.

A couple of joints and one more vodka later, and Spencer and his friend were ready to go. By now, Pete was out of it and when they rolled out into the cool night air, he'd no idea where he was going and didn't ask.

'We'll get a cab in Church Street,' said Spencer.

They walked down a couple of side streets, and then, on reaching the corner, a taxi appeared and miraculously stopped for them. They tumbled in. The motion of the cab started to make Pete's head swim and when the cab seemed to have to wait for an age at the junction of Ken High Street and Church Street for the lights to change, Pete felt he was going to throw up. But with the lights changing to green, his toxic moment luckily dissolved, the taxi sped down High Street Ken and turned into Earls Court Road.

For a short moment, a blurry Pete thought that he saw two people, looking remarkably like Baz and Brad, outside the Bolton's as the cab streaked by that pub. But this he promptly forgot and had no memory of what happened after.

Pete nursed a bumper hangover for two days after the party. It wasn't helped by getting the slowest train early the next morning, starved, thirsty and with no recourse to a buffet car. Despite that, he was still an hour late for work and, because of the way his supervisor scowled at him, he thought he was for the chop, but in the end, he got a warning.

Over the next weeks, he found he swung back into a good routine. He at last got round to writing to Georgy, after staring at the aerogramme he bought at the post office for a couple of weeks. A difficult task, he was totally stumped as how to address him. *Dear Dad* or *Dear Father* seemed too unreal, so in the end he just plumped for George. The phone rang as he was just going out to post the letter. It was Anton de Grande confirming the date for the opening in late January and asking him to travel up to London for a meeting.

And that was about the extent of his communication with the outside world during that period. He saw Connie, Nicola and Darren periodically, but he had no contact with Mel. Therefore, after the meeting with Anton, he decided to surprise her at the library. She seemed flustered when he arrived, as it transposed Miss McPherson was laid low with flu so extra duties devolved on her.

She was able to take a lunch break, though, and they decided to go for a walk in Holland Park. It had been a cold day when he'd left home, and halfway up, on the train, Pete noticed a sprinkle of snow on the Downs. And London was even colder, the temperature being hardly above freezing as they entered the park. Frost still covered the roofs of the surrounding buildings, the lawns and branches of the trees, and breath steamed out of their mouths as, while crunching across the hard ground, they talked.

With few people venturing out that day, the park seemed like a newly discovered fairy-tale land; they passed enchanted by intricate patterns made by frozen spiders' webs across newly naked trees. To crown this scene, the low-level bright winter sun exploded through the slight mist and quite blinded them for an instant.

'You know, Pete, this park is the best thing about my job,' Mel said.

They sat down on a bench; Pete could feel that Mel was perturbed, but she brushed off Pete's initial enquiries. But he knew her better, coaxed her, and it all came out.

After the party when she slept in Hazel's room, she made the decision to move to Wales.

'I'm going to give in four weeks' notice at the library around the middle of February and join Hazel in the commune in the early spring,' she told him.

Naturally, Hazel played no mean part in persuading her, but before she finally decided, she did go and meet other members of the commune who took to her, were keen for her to join them. She planned to have the baby there, a natural birth. To start with, she was going to share the top floor of a converted Routemaster bus with Hazel while the house was being renovated. Other members would live in a converted outbuilding. To be sure, the facilities were very basic, a kind of lime-filled affair of an outside toilet and hardly a bathroom as such, while clothes were washed in the stream on a convenient slab of slate overhanging the icy flow which ran down from a pool beneath a small waterfall.

'Imagine, Pete!' she said. 'Our very own waterfall in the garden; it is all straight in my mind, I will go. Honestly, Pete, I really feel it's right thing to do, but I can tell you that I was hesitating about telling Baz. He's been away a lot recently, Heaven knows where. I was finding it increasingly difficult to keep track of his comings and goings, and for a while, I could never find the right time to tell him. Then I told myself on the way back from work one night, that if he was at home when I got back, I would tell him there and then. Get it over and done with. And I know you understand how hard and sad for me it was because I still love him. But I just felt more and more constricted, like we'd been going nowhere for ages. You know, I rehearsed it over and over again, what I would say on the journey to the barge. Loud music was coming from *De Mooie Marieke* as I crossed the gangplank, and laughter and other kinds of noises, which I couldn't quite make out. But as I got nearer, I recognised Brad's laughter. Brad had left for Germany three weeks before, but evidently, he'd come back.'

Mel paused here.

'They didn't hear me as I walked into the cabin because they carried on and only stopped after I ran out, slamming the door, and because I must have cried out. I don't know what I said. I was like so really shocked, stunned. It felt almost like a car crash or something.'

'You mean… they were having… sex? You're… sure… they… Baz…? Brad? No way, surely,' Pete stuttered.

Astonishment and confusion prevented him from stringing a whole sentence together at all; his mind felt scrambled. He started to speak again but was stopped by words getting caught up in his throat. His mind raced over memories of past scenarios. Then out of the confusion, the pieces began to fit: Baz's sharpness, at certain times, like he was trying to deflect things; his particular cruelness to Mel on certain occasions in public; his strange and sudden disappearing acts; his flustering. And then Brad saying, what was it he'd said that first time? Yes, it was how he was sure he recognised Baz from Amsterdam. And Baz acting really unfriendly to him for quite some while after that. And then, of course, and he could have kicked himself for not realising, that time when Baz and Brad drove to Germany so Brad could get his plane and how, when Baz got back, his attitude about Brad was changed. And there was the business of the bail money. What an idiot he was for not realising who *that someone else* talked about in Berkeley indeed was. And Angel Dust had very nearly gave the game away when he made that comment about the Pan Am bag.

'I couldn't believe my eyes,' Mel continued. 'Baz with a man, and there's me been thinking he was knocking off some Dutch chick. And not with any man either – oh, Pete, I was more than shocked, really narked, not only for me coz, in many respects, it made my task easier, but for you, Pete, for you. That's why I hadn't rang you. I've been racking my brains thinking of how I would tell you.'

'Well, Hazel said Brad was a snake,' Pete said. 'But you know, I realise that he nearly told me once but somehow I headed him off; maybe I didn't want to know who it was. When he mentioned he met someone in Germany during those last few days, I just assumed the guy was German. But then, Angel Dust kind of mentioned a German staying or, at least, I thought he did. It was when he saw Baz's Pam Am bag, said he'd seen it before, that the other guy, oh yes, I remember now what he said, the other English guy who visited had one. And Brad became strangely sharp, said the guy was German. Oh, Mel, do you think that that means Baz was with Brad in California before me?'

Now it was Mel's turn to look incredulous.

'The bastard! Hazel's right. They're both snakes, dirty rats. How skilful they were covering their tracks? Though perhaps it's a little my fault as I do attract gay men.'

'Mel, it's your fault as much as the Vietnam War is. Come on, hardly!'

'So do you think Baz was always gay, Pete?'

'Who knows? Like, bisexuality is complicated. I don't really understand it.'

'Well, regardless of that, I just don't understand how they could do that to us when we were all so close. You know, meeting Hazel and the other women in the group is the best thing that happened to me. I adored Baz, but I knew it wasn't right, like, it was that I could never depend on him. He was always off somewhere, ducking and diving. Maybe that time with Tiny was supposed to happen. How strange relationships are? I've realised now that when I first got together with Baz I did what my mum did. She did everything possible to please my dad and he still put her down, constantly finding her weak spot, pushing in the dagger and twisting it. It's all just so perverse. Before she married she was a confident woman. She worked, did a job equal to anything a man could do, but his constant bickering, his embarrassing her in front of friends and strangers alike, and his bitchiness towards her wore her out, undermined her. She became a shell of what she'd been. I think that was happening to me with Baz. Imagine bringing up a child under those circumstances.'

Pete remained silent, gazing across to the Orangery; there was still a trace of frost on its roofs despite strong sunlight now. They both simultaneously started to shiver.

'Phew, I'm getting really cold here,' Pete said. 'Let's walk a bit through the wooded area and see if we can get some coffee somewhere. There's bound to be a café or, you know, I wouldn't mind a scotch. Or a whiskey mac like Mémé sometimes drank in the winter.'

'Well, no scotch for me, but a warm place would be good. I know, let's go to the Windsor Castle. You know, I'm really feeling quite peckish,' said Mel.

They started to make their way out of the park.

'And you know what he had the gall to say?'

'Who?' Pete asked.

'Baz, Brad didn't say much. He was, like, really embarrassed. But Baz said, "Doll. It's not what it seems." Not what it seems? It was very obvious what it was. I ask you. What did he think it seemed? You know, I feel a bit sorry for Brad. He'll have to put up with what I did, for a start.'

As they made their way towards Holland Walk, a rabbit scampered close by them.

'It's terrible, it's just terrible,' Mel said.

Pete was slow to agree, as this overwhelming revelation, together with the cold, had somehow contrived to anaesthetise him, leaving him struggling for a suitable reply.

'Yes, it's just terrible!' Mel repeated. 'Those poor rabbits, the park authorities ought to provide them with some warm hutches with plenty of straw in them for the winter.'

Pete, recalling the saga of the sheep in the cottage kitchen in Wales, laughed.

'After all this, you're still the same, Mel – don't change,' he said, giving her a hug.

As they carried on past the comprehensive school in silence, he did wonder whether her attitude to human beings might harden.

'So what did it seem like to Baz then? What did he say?' asked Pete as they were turning in Campden Hill Road.

'He said he could explain everything, but that was when I lost it and told him I didn't want to know. I was seething. You know how I hardly ever lose my temper. Anyway, like what was there for him to explain, I had seen crystal-clear what it was. But you know, the roleplay in the women's group started to surface, suddenly it all made sense, became useful, and I found myself assertive. Neither of them knew what hit them.'

She laughed.

'I still feel bad for Brad, though,' she added.

Apparently, Mel really exploded when Brad kept saying he was sorry. Mel knew enough about sex to know that most people, especially men, were never too sorry for having it, and it pushed her to snapping point.

'I just screamed out the words, "Sorry, like, fuck you, you dirty rat." It was then that Baz said, "Doll, there's no need to shout."'

Mel, although she didn't intend to, then slapped him on his cheek and called him a pathetic wanker. And with that, her anger quite abated and she began to feel strangely calm.

Yes, calm but powerful. She proceeded to tell him about her intentions to move to Wales.

'You know, Pete, he said, "But what about the baby?" "What I do about the baby is up to me," I told him. He looked so stung and humiliated, but you know what? I didn't feel sorry, or like a bad person, for the first time in my life. I was quite surprised by myself.'

The force of Mel's words and actions surprised Pete. It was evident, at that moment, she'd seen her relationship with Baz for what it was and confirmed she'd been right in her decision to leave him. She wasn't even going to bother to tell him about the baby being Tiny's, if indeed it was. After their discussion, if you could call it that, she, ignoring Baz, went around the barge, quietly packing up her stuff. Essential things she took to Vicarage Gardens, where she knew she could crash; the others, she told him, she would collect later.

'You know, Pete, it was sad, but I felt a sense of relief as soon as I walked away. It might well have been the end of something, but it really felt more like the beginning of something, something good, productive and meaningful.'

They arrived in front of the Windsor Castle. They entered. A roaring fire was burning in the grate and, luckily enough, there were two free seats close by it. Mel grabbed them while Pete went to the bar to order drinks and food. Poor Mel had to make do with orange juice, but Pete got his scotch and a bottle of barley wine. He needed warming up. Settling back in their chairs, having eaten their mushroom pies, they stretched their hands towards the fire, quite content to remain silent for some time. When they did speak it was almost simultaneously. They found that they were about to say more or less the same thing, for they both agreed that they felt like a great weight lifted. Content to stay in the present, while looking into the fiery world before them, it was only when the bell rang for last orders that they were jerked out of their reveries.

'Oh, Christ!' exclaimed Mel. 'I'm for the chop if Miss McPherson ever finds out that I've been away so long. What should I do? If I go back now—'

'Don't!' Pete replied.

'What, don't go back?'

'Yeah, don't go back, just phone and say you're not feeling well. You're pregnant, for heaven's sake. Surely, they'll understand. Ring them and we can go and hang out at Vicarage Gardens. I was thinking about asking you if I could stay the night, if that's okay. I was kind of thinking of going to the GLF meeting this evening.'

Mel broke out into a wide smile. She glowed in a way that Pete had never seen her glow before.

'That would be really great. To have you stay.'

They got up to leave and, from a nearby phone box, Mel called the library.

They then made their way to the health food shop and MacFisheries on the gate to buy food for later. There was an air of Christmas everywhere; it was as if like the cold clime had brought out the Yuletide spirit. They passed decorated shops from which festive music wafted out over hurried shoppers and it was also obvious that the season of Christmas parties had evidently begun as inebriates were swaggering along the pavements.

Christmas already, thought Pete. No, it was not possible, not another Christmas without Granddad at home and yet another, without Mémé and an idea he'd had in his head for a while, became a decision.

'I'm going to bring him home, Mel.'

'What?' Mel asked.

'I'm going to bring Granddad home. It'll be hard, but I'll manage.'

Later, after a bowl of steaming miso and seaweed soup, Pete strolled down to Powis Square. The weather quite changed after dusk, becoming warm and wet; winter had gone into reverse.

When he arrived at the hall, Pete imagined, because of the large crowd milling around at the door, some other function was taking place, but as he drew closer, he saw that people were having to queue to gain entry. And once inside, he found the corridor, the vestibule by the front door and even the staircase leading up to the first floor of the building to be jampacked. Managing to squeeze through the crowd, he eased himself into a gap by the door leading into the hall. Only if he stood on tiptoes was he able to see over the heads of people in front of him and get a view inside.

It wowed him to think that in the space of two years since that initial meeting, the movement had so exploded. Among many faces there, he saw the burly landlord of that pub in Bayswater Road, but as he scanned them, he realised what Hazel said was true: there were few women. But what was exhilarating was that nobody was queer, pansy or poof; they were gay and proud to be.

Clothes played a great part in this transformation, making both individual and collective statements. But they'd left Kings Road and Carnaby Street far behind; they were *of the street*; now it was for the media to follow. He saw guys with kohl around their eyes, glitter covering faces, beards and moustaches, wearing second-hand forties dresses over flared jeans and tee-shirts. A group of acid queens noisily exploded before him in an exquisite detail of riotous colours and patterns, their nails painted intricately and faces made up like masks in a mime show, clothed in silks, satins and chiffons, a couple of them leaving their hair in rollers. It was as if all the fashions of the last few hundred years had been put into a mixer and this was the result: a total anarchy. No more rules; just do your own thing; the magic of the Magi merging with the allure of Garbo and Gable. There were those dressed in workmanlike apparel like their business was infinitely more proletarian: dungarees like Mel's as well as old-fashioned boiler suits, plaid, denim and other kinds of work shirts. And as for footwear, plimsolls, Doc Martens, walking boots, platform-heeled boots and shoes, and sandals. And the accessories: diamantes brooches shaped as stars, earrings and studs, tattoos, agitprop badges, leather shoulder bags and pouches, granny glasses, Second World War airmen's shades could be seen. And what was linking all this together? A pungent mélange of fragrances: jasmine, rose, geranium, rosemary and, of course, patchouli – yes, *particularly* patchouli.

Yes, Pete thought, *people have become artforms.* Art produced in conventional media was no longer sufficient; it must be moving, and what better than the human body to project that? The body became the frame of the picture, but the picture obscured the frame; it was no longer encased by it.

On the side of the hall, opposite the entrance, was where various speakers were, but above the general noise, with no microphones, they were hard to hear. In fact, some people paid him no attention to the speakers and, as Hazel said, seemed to be there just for the purpose of cruising. Pete spotted Spencer approaching the group. Wearing a simple white cheese cloth shirt and white trousers, and Indian sandalwood beads around his neck, and with his long blond hair, the simplicity of his dress keenly contrasted with the surrounding flamboyance. For a second, Pete, wishing he had his camera, had a flash of some forgotten Italian renaissance religious painting, a kind of Sermon on the Mount scenario.

Now and then, he recognised faces from the magazine launch; sometimes he spotted other familiar faces, from where? Perhaps from being out and about during his summer in Portobello, or from pubs or parties, but then his eyes were drawn to a certain face and he felt disquieted. Those familiar eyes were searching for someone and that someone was presumably found as the face broke out into a smile. It was Brad's smile, the smile he'd first seen at the bottom of those steps, eons before. He was waving now, not to Pete but to someone beyond him, someone who now pushed past him. Baz's back receded before him. That intimate look Pete remembered so well, one that he'd once thought was exclusively his, was focused on Baz. They hugged, kissed while Pete experienced a plethora of feelings: jealousy and anger, confusion and rejection.

Be rational, it's Mel and not me who's the real wounded party, the deceived one. I deceived myself even if he is a fucking... don't go there, don't.

His view became obscured by someone in orange overalls squeezing past him, making him flinch, but then he thought of Henry Abercrombie. Where was he, he wondered? When he looked across again to where Brad and Baz had been standing, they were no longer there. Had they seen him, he wondered?

Spencer's speech was drawing to an end. Pete managed to get nearer and could hear it now. The man's oration was inspiring, a combination of the ancient and the hip, like Shakespeare and King James meets the Beats. It certainly got the crowd going.

His eyes again found Brad and Baz. As the speech finished, he watched Baz break out in applause; his exhilaration seemed like that of a born-again Christian. Initially unkind thoughts filled Pete's head, but he recognised, despite Mel and the pain caused, it must have been hard for Baz to reach that moment. He'd needed great courage. Both Baz and Brad had to fight themselves to be gay. Baz's subterfuge must have been well developed from boyhood; his ducking and diving and covering his tracks while life for Brad, because of his family, Joel's EST and suicide, there was no easy path. They'd obviously carried a lot of guilt, baggage, and maybe that was what drew them together. Guilt was something that Pete had never felt; his being gay seemed to him like a natural progression, organic. He'd always believed, regardless of society, he was born that the way. Society had it wrong, not him.

Pete and Brad's eyes fleetingly met, but like two spooked animals, they both looked away. Pete cursed himself, but when he looked again, Brad and Baz were lost in the swell of the cheering crowd.

When he eventually reached the street, he ran into Spencer and his friend. They invited him to the Elgin. It hadn't been in his plan. He intended to go back to Vicarage Gardens and get the first train the next morning. The decision he'd made earlier, about bringing Albert home, was still racing around in his head and he realised that he'd much thinking, planning to do. But he also recognised he needed to give himself some space as it had to be considered in the cold light of day. So he accepted their invitation and they started slowly walking towards the pub.

It was if there were a new river, never to be submerged in a conduit like the unfortunate Westbourne was, in Notting Hill that night, a river, its source being the hall in Powis Square that ran down to the sea that was the big bare function room at the back of the Elgin pub. This torrential flow quite alarmed many a passer-by. Strange time for a fancy-dress party, some were thinking, but any thought of derogative commentary or aggressive behaviour was stanched by the sheer number of gay men streaming past them. In fact, the only petty insults were delivered from the safety of cars, once foot was firmly on the accelerator. On its way the river split into two, reuniting at Ladbroke Grove. It stopped traffic, paying no attention to lights.

They all piled into the pub. The locals, in both saloon and public bars, appeared strangely unaffected by the spectacle; Notting Hill was getting used to diversity. No doubt, there were some who hoped to be gratified later in the darkness, their tracks already pre-covered, excuses worked out in advance.

The function room soon filled up. In the far corner, a turntable was set up and music started to blare out of the two speakers while a sole dancer was involved in an exercise of free expression on the dancefloor. The room might have been darkened, but the windows weren't curtained. It was all open; no more lurking in the shadows, walking down dingy steps to some strange drinking club where you were only allowed in if they liked your face and you bought temporary membership in the form of a meal ticket. No, people here were natural; their sexuality was no longer a perversion but a gift. Gradually people started dancing. And by the time the deejay started to play James Brown, the floor was teeming with over one hundred gay men dancing to 'Like a Sex Machine'.

Pete felt a tap on his shoulder. He turned around. The smile, no longer his, beamed towards him, and Brad and he drew nearer to each and danced while Spencer paired off with Baz. When the tune finished they made their way to the side of the room, found a table with free seats and sat.

'Sorry I didn't write Booby,' said Brad to Pete. 'I was confused. I did try to tell you. Like, it got so complicated and I didn't want to hurt you and I didn't want to hurt Mel. It got so messy. I'm sorry.'

'I'm sorry too,' said Pete. 'I probably expected too much. I really don't know what to say now I know the score, everything makes sense, but before, I was confused; I just didn't understand why. You know, that fear of rejection type thing and then it all got so complicated over there with the arrest. I got paranoid. And it was like I thought it was me, like I was a bad person.'

'No, you never were. You just fell in too fast and, well… it was like you were needy when you met me. I realised that after. It was kind of scary. I panicked. And I didn't know how to tell you. I did, I still do love you, but not in that way.'

'Well, Angel Dust nearly spilled the beans and now I realise that I stopped you from telling me,' Pete replied, looking down to the floor. There was an instantly recognisable bag at Brad's feet. He burst out laughing.

'Well, I guess that Pan Am bag could tell some stories,' he said.

It was a relief for him to talk to Brad normally. He felt no regret, no jealousy, no sense of abandonment, and it was clear that they still had great empathy for each other.

'But how is Mel?' Brad whispered.

'Really blooming, she's planning a move to Wales. I know she was stunned at first, but it's like the whole process has made her grow. She's so positive. Yes, the girl's got plans.'

And they spoke of their work: Brad's writing and Pete's photography and of their hopes and of Pete's plans to bring Albert home, and they talked about how they had both changed over the last two years and, despite all the heartache, that it had been a good thing.

One thing that had not changed, however, was the bell for last orders. The music was lowered as the bell clanged unmelodically in their ears. Then, the last bell clanged, plugs pulled and the *'orrible lot* unceremoniously told to *get lost*. Slowly, as jackets and other garments were found, the crowd started to file through the empty saloon bar, passing the pint glasses and sordid ash trays lined up on the bar waiting to be cleaned. Out onto the deserted Grove, where a sole plod on his beat was standing overlooking this exodus. He might have been a fly on the wall, but he dared not buzz.

A group remained on the corner chatting; nobody wanted to make the first move as if they'd no desire to the break up the magic of such an evening. Pete felt that dancing and the talk with Brad had increased his confidence about what he must do. A curtain had been drawn over past events and he had to admit that seeing Brad together with Baz made him realise how well they complemented each other.

'You ready, Doll?' Baz said.

'Yeah, I guess,' said Brad. 'I gotta go back to Germany tomorrow, Pete. So where are you staying?'

'I'm staying with…'

He was about to say Mel but he thought the better of it.

'…with friends.'

'Yeah, he's staying with us,' said Spencer's friend.

Of course, that was not his game plan, but he went along with it until they split.

He watched Brad and Baz get in the VW, the bus spluttering on its way up the hill back towards to the dock and *De Mooie Marieke*. Pete's eyes followed it till it got right up to the top of the hill and disappeared over its brow. Somehow, he was certain that he would never see it again, perhaps never Brad and Baz again either.

He turned. Spencer and his friend were locked into an embrace. For an instant, they looked like they were one, illuminated for the entire world to see by the street lamp above them.

'So you coming back to ours?' asked Spencer.

'Thanks, but no. I'm staying in Vicarage Gardens, you know, the house where we met.'

They said their goodbyes and Pete, a determined spring in his step, made his way back up the hill to Mel's squat. As he walked a sense of relief filled him. At last the air was cleared. Now he just wanted to be back home and continue creating. He felt at last there was light at the end of the tunnel.

But later, while falling asleep, the thought came to him that he'd only observed the evening, hadn't really been part of it, that he was an imposter, he didn't belong; it was all too unilingual and, being so, tended to exclude or dismiss different, albeit parallel ways of expression, definition, attitudes to sexuality.

Christmas crept up fast that year. So busy was Pete preparing for the exhibition that not even Darren's constant references to the festive season were able to raise enthusiasm in him. Cards started to arrive and most of them he put to one side to take up to Albert on Christmas Day. He planned a little party for him there. But the real party would be in the New Year after his exhibition as Pete was definitely going to bring his grandfather home.

Amongst the cards he did open were one from Susan and one from Laverne Jefferson. Susan wrote that Jim was working for a law firm in the city while she'd met a gold prospector and would be off to the desert with him in the New Year panning for gold. She would be back in that awesome environment which she both loved and respected.

When he opened Laverne Jefferson's there was a verse inside:

Love and peace across the miles,
Goodwill to all and Yuletide smiles.

Pete was touched Laverne remembered him. They'd only met once. There was also a letter inside. She wrote she was busy getting ready to spend Christmas with her family but was sad this year as Henry wouldn't be there. But there was a good reason for Henry's absence as his dream had come true for, in the autumn, he auditioned for and got a part with a musical theatre company which was soon embarking on an international tour and he'd be in Europe by the middle of the next year. She finished off the letter asking after Albert and saying she prayed for him. Pete, although doubtful about intercessory prayer, was nevertheless grateful.

He was glad to get news of Henry. He often thought of him; his mantra *Keep the faith* often raised his spirits in the lowest times; in those hours just before dawn when he'd sometimes awake haunted from a strange but quickly forgotten dream and the bald reality of his actual situation hit him hard.

Another card was from Georgy replying to the letter Pete wrote him in the autumn. Apparently he planned to visit *Old Blighty* in the summer, as he'd promised the twins, Isobel and Jane, a trip to the motherland as a graduation present, so he'd bring them down to visit their grandfather. Amber Mae was coming over too, but she'd stay with Cynthia, who'd been in London for the last eighteen months working as an *au pair*.

'Jesus, fucking hell!' said Nicola, after Pete read her the letter while they were drinking tea in the kitchen. 'That Cynthia looking after kids, the poor little blighters, I can't imagine their lives are worth living.'

Having been the recipient of Cynthia's bullying and unkindness, Pete could only but agree with her.

Christmas Day, when it came, started out blustery and warm. Pete went next door to Connie's for dinner, after which they played Monopoly. Their game, though, was interrupted by a knock on the door. It was Ernie coming round with a present for his nipper, a rare occurrence. Nicola scowled while it was blatantly evident that Connie was none too pleased to have her Christmas interrupted. She watched with horror as Darren unwrapped his present and, much to Darren's glee, a space hopper appeared from underneath many sheets of paper.

'Something else to get in the way, it's worse than that blooming dog,' said Connie, crossly.

As Pete got up to leave for his ride up to the hospital, he was bowled over when Ernie offered to drive him up there. He was calling in on a brother who lived nearby and Pete could put his bike in the back of his van, he said.

Pete certainly hadn't been relishing cycling up those hills after a large dinner, and although they'd never been friends, he'd known Ernie since Nicola started to go out with him when she was fourteen. So despite Ernie's reputation, Pete was never much worried by him, but as they drove out of town, it became apparent that Ernie had an ulterior motive for this generous offer.

'Season of goodwill, Pete, me old mate, you know what I mean, season of goodwill and all that, to all men and... women. Ha-ha!' Ernie kept saying, chuckling to himself while having to double declutch on the steepest part of the hills. 'Thing is, Pete, you can't sweet-talk Nicky round for me, can you?'

It transpired that Ernie wanted Pete to put in a good word for him with Nicola as he wanted to get back with her. Pete had to play it diplomatically as he was at a loss as for what to say to Ernie because the last time Nicola spoke to Pete about him, it had been obvious she was glad to see the back of him now their divorce was finalised. Besides, now Darren was older, she'd started a HND at the Technical College in Business Studies and Accountancy, having got a taste for numbers when she helped Zénaïde with the books and invoices for her business. But Pete wasn't going to spill those beans to Ernie.

'I don't know, mate. Perhaps you should just ask her what she wants, but I expect she'll say go straight,' Pete said.

Ernie dropped Pete off by Stockfield's main entrance, and once the bike was out, he sped off like he was taking part in a stock-car race.

In the ward Pete found Albert asleep so he quietly started to unpack his bag. He opened the cards and arranged those on the bedside trolley around a small Christmas cake, some mince pies and two presents: one from Connie, Nicola and Darren, and the other from him. He twisted streamers and tinsel around the metal frame of the bed and blew up three balloons, which he tied to the bed frame. Chocolate, tangerines, peppermint creams and a sugar mouse which, together with some small crackers from Connie, he crammed into one of Albert's old socks, the one which he'd actually used himself when a kid for Father Christmas's visit.

Albert woke up as the tea trolley was passing, and for an instant, his face, smoothed and soothed by sleep, looked for a brief moment like that of an excited child.

'Merry Christmas, Granddad,' Pete said as he let down the bed's headrest, puffed up the pillows and, lifting Albert up against them, kissed him on the forehead.

'Where's Zinny?' the old man suddenly blurted out. His mood quite changed. Every so often Albert would call for Zénaïde and, getting no response, could end up in a very distressed state. However, that day, as there was so much to divert him, he was easily distracted by the glinting of Connie's glitter-covered Christmas card which took over his attention, causing him to blink a number of times. After Pete had opened Albert's presents for him and feigned surprise at the pair of pyjamas he'd chosen for Albert, and Connie's woolly bed socks, Pete raised the spout of Albert's special cup filled with tea to his mouth and told his grandfather all about his day and how he had a Christmas card from a lady far away who asked after him and said she was praying for him.

'She's a lovely person, Granddad,' Pete told him. 'I think you'd like her if you met her. And Granddad, you know what else? Georgy is coming over next summer with Isobel and Jane, the twins, your granddaughters.'

As he finished saying this he could have sworn that he saw Albert's eyebrows rise in an expression of disbelief before he sank back into the pillows. He was soon snoring.

The bell to leave was soon sounded and, after saying farewell, he made his way down the aisle of the ward, offering the cake and other leftovers to the nursing staff. And through the labyrinth of corridors out into the suddenly purple, chilly and blustery night. But it was downhill all the way.

The snow started to fall not long after Pete returned, continuing till early morning. At first, it didn't seem like it would stick, but the flakes thickened, got heavier. Like he'd done as a toddler, Pete sat in the dark by the small round window halfway up the stairs and looked out along the street watching the flakes, illuminated by the yellow street lamps, as they danced to the ground. All of a sudden, he had a desire to be outside and, coatless, went out into the street.

'Peter, you'll catch your death,' a voice yelled.

It was Connie, struggling with a shovel load of cinders which she was spreading over the path between her front door and her gate. She saved a sprinkling for the pavement beyond before she turned and, wishing him goodnight, returned inside. Pete could hear her bolting her front door.

Shivering, he went back inside himself and, after making some coffee, settled in the living room. He hadn't spent much time in that room since his return from California. There was no tree this year; he'd not seen much point in getting one. Besides, there was a row of them along the fence in Albert's orchard, all constant reminders of past Christmases, the oldest, tall now, being around the same age as him.

He scrutinised the room, recalling parties, games and those hours spent with Albert, pouring over atlases, maps and books about their world while Zénaïde knitted, mended, read or was preoccupied with some kind of complicated piece of needlework or tapestry. He got up and switched on the television. Morecambe and Wise were on but that night he didn't find them funny. He switched it off and returned to the landing window. The wind was up and coming from the east, the snowfall now a blizzard. He felt cold and went to bed.

Waking the next morning, without even looking, he knew, because of the muffled sound, he'd not be able to visit Albert that day. How he'd longed for days like this in his childhood: no school because of blocked roads and sliding down the hill on an old tin tray, but that morning, all he could think was of his grandfather in that old draughty hospital, alone and confused.

Still, he had much to do. After breakfast, he carried on working. It wasn't long now and he needed to get it all ready by mid-January. Anton said he would arrange for some men and a vehicle to collect everything. But having been so buoyant about the forthcoming event for weeks, that morning he became downhearted by the thought of the immensity of it all.

He paced around the house, telling himself it had to be good, that it had to be a success. He couldn't just go and fuck up such a great opportunity, and now he knew that after the exhibition's close, he'd bring Albert home, he recognised no other opportunities might arise for some time.

When he told Connie, the day after Boxing Day, about his decision, she said he was mad. But she came offering not only an old commode that had belonged to her mother but also to sit with Albert when he needed to go out. Nicola did too. And as he dropped loose the idea with some of the neighbours, he was surprised how supportive some were. Old Mr Rye, who had given Pete such encouragement when he'd started out in photography, and his daughter Susan, who used to play in the street with Nicola and him, made offers of help.

Pete had an appointment to see the doctor the day before New Year's Eve. Initially, Dr Crammond was reticent about it, but Pete won him over, and he told him he'd get the ball rolling with district nurses and would make regular visits. After seeing him, Pete called by the Citizens Advice Bureau and a kindly woman, with prematurely white hair gathered up into a tight bun, put him right about Albert's financial affairs. The almoner at the hospital was a help too. In fact, the only thing left to do other than to get the house ready was to give in his notice at the Post Office, which he would do in mid-January. And after the exhibition's four-week run, at the end of February, Albert would come home.

The morning of New Year's Eve, waking later than normal as he had the day off, found Pete immersed in bright sunshine streaking through the gaps in the curtains. Outside, birds sang like winter was already over; the street sounds were back to normal. Getting up, he went over to the window. A thaw had set in overnight; the street, though glistening where shrouded in bright rays of sun, was wet, gritty, dirty-looking. He craved fresh air.

After breakfast, making a thermos of coffee and sandwiches, and putting them and his camera in his rucksack, he got on his bike and cycled towards the Downs.

Stopping halfway up, he looked back over the town. A faint, low-level mist of a yellowy-grey colour hovering over it made it seem toylike. The air was fresh and he felt the warmth of the sun on his face. The Opal Causeway, beyond the town, looked murky and flat, but then it turned, as if someone had flicked on a switch, to a steely grey. Despite the complete thaw in the town, up on the hills as Pete looked around him, he could see remaining in easterly exposed parts great chunks of snow, snow that had either drifted up on clumps of bottle-green gorse or been piled up by snowploughs. The green rounded hills glistened with moisture and, looking at the winding road ahead, he noticed streams of water cascading down its gritty surface. He got back on his bike.

Once the steepest hill was negotiated and he was as high as he could go, he started to follow in the direction of the cliffs a deserted lane, along which Zénaïde told him she'd driven ambulances during those nervous days in the summer of 1940 and on whose banks grew windbitten, puny hedges. He soon came to a row of dwellings high up on the cliffs near to where a memorial to Blériot was erected. He dismounted and looked around.

Many houses in front of him were incongruous-looking bungalows, strangely perched as near to the top of the cliffs as they dared and looking as if they were parachuted down from the sky during the nineteen-thirties. They brazenly seemed to deflect any passing thought or comment about bad taste, as their reply, no doubt, would have been that they didn't care what anybody thought because it was the view which was the most important thing, the everlasting environment, not the momentary one.

Pete wheeled his bike across the road, found a secluded spot which looked out far below to the cove, where scars of that first attempt to build a tunnel were still visible. After taking some shots, he sat on a gnarled tree stump, a rarity up on that chalky, windswept place, poured coffee and ate his sandwiches. The Opal Causeway, from that height and angle, appeared as flat as a mill pond, and the steely grey colour had now absorbed some blue, though in parts a sandy hue could be detected.

His eyes looked towards the horizon; there was no France today. But below, a ferry was negotiating the harbour mouth, and for an instant, he longed to be on it. These thoughts were suddenly distracted by the distant sound of a hunting horn. Of the hunt which had never knowingly caught a fox.

It was dark by the time he got back from visiting Albert. Nicola was on her way out and they stopped to talk. He'd not seen her since Christmas.

'Listen, I've been trying to make myself invisible. Sorry, me old mucker,' she called. 'Thing is, Ernie's been a right pain since Christmas, keeps coming round saying he wants us to get back together. You won't believe it. He only asked me if I wanted to get married again. He just don't get it. Doing my head in, he is, said something about going straight. As if!'

Pete laughed.

'Sorry, it's probably my fault. He asked on the way to the hospital what I thought he should do to get back with you. Go straight, I said, and he said he wouldn't know how to.'

'Yeah, that's what I said to him,' Nicola said.

Pete realised how she'd changed, intended to be a different person.

'Hey, Petey, come to the pub later? I'm meeting up with Susan Rye and some others in town, but we'll end up at the White Horse. See you in the New Year there. I think there's a party after and yeah, Mum's cooking Darren a special tea and says she'll save some for you, gotta go.'

Pete watched her as she strode off in her platform heels, her maxi coat floating out behind her and unbuttoned to disclose the hot pants which she'd brought in Kensington market.

Pete passed up on Nicola's invitation. He decided his New Year would start once Albert was home. There was a bottle of champagne left over from Zénaïde's last trip to France, waiting for the celebration.

It got to be stressful getting everything ready for the exhibition, but he couldn't allow himself any slack whatsoever. At times, during the run-up, he got addled, agitated by the weight of it all, the precision needed, the little details to be considered. He made that many lists, but somehow, something always seemed to be left out, only to be remembered as he was drifting off to sleep, to be forgotten again, come morning. And there were sudden last-minute bits because it had to be up to scratch, as perfect as possible, no half measures, no corners cut, no diminishing of the vision.

A week before the opening, a van arrived to collect his work. Pete'd been up half the night working on the final touches and overslept. He awoke to a battering on the door and the sound of some banter between the van driver, his mate and Connie.

'Blooming Londoners,' she scoffed as he opened the front door, blurry eyed. 'Snooty lot, full of themselves, aren't they?'

'Get her, what's her problem then?' the driver asked.

Pete smiled, shrugging his shoulders. It took no time to

load up the van, and after watching as it disappeared down the road, though excited, Pete felt utterly drained. But as he'd finished working at the post office early, having taken some holiday accrued, he at least would be able to relax over some days before going up London to oversee everything. The weather was a lot colder than previous days. Looking up at the sky, he saw it was a yellowy-grey colour. More snow was forecast.

In the afternoon, after visiting Albert, he built a fire in the front room. The kindling being dry, it took straight away, and after laying on a log, he sat gazing into it, fascinated by the fluidity of movement. Nicola was due later to help move furniture. But now he needed to rest, and as the day faded, in the twilight he recalled those invented monsters from his childhood which loomed large on the walls and across the ceiling of the room, as the fire's licking flames cast large shadows all around. He quickly fell asleep.

Nicola's knocking woke him. They'd already planned how they'd get the house arranged for Albert. Starting in the dining room, dismantling the table, they emptied it of all furniture and cleansed it thoroughly. Then they went upstairs to dismantle the bed.

'It's a shame, but it has to be done as, you know, I always felt safe in this room when I was a kid. Mémé would hide me here when my dad was on the rampage,' Nicola said, on entering the room.

Pete smiled at her. It was true. Zénaïde protected her from her father. They used to laugh about how she'd send him on a wild goose chase till he'd forgotten why he had it in for Nicola.

'I travelled in this room, you know. Through magazines or books, trying on Mémé's jewellery, her clothes, hats while I'd listen to her tales.'

'Yes, her tales!' said Pete.

They accomplished the change-around relatively easily. It surprised them. Even Mrs Robert's commode was found a place.

'What happened to that old porcelain basin and jug?' Nicola asked him.

'In the loft, I think. I'll have to look. There might be a screen up there. I'll go up later.'

'Well, I'm mashed, I'll be off.'

'Okay, thanks so much, Nicknick.'

After she left, still driven, he made his way to the loft. He'd had not been up there for yonks. The cold air suddenly embraced him, as, standing on a chair, he slid open the hatch and, with torch between his teeth, hauled himself up. The electric light was still working, and as his eyes slowly adjusted to its light, he made out in the far corner the glint of some large porcelain objects in a box. Yes, the bowl and jug. As he made his way across to them, he stumbled on another box and a dust-covered scrapbook slipped out from it onto the boards.

It was one Zénaïde kept since first married to Albert. He remembered from a young age so clearly what it contained: a programme from the Casino de Paris, when they'd seen Maurice Chevalier, around the time of the Munich crisis; menus from restaurants they'd gone to before the war; railway, ferry tickets and *billets doux*. Curious, he picked it up and opened it at a random page, on which were pasted some photographs taken around the time of the Coronation. They were of him, Nicola, Françoise, Jean-Luc, Susan Rye and her Labrador performing in a play Nicola had written.

He turned another page and now found a card addressed to Albert posted in France from Zénaïde informing him of Pete's and Zénaïde's safe arrival. And there were more items: photos from their journey to the battlefields of Flanders and visits to the house by the dunes; and a newspaper cutting about the death of Derek Rye, Susan's brother, shot by terrorists in Aden, together with a photo of Derek and all the children in the street, when last home on leave, and in Zénaïde's hand alongside were written the words: *It should never have happened!*

He could've looked at the scrapbook forever but for the job in hand! He took the jug and bowl to the kitchen, leaving them to soak while he had one last look in the bedroom.

Yes, the urn? How had he missed the urn containing Zénaïde's ashes before? He recalled Albert's wishes. Despite not associating it with Mémé, he put it away safely in the cupboard. He was ready now.

The exhibition was a success. Anton de Grande pulled out all the stops for the opening. The gallery in Kings Cross was teeming with people – journalists, other photographers, artists and guests – when he walked in. Plucked from his solitary comfort zone, he felt awkward and was taken back by the pretentiousness of some of the questions asked him, was quite stumped for answers, found himself stuttering, but his self-assurance was restored by the sight of Mel's friendly face smiling at him as she came through the gallery's entrance.

Extremely pregnant now, she came with Hazel, who'd driven from Wales that morning to move her. Mel's new life was just about to start; she was excited, positive about it and undaunted by the path she was choosing. She seemed to have a total sense of purpose. She told Pete that Baz, now open with her about his relationship with Brad, made a scene when she told him she was moving to Wales. He'd got heavy about his right of access to the baby when it was born. She placated him, but he was none the wiser about the baby's questionable paternity.

Towards the end of the evening, Anton drew Pete aside, telling him he was thrilled by the success of the exhibition and started spelling out to Pete grandiose ideas about touring it, perhaps with an Arts Council grant. He was also very enthusiastic about mounting it in Paris, in the gallery in the Rue St André des Arts.

'But you don't seem keen on that idea, Peter, I believe,' he said, sensing Pete's reticence.

'Oh no, it's not that I don't want to, it's just I might not be able to get there myself,' he said. 'The thing is that my grandfather is coming home from hospital. He needs a lot of looking after and has nobody else so it will be difficult to leave him.'

'Ah then,' said Anton, throwing up his hands. 'So when he's better. A month or two will make no difference, there's time yet.'

Pete didn't reply. He knew that Albert would not get better.

On a prematurely spring day, to the singing of one thousand birds and a welcoming party of Connie, Nicola, Darren, Mr Polly and the Ryes, an ambulance brought Albert home. Pete, and cycle, rode in the ambulance with his grandfather. Once in a wheelchair, Pete negotiated him through the front door into his bedroom and he was soon back in his own bed. He sank down in it with the greatest of pleasure, emitting a sound that could only have been taken for a sigh of relief.

After the ambulance left and everybody had dispersed, with Albert snoozing, Pete sat on a chair next to his bed. It was still hard to believe he was home and, with moistened eyes, Pete watched him for over an hour. He knew they'd never have conversations again, go to the orchard or the wild strawberry woods, never be able to look at books together or reflect on the colours of the Opal Causeway, but Albert was back where he belonged.

It was hard work, harder than he'd imagined, demanding utmost patience. But the satisfaction of knowing he was doing the right thing overrode the daily frustrations and trials. He always had to be always alert and, in those weeks, scarcely slept a whole night through. However, there were joyful moments when Albert had periods of lucidity, a sort of lucidity which evaded him before, and in those times, they sat together by the window and Pete talked and it seemed that the old man understood. He was definitely was less agitated; his shouting fits diminished significantly.

When the daffodil petals had become crisp and browning, their swordlike leaves withering, in that time, when a brief lull in the growing season can sometimes be observed as the earth is stoking itself up and summer plants still consolidating their strength, Albert died.

He died surrounded by *muguet*, lily of the valley, which Pete picked from the shady part of the garden to offer him for *le premier mai*, a tradition instigated long before by Zénaïde.

He died while Pete was asleep by his bed, dreaming that he was in a strange room with Albert, who was able to walk. There was a knock. They noticed a door at the end of this room and were drawn towards it. Instinctively Pete knew that he must guide the old man through it. He reached for the handle to open it and, leading Albert by the hand, they passed through. Another strange room, but there in the corner on a chaise longue, smiling and beckoning to them, was Zénaïde. Pete watched as Albert walked over to her, sat down beside her and they merged together, becoming as one before slowly evaporating.

At this point, Pete woke up suddenly. His eyes looked over to where Albert lay and he knew immediately his grandfather was no longer breathing. Calmly, he went to the phone and dialled the doctor. As he replaced the receiver, as if on cue, there was a knock; Connie was at the door.

'I've been knocking,' she said, with a quizzical expression. Then her eyes went straight past him and she walked into Albert's room, felt his pulse and raised her eyes upward. The doctor arrived not long after, confirming Albert's death. But, once he left, something strange happened as Connie and Pete were laying out the body. A strong wind blew up outside and a sudden gust suddenly rattled the window pane. Was someone tapping to get someone's attention? Pete probably wouldn't have thought much of it if he hadn't dreamed that dream, but for the rest of his life, he believed that it was Zénaïde come to claim Albert.

With much to arrange, the days leading up to the funeral in Pete's memory all merged into one. Strangely, the day after Albert's death, Pete received a letter from Laverne Jefferson, full of news and, as usual, a lot of smiles. But he had a sense of her reaching out to him like she somehow knew what had happened. He wrote back to her that day.

He also wrote to Germaine. He tried to ring her twice, but both times, there was no reply, but the mystery was cleared up as she herself rang him some days before the funeral, saying she'd been in Paris because Marie-Thérèse had suddenly been taken ill and she'd brought her back with her to the house by the dunes. She was desolate at not being able to attend Albert's funeral as she'd such happy memories of him. Pete was upset she couldn't be there. Was it because he saw her presence there as being a sort of a counterweight to that of his father?

For Georgy was coming. A few weeks before, he'd written to Albert with the address and number of the hotel in London where he would be staying. But when Pete rang the hotel to tell him of his father's death, he was told that Georgy wasn't there. He left a message. Georgy called two days later. He sounded curt on the phone but, once told of his father's death and given the details of the crematorium, told Pete to expect him and the twins.

But his greatest surprise was when, about to set off to the crematorium, there was a knock at the door. Opening it, to his surprise there were Mel, her baby daughter and Hazel.

The baby cooed gently throughout the service, adding a strange, haunting harmony to the hymns. There was a good turnout. At the wake in the house under the Downs, other than Georgy and the twins, Mel, Hazel and the baby, there were Connie, Nicola and Darren, together with a smattering of neighbours, including the Ryes. Mel's baby had pride of place, and Connie, Nicola and Darren unashamedly cooed over her.

'Mel, what you gonna call her?' asked Nicola.

'I haven't been able to decide what to call her up till now. She's had that many names, but none seemed right. But inside the crematorium, it came to me,' she said, and turning around, she started to address everybody in the room.

'Excuse me, everybody, but I have an announcement to make. I've been racking my brain as to what to call my baby. But there in the crematorium, it came to me. I want to call her Alberta Zénaïde.'

Pete smiled.

Darren was now completely monopolising the baby.

'I bet you I know what her nickname will be, Mel,' he said.

'What, Darren?'

'Little Zinny.'

'Oh, that's lovely, Darren,' Mel said.

'Son, me and the twins gotta get away now. We're going to Scotland tomorrow,' Georgy said, once everybody had left.

'Oh, I thought we were going to the solicitor,' said Pete.

'No can do, son. I'll be back in ten days. We'll go then,' Georgy told him.

He found it bizarre to hear someone calling him son so soon after Albert's death, particularly as they communicated like suspicious strangers. When they did visit the solicitor, Pete was astounded to learn Georgy was the sole beneficiary of Albert's will. He would be allowed to choose as many of the house's contents as he wished, but Georgy was to get the house, the orchard and any money that was in Albert's bank account. There was also a codicil to the will which specified Albert's wish that his and Zénaïde's ashes should be mixed together and one half be scattered from Shakespeare Cliff and the other from Cap Blanc Nez.

'Nice little job for you then, son,' said Georgy.

On their way back home, Georgy started talking about how he needed to, once all the paperwork was sorted, sell the house and orchard quickly, and what Pete didn't want from the house, he would put in an auction or sell to dealers.

'So better choose quick, son,' he said, ebulliently. 'Because I want to get back to Oz as soon as is possible, that's the life, what with this common market malarkey, this country is going to the dogs. I wonder if you don't see yourself emigrating to Australia or New Zealand, son, or South Africa even.'

Pete, feeling gutted, didn't reply. He was about to see his childhood home and many of the things which had surrounded him since he could first remember go under the hammer. And as for immigrating to South Africa? Where the fuck had Georgy been for the last twenty-five years?

Back home, after leaving Georgy looking at the china and silverware, the first thing Pete did was go up to the loft and bring down Mémé's scrapbook. Looking through it again made him recognise how he'd always have the memories of being in the house under the Downs because he realised that he'd always had a keen ability to recall objects, shapes and colours, as well as events and feelings. A parade of his past life was retained in his memory and he knew he'd be able to call it up at any time. He knew even if he wasn't able to take photographs, he could always take them with his brain. He became so deep in thought that he didn't hear Georgy calling up to him.

'Are you there, son? You got a visitor.'

Bounding down the stairs, Pete walked into the living room and was astonished to see Germaine. Overjoyed, he rushed towards her and they hugged.

'Eh, Peter, I am desolate that I could not come to Albert's funeral. I hope you got my letter. I am also desolate to tell you Marie-Thérèse died on the day of the funeral. Her funeral took place two days ago.'

He was silent; he had no more tears.

'Oh, how sad. She was such a lovely person. I'll always remember that first visit to the Louvre,' he said. 'But they have all died now, Mémé, Solange, Granddad and now

Marie-Thérèse. They aren't many of the older generation left, well, your parents, of course.'

'And me,' said Georgy, who'd been listening by the doorway. 'Right, son, I'll be off. I promised Amber Mae and the girls I'd be back in time to take in a show. Good day.'

After he left, Pete made some tea which they drank, while sampling some *petits fours* Germaine brought.

'But is *he* your father, Peter?' she asked, looking at Pete with a bemused expression on her face.

'Yes.'

'I didn't realise.'

'I don't think I have yet either,' Pete said.

They both laughed.

Germaine stayed for a night and the next day. Other than cooking some memorable dishes, she had some astonishing news. She told Pete that now Marie-Thérèse had died, the apartment in the building on the Rue Bonaparte, which had been owned jointly by Zénaïde, Solange and Marie-Thérèse, was left to him and, with that, went a *chambre de bonne* in the same building.

'It was decided long ago, Peter, naturally. Even, I believe, before my grandmother died. I was to get the house by the dunes and you the apartment, one for each grandchild — what could be fairer?'

Before she left, he and Germaine discussed the question of the ashes, deciding they would scatter them in September, by which time, they anticipated the house would be sold and Pete ready for his move to France.

September came quickly. It seemed to Pete the older he got, the faster time went, and the summers which lasted forever as a child now just went by in a flash. He was beginning to feel older too, now there was no one above him anymore. A new era was dawning in his life: the house was sold; its contents, once he'd made his choices, had been either auctioned off or brought by local dealers; the orchard was purchased by a property speculator for a new housing estate.

Georgy was very happy indeed and preparing to go back soon to Australia richer than he'd come. He stayed, after Amber Mae and the twins returned home, in Cynthia's box of a flat in Hampstead where she was au pairing and only came down to the house under the Downs when really necessary. Pete continued to find him a stranger, but it didn't worry him now. He'd soon be in France. Besides, he had more to think about, as Anton de Grande had now given him a date at the beginning of November for his exhibition in the gallery in Rue St André des Arts.

It was early in the morning, not much past eight. White cumulonimbus clouds were being blown fast across a pale blue sky.

'Peter, I hope it will not rain,' said Germaine.

They were outside in the street by Connie's house saying

goodbye to Nicola and Darren, who were off to Wales with Mel and Hazel. In the months since Albert's funeral, Mel and Hazel, with Alberta Zénaïde, whilst visiting Pete, had become closer to Nicola. It was Hazel who persuaded her she'd be a useful person in the commune, particularly as they were setting up a wholefood shop in the village and thought Nicola's expertise with bookkeeping would be an asset.

But what decided Nicola go was the fact that she realised she needed to make a proper break with the past. Besides, Mel and Hazel's description of their life in Wales had from the start got to her. Of course, they warned her that she wouldn't have much time to wear high heels, to which she replied, 'Thank fucking god for that! It's high time I's weaned off them.'

Darren was excited too as he'd go to a new school where some of the kids spoke Welsh; he'd be living where there were woods, mountains and lakes and where the night sky was clearer so he could better see and identify the stars, and there would be animals to look after, other children to play with and Little Zinny to care for. Mr Polly thought it was a good idea too, he told his nan.

Hazel's van was loaded up and they were ready to set off, Mr Polly, the gerbils Sputnik and Telstar, and the goldfish Gemini all secure inside.

'Yeah, Petey,' Nicola said. 'It will sad to come back and see the orchard no longer there. All built over.'

Hazel came around from the back of the van, where she had been fixing the door handles tight with some ropes.

'I guess we should get off. It's a long journey. This isn't the fastest vehicle in the world. I don't want to hit Spaghetti

Junction at the wrong time of day. And we've got to get through London first,' she said.

Connie started to cry as they said their goodbyes.

'Mum,' Nicola said as she hugged her. 'We'll be down to visit regular and you can come up and stay. But I will miss you.'

'But you are all going and I am the only one left,' she sobbed.

'But Connie,' said Germaine, now hugging her, 'you are always welcome to come over and visit me. I'm only twenty-two miles away.'

At this, Connie perked up. They were all crowded into the van now: Hazel in the driving seat, Mel with the baby on her lap and Darren holding the bowl which contained Gemini in his hands on the seat beside her while Nicola and Mr Polly were splayed out on a mattress laid in the back. The gerbils, in their cage secured with rope to one side of the van, seemed oblivious to everything around them. Hazel turned on the ignition, pumped on the accelerator for a short while and swung the van out into the road and they were off.

And now it was Pete and Germaine's time to leave. They were going to scatter half of the ashes from Shakespeare Cliff, then get the ferry. Germaine's car was packed, but Pete felt the urge to take one more look around the house, before locking the door and entrusting Connie with the keys. Leaving Germaine and Connie chatting, he wandered from empty room to empty room. It seemed strange without hardly any furniture. Had he really lived here? The phone rang when he was walking downstairs. He picked it up.

'Can I speak with Pete Jones?' a voice said.

'Yes?' Pete replied.

'Pete Jones?'

'Yes?' Pete said, not recognising the voice.

'Hey, Pete, this is Henry Abercrombie.'

'Henry, what, no, I don't believe it. How are you? You know, I got a card from your mum. She said you were somewhere in Europe.'

'Yes, I am. Been touring with this company for months. You know, it's been some trip, I can tell you. Far out. Hey, Pete, man, it's so good to hear your voice. You won't believe where I am. Made me think of you. I'm in Paris.'

'Paris? No, I don't believe it.'

'Yes, I am. And I landed me a little job in a cabaret.'

'You know what?'

'Say, tell me.'

'I'm taking the train to Paris tomorrow. Long story, but I'm moving there.'

'Wow, far out! What a coincidence. What time you arriving?'

Pete got out his ticket from his wallet and told Henry the time of his arrival. The line started to crackle and screech and Pete thought it had gone dead.

'Henry, are you still there?' he called, fearful that he'd lost contact.

'Yeah, man, no, I heard, Gare du Nord tomorrow, far out, you want me to come meet you?'

Later on the day, Pete and Germaine, once off the ferry, drove to the cliffs and walked up slowly to the edge of Cap Blanc Nez. There was a slight breeze. They clearly could see the White Cliffs.

'Eh, you are ready, Peter? It's strange to think we were across there this morning, walking on those cliffs. You know, I would like to imagine that perhaps some of ashes arrived here before us,' said Germaine, for on the English side, a substantial amount of the ashes was dispersed seaward by a sudden gust of wind.

Pete nodded and, after opening the urn, they both took turns in scattering the ashes over the edge of the cliff. As they were in the process, they both agreed that there seemed to be no satisfactory method for doing it, and they convulsed into laughter.

'I believe my aunt would approve,' said Germaine. 'She always saw the funnier side of things.'

'Yes, so did Granddad. I guess that's a reason why they made such a good team.'

'You know, I am so happy for them. Finally together again.'

'Yes,' said Pete, realising that he wasn't feeling at all choked up like he imagined he would've been. He felt he was doing something of great beauty. As the ashes disappeared out of their vision and became reunited with the universe which had given them birth, they stood silently while gazing out to sea and up at the vast blue sky above.

'How do those words in that song go? I think they would be very apt,' Germaine said as they started to make their way back to the car. 'You know, the one that Piaf sung after Marcel Cerdan died.'

'I know, Mémé used to sing it, "L'hymne à l'amour",' replied Pete.

'Yes, of course, that's it, *Dans le bleu de toute l'immensité.* That's where they are now.'

'Perhaps *Dans l'opale de toute l'immensité* might be their preferred resting place. Because it was the sea that made them.'

'Yes, as always, you are right. *Dans l'opale de toute l'immensité*, I like that... very much.'

The next morning Germaine drove Pete to the station to catch the train. As they were early, they remained sitting in the car chatting.

'You are always welcome to visit and come walk on the beach.'

'I'd like that, especially on a blustery winter's day.'

'Well, come over the New Year. Françoise should be back from Senegal around then and I promise I'll make the *pot-au-feu* you like so much.'

'Yum, it's a deal. I'll come. There's one thing I want to ask you. Granddad said in a period of lucidity in the hospital that Mémé's first husband was—'

'Like you, perhaps?'

Pete chuckled.

'So you knew then?'

'I was very close to my aunt, Peter. You should know that! Yes, Charles-Hippolyte was gay, not that they used that term then, of course. He was a dancer in the cabarets which my aunt worked in when she first arrived in Paris. The marriage didn't last long; they separated very amiably. But the poor man was shot by the Gestapo while trying to escape, when they were rounding up Jews.'

'That's terrible.'

'Yes, so many terrible things happened then. She actually came over on a secret mission and, although I'm sure that the authorities didn't know about it, formulated a secret plan to get him back to England, but she was too late.'

'A secret mission?' Pete said, incredulously.

'Yes, you surely knew that she did secret work in the war. It all started because of her photo collection.'

'Her photo collection?'

'Well, you see, she had so many photographs of Northern France, of the places where she lived and worked, of the docks at La Havre, Cherbourg, Calais and Boulogne. They were invaluable to the allies and she used to instruct agents, prior to their missions about things, like the lie of the land, accents, customs, you know, those types of things.'

'Oh, you know, they never mentioned much of what they did in the war, neither of them. But now it all makes sense. She was mysterious about some things,' said Pete.

'She landed near Cagnes-sur-mer, near my mother's. Jean-Daniel and I were in the area where she landed but didn't see her.'

'You were in the maquis? You were both so young,' said Pete.

How insignificant his troubles in California were as compared to what his cousins must have gone through.

'So did she see Charles-Hippolyte?'

'Briefly, from a distance, but she was too late to save him.'

'What was he like?'

'I only met him once when I was tiny. I think they'd been divorced for some time, but it was before she married your grandfather. It was around the time of *L'Assomption*, I believe. He was handsome, had great presence, the poise of a dancer. We can talk more when you come in the New Year as it's time for your train.'

Once he'd hauled up his luggage into the compartment

and said a final goodbye through the window, the whistle blew; the train was off.

Pete was too excited to read. He felt that at last his experience in America was expurgated and he could get on with his life. There was a large world out there, which embraced many different sets of tenets, had different ways of seeing things and of doing things, all of an equal validity. There was nothing to hold him back and he could only look out of the window and imagine a wonderful future while his eyes fed on the beauty of the sandy and marshy Canche estuary near Etaples, and the ponds and the mistletoe-covered trees in the Somme valley near Abbeville, until eventually the train reached the outskirts of Paris and he had a glimpse, crowning *la butte Montmartre*, of the *Sacré Coeur* to his right before passing on his left the Sernam depot, from which he would soon have to pick up a trunk that he'd sent on ahead.

The train came into the station and slowly halted; doors opened and shut; the sound they made echoed all about. Porters, suddenly and ruthlessly, began touting for business and Pete, overladen with luggage, stepped down on the platform and started to walk towards the exit.

'Hey, Pete, man, let me give you a hand with carrying that,' a voice said, from behind. He turned his head and saw Henry Abercrombie before him, smiling.